Adrian Mole: The Prostrate Years

Adrian Mole:
The Prostrate Years

SUE TOWNSEND

MICHAEL JOSEPH
an imprint of
PENGUIN BOOKS

MICHAEL JOSEPH

Published by the Penguin Group

Penguin Books Ltd, 80 Strand, London WC2R ORL, England

Penguin Group (USA) Inc., 375 Hudson Street, New York, New York 10014, USA

Penguin Group (Canada), 90 Eglinton Avenue East, Suite 700, Toronto, Ontario, Canada MP4 2Y3
(a division of Pearson Penguin Canada Inc.)

Penguin Ireland, 25 St Stephen's Green, Dublin 2, Ireland (a division of Penguin Books Ltd)

Penguin Group (Australia), 250 Camberwell Road, Camberwell, Victoria 3124, Australia
(a division of Pearson Australia Group Pty Ltd)

Penguin Books India Pvt Ltd, 11 Community Centre, Panchsheel Park, New Delhi – 110 017, India

Penguin Group (NZ), 67 Apollo Drive, Rosedale, North Shore 0632, New Zealand
(a division of Pearson New Zealand Ltd)

Penguin Books (South Africa) (Pty) Ltd, 24 Sturdee Avenue,
Rosebank, Johannesburg 2196, South Africa

Penguin Books Ltd, Registered Offices: 80 Strand, London WC2R ORL, England

www.penguin.com

First published 2009

1

Set in 13.5/16.25 pt Monotype Garamond
Typeset by Rowland Phototypesetting Ltd, Bury St Edmunds, Suffolk
Printed in Great Britain by Clays Ltd, St Ives plc

A CIP catalogue record for this book is available from the British Library

ISBN: 978–0–718–15370–0
TRADE PAPERBACK ISBN: 978–0–718–15426–4

www.greenpenguin.co.uk

This book is dedicated to Sean, with love and thanks. And also to Professor Mike Nicholson and the Renal team at the Leicester General Hospital.

Acknowledgements

Without the help of Bailey, Sean, Colin and Louise, I could not have written this book.

2007

Saturday 2nd June 2007

Black clouds over Mangold Parva. It has been raining since the beginning of time. When will it stop?

MAJOR WORRIES

1. Glenn fighting the Taliban in Helmand Province.
2. The bookshop only took £17.37 today.
3. Up three times last night to urinate.
4. The Middle East.
5. Do my parents have an up-to-date funeral plan? I can't afford to bury them.
6. My daughter, Gracie, showing alarming Stalinist traits. Is this normal behaviour for the under-fives?
7. It is two months and nineteen days since I last made love to my wife, Daisy.

I sometimes feel that she is less keen on me than she used to be. She hasn't taken the top off my boiled egg for ages. She has still not bought a pair of wellingtons despite living in Mangold Parva for three years. She is the only mother outside the school gate wearing five-inch heels.

This shows her total lack of commitment to me, and to the English countryside. In the first month of our marriage we picked blackberries together and she had a stab at making preserves. Now, four years on, the scars from the boiling jam have almost completely healed, and she is buying raspberry Bonne Maman at £3.50! It is ridiculous when you can buy the Co-op's own brand at 87p.

Yesterday I found her crying over her old briefcase. When I asked her what was wrong, she sobbed, 'I miss Dean Street.'

'Who's Dean Street?' I asked.

She slammed the briefcase down and savagely kicked out at a bag of John Innes.

'Dean *Street*, the place, *idiot*,' she said in that calm sarcastic voice I have come to dread.

But at least she was speaking to me, although she is still avoiding eye contact. Last week, whilst searching for my nostril hair clippers in my wife's handbag, I came across a Paperchase A5-sized notebook with a cover depicting harmless-looking monsters. On opening the notebook I was startled to find, on the first page, a note addressed to me.

ADRIAN, IF YOU HAVE FOUND MY DIARY AND YOU ARE READING THIS, DO NOT READ ANY FURTHER. THIS DIARY IS MY ONLY CONFIDANT. PLEASE RESPECT MY WISHES AND ALLOW ME SOME PRIVACY.

CLOSE THE NOTEBOOK AND REPLACE IT,
NOW!

I read on.

Dear Diary
I intend to write in you every day and I will hold nothing
back. I can tell no living person how I feel. Adrian would
have a nervous breakdown, my parents and sisters
would say we told you not to marry him, and my friends
would say we told you so. But the truth is, diary, that I
am utterly miserable. I hate living in yokel-land where the
populace have never heard of the White Cube Gallery or
macchiato coffee and think that Russell Brand is a type
of electric kettle. Do I love my husband? Have I ever
loved my husband? Can I live with my husband until one
or both of us are dead?

I heard the back door slam and Daisy came in from the
garden. I quickly replaced the diary in her handbag and
for some reason shouted, 'Daisy, when is the Queen's
official birthday?'

She came into the living room and said, 'Why do you
want to know? You haven't written her one of your
poems, have you?'

As she bent her head to light a cigarette, I couldn't
help but notice that she now has *three* chins. I have also
noticed recently that she has tampered with our 'speak
your weight' bathroom scales, so they no longer speak.

I have stopped accompanying her to the shops to buy
clothes since she had a temper tantrum in the changing
room at Primark, when she got stuck in a size 14 shirt
and had to be cut out of it by the manageress. All the way

home she was saying, 'I can't understand it, I'm only a size 12.' Even my friend Nigel, who is blind but can see shapes, said recently, 'By Christ, Daisy's piling on the pounds. She came to see me the other day and I thought it was my garden shed on the move.'

When she went into the kitchen, I was tempted to grab her diary and read on, but I daren't risk it.

After dinner (tinned tuna salad, new potatoes, beetroot salsa, own strawberries, Elmlea cream) I was washing up when Daisy came in and took a packet of chocolate digestives from out of the cupboard. Later, after I'd cleaned the kitchen surfaces and pushed the wheelie bin and the recycling boxes to the end of the drive, I went into the living room to watch Channel Four news and couldn't help but notice that Daisy had eaten three-quarters of the packet of biscuits. I should not have said anything. I should have kept my mouth firmly shut. The subsequent row was like the eruption of a volcano.

Gracie turned the volume up to full on her DVD of *High School Musical 2* and demanded, 'Stop shouting or I'll call the police!'

My mother came round from next door to find out if Daisy had actually killed me. She brought the row to an end by shouting above Daisy and me, 'Daisy, you are in denial! You are obviously a size 16! Get over it! Evans, Principles and even Dawn French supply clothes for fat women.'

Daisy hurled herself into my mother's arms, and my mother indicated with an angry gesture of her head that I was to leave the room.

*

6

This morning Daisy did not stand at the door and watch me mount my bike as I left for work as usual, and when I reached the lane and turned to wave, she was not at the window. Physically I am at a low ebb. I rise from my bed at least three times during the night, more if I allow myself a glass of wine after *Newsnight*. Consequently I am exhausted, and the next morning I have to put up with my parents (with whom I share a party wall) complaining that the constant flushing of our cistern is keeping them awake.

As I was cycling into a headwind it took longer than usual to ride to the bookshop, and when I reached the environs of Leicester I was further delayed. It seemed that every major road had been dug up so that new sewage pipes could be laid. As a reluctant cesspit owner this prompted me to be almost consumed with jealous rage. Is it any wonder my wife is yearning for the metropolis? I have denied her one of life's basic necessities. I blame my father for our primitive sanitary conditions, the money we put aside for mains drainage when we built the Piggeries was frittered away on wheelchair ramps for him. Yet it was his own fault he had a stroke – the only exercise he took for years was wagging his index finger on the remote control. To add insult to injury, he still smokes thirty cigarettes a day and gorges himself on fried bread and chilli-flavoured pork scratchings.

I rue the day my parents bought two dilapidated pigsties and converted them into living units. I was grateful to have a pigsty roof over my head in the early days of my insolvency, but I have certainly paid the price.

Another worry is my failure as a father. Gracie came home from nursery school yesterday with a felt-tip drawing of 'My family'. Diary, I looked amongst the stick people for the representation of myself but failed to find me. I was deeply hurt by my absence. When I asked Gracie why she hadn't included me, pointing out that it was the tax extracted from my wages that supplied her school with the felt tips and paid her nursery teacher's salary, her brow furrowed. To avoid the usual escalation – sobs, screams, snot and recriminations – I diverted her by opening a packet of pink wafer biscuits.

When I asked my wife why she thought Gracie had left me out of the family drawing, Daisy said, 'She has obviously picked up on your emotional detachment.' When I protested, she got ridiculously overemotional and shouted, 'When you come home from work you sit and stare out of the window with your mouth open.'

I defended myself, saying, 'I never tire of the view, the trees in the distance, the light fading from the sky.'

Daisy said, 'It's not fucking *Cornwall*. The view from the front window is of a boggy field and a row of leylandii your father planted to "protect his privacy". Not that anybody comes *near* the place.'

Sunday 3rd June

1 The Old Pigsty
The Piggeries
Bottom Field
Lower Lane
Mangold Parva
Leicestershire
Sunday 3rd June 2007

The Right Honourable Gordon Brown MP
Chancellor of the Exchequer
11 Downing Street
London SW1A 2AB

Dear Mr Brown

I wrote to you at the Treasury recently regarding a great injustice. According to my local tax office, I am still in arrears to the sum of £13,137.11. This 'debt' was incurred during a time when I worked for a duplicitous employer as an offal chef in Soho.

I realise that you are an incredibly busy man, but if you could find the time to cast your eye over my paperwork (sent 1st March 2007 by registered post) and then forward me a note confirming my innocence in this matter, I would be eternally grateful.

Your humble and obedient servant,
A. A. Mole

PS: May I suggest that you sort this out before you take over as prime minister.
PPS: Congratulations on doing so well with only one eye. You join the ranks of other illustrious one-eyed men: Peter Falk (Columbo), George Melly, Nelson and, of course, Cyclops.

Monday 4th June

What started as a minor disagreement about the correct way to boil potatoes (I cook them from cold, Daisy throws them into boiling water) turned into a tearful and angry denunciation of our marriage.

The list of my marital crimes included eating crisps too loudly, ironing creases down the front of my jeans, refusing to pay more than £5 for a haircut, wearing the same poppy (first purchased in 1998) during the month of November every year, putting too many dried herbs in spag bol, writing mad letters to famous people, failing to earn enough money to enable us to move out of the pigsty.

At the end of her diatribe I said, 'I don't know why you married me.'

Daisy looked at me as if seeing me for the first time and said, 'I honestly don't know why I married you. I suppose I must have loved you.'

'Loved?' I queried. 'Did you mean to use the past tense?'

Daisy went mad again, shouting, 'Our marriage is breaking up and all you can do is talk about my grammar.'

'That's grossly contrapositional of what I actually said,' I protested.

'Listen to yourself,' she said. 'Nobody speaks like that, Adrian. Nobody actually says "contrapositional".'

'"Contrapositional" almost certainly makes up part of Will Self's daily intercourse,' I said. Even to my own ears I sounded like Mr Pooter.

I do not enjoy such confrontations. Am I turning into one of those middle-aged men who think the country has gone to the dogs and that there has been no decent music since Abba?

Tuesday 5th June

Diary, I've been thinking about yesterday's entry and I am a little disturbed to find that I think the country has gone to the dogs and that there is nobody to beat Abba.

Wednesday 6th June

The sun came out today. I do not mean in the metaphorical sense, I mean the actual sun came out from behind the low grey clouds that have been hanging about for months. The smell of hawthorn was thick in the air and most of the water had evaporated from the potholes in our drive. I remarked to Daisy that the sunshine would do us all good, boost our serotonin levels and prevent rickets.

Daisy said, 'All that sunshine means to me, Adrian, is that I have to shave my legs.'

She is not the woman I married. The old Daisy, who delighted in the sun, would be lying on a towel in a bikini on the flat roof of our pigsty to soak up every last ray.

When I suggested she could sunbathe, her eyes filled with tears. 'Have you seen the size of me recently?' she said.

Diary, what has happened to my wife? Did she mean what she wrote about me in her notebook? Will we ever have sex again? Even my parents manage it every other Thursday. I have to wear earplugs because of the disturbing noises through the party wall.

Monday 11th June

Mr Carlton-Hayes is ill. Leslie, his friend, rang me at the bookshop first thing this morning. For years I have been wondering if Leslie is a man or a woman. I am still none the wiser. Leslie could be a deep-voiced woman, à la Ruth Kelly the cabinet minister, or a high-voiced man like Alan Ball the footballer.

All I know about Leslie is that he/she shares a house with Mr Carlton-Hayes, is unsociable and has a liking for Sibelius and the pink coconut and liquorice ones in a box of Bassett's Allsorts.

I asked Leslie what was wrong with Mr Carlton-Hayes, and he/she said, 'Did he not mention it? Oh dear,

I'm afraid I'm going to give you rather bad news. Oh dear . . .'

I said, hastily, 'I'll wait, shall I, until he's better?'

I could hear Leslie breathing. It sounded as if he/she had a bad chest.

A customer, a woman with one large eyebrow, asked me if we stocked anything on the early surrealists. I directed her towards a Man Ray biography. I was glad of the temporary diversion – I kept Leslie on hold and gave the eyebrow woman the hard sell. Mr Carlton-Hayes had badly misjudged the interest for books about early surrealists in Leicester and the five copies of the Man Ray had been hard to shift. On the other hand, he had severely underestimated the demand for Wayne Rooney's ghosted autobiography.

When I returned to the phone, Leslie had gone. I meant to ring back immediately but the woman came to the till with the Man Ray. When she had left, I dialled Leslie's number but after only two rings I put the phone down and disconnected the call.

Sunday 17th June
Father's Day

Woken up at 6.20 this morning by the smell of burning, and Gracie yelling into my right ear, 'Wake up, Dad, it's Father's Day!'

Rushed into the kitchen to find smoke pouring out of toaster, cornflakes underfoot, milk spilt on table, butter knife in sugar bowl. Gracie ordered me to sit down at the table and gave me a card she'd made with Daisy's help. Quite frankly, Diary, I was distinctly underwhelmed. A piece of card had been folded in half and the word 'Dad' written in bits of pasta, most of which had fallen off leaving only traces of glue. Inside it said, 'form Gracie'.

I gently pointed out to her that 'from' was misspelled.

She frowned down at the card and said defiantly, 'That's how children spell "from" in America.'

I said, 'I think you might be wrong there, Gracie.'

She said, 'Have you been to America?'

I had to admit that I had, in fact, never been to America.

Gracie said, 'Well, I have. I went with Mummy one day while you were at the bookshop.'

I let it go. She is a formidable opponent.

I am now regretting having volunteered to be the writer/ director and producer of the Mangold Parva Players. Rehearsals are not going well, I break into a sweat when I realise we have only got eleven months before the opening night.

1 The Old Pigsty
The Piggeries
Bottom Field
Lower Lane
Mangold Parva
Leicestershire

Dear Sir Trevor Nunn

Your name has been passed to me by Angela Hacker, the author and playwright, who is a neighbour of mine. I have written a play, *Plague!*, set in the medieval countryside. It is an elegiac piece and features sixty human actors and quite a few animals, mostly domestic.

Angela thought you might be able to give me a few tips on handling such a large cast.

As you cannot fail to see, I have enclosed *Plague!* for your perusal. If you would like to get involved, please let me know as soon as possible.

I remain, sir,

A. A. Mole

SCENE I

A storm. A group of monks enter, wearing habits and sandals.
A more distinguished monk is carrying a casket. This is ABBOT
GODFRIED, a holy monk aged about fifty. [Note to stage
management: A vacuum cleaner with the pipe in the blowhole set
at the side of the stage can create the wind of the 'storm'.]

ABBOT GODFRIED: Hark, Brother! The wind doth blow
very hard, methinks we must take shelter in this
cursed place.

A yokel appears. He is called John and is going home for his
dinner of maize dumplings in pig's ear broth.

ABBOT GODFRIED: Halt, yokel! Where is't thou goeth
with such haste?
YOKEL JOHN: I be going home to my dinner, holy
one.
ABBOT GODFRIED: What be this foul place called?
YOKEL JOHN: 'Tain't got no name, 'tis just an 'ill an' a
few fields and an 'ovel or two.
ABBOT GODFRIED: In a storm a hovel is as meritorious
as a palace, yokel.

They have reached the Village Square, where thirty-five assorted
men and women are standing around. A pack of dogs enter from
stage left and cross. Chickens peck between the villagers' feet.
ABBOT GODFRIED holds the casket aloft. He is followed by a
fat monk, BROTHER DUNCAN, who enjoys birdwatching, and

a thin monk, BROTHER ANDREW, *who suffers from panic attacks.*

YOKEL JOHN: What have you, in the box?
ABBOT GODFRIED: I have the entrails and anus of King John.

The villagers and animals fall to their knees.

ABBOT GODFRIED: His heart was buried at York. And this benighted place, methinks, will serve the King's anus well.

The villagers cheer and the dogs bark.

END OF SCENE I

Monday 18th June

I have just seen a photograph in an old copy of the *Leicester Mercury* of a bloke called Harry Plant who was celebrating his one hundred and ninth birthday. One hundred and nine! He fought at the Battle of Passchendaele in the Great War when he was nineteen.

Mr Plant had a full head of hair, in fact he could have done with a haircut. I wonder what his secret is?

1 The Old Pigsty
The Piggeries
Bottom Field
Lower Lane
Mangold Parva
Leicestershire

The Willows Nursing Home
Bevan Road
Dewsbury
Leeds

Dear Mr Plant

Congratulations on reaching the grand age of 109. I wonder if you would mind letting me in on the secret of your longevity? I am particularly interested in how you managed to retain your hair.

Advice on diet, habits etc. would be most gratefully accepted.

I remain, sir,

Your most humble and obedient servant,

A. A. Mole

A letter (in quivery writing).

Dear Mr Mole
  I thank you for your kind interest. I have no
dietary habits, I just eat the food of the average
Englishman.
  As for my hair, I pulverise an onion and apply the
juice to my scalp before retiring for the night.
  With regards from,
  Mr Plant

                                    1 The Old Pigsty
                                      The Piggeries
                                       Bottom Field
                                        Lower Lane
                                    Mangold Parva
                                    Leicestershire

The Willows Nursing Home
Bevan Road
Dewsbury
Leeds

Dear Mr Plant
  Thank you very much for your reply to my letter of Monday.
  I wonder if you would indulge me further by advising me on
the type of onion you use?
  I look forward to your reply.
  Yours,
  A. A. Mole

Tuesday 19th June

Today I asked Daisy if she would consider playing Eliza Hepplethwaite, the village whore, in *Plague!*. I told her that she would have to wear red stockings and a matted hair wig, stick on warts and have her teeth blackened. I said, 'Remember, *Plague!* is set in pre-Colgate days.'

Daisy said, 'Would it surprise you if I said no? Ask Marlene Webb from the boarding kennels, her teeth are positively medieval.'

I said, 'I confess myself bitterly disappointed, Daisy. I had hoped that you would support my theatrical activities. Don't tell me that *Plague!* is no good. It's the best thing I've ever written. I gave a copy to the vicar and he wrote to congratulate me.' I took the note out of my wallet and showed it to Daisy.

Dear Adrian

A short note. I'm stunned. Congratulations on the first draft of Plague!. It is quite an achievement to give over sixty cast members at least two lines each.

I fear a prior commitment prevents me from accepting your kind offer to play Daft Dick.

I have, as you requested, passed the script on to my wife. She says she will read it when she has finished working her way through the complete Iris Murdoch.

Yours in God,
Simon

Wednesday 20th June

Tony Blair is flying around the world on his farewell tour. My mother says she half expects him to break into 'My Way' at the top of the aeroplane steps.

Watched a Channel Five documentary about an American woman, *The Fattest Woman in the World*, with Daisy. The woman, named Cindy-Lou, cannot move from her reinforced bed. She is so gargantuan that her nightgown is made up of two king-sized sheets stitched together.

Daisy said, 'I could land up like Cindy-Lou if I'm not careful.'

Sunday 24th June

Rain, torrential. When will it stop?

Woken by church bells at 7 a.m. As usual, felt guilty for not going to church even though I am 20 per cent agnostic and 80 per cent atheist. Went back to sleep; woken again by phone.

It was Glenn in Afghanistan, using up some of his free family contact time. He asked me to give 'a girl what I met in Dude's Night Club my BFPO address. I can't get her out of my head, Dad. I think she might be the one.' When I asked him for the girl's name and address, he said, 'I cou'n't 'ear, Dad, the music was too loud. But if you 'appen to come across Tiny Curtis, the head bouncer at Dude's on Saturday night, can you pass this message on? Have you got a pen or pencil, Dad?'

I scrabbled in the bedside drawer, but could not find a single writing implement that worked. Conscious that precious seconds were ticking away, I reached for Daisy's black eyeliner pencil, which is never far from her side, even when asleep, and took down the following message.

Yo, Tiny. How's it hanging, Bro? Do you remember that girl I was with last time I was in? Well, can you tell her I think she's lush and that I want her to write to me in Afghanistan? Tell her to send a photo. Thanks, Bro.

You would think the boy had grown up in Harlem rather than a post-war council estate in Leicester. I protested to Glenn that I was never likely to 'come across' Tiny outside Dude's on a Saturday night since I never went into the city centre after dark if I could help it.

Glenn said, 'Please, Dad, it could be the last thing you ever do for me. The Taliban is closing in.'

I could hardly refuse.

Walked under dripping trees into Mangold Parva to the Bear Inn for lunch.

My mother said, 'If the sun doesn't shine soon, the whole of England will have a nervous breakdown.'

Gracie refused to walk through the puddles in the lane, even though she was wearing her red boots for the first time, and demanded to sit on my father's lap in his wheelchair.

My mother said, 'That child will never walk anywhere if you keep giving in to her, Adrian. And anyway, she won't be comfortable. There's not an ounce of fat on your father's legs now.'

Daisy said, 'Leave her be, Pauline, she'll only kick off. I want to eat my lunch in peace.'

My mother stomped off ahead, muttering, 'You're making a rod for your own bleeding backs,' as she attempted to light a cigarette in the stiff June gale.

I was surprised to hear a cheer as we entered the pub. Surprised, because the Mole family is not particularly popular around here since the incident with the wheelie bins. However, the cheer was for the news that Tony Blair has finally resigned as leader of the Labour Party and will be standing down on Wednesday as prime minister. I should have been joining in the cheers, instead I felt tears prick my eyes. Mr Blair squandered my affection and respect for him on a war that killed my son's friend.

I was transported back to that glorious May Day when cherry blossom floated in the spring sunshine – as if the trees were throwing confetti to celebrate New Labour's victory. I was young then and full of hope and believed that Mr Blair – with his mantra of 'Education, education, education' – would transform England into a land where people at bus stops spoke to each other of Tolstoy and post-structuralism, but it was not to be, my own father thinks that Tate Modern is a new type of sugar cube.

As we took our places in the 'Carvery' queue, my mother rhapsodised about Gordon Brown, saying he was dark and craggy and solid. Daisy broke off from comparing the relative succulence of the beef, pork, lamb and turkey joints and said, 'The north face of the Eiger is craggy and solid. The difference is, the north face has more emotional intelligence.'

Daisy claims that when she was a PR girl in London, rumour had it that Gordon Brown had a syndrome of some kind. My mother said that Gordon Brown still had all the qualities she looked for in a man – he was introverted with an air of menace about him, just like Mr Rochester in *Jane Eyre*. My mother is getting quite literary lately. She is reading four novels a week in preparation for writing her autobiography. Ha! Ha! Ha!

Lunch at the Carvery was adequate, but I still miss my grandmother's Sunday dinners. No carvery can replicate her crisp Yorkshire pudding and her rustling roast potatoes. As we were hacking at our meat (we had all gone for the beef apart from Gracie, who had the 'Pirate's Special' – fish fingers and an eye patch), my father said, 'I've been working it all out in my head. It's just cost us as good as six pounds each for this bloody muck, and Gracie's was near on four pounds. That's twenty-eight quid! How much is a decent joint of beef?' He looked at my mother and Daisy, they stared back at him blankly. Neither of them appeared to know. 'A bit of beef, a few vegetables . . . !' my father said. 'He's making a profit out of us!' He resumed scraping the last vestiges of gravy from his plate.

I said, 'But that's capitalism. I thought you approved of the capitalist system, or have you had a change of heart?' Was this failure to grasp the basic rules of business an early sign of Alzheimer's?

Tom Urquhart, the landlord, strolled over. For some reason, he has never liked our family. I haven't had a proper conversation with him since the day I asked him if he would install a disabled toilet for my father. His pathetic excuse was, 'A disabled toilet would spoil the character of the pub – The Bear has been 'ere since before the monasteries were dissolved.'

When I pointed out to him that Cromwell's army had a high incidence of disability (it was rife with amputees) he turned his back on me and started fiddling with the optics behind the bar.

We had run out of gravy, but I didn't want to ask Urquhart. Instead I went to the kitchen door with the empty jug and was shocked at the sight of Kath Urquhart, the landlady, having the back of her neck kissed by Jamie Briton, the trainee chef. I quickly moved away from the door but I think they may have seen me.

I returned to our table with the empty jug, much to my mother's disgust.

My father whined, 'I'd go myself but I don't know if my wheelchair will fit through the gaps between the tables.'

My mother grabbed the empty jug and almost ran towards the kitchen, disappeared through the door, then reappeared only half a moment later. I searched for a sign that she had witnessed more of Mrs Urquhart's scandalous behaviour, but her face was its usual mask of Max Factor foundation and disappointment with life.

Monday 25th June

Rained all day. The brook at the end of our field is babbling. My mother asked me if I thought our field would flood. I reassured her that according to Tony Wellbeck in the post office our field had only flooded a few times in the last ten years.

A letter from Mr Plant.

Dear Mr Mole
  Spanish.
  Yours,
  Mr Plant

PS: Please do not write to me again.

Tuesday 26th June

Today is Mr Blair's last day as Prime Minister of Great Britain. I expect he will have a full day trying to repair his reputation.

Perhaps he will visit a hospital and see some of the badly injured soldiers who served in Iraq.

On his last day in office Mr Blair entertained Arnold Schwarzenegger.

When I look at Mr Blair now I see a weak man who

took us into a war because of his own personal vanity. Everything he did for the country seems to be unravelling. I am an atheist but, should it turn out there is a God, I might think that He had arranged for biblical rain to fall on Blair's legacy of sin – casinos, television pornography, binge drinking, knife crime and instant credit. I have great hopes for Mr Brown, a man of substance, gravitas and numeracy. I think he is a secret socialist who will go into Number Ten much as Clark Kent went into a phone box. I am convinced that Mr Brown will emerge as Superman.

My mother is obsessed with misery memoirs, she is currently reading *A Child Called 'It'*. She said tonight, 'I could write a book.'

I expect she thinks it will validate her life.

Wednesday 27th June

The country is on flood alert. The people of Hull are already experiencing the worst.

Went round to see my parents and pay them our share of the mortgage. The television news was on. I studied the new incumbents as they stood outside Number Ten on Mr Brown's first day of office. He looked as if he had had a mouth transplant and was trying his smile out for the first time, and his wave is pathetic.

My mother said, of Mrs Brown, 'Poor Sarah, two little kids to look after, a workaholic husband and all those canapés to arrange and dignitaries to meet.'

I said, 'Why are you calling her Sarah? You don't know her.'

My mother said, 'All women are sisters to me. That's something you'll never understand, Adrian.'

My father said, 'She looks like a decent sort of woman, and at least she's got a normal-sized mouth on her.'

So Gordon Brown is now the captain at the helm of the country's ship. Let us hope he will steer Great Britain away from the rocks so that we may voyage on calm and prosperous seas and towards the light at the end of the tunnel. I expect Mr Brown to denounce Tony Blair's decision to invade Iraq any day now.

Still raining. River Sense – high. It has broken its banks in places. I have had to micturate twelve times today.

9 p.m.

1 The Old Pigsty
The Piggeries
Bottom Field
Lower Lane
Mangold Parva
Leicestershire
Wednesday 27th June 2007

The Right Honourable Gordon Brown
Prime Minister & First Lord of the Treasury
10 Downing Street
London SW1A 2AA

Dear Prime Minister

A quick note to ask if you have had a chance to glance at the papers concerning my tax affairs?

Yours,

A concerned citizen,

A. A. Mole

Thursday 28th June

Daisy has joined Weight Watchers at the village hall, I had to give her a lift on the back of my bike because she will not wear wellingtons and the lane is flooded due to the non-stop rain.

It wasn't worth going home again – she was only going to be an hour – so I arranged to meet her in The Bear after she'd been weighed and done whatever else it is that Weight Watchers do.

Daisy came in and slumped down next to me, saying, 'I'm thirteen stone twelve ounces.' She lit a cigarette.

'Thirteen stone twelve ounces, is that good or bad?' I asked.

'It would be great if I were a light-heavyweight boxer,' she said. 'But as I'm only five foot three and small boned, yes, it is a bad thing, a very bad thing.'

She picked up my beer glass and drained the contents, then wiped her mouth with the back of her hand and said, 'I was nine stone one pound on my wedding day.'

I could see that she was descending into one of her depressions, so I said, 'There's more of you to cuddle now.'

That obviously didn't help.

I went to the bar to get her a double vodka and tonic (drinking straw but no ice, no lemon).

A group of hefty women in tracksuits bulged into the pub and crowded round a small table where they all lit cigarettes. The bar soon resembled the last scene of *Casablanca* with fog on the runway.

'Are they your fellow Weight Watchers?' I asked.

'No,' said Daisy, who knew everything that was happening in the village. 'They're training for a sponsored run to raise money to save the post office.'

'Save it from what?' I asked.

'Closing,' said Daisy, lighting yet another cigarette.

I said, 'You've just put one out, and that was only half smoked.'

She replied, quite savagely considering we were in public, 'Listen, Mr Clean Lungs. On Sunday it will be against the fucking law to smoke a fag in a pub. I'm getting as many in as I can before then.'

To divert her I brought us back to our conversation about the post office. 'It can't close,' I said. 'I use it at least three times a week. And what about Dad? It's his only regular outing, he loves pension day.'

Daisy slammed her glass down and shouted to Tom Urquhart behind the bar, 'You could feed a newborn baby on this Stolichnaya. You're not supposed to water it down, it's not Rose's effing lime juice!'

I sometimes wish that Daisy had not been brought up to be a free spirit, and had learnt to be inhibited in public. She didn't care that Urquhart was muttering about her, or that everyone in the pub was looking at her.

I approached the tracksuited women to ask if I could join the Save the Post Office Campaign. I explained that due to personal reasons I was unable to do a sponsored run, gesturing vaguely at my legs.

'I know who you are,' said one of the women, wearing a pink and white tracksuit the exact shade of coconut ice. 'I've seen you at the school gate. You live in one of them pigsties – you're writing the community play. Can we all have a part?'

I told them that I would write a scene for them, and they laughed and did high fives with their porky arms across the table.

10 p.m.

On our way home the rain was thundering on to the umbrella. Gibbet Lane was more puddle than road. I had to push Daisy most of the way. It was no easy matter having a light-heavyweight boxer on the crossbar.

I told her that unless she bought a pair of wellingtons I would . . .

'You'll do what?' she said, her hands tightening around my neck.

I did not reply. She knows I am a fool for love.

The field was so flooded that the water came ankle height up my wellingtons and I had to carry Daisy right up to the front door.

As I was putting the key in the lock, my mother came to her front door and said, 'I saw you staggering up the drive – is she drunk again?'

Daisy slid off my back and said, 'Again, Pauline? Again? I can't remember the last time I was drunk!'

'I can,' said my mother. 'It was yesterday. I nipped in to cadge a fag and you were lying on the settee.'

'I was playing at casualty with Gracie!' said Daisy heatedly.

By now we were in the cramped hallway. I took off my sodden coat and trousers, put on my dressing gown and went into the living room. My mother and Daisy remained in the hall, having a whispered con-versation. Then I heard my mother's raised voice. 'You might think you can fool *him*, Daisy. But you can't fool *me*!'

Before we went to bed, I checked the alcohol supplies in the kitchen cupboard. There was very little vodka left in the bottle and all the leftover Christmas liqueurs and novelty drinks (Nigel's birthday gift of scorpion tequila) had gone.

Friday 29th June

Mr Carlton-Hayes, who returned to work on Monday, said the incessant rain reminded him of the floods of 1953 when his aunt was swept from her bungalow in Skegness, carried downstream and ended up on the roof of the bus station. He didn't say why he had been away from the shop, but I noticed that he is walking very gingerly.

Sunday 1st July

NO SMOKING DAY

A momentous day! Smoking in a public place or place of work is forbidden in England. Though if you are a lunatic, a prisoner, an MP or a member of the Royal Family you are exempt.

Smoking has blighted my life. There is a photograph

33

of me in my mother's arms, the day I was released from the maternity hospital. She is standing in the hospital car park with me cradled in one arm, the other arm is hanging at her side and in her hand is a lit cigarette.

I have been ingesting smoke since I was five days old. My childhood memories are clouded by smoke-filled rooms and car journeys made miserable by my chain-smoking parents. From my subservient position in the back of the car I would plead for a window to be opened, but my father would refuse angrily, saying fresh air was bad for his bronchitic chest. I remember, on a long traffic-choked journey to Hunstanton, improvising a facemask out of a Kleenex Mansize tissue. My parents found this to be hilarious and called me 'bandit boy' throughout our short stay.

After breakfast (two Weetabix, chocolate croissant, banana) I went next door to invite them to Sunday lunch at The Bear. I said, 'I want to experience *for the first time* what it's like to enjoy a meal with you without both of you blowing smoke in my face.'

My father went into a rant, saying, 'This bloody authoritarian government, they're a bunch of fascists, Nazis!'

My mother looked broken. 'This is a sad, sad day,' she said.

'It's hardly the end of civilization,' I said, as I went around the room emptying ashtrays into the pedal bin.

My mother said, 'Well, it's the end of my little world.'

She went into a lamentation about what will be lost.

'What will be lost,' I said, 'will be your hacking cough, the foul stink, the experience –'

Interrupting, my mother reached for her cigarette packet and said dreamily, 'I've smoked since I was thirteen. At fifteen I wore three-quarter-length gloves and used a tortoiseshell cigarette holder.'

'They'd lynch you nowadays,' my father said.

'Who would?' I asked.

'Bleedin' animal rights tossers, save the bloody tortoise.'

My mother continued, 'At sixteen I was going to the Hot Sounds jazz club in Norwich. It was there I smoked my first Disque Bleu.'

'I was on Capstan Full Strength by the time I was sixteen,' boasted my father.

I left them to their smoking reminiscences, I could hear Daisy and Gracie shouting at each other through the party wall.

When I got in, I found them engaged in yet another ridiculous argument about clothing. Why does my daughter always have to be dressed as a Disney character of some kind? She is a merchandiser's dream. I still remember her first day at nursery school, her pirate costume did not go down well with the reception class teacher, and it took for ever to wrest the cutlass from her tiny fingers.

Gracie shouted, 'Why can't I wear my Tinker Bell costume to the pub?'

Daisy said, 'You can, but you're not wearing the wings.'

'Fairies have to wear their wings, or they can't fly,' said Gracie.

'You're not wearing those bloody wings,' said Daisy. 'The last time you wore them in the pub, they knocked every glass off the next table and it cost your dad twenty-five quid to replace the drinks.'

Gracie shouted, 'Well, if my wings knock anything over today, I'll pay with my million pounds in the bank.'

Daisy and I looked at each other guiltily. We had pillaged Gracie's saving-for-the-future bank account to pay the last electricity bill. She stomped off to her bedroom and returned wearing the Tinker Bell dress and wings. I did not have the heart to remonstrate. When Gracie said, 'I look beautiful, don't I?' I weakened and said, 'Yes.'

Daisy exploded, saying that I was ganging up against her and undermining her authority. I took a tea towel and began to dry the breakfast things that Daisy had left on the draining board and remained calm as she berated me for actual and imaginary wrongs. It was a long and familiar list.

The cesspit.

The fact that she doesn't have a car.

I earn a pittance at the bookshop.

She is tired of colouring her own hair and the lack of Sky Plus.

She hates the taste and texture of the bread I make twice a week.

She thinks the villagers of Mangold Parva are
   imbeciles.
She hates giving the pigsty address to anybody.
She is sick of my parents interfering in our lives.

She sat down at the kitchen table and began to cry. It
was a heartbreaking sound and I suddenly became afraid.
Gracie wriggled out of the contentious Tinker Bell
costume and waved the twinkly wand over her mother's
head as though magic would stop her tears.

I don't know how I can make my wife happy.

Gracie and I sat on our own for most of our meal at The
Bear. Daisy and my mother and father were outside,
smoking in the rain, together with most of the regulars.
Tom Urquhart, the landlord, said, 'This no-smoking
malarkey is going to finish The Bear.'

I did not enjoy my meal. It was overcooked and had a
curious texture that set my gag mechanism off, I suspect
because Lee Grant, the chef, was constantly nipping out
to have a cigarette. Also, Gracie kept up an interminable
monologue about a boy at nursery school called Mason,
who lives in one of the council houses. She told me
that he has a packed lunch of two bags of crisps, a bottle
of Coke, a bag of Haribo sweets and a cheese string.
According to Gracie, Mason was made to stand in front
of the assembled school whilst the contents of his lunch
box were displayed and condemned by Mrs Bull, the
headmistress. The box reference reminded me that it was
months since I had last spoken to Pandora. I think about

her several times a day but I am a proud man and I have been waiting for her to ring me. I saw that the smokers had been joined in the drizzle by Hugo Fairfax-Lycett, the heir apparent of Fairfax Hall. As I watched, he lit Daisy's cigarette and she threw her head back and did her party trick of blowing a succession of smoke rings. I saw the admiration on his face and watched as my mother undid the top button of her mock-satin shirt. I don't see why women go so barmy about Fairfax-Lycett. He is far too tall, looks like a ravaged Hugh Grant and is vulgarly ostentatious with his sports cars and Savile Row tweeds. I bet he has never opened a book since leaving Cambridge. Pandora would make mincemeat of him.

After an interminable-seeming ten minutes I heard the roar of Fairfax-Lycett's car and my family came back inside for their pudding.

My mother pushed her soggy peach cobbler to the side of the bowl and said, 'The food in this place has gone off.'

My father said, 'Everything has gone off since New Labour took over. Do you know who owns our water now? The fucking French! And you can't even pick your nose in private any more, there'll be a bloody CCTV camera watching where you put your bogeys. You've got nutters in Glasgow bombing the bleeding airport, and soon we're all going to be up to our waists in floodwater. What next?'

Tony Wellbeck from the post office said, 'Foot and mouth, George. They've got it in Hardton, less than a mile from Mangold.'

Diary, if somebody had walked into the pub and said,

'There's a plague of locusts outside,' I would not have raised an eyebrow.

Is this the end of the world as we know it?

Later, I was going to have it out with Daisy, but then I noticed she was reading *For the Sake of Argument* by Christopher Hitchens and again decided against it.

Monday 2nd July

Mr Carlton-Hayes phoned to say that he was 'incapacitated'. I don't like it when he's not at the shop. It's not that he does very much these days, but I feel better when he's there.

He truly loves books, to the detriment of the business. The other day a middle-aged woman with John Lennon glasses and overlarge breasts came in and tried to buy a second edition of *The Mill on the Floss* for £150. She introduced herself as Dr Pearce and said she was looking for a retirement present for the head of the English Department at De Montfort University. Mr Carlton-Hayes unlocked the glass cabinet where the antiquarian books are kept, and took the two-volume edition down from the shelf. He handed volume one to the woman, watched her leaf through it, then took it back and replaced both books in the cabinet. When Dr Pearce had left, empty-handed and bewildered, Mr Carlton-Hayes said, 'I thought she handled it too roughly,' as though the book were an RSPCA rescue dog.

It's no wonder the accountants are advising him to sell the shop premises to Tesco. When he told me this, I saw a rare flash of anger pass over his face. He spread his arms out to the shelves and stacks of books and said, 'But where would they go?' as though they were a displaced people.

I took advantage of Mr Carlton-Hayes's absence, phoned De Montfort University and left a message for Dr Pearce to the effect that *The Mill on the Floss* was now for sale. She came in only minutes before I closed. We talked about George Eliot and she seemed pleased to find a fellow enthusiast. It was 6.30 before I noticed the time. She waited while I locked up, then we walked down the High Street together, me pushing my bike, she holding an umbrella over our heads. She kept me talking on the corner of the Holiday Inn car park for another half an hour.

When Daisy asked why I was late home, I told her that the chain had come off my bike. Don't ask me why.

Thursday 5th July
Mr C-H back

Received a disaster alert text on my mobile as we were eating our sandwiches in the back of the shop. Twenty-five killed and thirty-three injured in an explosion in a karaoke bar in Tianshifu in China.

'Shocking, isn't it?' I said to Mr Carlton-Hayes.

'It is indeed,' he said, sighing. 'Karaoke in Chin, Weep, Confucius, weep!'

Friday 6th July

Woken up by the phone. It was my mother. 'Have you looked outside?' she shrieked.

I took the phone and drew back the bedroom curtains. The fields had vanished and been replaced by shimmering floodwater as far as the eye could see.

'Have you got any sandbags?' my mother asked.

I said, 'You *know* I haven't got any *sandbags*. Why would I have sandbags?'

I phoned Mr Carlton-Hayes to tell him that I wouldn't be in today and he said, 'Yes, it was rather exciting driving through the floods. The water came up to the wheel arches of the Rover.' I spent most of the rest of the day trying, Canute-like, to prevent the water from breaching our doorstep.

When the flood had receded somewhat, I sat down with Gracie to watch television. Postman Pat has been promoted, he has got to leave Greendale Village and his red van to move to a middle-management position at Head Office. Some fool at the BBC said, 'We are taking Postman Pat into a dynamic new environment. There will be highly charged storylines.' So even Postman Pat is sacrificed on the altar of progress. Without his uniform and his red van, Pat is nothing. NOTHING!

This is just a blatant attempt to exploit the commercial

arm of the BBC. I expect there will be a new range of Postman Pat merchandise. Will I have to buy Gracie a Postman Pat Montego and a suit and briefcase set?

Wednesday 11th July

Day off today. I intended to spend it diligently colour coding my CDs and updating a few pages of my serial killer comedy, *The White Van*. I lay awake last night thinking about it. Obviously Pauline Quirke and Harry Enfield are a bit old now to play the serial killer and his wife, but Russell Brand and Amy Winehouse would make good substitutes.

I was also going to offer to do half the ironing, but something came over me, and I did nothing but watch television. At 4 p.m. I tore myself away from *Flog It!* (I really wanted to know how much a Clarice Cliff egg cup set went for at auction) and ran in my wellingtons through the last few inches of floodwater to the post office, to post a birthday card to my sister-in-law, Marigold, and a parcel for Daisy. She had eBayed her Louis Vuitton holdall to a woman in Nuneaton to pay the Severn Trent water bill before they cut us off. The postmaster and postmistress, Tony and Wendy Wellbeck, were both behind the counter bickering over the cost of airmail stamps to Timbuktu. I signed the Keep Our Post Office Open petition and waited. They both smiled politely when they noticed me at the counter.

'Who in Mangold Parva is writing to Timbuktu?' I asked.

Wendy looked around the post office, then lowered her voice and said, out of the corner of her mouth, 'I'm not allowed to say — confidentiality or data protection — but if you nip out and look up Gibbet Lane . . .'

I went outside and saw old Mrs Lewis-Masters inching her way up the hill behind a Zimmer frame. Timbuktu? She looked like the type of woman who only ever wrote to some distant relation in Sydenham about knitting patterns and the trials of dealing with one's bank via their call centre in Calcutta.

As she weighed Daisy's parcel, Mrs Wellbeck said, 'She writes to Timbuktu once a fortnight, sends cards at Christmas and Easter and a birthday card in early July.'

The Mangold Parva post office is like an illustration out of one of Gracie's books, apart from the fact that Mr and Mrs Wellbeck are not squirrels in Edwardian clothing. Every inch of the interior is lined with shelving and stuff for sale, though I think the Wellbecks lost control of their stock years ago. There are tins of beans next to a box of Jiffy bags. Pots of pens and pencils share a shelf with tins of cat and dog food. Greetings cards are jumbled together in shoeboxes: 'Happy First Birth-day' shares a box with 'Condolences On Your Recent Bereavement'.

The stationery shelves tempted me with their luscious spiral-bound notebooks containing virginal white, black-lined paper with margins in red. I was drawn to them as other men are drawn to adult toys in sex shops.

43

'Another notebook?' said Mrs Wellbeck. 'What are you doin', eating 'em?'

'Mr Mole's a bit of a writer,' said Mr Wellbeck. Everything he said sounded faintly insulting, as though he was having a private joke.

'*I* could write a book, working 'ere,' said Mrs Wellbeck. 'You wouldn't believe the things we see and hear.'

It is my habit to challenge people like Mrs Wellbeck, who make such empty boasts. 'Why don't you write a book then?' I said.

Mrs Wellbeck sighed. 'I would if I 'ad the time.'

'Wendy's a brilliant writer,' said Wellbeck. 'Her letters are famous in the family.'

'A book is a very different thing, though, isn't it?' I pressed. 'A book needs structure, plot, characterizations.'

'Her punctuation is second to none,' said Wellbeck. 'She knows exactly where to place her full stops.'

'Then she must go ahead and write her book,' I said.

'I told you, I haven't got the time,' she said quite irritably, I thought, considering I was a customer.

'Why? What do you do with the hours you are not working?' I asked, genuinely wanting to know.

'I sleep for eight of them,' she said.

'And the rest?' I asked. I couldn't stop, even though I could see that our conversation was leading to a confrontation about the artistic sensibility.

'I cook, I clean, I wash, I iron, I do a daily sudoku, I garden . . .' She went on in this vein.

I happen to know that Mrs Wellbeck is an ardent follower of various soap operas. I have often heard her talking proprietorially about characters in *EastEnders*, *Coronation Street* and *Emmerdale*.

'And television,' I queried. 'Does that take up the time when you could be writing?'

Mr and Mrs Wellbeck exchanged a glance. She'd been caught bang to rights. However, I felt no joy at my victory, and to show compassion to Mrs Wellbeck I bought yet another notebook to add to my collection.

On the way home, I easily overtook Mrs Lewis-Masters, who was still inching up Gibbet Lane in the rain. I walked at a funeral pace beside her, sheltering both of us from the heavy downpour under my umbrella. She looked a little afraid of me and moved her handbag, so that it hung on the other side of the Zimmer frame. I put her at her ease by discussing the merits of the hanging baskets which were displayed on every cottage and lamp post.

She looked at the floral baskets disdainfully. 'Were I younger,' she said in an accent the Queen would have felt at home with, 'I would steal out at night and destroy the gaudy horrors.'

She stopped and stared at some bright orange flowers that spilt out of a green plastic tub, hanging from a bracket on the wall of Pamper Yourself.

'What are they?' I asked.

'Begonias,' she spat. 'They are abominations, the Margaret Thatcher of the plant world. Shrill, domineering, ubiquitous.'

I looked at the old woman with new eyes. I would have put her down as a certain Thatcherite.

*

Before we parted company at the top of the hill, I determined to find out why she regularly corresponded with somebody in Timbuktu.

'Do you live far from here?' I asked.

'No, that's my house there.' (No, thets my harse thare.) She nodded at an imposing flat-fronted brick house at the crest of the hill.

'So not as far away as Timbuktu?' I said, feigning a laugh.

'Timbuktu?' she said, lifting her head and focusing her grey eyes on me. 'Why bring Timbuktu into the conversation?'

I said, 'It's an expression my father uses to denote distance.' I wished her 'good day' and hurried away.

When I got home I Googled Timbuktu and learnt that it is the main city in the landlocked state, the French Sudan, where the river meets the desert. Arab tribes brought gold from the south and salt from the north. Once described as the place where the 'camel meets the canoe'.

Thursday 12th July

Gracie had a horrible tantrum this morning, demanding that she be allowed to wear her Little Mermaid outfit rather than her school uniform. Daisy and I were quite helpless in the face of the child's rage. I explained that it would impede her movements, and the fishtail dragging through the puddles in the lane would prevent her from walking to school. Besides, Little Mermaid has to be carried everywhere and then lowered on to 'rocks'. Gracie was screaming, 'I am a fish! I can *swim* to school!' as I abandoned my wife to my by now hysterical daughter, costumed in her half-bimbo, half-fish dress. It was pouring with rain again, but I didn't care. I would have cycled in a typhoon to get away from the din in that house.

Mr Carlton-Hayes was away again. A young man in black square-framed glasses asked me if I had anything on tropical diseases. He looked a bit peaky, so I kept my distance and directed him to the medical shelves where he opened *Rapid Infectious Diseases and Tropical Medicine* by Rachel Isba, read for twenty minutes looking increasingly worried, then hurried from the shop without buying anything.

    After he had gone, I sprayed the shop with Dettol Antiseptic Disinfectant, just to be on the safe side. I can't afford to be ill.

Saturday 14th July

Nigel rang me at work to tell me that he's in love '*with a fellow blind man*'! How stupid can you get? It would have been better all round if Nigel had fallen for a man with good eyesight. But as it is, Nigel and his new partner, Lance Lovett, will be blundering around, bumping into furniture, spilling drinks and walking into the traffic together!

    I told Nigel that he has made a rod for his own back.

47

He said, 'I've still got Graham to help me.'

I said, 'Graham is a *dog*, Nigel! And he's on his last legs, it's not fair to expect him to look after *two* blind people. It's extra work for him.'

'Don't feel sorry for *Graham*,' said Nigel, bitterly. 'He's been a lazy bastard lately. I asked him to fetch a clean towel from the airing cupboard yesterday and he wouldn't move out of his basket.'

Sunday 15th July

Nigel rang. Hysterical.

Graham is dead. The vet said he'd probably been dead at least twelve hours.

'And you didn't realize the poor dog had stopped breathing?' I said scathingly. 'I thought blind people were supposed to have superior hearing?'

'You're confusing me with Superman,' said Nigel, through his sobs. 'Anyway, Mole, I want you to come over and bury Graham in the back garden.'

Later I said to Daisy, 'Why me? Why are people *always* asking *me* to bury their dead dogs?'

'Why, how many dead dogs *have* you buried?' she said.

'Two,' I said. 'Bert Baxter's dog, Sabre, and my family's old dog.'

'What was its name?' she asked.

'The Dog,' I said. 'It didn't have a name.'

'Well, two dead dogs in how many years?'

'Nearly twenty.'

'Well, that's hardly a regular supply of dead dogs, is it?'

10 p.m.

Nobody is on my side over the dog burial thing.

My mother accused me of being callous, saying, 'You're breaking the hearts of two blind men.'

I pointed out that Nigel and Lance are planning a kayak expedition through the Norwegian fjords, so they are more than capable of digging a hole big enough for a golden Labrador together.

My father thumped me on the arm from his wheelchair. 'I'd dig the hole myself if God hadn't given me a stroke.'

'It wasn't God, George,' said my mother, curling her lip. 'It was pork scratchings and forty fags a day.'

I rang Nigel when I got home and asked him if he'd got a spade.

'I didn't own a spade when I could bloody *see*. Why would I own one now?' he answered.

I could hear Lance sobbing in the background over the theme tune to *Newsnight*.

Monday 16th July

Left Mr Carlton-Hayes in charge of the shop and called for a taxi. Daisy, who had previously shown no interest in Graham whatsoever, insisted on accompanying me to the funeral, saying, 'We never go out together.'

I said, 'Since when did attending a dog's funeral count as taking you out?'

She said, 'There'll be a few lovely gay people there, so it should be a laugh.'

She was in black from head to foot and had even painted her fingernails with Chanel Noir. I did point out that wearing all black was a futile gesture because Nigel and Lance, the chief mourners, had only got 2 per cent eyesight between them.

Daisy said, 'I'm in all black because I'm in mourning for my fucking life!' I saw the taxi driver glance at Daisy in his rear-view mirror. I could tell that he disapproved of my wife, and I felt a little ashamed of her myself.

She sounded desperate.

To cheer her up I held her hand and suggested that we go to Wayne Wong's for a Chinese after the funeral. She squeezed my hand and smiled. It was like a shaft of bright sunlight piercing lowering storm clouds.

We arrived at Nigel's house by 9.30 a.m. There was a black wreath on the front door. I hadn't realized that Graham's interment would be such a big deal.

Nigel had invited guests. There was a sort of shrine to Graham on the corner unit in the living room and a large framed photograph of him smiling with his tongue lolling out. On a velvet cushion next to it lay the dead dog's collar and identity disc, and a Bonio that had been sprayed silver. Lance looks at least ten years older than Nigel, and has shaved his head, though not very well, as his scalp is covered in tiny scabs and more recent nicks. He was dressed in a dark suit and has a gold earring in his right ear, which I expect he thinks is rather dashing.

A candle burned in a black candlestick. Nigel choked, 'I'll never let that flame go out.'

I said, 'You should blow it out before you go to bed. The statistics for house fires have gone through the roof since candles became an interior design must-have.'

The deceased Graham lay in a Habitat storage box, surrounded by potpourri. His mouth was half open, displaying his teeth and giving him, even in death, the look of aggression that always kept me from being entirely comfortable in his presence.

While the guests ate the Iceland canapés and sipped pink champagne, I went into the little back garden and began the laborious business of digging a grave in wet clay. Every now and again I would stop to wipe my brow and look back at the living-room window, where one of Nigel's friends would wave encouragingly. I could see Daisy, surrounded by a crowd of admirers, talking and occasionally shouting with laughter. From this distance she appeared to have lost a little weight. Her resemblance to Nigella Lawson was remarkable.

Nobody offered to help. Though I must admit, when it started to rain, a gay friend of Lance's – who introduced himself as 'I'm Jason, I'm mad, I used to have green hair' – brought out an umbrella for me before running back inside to avoid getting wet.

Has Jason, or anyone else, tried to dig a hole with one hand, whilst holding an umbrella with the other?

I intended to take no part in the actual interment ceremony. In my opinion it was grossly over the top to have a CD of Elvis singing 'Old Shep' and a procession carrying the storage box and contents to the grave.

When the time came to lower the box, there was a horribly emotional scene. Nigel's grief was pitiful to see and hear. He almost stumbled into the grave at one point. To my great annoyance, the storage box was too wide for the hole and I had to retrieve the spade and resume digging. I am no homophobe, but digging a dog's grave whilst being watched by a dozen or so critical gay men is not an experience I want to go through again.

Eventually the lid of the storage box was put on and Graham was laid to rest. I was the only person present to remain dry-eyed throughout.

Diary, should I worry about my emotional detachment? Or should I congratulate myself on my self-control?

Nigel recited a poem Lance had composed.

'Graham' by Lance Lovett

Graham, is that your bark I hear?
Is that your growl, dear?
Graham, are you there in the daytime,
Are you there in the night?
Is it true that your bark
Was worse than your bite?
You lightened our darkness,
You shouldered our load,
Your eyes were appealing,
Your fur it was gold.

You shouldn't have left us
Before you grew old.

It was everything I hate about amateur poetry. It was sentimental, bathetic, it failed to scan and was riddled with clichés, but everybody else lapped it up and Lance was congratulated over and over again.

We didn't go to Wayne Wong's. Daisy drank too much pink champagne and became quite abusive about my cardigan, so I took her home before there was a scene.

Times visited the loo: twelve.

Wednesday 25th July

Half the country is underwater. The television news is showing cars and whole trees floating in the rapids that used to be roads. I walked down to look at the brook, it has turned from being a trickle of clear water into a white-water hell and it is encroaching on to the piggeries' land.

Gordon Brown has taken charge of the flood crisis. He is holding many emergency meetings. The newspapers have been over the top, with headlines such as 'Gordon Saves Flooded Brits'. Anybody would think he was lugging sandbags about or pumping the water out himself.

Wednesday 8th August

Took advantage of my parents' absence. They are at a protest meeting at The Bear, called about the proposed closure of our post office. I wanted to find the copy of *Jane Eyre* that my mother borrowed and swore she had given back to me. Sure enough, I found the missing book on the battered table she calls her 'desk', underneath a pile of misery memoirs.

A Child Called 'It', *Angela's Ashes* by Frank McCourt, *Running with Scissors*, but more interesting to me was a box file labelled *A Girl Called 'Shit'*. I opened the lid, there were a few pages of manuscript inside. I read them, standing at the desk. It was an account of her childhood in the Norfolk potato fields. My mother's book is a tissue of lies. In fact, it's a brown paper of lies – tissue is too delicate a simile to be attached to such a fraudulent enterprise.

A Girl called 'Shit' by Pauline Mole

I was born in the middle of a potato field near the village of Hose in the county of Norfolk. A bitter east wind chilled my mother's thighs as I made my way into the world of poverty and pain.

My father was a brutal giant of a man, with a head of black hair and a matted beard. He was taught to read and write at the village school and proved to be a brilliant pupil. His teacher, Mr Chipper, encouraged him to apply for Cambridge. However, on the day he was due to take the exams he was five minutes late, having walked barefoot from his village. He was turned away, and on his return home he burned every book and vowed never to read again.

My mother had been one of the great Norfolk beauties, she was of aristocratic birth and had met my father when she was riding with the Sandringham Hunt. She had fallen off her mount whilst crossing a potato field, and my father had gone to her assistance. Their liaison caused a great scandal and my mother, Lady Clarissa Cavendish-Stronge, married my father and became Mrs Sugden. I never heard my father call my mother by her name, it was always 'You'.

Within half an hour of giving birth, my father dragged my mother to her feet and insisted that she continue her work of picking potatoes from the black earth. I, having been wrapped in a potato sack, was pushed inside my mother's ex-army greatcoat. She worked until nightfall, only after she had cooked my father's dinner and cleaned out the ferret cages was she allowed to sit down.

My father's first words on seeing me were, 'A fookin' girl child ain't no use to me. I wanted a strong-armed lad to chuck a full sack o' spuds on't back of fookin' cart. Tek the girl child to yonder dike and let the crows 'av 'er.'

Luckily for me, my father drank himself into a stupor on turnip wine and in the morning had forgotten his directive. He refused to acknowledge me or register my birth and only ever referred to me as 'Shit'.

This is a complete lie. I have seen my mother's birth certificate, she was born in the cottage hospital at Burnham Market and was given the name Pauline Hilda

Sugden. Her father is a timid man who has never been known to raise his voice. Her mother was not beautiful. There is a story in our family that Grandma Sugden's face once frightened the horses at a local gymkhana and she was asked to leave.

Thursday 9th August

Got home from work to find Daisy in a state of excitement: eyes shining, cheeks pink, dark lipstick freshly applied, smelling strongly of Sarah Jessica Parker's *Lovely* and Jim Beam.

As soon as I put my key in the lock, she yanked the door open and said, 'Guess who's next door?'

I said nothing to Daisy but my actual first thought was that my dear younger son, William, had returned from Nigeria where he has been living with his mother and her new husband. I never talk about William – the subject is too painful.

'Not Glenn, back from Afghanistan?' I said.

She shook her head. A few hairgrips fell from her Amy Winehouse beehive.

'It's your brother!' she said.

I took my bicycle clips off and put them on the hall table. 'Half-brother,' I corrected. 'He's only got my father's blood.'

'Yes, Brett Mole. Oh, Aidy, he's amazing! You'd never think you were related.' She said, 'You didn't tell me he'd been to Oxford.'

I asked where Gracie was.

'She's next door with her Uncle Brett,' said Daisy. 'He's wonderful with children.'

I said, 'What's brought him here.'

'His mother. I don't know her name,' she said.

'Stick Insect,' I said. 'Otherwise known as Doreen Slater.'

'Well, she's dead. She died yesterday. Brett wanted to tell your dad himself, face to face. He's so thoughtful,' she said.

'Stick Insect dead,' I said, shocked. 'Was it anorexia?'

'Motorbike accident,' said Daisy.

'What was she doing on a motorbike?' I asked.

'According to Brett, she got in with a bad crowd.'

'She must have been sixty at least. You don't get in with a bad crowd when you're sixty,' I said.

'You do if it's the Bournemouth Chapter of the Hells Angels,' said Daisy. She checked her reflection in the hall mirror, gave a little smile and went next door.

I sat down on the bed and tried to control my breathing. Whenever I think about Brett Mole, I feel a deep sense of inadequacy. I remember that awful day in Skegness when my father told my mother that he had been having an affair with Doreen Slater and that she had just given birth to Brett. He is taller, better looking, better educated, he's a sportsman par excellence, and he does something mysterious involving hedge funds (whatever they are) in London, Tokyo and New York that has made him immensely rich.

My mother never stops telling me about the bunga-low that Brett bought for Stick Insect. Apparently, all

Doreen had to do was press a few buttons and the lights would come on, the curtains would close and music would play in every room.

My mother used to sigh and say, 'I wish ...' She never, ever finished the sentence but I know that her wish was that I had bought her a similar type of push-button house.

I had a good wash, changed out of my cardigan, combed my hair and went next door.

1 a.m.

What a bore! How can anybody talk about themselves for four solid hours? I blame the women. Every time he appeared to be running out of things to say about himself either Daisy or my mother would ask him a question about his very fascinating life and he would be off again. Yak, yak, yak.

How his lavatory in Tokyo washes and dries his bum automatically, what a great view he has of Central Park from his apartment in New York, how he loves to watch the boats on the river from the terrace of his Thames-side flat.

He seems to know every chef in London, constantly talking about Gordon, Marco and Jamie. And, according to him, his name is embroidered on Tracey Emin's tent.

He has got the whitest teeth I have ever seen, freakishly white. They could light up our dark field. I suppose he is conventionally good looking in a sort of vacuous George Clooney way. He told us that his casual suit had

death throes, claiming that her last words had been, 'Lift me up so that I can see the buds on the trees.'

This is when I first began to suspect that Brett Mole was an unreliable narrator:

a) Doreen died yesterday, long after the buds had developed into leaves.
b) I know for a fact that Doreen Slater hated trees. She used to say, 'Look at them, they just stand there.'

My father put himself to bed at ten o'clock, which is early for him.

My mother said, 'Poor George, he wants to grieve for Doreen.'

I don't think it was grief that sent him to his bed early, I think it was yawn-inducing, brain-deadening, buttock-clenching BOREDOM.

At 11.45 a young man with blond highlights knocked on the door. Brett introduced him as Logan, 'my driver', kissed everybody on both cheeks and nuzzled Gracie (who was sleeping in my arms), whispered, *Dors bien, ma petite*,' then climbed into the back of his car and was driven away. Stick Insect's funeral is next week.

When we got home and had put the sleeping Gracie into bed, Daisy said, 'Brett has invited us to stay with him in Bournemouth after the funeral.'

I said, 'No thank you. He's got to be the most boring man in England.'

'Boring?' she said. 'I thought he was totally fascinating. And he was so funny about Guy Ritchie and Madonna.'

My wife baffles me.

Friday 10th August

Daisy managed to mention Brett's name at least a dozen times before I left for work.

As I was putting my cycle clips on in the hall, I heard her on the phone to my mother, speculating on whether Brett was gay or not. 'There was no mention of a wife or girlfriend,' said Daisy. 'And he's incredibly well groomed.'

Monday 13th August

I went to see Nigel and asked if I could borrow his car. He refused, saying that the last time I borrowed it I brought it back with the petrol tank empty.

I said, 'What's it to you? You can't use the car yourself – you're blind, as is your life partner, Lance.'

Nigel said, 'He might not be my life partner for ever. I might fall in love with somebody with good sight and a driving licence.'

I said, 'In that case, stop introducing Lance as "My Life Partner".'

Nigel said, 'Yes, I should. He's getting far too complacent, he's let himself go a bit, he's now only shaving every other day.'

After I'd promised to return the car with a full tank, Nigel reluctantly agreed to let me borrow it 'for a couple of days'.

As I left, I passed Lance in the kitchen. He was at the sink, wearing a shirt and tie, football shorts and old man's slippers.

Cut down on liquids. Only ten visits today.

Thursday 16th August

In the week between Brett breaking the tragic news and Doreen Slater's funeral there has been much agonizing about the etiquette involved. Would it be even proper for my father to attend the funeral of his ex-mistress? And should my mother accompany my father? Did the fact that I was Brett's half-brother justify my place in a pew at the crematorium, and was it right that my wife should accompany me? And did her grandfather's ex-mistress's funeral justify Gracie having a day off from nursery?

Google tells me that Mangold Parva to Bournemouth is a distance of 175.7 miles and should take three hours and forty-six minutes.

I am allowing three toilet stops at approximately ten minutes per stop, then an additional ten minutes for getting the wheelchair in and out of the boot, thus working out that because the funeral is at 11.30 we will need to leave the pigsties at 7.04 a.m. on the dot.

Friday 17th August

Left on time but had to queue for half an hour to get on to the M1 at junction 21. Why are there so many idiots on the motorway, getting in the way of legitimate travellers? Isn't it time that the government bit the bullet and made lorries travel in tunnels underground? If they can run a train under the English Channel, surely we could have subterranean lorry routes connecting the major cities and towns.

To save money we ate our own sandwiches on the way. I thought it was incredibly selfish of my father to insist on Camembert as his main filling. Even before my mother opened the Tupperware box the smell was bad. When the lid was removed, Gracie started to cry. I immediately opened the windows, and everybody screamed at me to close them again.

I made up some of the lost time on the A43, but the traffic was slow going round Oxford, then it speeded up on the A34 down to Newbury.

We arrived at Stick Insect's bungalow just as the hearse pulled up with the coffin inside. There were dozens of motorbikes parked in the driveway and many people clad in black leather talking quietly in groups.

By the time I'd got the wheelchair out and put my

father in it, the hearse was ready to leave for the crematorium. There was no time to have a look at the interior of the amazing labour-saving bungalow. The outside looked very unprepossessing, and the sea view was rather dull in my opinion, there were no breakers, and no waves. The sea was just lying there doing nothing much.

The Hells Angels were not so much angels as baby boomers. They were mostly grey-haired under their helmets. They gave Doreen's coffin a motorcycle escort, which turned a few heads as we processed along the front.

At the crematorium, a tall man with a familiar face gave me an order of service with Stick Insect's photograph on the front and said, 'Hello, Adrian, I'm Maxwell – Doreen's elder son.'

'Maxwell House!' I exclaimed.

He said, testily, 'Nobody calls me that now.'

I gave him my condolences.

He said, 'She had it coming to her. She rode that bike like a maniac.'

Brett was already sitting in a pew at the front, sobbing ostentatiously. When my mother pushed my father down the aisle, Doreen's side of the family gave a collective grumble of disapproval. My father kept his eyes down, as though he was particularly interested in the flagstone floor.

There was confusion about where we, the Moles, should sit. In the end we sat immediately behind Brett. Then Meat Loaf filled the little chapel with 'Bat out of Hell' and a man with long greasy hair and black leathers came in from a side door and climbed into the pulpit. He said that Doreen had requested in her will that she should have a humanist service because, I quote, 'After George Mole left me, and went back to his wife, I knew there was no God.'

All heads turned to look at my father, who bowed his head even further. My mother, in contrast, stared people down defiantly and muttered under her breath, 'He knew which side his bread was buttered.'

The humanist, who said his name was Rick, invited various people to come to the front and say a few words. Maxwell House (Stick Insect's illegitimate first son) got up and said that although his mother had suffered depression after George Mole left her, in later years she had found great happiness and companionship in the Bournemouth Chapter.

Her last boyfriend Yeovil Tony's voice broke as he told the congregation that he had asked Doreen to marry him, but she had refused, saying, 'No, I live in hope that George Mole might come back to me.' Tears glistened in his eyes as he said, 'She was a lovely lady.'

Then Robbie Williams sang 'Angels' and Brett came to the front and said his mother had lived a very difficult life. Her anorexia had caused her a lot of misery, some unkind people had taunted her, and called her Stick Insect. He said, 'Yes, it's true that my mother's heart had been broken by my father, George Mole, but I think I managed to make her last years happier. I imported a Harley-Davidson for her sixtieth birthday, and she became a well-known Bournemouth character.'

*

Afterwards we went back to the bungalow with the rest of the mourners. Brett had paid for caterers. Most of the food consisted of towers of vegetables, and my father grumbled, 'I don't recognise any of this stuff. Is there a bit of ham or a pork pie, son?'

Suddenly the curtains began to open and close, the lights went on and off, and music blasted through the speakers which were in every room of the house. The mood controller remote could not be found, even though everybody searched thoroughly for it. My mother tried to wrestle the curtains open but Brett screamed, 'Step away from the curtains, Pauline! You'll ruin the delicate electronic timers.'

The journey back was complicated by the fact that each of my family's respective bladders needed emptying at different times. In all we stopped on nine different occasions. At Watford Gap Services, when Daisy searched for a wet wipe in Gracie's bag, she found Brett's mood controller.

Gracie denied hiding it there.

My mother said, 'If you carry on lying, our Gracie, your nose will grow like Pinocchio's.'

Gracie said, 'I don't care. I *want* to be a wooden boy.'

I said, sotto voce to Daisy, 'I'm going to ring the school psychology service on Monday.'

There was a ray of sunshine at the end of a gloomy day when Glenn rang from Afghanistan. He is coming home in ten days. When he asked me if I'd been to Dude's yet

67

and spoken to Tiny Curtis, I lied and told him that I had. I will have to go next week.

As we were falling asleep, I told Daisy that I was envious of Brett's vast wealth.

She said, 'He's empty inside, Adrian. He says he envies you.'

'Me,' I said, 'Why?'

'Because you're married to me,' Daisy said. Then she turned over and was almost instantly asleep. I lay awake, listening to my mother coughing through the party wall. At 3.10 a.m. a lone bird started to sing. The song was somehow heartbreaking in the pre-dawn darkness.

Sunday 19th August

We cycled four miles through idyllic countryside, me towing Gracie in her little trailer past fields where harvesters were turning corn into bales of hay, to Beeby on the Wold to Daisy's dad's house, to give him the 'dozen sturdy white handkerchiefs' he had requested for his birthday. It's a few months since I saw him in person and I was shocked at how old he suddenly looks. He has taken the failure of Orgobeet very badly.

Daisy warned him not to put the last of his money into all that beetroot crushing machinery, but he was full of bombast as usual and refused to listen to any advice.

When he went on *Dragons' Den* and asked for £250,000 for 10 per cent of the business, the TV Dragons told him to cut his losses and pour the beetroot juice down the drain, but he shouted at them that they were short-sighted fools and that one day they would see his name in the *Sunday Times* Rich List. The episode was never shown – apparently, the Scots dragon with the health clubs, Duncan Bannatyne, turned nasty.

Michael Flowers was in his study on the telephone, having a maudlin conversation with his ex-wife, Netta. He had a glass of Orgobeet at his elbow. It looked as though he was wearing carmine lipstick – quite an unsettling sight. One of Orgobeet's disadvantages is that it stains the lips. Gracie refused to sit on his knee and said, 'Grandpa looks like a lady with a beard.'

His house is too big and dark to be comfortable, as he will only burn low-energy light bulbs. And he doesn't believe in central heating, claiming that it robs Mother Earth of her precious resources. So we sat in the kitchen, huddled round the log-fired Aga, and looked out at the rain, waiting for Flowers to finish his phone call and join us for his birthday tea. Daisy had made him a cake and allowed Gracie to decorate it with 'Happy Birthday, U R 62'.

Sixty-two! And the man still wears his hair in a ponytail.

I feigned interest in his remaining stock of Orgobeet and he took me out to the garage to show me the casks.

'My only hope now,' he said, 'is that an arsonist should set the garage on fire.'

He lifted a grey straggling eyebrow, and looked

pointedly at me. I asked him if he had taken out business insurance.

Flowers snarled, 'Do I look like a fool? Of course, can one do anything in this hideous modern world without insurance? Don't the insurance companies have us all by our balls? Yet when I claimed for a stolen camcorder, the bastards refused to pay out.'

'But that's because you had never had a camcorder, so you couldn't furnish the Zurich with a Currys receipt as proof of purchase,' I said.

'There was a time when a gentleman's word was his honour,' he boomed.

'But you were lying to Currys,' I protested.

'They weren't to know that,' he said through gritted teeth.

He is an impossible man.

As we walked back to the house, he asked me if I had sorted out my tax affairs. I told him that I had written to Gordon Brown again and was expecting a reply any day.

He said, 'I hope you didn't mention that I was your father-in-law.'

When Daisy's sister Marigold turned up with Brain-box Henderson, her husband, my spirits were lowered further. I cannot get over the fact that I was once engaged to Marigold. I had a narrow escape. Neither of the Hendersons likes children, preferring to spend their spare time as active members of the *Star Trek* fan club. Both are fluent in Klingon and converse in it when they share a private joke, which I think is the height of rudeness.

*

70

Tea was a gloomy affair.

Daisy said, 'Only three years to go before you retire, Dad.'

He laughed scornfully and said, 'If I live that long.'

Daisy said, alarmed, 'Are you dying, Dad?'

Flowers said, 'We're all *dying*, Daisy. Nobody is immortal.'

Gracie said, 'Are you going to die soon?'

Flowers gazed out of the window and said, 'Who knows?'

After tea Gracie entertained the company with her improvised one-woman *High School Musical* show. She 'sang', in an appalling American accent, into a pink plastic microphone which amplified her voice. When any of us lost concentration, Gracie would shout, '*Look* at me! *Look* at me!'

As she frolicked in the big bay window of the sitting room, drawing the dusty velvet curtains between scenes, I envied the child's self-confidence. I can remember fleeing from the house at family parties when my parents urged me to recite my poetry.

On the way home I told Daisy that she could visit her father alone in future.

She said, 'That's so unfair, I put up with your parents every day of my life.'

Later that night we climbed into our cold marital bed in silence, and turned away from each other.

Monday 20th August

After work I bumped into Dr Pearce outside the bookshop. She was struggling to carry a large box which contained a single goose down duvet (9 togs), and I offered to wheel it to her car. I could not help but notice that her breasts were rather prominent in her low-necked summer frock, and I had a vision of her slipping naked under the duvet. My mouth went dry and I developed a tremor in my left hand, the one holding the box on the saddle of my bike. We walked to her car and I helped to put the box in the hatchback. Each time I attempted to leave she engaged me in conversation, telling me that she was enjoying the long summer holiday. She volunteered that she was the mother of four children and that her youngest had just moved from a cot to his first bed.

I had another vision of Dr Pearce, haggard and harassed, stumbling from her bed to quell the noise of several bawling children. I said goodbye, mounted my bike and left.

When I got home, Daisy, Gracie, my mother and father were sitting outside in the early evening sun. I went into my parents' house to find another deckchair and couldn't help but notice my mother's handbag was on the hall table, with her manuscript poking out.

CHAPTER SIX

I Escape

On the night of my twelfth birthday, administering a brutal beating, my parents took it in turns to beat me with the buckle end of Father's leather belt. I lay in the dark in the understairs cupboard, where I slept on a pile of rags, and planned my escape. I heard my parents speak of the town Spalding and, judging by the way in which they spoke of it, I surmised that Spalding was a gateway to the world. I planned to make my way there as soon the fractures in my ribs had healed.

I had no clothes apart from potato sacks with holes cut for my head and arms, and no shoes apart from sandals made from old lorry tyres and rope. Why did nobody notice my neglect? Shouldn't my teacher have enquired as to why I was the only child not in school uniform? Did no social worker drive by as I was pulling a laden potato cart with a yoke across my slim shoulders?

Friday 24th August

A family came into the shop this afternoon. Judging by vividly coloured cheap clothes, trainers etc. and low brows I would guess socio-economically they were CDs.

All but one of the children displayed Attention Deficit Disorder. The mother, who was missing several teeth, said to the exceptional child, a tall grave-faced boy, 'Why have you chose *this* shop?' She looked around suspiciously.

'I want to buy a book,' said the child.

'You've gorra book,' said the mother.

'I want another one,' the child insisted.

At this point I intervened and led the boy to the children's classics section. The mother drummed her fingers on the counter, impatiently. The father sighed deeply, went outside and lit a cigarette.

I demonstrated to the boy how he should handle a hardback book, and asked him if he was interested in pirates.

'Yeah, I seen the film,' he said.

I found a copy of *Treasure Island*. He opened it and leafed through, reading a few lines, moving his lips.

'You might find bits of it hard, but it's worth persevering,' I said.

He looked at the coloured illustration. Long John Silver was crowing over a treasure chest. He took a £10 note out of his pocket. I almost said the book cost £15, but instead I kept quiet.

After I had paid the money into the till, the mother said, 'Don't he get no change out of a tenner?'

I said, 'No, sorry.'

As they were leaving the shop, the mother said, 'You must be bleddy mad, spending your birthday money on a book.'

Saturday 25th August

I told Daisy that I would be very late home because I had to call in at Dude's nightclub and attempt to contact Tiny Curtis.

She said, 'I could meet you there, it's ages since we danced together.'

I said, 'I don't intend to enjoy myself, Daisy. I'm simply doing an errand for Glenn.'

She put her arms around my neck and kissed me and said, 'Do you remember how we used to dance, before we were married?'

I said, 'Yes, we were naked and I never wanted to let you go. I thought about you day and night. I lost half a stone in weight, colours were more vivid and everything I heard or read reminded me of you.'

Gracie came between us and pushed us apart, saying, 'Stop kissing.'

Had she not interfered, we might have made love. It would have been worth being late for work.

Sunday 26th August
1 a.m.

Not being a regular clubber, I hadn't realized that Dude's did not even open its doors until 11.30.

Leicester city centre was like the Wild West. I tried to find a quiet pub where I could sit and read my book, but there was nowhere. In the end I went to Wayne Wong's and had the Special Dinner for One. I asked Wayne if I could swap sweet and sour chicken for beef in black bean sauce, but to my astonishment (this is a man I have known for thirty years!) he refused, saying, 'If I do it for you, Moley, I'll have to do it for everybody and we'll be in chaos – chaos.'

Wayne has not aged well, he has lost most of his hair and has ballooned in weight and now looks like the Michelin Man.

When he brought me my meal, I said, 'Did you ever achieve your ambition of owning a Lamborghini?'

'No,' said Wayne, 'but thanks for reminding me.'

I asked if he knew what time 'Dude's' opened its doors. 'Do I look like somebody what would know that?' said Wayne. 'I'm in this place twenty-four seven. I work my bollocks off.'

I said, 'Money is not everything, Wayne.'

He flicked a stray noodle off the tablecloth and said, 'Money *is* everything, Moley. I got two kids at private school, parents in a nursing home and I've just had to replace two koi carp at five hundred quid a throw.'

At eleven o'clock I was outside Dude's. The doors were still closed. A queue started to form behind me.

A youth in a string vest came up to me and said, 'You won't get in looking like that, Bro, you're violating the code.'

A girl shrieked, 'No Burberry!'

I took my M&S Burberry scarf off and stuffed it into a pocket.

At exactly 11.30 the doors opened, releasing a blast of

stale air, and a handsome black giant put portable stands and a velvet rope across the door. I approached him and he said, 'Easy, professor, we ain't open yet.'

I asked him if he knew Tiny Curtis.

He said, 'That's me.'

I said, 'I'm here with a message from Afghanistan.'

The giant laughed.

'I'm Glenn's dad,' I said.

Tiny checked, '*Glenn* Glenn?'

'Yes, I'm Glenn's dad, Mr Mole.'

A girl near the front of the queue shouted, 'Let us in, Curtis. It's freezin' out here.'

'He wants the girl he was with last time he was in to contact him in Afghanistan,' I said.

The giant took the slip of paper with Glenn's BFPO address and mobile number. 'That would be Finley-Rose,' he said. 'I'll let her know. I appreciate what your boy's doing for us out there, Mr Mole.'

I wished him goodnight, collected my bike from the bookshop and cycled home.

Daisy hadn't waited up for me.

Monday 27th August

The Jeremy Kyle Show has written to my mother, inviting her to appear on the programme to 'settle once and for all the question of your daughter Rosie's paternity'. She has not told my father because she thinks it would kill him, and has sworn me and Daisy to secrecy. If my mother agrees to go on *The Jeremy Kyle Show*, I will have to leave the village, the country, Europe.

Apparently, Mr Lucas – my mother's one-time lover – contacted the show, claiming to be Rosie's real father. I got a text from Rosie in the middle of a staff meeting at the bookshop.

Hoo the fk is Alan Lucas?

Before I could reply, another text pinged through from Daisy.

Come home soonest. Yr mum in bits.

Mr Carlton-Hayes must have sensed my agitation because he paused in his introduction of the new titles and said, 'Adrian, has your telephone conveyed bad news?'

I said, '*The Jeremy Kyle Show* have been in touch with my mother.'

There was an audible gasp from Hitesh, the work experience boy that Mr Carlton-Hayes had agreed to take on in a weak moment when I was not in the shop. He understood the significance of *The Jeremy Kyle Show*. However, Mr Carlton-Hayes does not own a television and relies on *The Archers* for his knowledge of current affairs. In Mr Carlton-Hayes's world, Wagner's *Ring* cycle is popular culture.

I explained to him that *The Jeremy Kyle Show* is a

television programme that encourages not-very-bright people to confront other inadequate people with their grievances. Issues of adultery and the paternity of children are increasingly solved by the miscreants taking lie detector or DNA tests. People cry and scream and are confronted by angry former loved ones who are spurred on by Jeremy Kyle himself.

Mr Carlton-Hayes looked bewildered. 'But why would a person agree to such an unpleasant public exhibition?' he asked, genuinely wanting to know.

Tuesday 28th August

Email from Rosie:

Hi, Bro

Listen, a bloke rang me on the landline and told me that he was my real dad. His name is Alan Lucas. He said that he was Mum's lover in the eighties. He said that you and him got on like a house on fire and that he took you on holiday to Scotland and bought you a Swiss army knife, with seventeen attachments. Is this true? He wants to meet me and 'forge a relationship'. He says he is lonely and hasn't got nobody in his life. He says he has been unlucky with women. They have all turned out to be evil scheming bitches who have taken his money, houses and cars and left him with nothing. I am severely pissed off with BT. I went ex-directory to avoid this sort of shit. I was hanging on the end of my phone for fucking *months* trying to go ex-directory, what a fucking waste of time *that* was. Do you think I can get some compensation? I missed signing on today because of his phone call.

Love U,
Rosie

I emailed back:

Dear Rosie
As usual, you are failing to grasp what is important and what is not. You should be exercised by the fact that 'Rat Fink' Lucas is claiming to be your father. (Yes, I remember him well. The Swiss army knife did have seventeen attachments. The scissors once came in handy when I caught my pubes in a zip, only minutes before my second wedding.)

The fact that Lucas somehow came by your landline number is of trifling importance. Surely you can see this? What is causing me anguish is Lucas's assertion that you are his child. This could kill Dad (George Mole). You have always been his favourite. Whatever happens, Rosie, please don't tell Mum and (especially) Dad about Lucas's call.

Wednesday 29th August

Another email from Rosie:

Aidy, Mi Bro

Yeah, perhaps it's a nightmare about Alan Lucas claiming to be my dad. But if you think that BT giving out information about their customers is ethical, then I feel sorry for you. We live in a Stalinist society, Adrian, watched and spied on 24/7. Quite honestly, Aidy, at the end of the day it doesn't matter whose sperm fertilised Mum's egg. Rizla says he is getting bad vibes from you and your emails. He says that Lucas sounds like he's a cool dude. Rizla's women have let him down, it's the reason why he can't work. The women have taken all his confidence away.

I think Dad ought to be told, Adrian. Me and Rizla believe in being totally honest.

I replied:

Rosie, I'll be honest. Rizla is a lazy middle-aged poseur who smokes so much skunk that his brain is a scrambled mess of paranoia and self-pity.

I beg you, do nothing until I talk to you in person. Where will you be this evening?

Aidy

Aidy

Rizla says that you are a typical bourgeois and materialist who lives a lie and colludes with society to 'stifle the world of the dreamer'. He asks if you could send him some money so that he can buy a hundred toilet rolls. He is making an installation. He wants to wrap toilet paper around a BMW car for an exhibition in December. He has written to various artists and Tate Modern but they have all turned him down. He has been offered various cheap brands but he is holding out for Andrex. Two hundred quid should cover it.

Love,
Rosie

PS: If you know anybody with a BMW who wants to sponsor an artistic genius, please let me know.

PPS: As for the identity of my real father, Rizla says that sperm is universal and that in the end we all have the same mother and the same father. He says that he would welcome the opportunity to go on *The Jeremy Kyle Show* and present the country with his manifesto.

I showed this latest email to Daisy, who snorted, 'He's ten years behind the times. The Black Box Gallery in Shoreditch exhibited a Robin Reliant wrapped in ASDA's Own Brand!'

I pointed out to Daisy that the art installation was not the most important detail in Rosie's rambling email. I said, 'This could actually kill my father.'

Daisy muttered under her breath, 'We all have to die someday.'

I rang my mother on her mobile and arranged to meet her in The Bear. I stressed that I wanted to talk to her and her alone. We walked to the pub in a stiff breeze, under a constant fall of gold, brown and red leaves. My mother complained that we were now in autumn and that we had never had a summer.

Midnight

Spent most of the evening outside in the cold. My mother said she could not talk about Lucas, Rosie or *The Jeremy Kyle Show* without smoking 'many, many cigarettes'. We sat at an incredibly uncomfortable picnic table, under an inadequate parasol advertising Carling Black Label. We hardly had any time to talk privately. Smokers kept coming out to join us, including The Right Honourable Hugo Fairfax-Lycett from Fairfax Hall, who complimented my mother on her leopard-skin raincoat and matching hat. He drawled, 'Bloody tiresome having to pop out for a puff every five minutes. One wants to support the local pub, but what's a drink without one's packet of cigs and one's Ronson on the table in front of one?'

My mother went into a diatribe about New Labour's propensity for 'spoiling our simple pleasures'.

Fairfax-Lycett went on about fox-hunting, banning conkers and political correctness. Normally this kind of talk would act like a red rag to a bull, and I dreaded my mother's reaction. But to my astonishment, she nodded and simpered as she gazed into Fairfax-Lycett's battered but aristocratic face. When he offered her a Dunhill, I noticed that their hands touched, and when he lit her cigarette, they exchanged a look. I have seen that look before and it always presages disaster.

On the way home, as we circumnavigated the potholes in the lane, I managed to stress that she must on no account agree to an appearance on *The Jeremy Kyle Show*. I made her promise on Gracie's life that she would not even speak to anybody from the production team, should they be in touch.

She said, 'It would be an opportunity to clear the air.'

I said, 'If you need the air clearing, buy an extractor fan. But on no account are you to wash our family's linen in public.'

My mother said, 'Adrian, to be honest, I've always wondered who Rosie's dad was. She hasn't got the Mole awkwardness. You know, that gormlessness, that cack-handedness, the inability to walk through the china section of a department store without your coat catching on something valuable ...'

This referred to the time when I was eight years old and dislodged a Wedgwood soup tureen with the sleeve of my too-big winter overcoat in John Lewis in Leicester.

I said, 'More to the point, Rosie is the spitting image of Rat Fink Lucas: that dark skin, black hair, brown eyes. She's always been a cuckoo in the nest, Mum.'

We continued walking in silence until we got to our respective front doors. I could hear the theme music to *Big Brother* blasting from the television in my parents' house and the mournful tones of 'Hallelujah' seeping through the crack in my own front door.

When Daisy enters a Leonard Cohen phase, it means trouble for me.

Thursday 30th August

In the middle of the night I got up to pee and found Daisy on her laptop in the living room. Leonard Cohen was mumbling in the background about somebody called Alexandra who was leaving.

When she saw me, she clicked on the screensaver and said, 'You should take that bladder to the doctor's, Adrian.' I pointed out to her that it was 4 a.m. and she said, 'I prefer to keep rock 'n' roll hours.'

The bed was cold when I returned to it. Melancholy autumn is closing in on us.

Friday 31st August

Took Daisy home a present of Nigella's *How to Be a Domestic Goddess*.

She muttered a thank you and opened it at random, then said, 'Anchovies, I hate anchovies,' and closed it again.

I was cut to the core and had to leave the room before I said something.

The house was very untidy and the sink was full of dirty pots. When I mildly asked Daisy what she had been doing all day, she went into a tirade about me having Obsessive Compulsive Disorder, and said that all civilised people had a dishwasher. I listened to *The Archers* as I ploughed through the washing up – Ruth Archer is having trouble with her prosthesis, she plans to talk to David about having breast reconstruction. The running water made me go to the loo twice, which is ridiculous. There is obviously a nervous causation because, after I have voided urine, my bladder still feels full. Perhaps I should see a therapist.

There is nobody I can talk to about my problems, apart from Nigel. After checking my bank balance online (£349.31 overdrawn), I rang and asked if I could call in and see him on my way home from work tomorrow. He grudgingly agreed.

Gracie was in her bedroom playing at social workers with her dolls. Barbie and Ken were each married to one of the Bratz dolls and Sindy (dressed in a business suit and carrying a briefcase) was threatening to take Barbie's child (Baby Annabelle) into care. The fact that Baby Annabelle dwarfs spindly Barbie does not seem to bother Gracie. Where does my little daughter get her knowledge of social work practice? I intuit the influence of my mother, who is fond of relating lurid anecdotes about the unfortunates who live in the council houses in the village. I stayed and watched Gracie's game until Baby Annabelle had been taken to live with Paddington Bear and his wife (a purple My Little Pony) in their Wendy house/orphanage. Whilst playing the part of best man at Postman Pat and Tinky Winky's wedding, I told Gracie that most mummies and daddies love each other and their children. I asked her why she didn't play happy families, but she didn't answer and busied herself by fiddling with Postman Pat's bridal veil.

2 a.m.

Made my usual moves on Daisy tonight, i.e. stroked outer thigh, kneaded shoulder, but she did not respond. After a while I gave up and turned my back on her.

Saturday 1st September

We were busy in the bookshop today. Only half of the customers were mad. When one such madman came in asking for a book on UFOs, and on the way to the shelf told me that he had seen seven-foot extraterrestrials walking around a field outside Market Harborough, I handed him over to Hitesh, who believes that the American CIA exploded the Twin Towers.

Nigel and Lance Lovett were watching *Hollyoaks* in the dark when I arrived. I know it's unreasonable, but it annoys me that they do not switch any of their lights on.

When I remarked that it was strange to see two blind men 'watching' television, Nigel said, 'We can still hear the sound effects and dialogue, Moley, and we only have to pay half the licence fee.'

God knows what they get out of listening to *Hollyoaks*. The sound consists of slamming doors, sobbing, fighting, love making and revelations about the paternity of children. When the adverts came on, Nigel turned the sound down and gave me his full attention. I had wanted to talk to him alone, but Lance made no attempt to leave us and I could hardly ask a blind man to go somewhere and sit in the dark, so I told them both about my many and various problems, starting with *The Jeremy Kyle Show* and finishing with Daisy's obvious unhappiness. Nigel said (using, to my mind, an excessive amount of metaphor), 'You've taken a rare orchid and shut her away in a dark outhouse. You haven't nourished her or paid her enough attention. Is it any wonder that her roots are struggling to survive? Daisy is a trapped bird whose wings have been broken, she is a Fabergé egg that you have boiled for four minutes and eaten for your breakfast.'

I stopped him just as he was embarking on a new metaphor to do with Daisy being a submerged volcano.

Lance said, 'I had a long conversation on the phone with Daisy this morning. She said that your love life is like the Kalahari Desert. She said that you struggle through shifting sands to the summit of a dune but rarely reach it together.'

Nigel and Lance found this amusing.

I said, 'I am shocked and feel betrayed to hear that my

wife has been blabbing out the most intimate details of our love life.'

Nigel said, airily, 'Don't get your boxers in a tangle, women always tell gay men their most intimate secrets.'

'We are the keepers of the knowledge,' Lance said, 'and he's not talking about interior design.'

They laughed again.

I looked around their living room. Somehow, although unable to see, they have managed to coordinate the carpet, curtains and cushions.

Do gay men have an extra, soft-furnishing gene?

When I got home, my mother was there talking to Daisy about the Lucas/Jeremy Kyle problem. I was alarmed that they seemed to be considering the benefits of, as my mother said, 'getting it all out in the open and finally having closure'. I spoke passionately and, I think, eloquently about the benefits of keeping family secrets hidden and unresolved, but they looked at me with what I can only describe as incredulous pity and resumed their discussion. Gracie was next door with my father, watching a DVD of *The Wizard of Oz* for the 79th time (my father keeps count) so I went into the kitchen and resumed work on *Plague!*. I wrote a monologue for a plague victim.

SCENE VI

Village Green, Mangold Parva. It is market day. A pack of dogs cross from stage left and exit stage right. A chicken comes to centre stage and lays an egg, then exits stage right. Villagers are selling and buying produce. It begins to snow. A plague victim staggers from stage left and addresses the audience. The villagers draw back in fear.

PLAGUE VICTIM (addressing audience): Ay, see thee draw yon selves away from my poor diseased body. No man nor woman will touch my putrid flesh, nor will they give me comfort and kindly words. Death waits around the corner for me, for no man can survive once the plague hath touched him. I do not want to leave this world. There are many delights I have not seen. I have heard that to the east there be a sea where ships do sail to foreign lands, to the south a pile of holy rocks they do call Stonehenge and to the west there lieth the great city of Leicester where there are many glittering buildings of such magnificence that humble folk do rub their eyes in wonder thinking that what they see is but a dream.

A peasant woman approaches the plague victim.

PEASANT WOMAN: Be gone, ye diabolical plague victim! Take thy filthy personage to a hole and die! Thou art not fit to be in a public place!

GODFRIED pushes through the crowd to centre stage.

GODFRIED: Have mercy on this poor wretch. Hath he not flesh like yours? Hath he not a heart and soul and loins that God hath made?

GODFRIED holds his arms out and approaches the plague victim.

GODFRIED: Come to me, scurrilous one. I will embrace your common humanity.

GODFRIED embraces the plague victim. There is a gasp from the crowd. The pack of dogs enter stage left and surround GODFRIED and the plague victim. The dogs act in unison, and dip their heads as if in prayer.

I'm quite pleased with this. It may be difficult to get the dogs to lower their heads simultaneously, but there is plenty of time to train them. The chicken may be more problematical.

Monday 3rd September

Daisy rang me at work to say that she had rung the surgery at 8 a.m. for an appointment re my bladder but that the line was constantly engaged.

When she finally got through, Mrs Leech, the receptionist, said, 'It's eight thirty-five. You must ring before eight thirty to book an appointment.' When Daisy pointed out that she had been trying since eight o'clock, Mrs Leech said, 'If I don't keep to the rules, it will be anarchy here.' When Daisy asked if she would make an appointment for tomorrow morning, Mrs Leech said, 'No, you must ring tomorrow between eight and eight thirty.'

Daisy admitted to me that she had muttered a swear word and that Mrs Leech had said, 'I heard that, Mrs Mole. Perhaps you ought to know that our conversation is being recorded for the purpose of staff training.'

Daisy said that, as she had not given her permission for her voice to be recorded, she would be making a formal complaint to the BMA.

In my opinion, it is always a mistake to antagonize a doctor's receptionist.

Tuesday 4th September

Started ringing the surgery at 7.59 a.m. Mrs Leech answered immediately and told me that I must ring again at 8 a.m.

Rang at 8 a.m. The line was engaged. Rang again at 8.15 whilst cycling to work. Got through at 8.25 but couldn't make myself heard to Mrs Leech because at that very moment a fire engine passed me with its siren blaring. Rose on to the pavement and dismounted but Mrs Leech had disconnected the call. Tried again but line busy. It's a good job I am not suffering a serious illness that requires immediate treatment.

*

Got through at 8.31, to be told by Mrs Leech that it was too late to make an appointment.

10.15 p.m.

Dr Pearce has just rung me on my mobile to ask if the shop has a copy of *Yes, I Would Like to Have Sex With You*. I was very surprised to hear from her, especially as it was such a late hour for a phone call from a mere acquaintance.

Unfortunately, Daisy overheard me say 'yes, I would like to have sex with you' as I was writing it down. When I put the phone down, after I had told Dr Pearce that I would 'deal with your request tomorrow', Daisy burst into the kitchen and accused me of having an affair. I protested my innocence but she screamed, 'I heard you with my own ears, you cheating bastard!'

I informed her that *Yes, I Would Like to Have Sex With You* was subtitled *A Teenager's Guide to The First Sexual Encounter*, but she was too angry to listen.

The last time I sneaked a look at Daisy's diary she was writing admiringly about Hugo Fairfax-Lycett's commanding air as he took charge of bailing out the floodwater from old Will Frost's semi-submerged cottage in Hollow Lane last month.

Diary, it is a well-known fact that adulterous partners often suspect their spouses of infidelity. Is it coincidence that Fairfax-Lycett always turns up at The Bear within minutes of our arrival?

Wednesday 5th September

A police forensics expert from Michigan has been sacked for using lab facilities to test her husband's underpants for DNA. Ann Chamberlain, aged thirty-three, admitted during divorce proceedings that she had run forensic tests on her husband's underwear at the State Police laboratory because she suspected he was cheating on her. When asked what the results showed, she replied, 'Another woman. It wasn't me.'

I showed this news item to Daisy and offered her all the underpants I have worn since Sunday. She replied, coldly, that it was too late, she had done a 'white wash' at sixty degrees.

Thursday 6th September

Faxed the surgery at 8.01 a.m. requesting an appointment. Received fax back immediately from Mrs Leech stating that 'appointments can only be given over the telephone'.

Friday 7th September

Emailed Mrs Leech asking her to be prepared to take my telephone call at precisely 8 a.m. Received an email at 8.02 to say that 'at this moment in time' there was a queue of thirty people on hold.

*

When I got to work, I went into the back room and rang NHS Direct. I spoke to a kind woman and explained my symptoms (frequent urination, pain whilst passing urine, dribbling whilst passing urine and occasional pain in organ). I heard her clicking on a keyboard and then she said, 'You should go and see your GP immediately.'

I explained my difficulties in getting an appointment. She said that I must go to the Out Of Hours Clinic at my local hospital. She stressed that I must not delay. I thanked her and put the phone down. All day I had a terrible feeling of apprehension. I went to the medical shelves and found *Symptoms and Diagnosis*. After doing a self-diagnosis, I concluded that I have a severe bladder infection. The book also diagnosed prostate cancer but, thank God, I am too young for that. Prostate cancer, as any fool knows, only affects very old men and I am not forty until April next year.

Saturday 8th September

I looked for *Yes, I Would Like to Have Sex With You* and found it in the teen fiction section. When I pointed out to Hitesh that it was a non-fiction book and should have been placed in the medical section, Hitesh said, with the arrogance of youth, 'I'm sorry, Mr Mole, but I thought sex was mostly a teenage interest.'

Hitesh has just started going out with an English girl called Chelsie Hoare, who had a breast augmentation for her 18th birthday. He has to meet her secretly, his parents would kill him if they found out.

I felt I had to explain to him that people of my age also have an interest in sex.

He pulled a face.

The kid has a lot to learn. He keeps putting books about the Labour Party in the history section.

Just as I was locking up, Dr Pearce dashed in with two Mothercare bags and asked if she could pick up the copy of *Yes, I Would Like to Have Sex With You*. Her hair needed washing and her stomach was straining against a too-tight skirt. I went into the back room and was startled to find that she'd followed me.

She said, 'Goodness me, what a lot of books. There's hardly room to move in here.'

It was with relief I heard the shop bell ring, but when I went out I was alarmed to see that it was Daisy and Gracie.

Gracie said, 'Why are you standing in the dark?'

Before I could answer Dr Pearce reappeared and said, 'Thank you for your personal service. It will be a sad day when we lose our independent bookshops.'

When Dr Pearce had picked up her Mothercare bags and left, I asked Daisy what she was doing in town. She said that she regretted her accusations of the other night and thought that it would be nice to have an early dinner at Wayne Wong's. Unfortunately, as we were walking towards the Chinese restaurant, Dr Pearce drove past, stopped the car and said, 'I forgot to ask you, Adrian, could you order me the sequel to *Yes, I Would Like to Have Sex With You*? I think it's called *Sorry, I no Longer Want to Have Sex With You*.'

I knew then that I would not be manipulating the chopsticks that night or for many nights to come. Daisy let go of Gracie's hand, turned round and clattered down the high street in her high heels.

Diary, nobody could have judged me if I had carried on to Wayne Wong's. After all, I had only eaten a Twix since lunchtime, and I was looking forward to deep-fried wontons and beef with ginger and crispy noodles, but I turned round and followed my wife.

When Gracie said, 'Why is Mummy running away from us?' I told her that Mummy was jogging in preparation for running a half marathon.

Sunday 9th September

The Pearce row went on all day and well into the night. I am exhausted and distraught. Daisy said some cruel and heartless things about me, my personality, my looks, my clothes, my parents, my friends, the way I eat, sleep, drink, walk, laugh, snore, tap my teeth, crack my fingers, belch, fart, wipe my glasses, dance, wear my jeans up around my armpits, put HP sauce on my toast, refuse to watch *The X Factor* and *Big Brother*, drive . . . The litany went on and on and was interspersed with tears and sobs. I tried to take her in my arms and comfort her but she pushed me away, saying, 'Why don't you put your arms around Dr Pearce? You know you want to!'

I protested that frequent childbearing had taken an obvious toll on Dr Pearce's sexual allure and that she had let herself go.

Daisy said, 'Your mother warned me that Mole men will not tolerate their Mole women going over nine and a half stone! I have *tried* to lose weight, Adrian, but you will insist on having chocolate digestives in the house!'

At midnight, when Daisy was finally sleeping, I left the house. The moon was bright and an east wind was buffeting the tops of the leylandii as I stumbled down the potholed drive to phone Pandora. I expected to leave a message – she almost never picks up the phone herself – but to my surprise she answered immediately, saying, 'Oh my God, what's happened? Is somebody in Leicester dead?'

I apologised for ringing her at such a late hour and said that I needed to talk to her urgently.

She said, impatiently, 'Look, you've interrupted me in working on a policy document for Gordon Brown's office. It has to be on his desk at eight in the morning.'

To be polite I asked her what sort of policy demanded Mr Brown's urgent attention.

She said, somewhat reluctantly I thought, 'Newts – do they deserve protected species status?'

I said, 'Perhaps I can help you there. Do you remember when I was working at the Department of the Environment?'

'I certainly do,' she said.

'Well, my expertise was in newt population.'

'Yes,' she said, 'and you made a terrible balls-up by estimating that there were 120,000 newts in Newport Pagnell, when in fact there were only 1,200, and consequently held up the new bypass for ten years.'

'How could you possibly know that?' I asked.

'From the net,' she said. 'Your report is on a website called www.planningblunders.com.'

'Why is Mr Brown so interested in newts?' I asked.

'The government is trying to streamline the planning laws,' she said, 'and bloody newts and rare orchids are preventing hard-working stakeholder families from living in decent housing in our proposed eco-towns.'

'Hasn't Mr Brown got more important things to address?' I asked. 'Such as Iraq, the Labour Party's twenty-million-pound debt and the fact that National Health Service hospitals are full of rampant life-threatening infections.'

Pandora said, 'He's an obsessive micro-manager. He's down to three hours of sleep a night. I heard a rumour that he's started using Elizabeth Arden's concealer on his eye bags.'

Pandora enjoys giving me these titbits of gossip. She was halfway through telling me about Geoff Hoon's use of Garnier's Grey Coverage, when I interrupted and told her that my wife appeared to hate me.

Pandora laughed and said, 'You should be used to it by now. Aren't all your relationships with women disastrous? Didn't you have one girlfriend who burned down your house?'

'She was clinically insane,' I protested.

'Yes, but you *chose* her,' said Pandora.

An owl hooted in the sycamore tree opposite, reminding me that unless I went home and got some sleep I would be good for nothing the next day. I said goodnight to Pandora and added, 'I will always love you.'

Pandora was silent for a long time, then said, 'Was that an owl I heard?'

I said yes and she disconnected the call.

Monday 10th September

Neither Daisy nor Gracie spoke to me this morning. It's a bit much when your own child gives you the cold shoulder.

I was halfway through serving a young man who had terrible teeth with *The Oxford Companion to English Literature* by Margaret Drabble when I excused myself and went to the toilet. Mr Carlton-Hayes took over the sale.

When the terrible teeth man had gone, Mr Carlton-Hayes said, 'Adrian, dear, I could not help but notice that your visits to the lavatory are becoming more frequent. Are you physically ill, my dear, or is it a nervous affliction?'

I felt myself blushing and was saved from answering when a woman in a salmon-pink smock and olive-green pedal pushers barged in and asked for a copy of *What Not to Wear*.

Mr Carlton-Hayes and I would usually have a cup of tea or coffee on the go all day, but for the rest of the day I cut down dramatically. Even so, I still had to make several urgent dashes into the back. The last time, when I had emerged and was washing my hands, Mr Carlton-

Hayes came to me, put a hand on my shoulder and said, 'Adrian, please go and see somebody about your urinary problem. Do you have any other symptoms?'

I would rather have crawled over broken glass than tell Mr Carlton-Hayes about the occasional pain whilst urinating, but I agreed to go and see a doctor.

I rang Daisy at five thirty and told her that I was going to the Out Of Hours Clinic at the Royal Hospital.

She said, 'About time.'

The Out Of Hours Clinic was a bit Third World. The waiting area consisted of a dimly lit rectangular room with patients sitting around the edge on plastic chairs. Some were bloodied, some were bowed, most were obviously poor and at least three had the flattened noses and beaten-up faces of the alcoholic homeless. There were frightened young parents with crying babies, a toddler with a nosebleed and an old lady with a hacking cough. It was nine thirty before I was seen. The doctor was a young man with ginger hair. He yawned several times during my description of my symptoms. Then he said, 'Haven't you got a GP?'

I explained about my difficulty getting an appointment. He said, nodding towards the waiting room, 'Yeah, that's why we're open twenty-four seven. Has your GP changed his car recently?'

I said, 'As a matter of fact, he has. He used to drive an old Volvo Estate but he swapped it a few months ago for a new Mercedes four-by-four.'

The doctor, whose ID said he was Tim Coogan,

laughed triumphantly and said, 'Yeah, GPs are the new rich, the jammy bastards are working half the hours for twice the money.'

He seemed to have forgotten me and my symptoms so I asked, 'Is my frequent urination something to worry about?'

He said, 'I dunno. Let's have a look at you.' He snapped on a pair of blue gloves and said, 'Climb on the examination table. Take your pants and trousers down and pull your knees up to your chest. I'm gonna give you a DRE.'

I regretted wearing boxer shorts that had gone pink in the wash as I watched Dr Coogan stick his index finger into a jar which said 'lubricant'.

'DRE?' I asked.

'Digital Rectal Examination,' he said, sticking his index finger into my rectum and wiggling it about. 'You've presented with the classic signs of prostate trouble.'

'No, it won't be my prostate,' I said, trying to smile. 'I know I look old beyond my years, but I'm only thirty-nine and a half.'

Diary, I feel that a man more at ease with himself and his body could well make light of Dr Coogan's examination. Could laugh it off, or use crude rugby-player-like terms. However, I am not that man.

'Try to relax,' he said.

God knows I tried, Diary. I tried to remember a relaxation exercise I had been taught by one of my therapists years ago. It consisted of swimming in a dark blue sea, past a small desert island.

Dr Coogan said, with an attempt at humour, 'If you don't relax, Mr Mole, you could trap my finger up your bum for ever.'

I made a conscious effort to relax my rectal muscles and he finally retrieved his finger.

'Wow,' he said, 'I've rarely come across such powerful muscles.'

I pulled my pants and trousers up and said, 'Yes, I have been described as being an anal retentive before.'

He threw his blue gloves into a waste bin and washed his hands at a little basin. 'I'll write a note to your GP asking him to take some blood.' He scribbled a note and put it in a brown envelope.

I read it on the way to the car park. It said:

Dear Dr Wolfowicz

I saw your patient, Mr Adrian Mole, at clinic this evening.

I gave him a DRE and request that you take bloods to include PSA. This man has tried and failed to book an appointment to see you and had to resort to attending this Emergency Clinic. Please ask a member of your staff to ring Mr Mole with an appointment as soon as possible.

Yours,

T. Coogan

Registrar

I was greeted with icy politeness when I got home. I ate alone. Daisy had made a bolognese sauce but, as usual, she had been heavy-handed with the oregano. When she came in and found me scraping most of it into the bin under the sink, she said nothing but the look she gave me was worthy of Lot's wife.

Watched a documentary about 9/11 for a few minutes, but I had to turn it off. Daisy did not ask me what happened at the hospital. We slept apart for the second night running.

Tuesday 11th September

I left the house in pouring rain, wearing my wet weather gear.

Daisy looked me up and down and said, 'You look like that old bloke they used to have on tins of John West's pilchards. It's not a good look.'

I was nearly mown down on the dual carriageway by a petrol tanker. I dismounted my bike and walked the rest of the way to work. When I arrived, Mr Carlton-Hayes asked me how my hospital consultation had gone. My eyes filled with tears and I had to turn away before I trusted myself to speak.

Thursday 13th September

Mrs Leech rang this morning at 7.45 and told me that she had made an appointment for 8.20. Dr Wolfowicz lives in an Edwardian house just outside the village. He has converted the old stable block into a surgery. While I waited I read a peeling copy of *Sainsbury's Magazine*.

Jamie Oliver had written an article about bolognese sauce. He gave several recipes but at no point did he mention oregano. I carefully tore the page out and put it in my pocket.

Mrs Leech was permanently on the phone telling people that there were no appointments. When it was time for me to go in, she handed me my medical records and said, 'You'll need the old-fashioned handwritten notes. Dr Wolfowicz is technically challenged and doesn't know a mouse from a modem.'

Dr Wolfowicz looked as though he had just finished a shift at a steelworks in Gdansk. His huge face could have been carved out of rock. Isn't it time he bought himself a decent suit? After all, he has been in this country for at least three years. I must admit, though, his English has improved.

He muttered, 'I will just try to get you up on the system.' He turned to the computer on his desk and pressed a few keys. After typing in my name and asking me if I now lived in Belfast, to which I answered, 'No, I live at Number Two, the Piggeries,' he sighed and took my medical records from me. He read the last few pages, including the letter from Dr Coogan, then said, 'So you've had a DRE?'

'Yes,' I said, 'so I don't need another. All you need to do is take some blood.'

Dr Wolfowicz frowned and said, 'Please, Mr Mole, do not tell me how to do my job. I will need to examine you myself. Now you are getting on the couch?'

He put on a pair of gloves and I pulled my trousers down and got into the foetal position for the second time in two days. It wasn't quite as bad as the last time. When I had dressed myself again, he said, 'Your prostate is not what I would like. I will take some bloods and then we will wait . . .'

I said, 'But I can't have prostate trouble. I'm too young.'

He said, 'Do you have penis pain?'

'Occasionally,' I said.

'And is there any erectile disfunction?'

I said, 'I haven't tried for a while, my wife and I are having a few difficulties . . .'

Dr Wolfowicz smiled sympathetically and said, 'My wife, she is in Warsaw, also . . .' He put a tourniquet around my arm and said, 'A little prick.' Then he took three vials of blood and said, 'I will send these off today. Maybe we know the results next week . . .'

As I was leaving, Mrs Leech said, 'In future, Mr Mole, please desist from destroying our magazines. You are depriving other patients of reading matter.'

I pointed out to her that the magazine from which I had torn Jamie's recipe was first published in 2003.

She snapped, 'Please don't speak to me in that tone of voice, Mr Mole. I am simply trying to do my job.'

Why didn't I leave it there, Diary? Why did I have to further antagonize her in front of a waiting room full of villagers?

Our argument continued until Dr Wolfowicz came out of his room and in a calm voice, like somebody training a dog, said, 'Mrs Leech, am I waiting for the next patient for ever?'

Mrs Leech shouted, 'Mrs Goodfellow!' and an old lady hobbled towards the doctor's room.

As I cycled to work, I looked down and saw that my fingers were crossed on the handlebars.

When I reached the shop, my heart sank. Dr Pearce was standing outside waiting for it to open. She said she had time to kill before her next tutorial, so I brewed some coffee and we made small talk about children. She said the children and the house were getting on top of her recently because her husband, Robin, was in Norway measuring glaciers. I talked about the Norwegian leather industry and I think she was surprised at my knowledge. She is a fan of Norwegian mythology and compared Odin's wife to Boudicca. I was relieved when a regular customer came in, and Dr Pearce said, 'I must fly.'

After she had gone, I had a reverie. I was standing on the prow of a ship next to Pandora, her heavy flaxen hair was streaming in the wind as we entered a fjord.

Friday 14th September

Worked on *Plague!* this evening. Until I finish it I don't know how many acting parts there are and how many animals are needed. The Mangold Parva Players have not performed together since they fell out over a production of *Fame* when the choreographer, Marcia from the Saturday morning dance class in the church hall, accused Garry Fortune, who was playing Angelo, of sabotaging the finale by making lewd gestures to his girlfriend who was sitting in the audience.

Daisy was quite civil to me this evening, until I remembered and gave her the Jamie Oliver recipe for bolognese.

Saturday 15th September

I thought that my mother had forgotten about *The Jeremy Kyle Show*, but no such luck. She was on the phone to Rosie when I went round after work to borrow my father's nose hair clippers, and I heard her say, 'I don't know which would look better on television, my lilac trouser suit or my fuchsia dress 'n' jacket.'

When she came off the phone, I said, 'If you are so desperate to go on television, why don't you audition for *The X Factor*, and then you could meet your hero, Simon Cowell.'

She said, 'I used to sing with a rock band in Norwich – Pauline and the Potato Heads. I could have been famous if your dad hadn't held me back.'

Sunday 16th September

A miserable day. The air was damp. Took Gracie for a short walk to the woods. Leaves coming off trees but no crackle underfoot yet. Heard gunfire coming from grounds of Fairfax Hall so turned and went back home. Had crumpets and cocoa. Watched *Antiques Roadshow*.

Daisy and I slept in same bed but apart.

Monday 17th September

Brett phoned the bookshop at lunchtime to tell me that he had 'made a killing' from derivatives (whatever they are) by ten o'clock this morning. He asked me if I wanted to invest any spare money I had in a new hedge fund he had set up. I said I didn't have enough money to buy a modest privet hedge let alone pay out for my mortgage, food, gas and electricity bills. I mentioned that I had been tested for prostate trouble and told him that I was anxious about the results.

He said, 'You're absolutely right to be worried, I've known two good blokes die from prostate cancer within the last six months. One of them was going to be the best man at my wedding.'

Although I was annoyed that the focus of the conversation had veered away from me yet again, I asked, 'So when are you getting married?'

He said, 'I don't know. I haven't found the right girl yet. I'm looking for a stunningly beautiful, rich and independent woman, who isn't a feminist.'

I said, 'I think you'll find that they are thin on the ground.'

He said, quite nastily, 'Do you think I don't know that? It's the reason I'm not planning my wedding in the immediate future.'

Nigel was only marginally more sympathetic, when I called round after work.

He said, '*I* had a prostate scare a couple of years ago. It turned out that I had a bladder infection. It cleared up with antibiotics, so don't go around wittering that your time is up, Moley.' Then he turned the conversation to his household worker dog. He said, 'We don't know what to call him. He's not a patch on Graham. He's a lazy sod, he wouldn't get up to answer the door to Parcelforce this morning, so that means I've got to schlep down to the depot to pick the bloody thing up. Unless you could go, Moley?'

After groping along the kitchen table, he found the 'sorry you were not at home' card and gave it to me. I had no choice but to go and collect his parcel. When I asked him what was in it, he said, 'It's a set of matching bed linen and curtains from QVC.'

I put the card in my pocket and left. The housework dog saw me to the front door. I can foresee trouble with this cur. The dog looks sulky to me and has quite a martyred air about him.

*

As soon as I arrived home, Daisy rushed to tell me that my parents had gone to town and were queuing outside the Northern Rock branch in Horsefair Street intending to withdraw their savings first thing in the morning.

I said, 'They can't possibly queue all night. They'll freeze to death.'

She said, 'They've got sleeping bags and Thermos flasks, and I said that you would top their flasks up sometime in the night.'

I said, 'Why are they so desperate? Can't they wait until the weekend?'

Daisy said, 'You haven't seen the news, have you? Northern Rock has gone bust.'

I said, 'Impossible. That bank is as solid as a, well, rock.'

We switched on the news and saw long queues of mostly pensioners waiting outside a Northern Rock branch in the City of London. The camping stool and Thermos flask quotient was high. One elderly woman with a frazzled grey perm told a BBC reporter, 'I've worked hard all my life. I'm not leaving here until I get my life savings out of that bank.'

The reporter asked, 'And where will you put it?'

'Under my mattress,' she said, defiantly.

At 11 p.m. I drove into town, stopping for fish and chips on the way. My parents were huddled in their sleeping bags outside Northern Rock. They were the only people in the queue. They fell on the fish and chips like savages.

My father said, 'There's nothing like fresh air to give you an appetite.'

I tried to persuade them to come home, but my mother said, 'Not until I've got that money in my handbag. What if your father has to go into a nursing home? How will we afford the fees?'

My father pulled the sleeping bag over his head. 'And how are we meant to pay our half of the mortgage if the bank goes bust?'

When they had finished their fish and chips, I handed them each a wet wipe and replenished their flasks. I asked, 'Where will you put your money if you don't trust the financial institutions?'

They discussed where to put their money.

My mother said, 'You can get hollow tins that look like Heinz beans, nowadays.'

My father shook his head in wonder at this latest evidence of hi-tech Britain.

'They're burglar proof,' she said.

'Unless the burglar fancies beans on toast,' I said. 'According to police statistics, four per cent of burglars make themselves a snack before leaving with their swag.'

After trying and failing to persuade them to come home, I gave up and went to my own bed.

Tuesday 18th September

When I got home last night, Daisy had prepared my favourite three-course dinner: a prawn cocktail, without the yucky pink stuff, rack of lamb, mashed potatoes and green beans, gravy and mint sauce. The pudding was peach cobbler made with fresh peaches and served with thick Bird's custard. With it we drank a bottle of rosé wine that Daisy had picked up at the post office. It was predictably vile, but I didn't care.

I moved the custard jug aside and squeezed her hand, she squeezed back so perhaps our marriage is back on track. We didn't get to bed until 2 a.m. There was no sexual contact, but we went to sleep in the spoon position.

Wednesday 19th September

I told Mr Carlton-Hayes about my prostate trouble today.

He wrinkled his brow and said, 'I'm so sorry, my dear. If you need some time off, I'll ask Leslie to cover for you.'

To my great alarm I felt tears well in my eyes again.

Mr Carlton-Hayes said, 'You are a young man. The probability is that you will not be diagnosed as having cancer.' (Which he pronounced 'kenser'.)

It was the first time anybody had uttered the 'C' word out loud, although I have hardly thought of anything else since my first medical examination.

I said, 'But what if it is cancer? I can't die yet. I've got responsibilities and a family and I have to look after my parents, they're completely irresponsible and couldn't survive without my help. And there are so many places I haven't visited: the Taj Mahal, the Grand Canyon, the new John Lewis department store they're building in Leicester.'

Mr Carlton-Hayes put his hand around my shoulder and said, 'Should the diagnosis be the very worst, remember that you are otherwise healthy and have youth on your side. Many men make a complete recovery with the various forms of treatment.'

I said, 'I can't have chemotherapy, I would look terrible with a bald head.'

A customer came in asking for Krafft-Ebing's book on sexual deviants. It took both of us twenty minutes to find it, and then we didn't resume our conversation because it was time to go home.

My parents have successfully withdrawn their life savings but will not say where they have deposited the money. I hope they haven't stuffed it into a fake tin of beans, burglars are wise to this trick. Hitesh told me that the burglar that broke into his parent's house opened every tin in their food cupboard and left the tin opener behind. I asked Hitesh if his parents lost any money.

He said, 'No, they keep all our cash inside a five-kilo bag of basmati rice.'

Thursday 20th September

An old man in a tracksuit, wearing trainers the size of tanks and with a scraggy grey ponytail came into the shop this morning and asked me to value a first edition paperback of Harold Robbins's *The Carpetbaggers*. I told him that it was of no value at all and pointed out that the pages were curled, the cover was torn and it looked as though somebody had been using slices of bacon as a bookmark.

Tracksuit man bridled at this and said, 'So it ain't worth nothink?'

'No,' I confirmed.

'I'll kill that lyin' bastard,' he said. He then told me that he had accepted the 'first edition' in exchange for helping his son-in-law dig his garden.

I sympathised with the old man and told him to go home and read *The Carpetbaggers*, saying, 'At least you will get something out of your transaction.'

He said, 'I can't read. I was away from school with TB and I din't catch up.'

I told him that it was never too late to learn and said that he could attend adult education classes.

He said, 'No, you can't teach an old dog new tricks.'

I said, 'On the contrary, have you never seen *Dog Borstal*? They teach the most recalcitrant old dogs how to behave themselves and to compete on a dog assault course.'

Then my mother breezed into the shop, halfway through a shoe-buying expedition. She said, '*The Carpetbaggers*. What a brilliant book that is.'

The old man said, 'You can 'ave it, girl.' He slumped out of the shop with his shoulders down.

My mother turned to me and said, 'We've got to talk about Jeremy Kyle. The researcher has been on to me again. She said that Lucas is going on the show anyway, whether I agree to go on or not.'

I said, 'Let him go on, he'll look stupid on his own.' She looked down at *The Carpetbaggers* and turned a few pages, then said, 'He won't be on his own. Rosie is going with him.'

I said, 'Doesn't she realise that this will kill Dad? Rosie has always been his favourite child.'

'At least your father has got two children to choose from. Lucas hasn't got any children apart from ...'

'Apart from Rosie,' I said, completing her sentence. I asked her outright if she wanted to go on the show.

She turned *The Carpetbaggers* over and appeared to be reading the back cover. 'I ought to go on and support Rosie,' she said.

'And what about Dad?' I asked.

'Can't you take him to work with you on the day the programme is going to be transmitted?'

I pointed out to her that *The Jeremy Kyle Show* is on three times a day – 9.30 a.m., 1.30 p.m. and again in the early hours at 1 a.m.

She said, 'I'll put a hammer through the screen so that he can't watch it.'

I said, 'But, Mum, somebody is bound to tell him.'

'Why?' she said. 'He never talks to anybody outside the family lately.'

I could see that nothing I said would stop her. Mr Carlton-Hayes came in from doing an evaluation of somebody's dead father's book collection. He was delighted to see my mother. He kissed her three times in the continental style and told her that she was looking 'splendid'.

She laughed like a girl and said, 'Why don't you take me for a cup of coffee? Adrian can look after the shop.'

'Nothing would give me greater pleasure, my dear,' he

said, and they left me to cope with the sudden rush of students looking for second-hand course books. One of them, who was doing American studies, saw *The Carpetbaggers* on the counter and asked how much it was.

'It's free,' I said, and gave it to him.

Mr Carlton-Hayes returned half an hour later and said, 'Your mother has explained her dilemma to me, Adrian. Your sister's paternity has the makings of a Greek tragedy.'

I said, 'Personally, I think it is more of a French farce.'

When I got home, Daisy told me that Mrs Leech had rung from the surgery to say that Dr Wolfowicz wanted to see me urgently. I phoned immediately, but the surgery was closed.

Friday 21st September

Last night Daisy put her arms around me in bed and said, 'I hope everything will be all right tomorrow, Aidy.' It is ages since she called me Aidy. Perhaps she is worried about me. I left a message on Mr Carlton-Hayes's phone to say that I wouldn't be in this morning.

As I walked down the lane towards the village and Dr Wolfowicz's surgery, a golden sun shone through the branches of the trees and somebody was burning leaves somewhere. I realized that I was as apprehensive about facing Mrs Leech as I was about my diagnosis. However, she gave me a charming smile, sat me down in the waiting room and even handed me a pile of fairly recent magazines. Her ministrations filled me with alarm. Had she seen my results? Or had she been rebuked by Dr Wolfowicz for shouting at his patients? The longer I waited, the more nervous I became. Was Dr Wolfowicz sitting in his surgery trying to work out how to break the bad news?

When I was finally called in, he said immediately, 'Mr Mole, I have had your results back and I am going to refer you to a consultant urologist for further examination.'

It felt as though my blood had turned to water. I looked him straight in the eye but he avoided looking back at me and turned to his computer screen.

'I have written to Mr Tomlinson-Burk at the Royal Hospital, he's one of the best urologists in the East Midlands.'

I said, 'Yes, but how is he rated in the British Isles?'

Dr Wolfowicz said, 'He is good, very good. You will be in good hands.'

'And how soon will I be in good hands?' I asked.

'I have written to him and asked him to see you in his Wednesday clinic next week.'

I made a mental note to take my suit into the cleaner's. Something, perhaps Mr Tomlinson-Burk's name, told me that casual clothes would not be suitable apparel.

I stopped at the post office on my way home and bought another notebook. Mrs Lewis-Masters was at the counter drawing her pension. She gave me a nod of recognition.

Wendy Wellbeck said, 'That's the third notebook in a month, Mr Mole. Are you writing another *War and Peace?*'

Mrs Lewis-Masters said, 'So you are a writer?'

I told her that I had managed to publish two books.

'Would I have read them?' she asked.

'Not unless you were interested in offal,' I said.

'Offal,' she repeated. 'Actually I once lived exclusively on offal. Camel's brains were considered to be a delicacy when my husband and I were travelling in North Africa. As honoured guests we were served only the best part of that prized animal.'

We left the shop together and for some reason I found myself telling her about my prostate trouble. She stopped walking and said, 'The men of the desert called it the Old Man's Curse. Their cure was to take camel dung and use it as a poultice around their genitals.'

'And did it work?' I asked, as we resumed walking.

'Of course not,' she said, 'but it seemed to relieve the symptoms somewhat.'

When we reached her house, I asked her its age.

'Georgian,' she said and asked me if I would like to join her for coffee.

I was curious to see inside so I said that I would be delighted.

When we entered the hall, there was a fat woman in an apron polishing the floor on her hands and knees. Mrs Lewis-Masters said, 'Mr Mole, this is Mrs Golightly, my housekeeper.'

Mrs Golightly hauled herself to her feet and said, 'Yes,

I've seen Mr Mole in The Bear. I put my name down for the community play. 'Ave you finished it yet, Mr Mole?'

I lied and said I had a few revisions to make but that otherwise it was completed.

Mrs Golightly giggled and said, 'I 'ope you've written me a good part.'

I forced a laugh, and she left to make the coffee.

Mrs Lewis-Masters showed me into a reception room at the front of the house. It was like entering a museum of anthropology. There were animal heads on the walls and crudely fashioned African statues scattered around. There was a large tiger-skin rug, with the beast's head attached, in front of the marble fireplace where a log fire smouldered. After inviting me to sit down on a sofa draped with a zebra skin, Mrs Lewis-Masters poked at the fire until sparks flew up the chimney. When Mrs Golightly brought the coffee pot in on a tray together with cups and saucers and a plate of shortcake biscuits, she put it down on an elephant's leg footstool and said, 'So what's the play about, Mr Mole?' I told her that it was called *Plague!* and was about the Black Death and how it had impacted on Mangold Parva.

Her face fell and she said, 'Shame. I 'ave been compared to 'Attie Jacques. And my 'usband reckons I'm funnier than 'er.'

Mrs Lewis-Masters said, 'Thank you, Mrs Golightly, you can go now.'

Mrs Golightly stomped out of the room and slammed the door.

Mrs Lewis-Masters said, 'Like all fat people, Mrs

Golightly is ultrasensitive. She claims she's fat because of her glands, but I put it down to her living almost entirely on Swiss rolls. I wanted to bring my African servants with me when my husband and I repatriated back to England, but the authorities would not let them in. Mrs Golightly is a poor substitute.'

I admired the heads on the wall and the animal skins, and she said that either she or her husband had killed them all, adding, 'I hope you're not one of those dreadful politically correct people who thinks that killing a wild animal is bad form.'

I made a neutral noise in my throat.

She said, 'I happen to think that anybody who eats the flesh of an animal cannot claim moral superiority over those of us who kill for sport.'

I asked her if she was still killing animals.

She said that she could no longer handle a rifle because she had cataracts and a tremor in her trigger finger.

I asked her what she had been doing in North Africa.

She said, 'My late husband and I imported camel accessories. The Sudanese value their camels and like to dress them up for festivals.'

I had a mental image of camels wearing shoes and matching handbags. She took an album out of a leather trunk and showed me photographs of her and a distinguished-looking white man surrounded by dark-skinned robed Africans and some very attractive camels wearing garlands and bells and tassels.

Mrs Lewis-Masters pointed a trembling finger at a particularly gorgeous camel and said, 'He was my favourite.

He carried me hundreds of miles across the desert. His name was Duncan.'

When Mrs Golightly saw me to the front door, she whispered, 'Thank you for taking the trouble to listen to 'er. I've 'eard them camel stories over and over again. Will you come back?'

Why does this always happen to me? Why do pensioners crave my company? I can't get involved with another one.

Saturday 22nd September

Yesterday, when I told Daisy that I have been referred to a consultant urologist, she burst into tears and said, 'I've been looking up the prostate on the net. I'm sure you'll be OK, Aidy. You're youngish and strongish, and if it's the worst ... well, I'm sure you'll make a quick recovery.'

I would like to have made love to my wife last night but my prostate, like a jealous lover, got in the way. Daisy said it didn't matter, but it does.

Sunday 23rd September

I have kept my illness from my parents, fearing hysteria from my mother and indifference from my father, who is consumed by his own poor health. I went round this morning to break the news to them, but they were listening to *The Archers* omnibus so I said I would call back later.

I busied myself clearing out the flowerpots on the patio at the back of the house, picking the last tomatoes. Daisy came out with a cup of coffee for me and we sat in the weak sunshine for a while.

I said to Daisy, 'We ought to do something with all this land.'

She laughed and said, 'Such as what, Bob Flowerdew?'

I got quite carried away, went inside for a pencil and paper, and made a rough sketch of my ideal garden. I diverted the stream and made a central water feature. I planted an avenue of horse chestnuts (for the conkers, I told Daisy). I constructed a revolving summer house and built a pergola and covered it in old-fashioned sweet-smelling roses and honeysuckle. Gracie came out to join us dressed in her Leicester City football strip. As she contentedly kicked a ball against the side of the house, for a few brief moments I felt happy to be alive.

In the afternoon I told my parents about my appointment with the consultant urologist.

My mother wept and said, 'As if I haven't got enough on my plate.'

My father said, 'At least you're not in a wheelchair like me, son.'

Monday 24th September

Nothing much happened today. I am dreading Wednesday.

Tuesday 25th September

When I went to get my suit out of the cleaner's, the woman showed me up in front of the queue by saying, 'You've ruined one of our machines because you left a packet of Starburst in your suit jacket.'

I pointed out to her that it was incumbent on the employees of the dry-cleaner's to check the clothes before they went into the machines.

She said, 'I think you'll find, if you read your ticket, that it is incumbent on you to remove anything that might cause harm to our machines. We've had to fly an engineer over from Germany to repair the damage.'

I said that if she had bought British machines she would have been spared the expense of an aeroplane ticket.

She said that the German machines were cheaper than the British ones and were state of the art.

I said, 'You can't blame me for the demise of British manufacturing business,' and asked if I could have my suit.

She said, 'Nothing would give me more pleasure than for you to take your suit off the premises.' She took it from a rack behind her and even through the plastic wrapper I could see multicoloured stains on the jacket and trousers.

We got into a heated argument which only came to an end when a brutish-looking man in the queue slammed his ticket down on the counter and shouted, 'Gimme my suit! I've gotta be in court in 'alf an hour.'

After she had served the brute, she said, 'You are banned from using this dry-cleaner's ever again.'

This is typical of my life: other men get barred from pubs and wine bars, I get barred from a dry-cleaner's.

Wednesday 26th September

Mr Tomlinson-Burk was not at all the patrician-looking man I had expected him to be. He looked like the type of man who jumps on the back of the dodgems at a fairground. He was swarthy and had the hands of somebody who worked in the building trade. I hoped that he wouldn't give me a rectal examination. For one thing, I didn't think that they made disposable gloves big enough to encompass his sausage-like fingers, but he was very kind and efficient. The rectal examination didn't hurt (perhaps he used his little finger – I was not in a position to know).

He said, 'Your blood tests show an increased level of benign prostatic hyperplasia or BPH, which indicates a problem.'

'A problem,' I repeated.

'Yes,' he said.

I looked at his hair, which was thick and black and

wavy. The word 'cancer' hung in the air, but neither of us spoke it.

He said, 'Your rectal examination shows that your prostate is very enlarged. I think it would be sensible to start treatment as soon as possible. I'm going to refer you to my colleague, Mr Rafferty.'

I asked him what Mr Rafferty was a specialist in.

He said, 'He's an oncologist.'

'Is oncology a euphemism for cancer?' I asked, although I didn't especially want to hear the answer.

'Oncology is the study and treatment of tumours,' he said.

'So I have a tumour?' I checked.

'You certainly have a tumour,' he said. 'What we don't know is how advanced it is. With luck we'll have caught it early.'

I wished at that moment that I had allowed somebody to accompany me to my appointment. Daisy, my mother and Mr Carlton-Hayes had all offered. Even my father had mumbled that he would hire a wheelchair-friendly taxi to take us to the hospital. Now I wished that there *was* somebody in the waiting room.

On my walk back to the bookshop I felt like a ghost of myself. I was wearing my own underwear, socks, shoes and second-best suit, but I felt hollow. I had promised to ring Daisy as soon as I left the hospital, but I couldn't speak, my mouth was dry and I couldn't find the words. So Mr Carlton-Hayes was the first person I told.

He made me a cup of tea and added two full teaspoons

126

of sugar, then sat me down in the back room. He told me that when he was a young man he had been taken seriously ill with a brain tumour. He said, 'Fortunately, I was in Switzerland at the time, preparing to climb the Matterhorn. The doctors feared that I would lose some mental capacity.'

'But you didn't, did you? You're the cleverest man I know,' I said.

'Well, for a time I quite forgot my Greek and Latin, but happily both came back.' He put a hand on my shoulder and said, 'Why don't you go home, my dear? You've had a dreadful shock.'

I said that I would rather stay in the back room and collect my thoughts. The bell rang and he went out into the shop. I heard a woman asking if he had a book about casting spells. She told him that her next-door neighbour wouldn't cut her side of the privet hedge that was a boundary to their gardens, and that she wanted to cast a spell on her.

Why are at least half the people who frequent our bookshop mad?

Thursday 27th September

I never want to live through a night like that again. Daisy took the news very badly. After sobbing for a few minutes, she flew into a rage, shouting, 'Why you? You've never hurt anybody or anything, and the next time somebody tells me that God exists I swear I'll stuff my bloody fist down their throat. If He or She exists, why does He or She allow violent thicko bastards to walk the streets in perfect health?'

My mother heard the shouting and came round. She wept, 'Why is God punishing you and not me? If I could have your tumour for you, I would. I've had my life, such as it was. I've not got anything to live for, apart from my family and the two weeks your father goes into respite care.' She added, lighting a cigarette, 'This will kill your father, we can't tell him.'

I said, 'We're already keeping *The Jeremy Kyle Show* from him. He can't be protected from the tragedies of life for ever.'

Gracie woke up and came into the living room She looked so adorable in her Disney princess pyjamas that I picked her up and held her until she said, 'Daddy, you're squeezing me too tight. Put me down.'

Later on, when everybody had calmed down a bit, we went round to tell my father. His reaction on hearing the word 'tumour' was to thump the sides of his wheel-chair and shout at the ceiling, 'Call yourself merciful, God? You murdered your own son, and now you're murdering mine!'

My mother opened the bottle of champagne she keeps in the fridge for celebrations, saying, as she handed me a glass, 'Let's celebrate the first day of Adrian's recovery.'

I had not had anything to eat that day so the champagne went to my head and for a few minutes I was full of optimism, but it soon wore off. When we returned home, I was putting Gracie back to bed and I felt fear grip me around my heart. Would I see my little girl grow up?

Friday 28th September

Can't write anything.

Saturday 29th September

I received an appointment in the post to see Mr Rafferty at his clinic on Tuesday morning.

Sunday 30th September

Me, Daisy, Gracie and my parents went to The Bear for lunch.

Mrs Golightly was in the pub with her hangdog husband. She shouted, 'Mrs Lewis-Masters enjoyed your visit the other day.'

Daisy raised her eyebrows and said, 'What visit?'

I told her about old Mrs Lewis-Masters and she said, 'Aidy, don't get involved with another pensioner. You've got to think about yourself now.'

As usual, the food was horrible.

When I complained to Mrs Urquhart that my York-shire pudding had shattered and that my Brussels sprouts were waterlogged, she said, 'Nobody asked you to come here.' Which was quite a reasonable statement because obviously nobody had.

I said, 'I thought you would welcome my comments on your food.'

She said, 'You want to try cooking and serving sixty or so Sunday lunches in a tiny kitchen with no ventilation.'

My mother took my arm and said, 'Adrian, you mustn't get upset. It's not good for your prostrate.'

Is this how my life is to be from now on? Is my prostate going to take centre stage?

In the afternoon I went for a walk by myself. The autumn trees were spectacularly beautiful. In the little spinney behind the Piggeries I sat down on the trunk of a fallen silver birch tree and phoned Pandora. Judging by the noises off, she was in a busy restaurant.

I asked her where she was.

'I'm in Wagamama. Halfway through a bowl of noodles,' she said.

I told her that I had some bad news.

'Is it my mother?' she said.

'No,' I said.

'Are you getting a divorce?' she asked.

'No,' I said. 'I've got a tumour.'

'What kind of a tumour?' she said, her voice quavering.

'Prostate,' I said.

I heard her shout imperiously, 'For fuck's sake be quiet!' The restaurant fell silent and she said, 'Who's looking after you?'

I told her that Mr Tomlinson-Burk was, and that I was due to see Mr Rafferty on Tuesday.

She said, 'You can't put your life in the hands of provincial doctors. I have contacts in Harley Street. I'll make some enquiries and ring you back tomorrow.'

We talked for a few moments about inconsequential things and then she said, 'You know I love you, don't you?'

I said, 'Yes, and you know I still love you, don't you?'

'Yes,' she said, and then she rang off.

A small part of me was glad that Pandora was back in my life and that, for once, *she* was going to ring *me*.

Dear Diary, I will not die until I have seen all seven modern Wonders of the World. They are: the Great Wall of China, Petra in Jordan, the Christ the Redeemer statue in Brazil, Machu Picchu in Peru, some ruin in Mexico I've never heard of, the Colosseum in Rome and the Taj Mahal in India. I am almost forty years of age and I have never seen a single one. I broke into a sweat when I realized that I could die any day without seeing a single Wonder! I hereby vow, Diary, that I will make it my life's purpose to knock off all seven.

Monday 1st October

Nigel took my prostate news very badly. 'And they say there's a fucking God,' he said. 'Well, if there is, he's a total bastard who sent me blind and lets little kids die like flies in Africa.'

Barbara Boyer, from our old school – Neil Armstrong Comprehensive – was there, celebrating her birthday.

131

She is as beautiful as ever, which is a miracle considering that she has been married five times and is the mother of seven children. She told me that her third husband, Barry, is still in remission from 'prostrate' cancer, eleven years on, and that he lives a very active life, snorkelling in the Maldives and hot-air ballooning. She added, 'And he's sixty-one. They do call it the old man's disease.'

'So I could live until I'm fifty-one,' I said. And for some reason we all laughed.

Lance processed in, flourishing a birthday cake, blazing with forty candles. It's a wonder they haven't burned their house down by now. They both smoke and are constantly missing the ashtray.

Later on, Parvez came round and gave Barbara a birthday card and a box of After Eights. Then Wayne Wong arrived with an orchid in a pot and, having been told my news, said, 'My uncle had prostate cancer.'

I asked how he was.

Wayne hesitated for a second and then said, with his eyes downcast, 'He died five years ago.'

As I was about to leave, Pandora rang and gave me the names of two Harley Street doctors. When they heard that Pandora was on the phone, everybody insisted on speaking to her. Barbara asked Pan if she was seeing anybody. Apparently, Pandora answered that she was having a secret affair with a shadow cabinet minister. When the call was terminated, we speculated on who the shadow minister might be. None of us could think of a single Conservative minister's name apart from David Cameron. For a few moments I forgot about the tumour inside me, and had a laugh and drank some wine and ate birthday cake with my friends.

It was not until I was on the way home that I realized I had not been invited to Barbara's birthday party and, if I had not called on Nigel, I would have known nothing about it.

Why didn't they invite me, Diary? Is it because Daisy once told Barbara that anybody marrying more than twice was a glutton for punishment and deserved everything they got?

Why do so many people mispronounce 'prostate'? I am sick of correcting them.

Tuesday 2nd October

Mr Rafferty did not look like a doctor either. He had a Belfast accent and reminded me of the Reverend Ian Paisley. He wore chinos, Timberland boots and a Ralph Lauren sweater. He went into detail about the various possible treatments for my tumour: radiotherapy, external-beam radiotherapy, Brach therapy, internal radiotherapy, surgery, high-intensity focused ultrasound and photodynamic therapy.

I told him that I didn't like the sound of the internal radiotherapy, where they insert radioactive pellets through a tube in the penis.

He said, 'No, it fair makes the eyes water, doesn't it? But it's an extremely effective method of zapping the tumour.' He told me he was going to send me off for a transrectal ultrasound examination and that he would see me later, when he had reviewed the resulting video, which he invited me to watch too.

'Then,' he said, 'with the knowledge gained, we can make an effective treatment plan.'

I was reluctant to remove my boxer shorts in the company of a young nurse and the ultrasound operator, but they were very matter of fact and told me that they do dozens of such examinations every day. When the probe was inserted, the young nurse squeezed my hand and said, 'That's the worst over.'

When the probe had been withdrawn, I got dressed and went back to Mr Rafferty's waiting room. I had read fifty pages of Graham Greene's *The End of the Affair* before Mr Rafferty called me in to see the video. He pointed at something on the screen and said, 'You see here that there are changes in the capsule of the prostate, and it may have been breeched. I will arrange for you to have an MRI scan in the next few days, then perhaps the dog will be able to see the rabbit, eh, Mr Mole?'

Wednesday 3rd October

I am sick of thinking and talking about my prostate. Pandora rang to ask if I had contacted the Harley Street doctors yet.

I told her that I had been too busy and that, anyway, I didn't have the money for private medicine.

She said, 'Take out a loan, then.'

I pointed out to her that I was still paying back tax on

the salary I had earned in 1997 and was waiting to hear from Gordon Brown. 'Perhaps he's too busy taking tea with Margaret Thatcher,' I said. I could not keep the bitterness from my voice.

She said, 'I will gladly lend you the money, Moley. I don't want you to die.'

I sometimes wish that Pandora would temper her language. She prides herself on calling a spade a spade, but I am with Gwendolen from Oscar Wilde's *The Importance of Being Earnest* who, when the Reverend Chasuble says, 'I call a spade a spade,' replies, 'I'm glad to say that I have never *seen* a spade.'

I asked Pandora if she knew when Mr Brown was going to announce a snap election.

'Snap is not a word I would associate with Gordon. He can't decide between tea or bloody coffee when asked,' she said, 'but I'd love to see you in the flesh, Aidy, perhaps when I'm electioneering? Though I must admit, it's some time since my constituents saw me in Ashby de la Zouche.'

Diary, am I not worth a special visit, whether or not there is an election to be fought?

Thursday 4th October

I have just read that the government has passed a law whereby 652 agencies of the state will be able to find out who I have phoned and who has phoned me. It is the end of privacy. The government claims, in the sacred names of terrorism and criminal activity, that these measures are vital to our security. But how secure am I going to feel when I phone Parvez and we talk about my finances? Is some government snooper going to be listening and assume that I am laundering money or smuggling Kalashnikovs into Leicester?

Parvez now wears Muslim dress and goes to Friday prayers at a radical mosque in Leicester. Only last week he said to me, 'Moley, don't ask me out for a drink no more, and don't invite me to the ex-pigsty you live in. I ain't comfortable knowing that pigs lived there before you. I'm strictly halal now.'

I said, 'I hope you're not going to try and make your wife wear a veil?'

He said, 'Fat chance. My wife has joined the Townswomen's Guild and is making potpourri baskets for the Christmas Fayre.'

Friday 5th October

Wrote another letter to Gordon Brown.

Dear Mr Brown

I wonder if you've had time to glance at my letter of 3rd June 2007.

I realise that you are busy trying to decide whether or not the country should go to the polls, but just five minutes of your time would put my mind at rest.

Also, do you think it fair that persons such as myself, who live in converted pigsties, should pay the full council tax?

136

After all, we are helping to preserve England's farming heritage and surely deserve to be recompensed for our commitment to the days of yore.

Yours sincerely,

Adrian A. Mole

PS: By the way, I quite often phone my friend and accountant, Parvez. He is an ardent Muslim and attends a mosque led by a loquacious imam. However, Parvez poses no threat to the state. Perhaps you would apprise the security forces of this fact.

A.A.M.

Saturday 6th October

Daisy phoned me at work to tell me she had opened a letter addressed to me and that an appointment has been made for me to attend the hospital for an MRI scan on Tuesday morning at 11.15.

She said, 'I'm going with you this time, Aidy, and nothing you say will stop me.'

I made a window display out of Katie Price's (aka Jordan's) new book *A Whole New World*, her ghosted autobiography. Mr Carlton-Hayes had ordered twenty-five hardback copies in the mistaken belief that Price's book was something to do with Jordan's role in the Middle East.

All twenty-five copies had been sold by lunchtime. Mr Carlton-Hayes was very relieved and said, 'Perhaps I'll leave the ordering to you in future, my dear.'

I am getting increasingly worried about him. Yesterday he forgot who had written *Scoop*, one of his favourite books. He kept saying, 'Don't tell me, Adrian. I know it's written by a woman.'

I gave him a clue and said, 'No, it's written by a man with a woman's name.'

Halfway through the afternoon he shouted, 'Evelyn Waugh!'

The more doddery and forgetful he becomes, the more I have to do in the shop. I told him three times that I had to go to the hospital on Tuesday morning, but as we were closing the shop he asked me again when my appointment was.

I know he is worried about me. Sometimes I think he regards me as the son he never had.

Sunday 7th October

Spent most of the day working on *Plague!*. Wrote a scene for Mrs Lewis-Masters' housekeeper, Mrs Golightly.

Plague victim is slumped on the Village Green. Enter a fat jolly woman. She crosses to the plague victim.

FAT JOLLY WOMAN: Thou lookest under the weather.
PLAGUE VICTIM: 'Tis true, I have got munificent sores cast about my body.
FAT JOLLY WOMAN: Have you the pox?
PLAGUE VICTIM: No, for I have never lain with a

woman, a man nor one of God's beasts of the field. I was keeping my corporal body pure so that I may enter the gates of Heaven.

FAT JOLLY WOMAN: I fear that I will go straight to Hell and be tortured evermore by the flames and the Devil's pitchfork, for I have lain with many in this village, maids and men.

PLAGUE VICTIM: I feel death at my shoulder. He hath his hands about my heart.

A carrion crow enters stage right and circles overhead.

FAT JOLLY WOMAN: I will hasten to the abbey and fetch Brother Andrew. He doth have potions and plants that may cure you of this evil scourge.

The carrion crow lands at the plague victim's feet and pecks at his boots. The fat jolly woman exits stage left.

I am pleased with this scene. I think I have captured the atmosphere and the language very well. I strongly identify with Plague Victim. Next week I will have to start casting, which I am dreading. The Mangold Parva Players are notoriously quarrelsome if they are not allocated the best parts.

Monday 8th October

My father told me that when he had an MRI scan he terminated the session after five minutes and demanded to be let out. He said that the doctors were extremely annoyed and told him that there were hundreds of people on the waiting list. My father said, 'It's not my fault I suffer from claustrophobia. I was locked in the cupboard under the stairs in 1953. My mother and her sister went to see *Gone with the Wind* and forgot about me.'

I asked my father why he had been locked in the understairs cupboard.

He said, 'It was a trivial thing. I fed two of her goldfish to the cat.'

I told him that cruelty to animals was an early sign of psychopathic behaviour.

He said, 'Those goldfish didn't suffer, the cat bit their heads off quick and clean.'

Tuesday 9th October
MRI Day

Daisy was making a disproportionate fuss last night about what she should wear to the hospital today. She went through her wardrobe, trying on her favourite clothes, before throwing them into a heap in the corner of our bedroom and saying plaintively, 'Nothing fits.'

I tried to calm her down by saying, 'You always look

nice in black,' but she said she couldn't possibly wear black, that it was far too 'funereal' and she wanted to feel optimistic about the results of the scan.

Diary, I could not help thinking, as I picked her discarded clothes up from the floor and rehung them in the wardrobe, that it would have been easier to go by myself.

Nevertheless, I felt proud of my wife, in her purple kaftan, as we walked into the room where the MRI machine was purring. A doctor told Daisy that she could sit in the waiting room. When she said, 'I would like to stay with my husband,' they told her that she wouldn't be able to hold my hand and she wouldn't be able to see me once I was inside the cylinder.

On the advice of my father I kept my eyes completely shut throughout the procedure. The machine clicked and whirred and occasionally a doctor would ask me to breathe in, hold it and then breathe out. For some reason I found it difficult to follow these simple instructions and kept breathing out when I was meant to be breathing in. I was very relieved when the hard surface on which I was lying slid me out into the room again. I had to be helped to my feet because my legs were wobbly. I dressed in a cubicle with Daisy's help. She even tied my shoelaces. Is this my future? Will I be reliant on my wife for my personal care?

Before we left the hospital we went to the Women's Royal Voluntary Service café for a cup of tea and a toasted teacake. As I looked around at the other people in the café, I wondered how many of them had an invisible illness, like me.

We walked to the bookshop together. Mr Carlton-Hayes said that not a single customer had been in that morning. I didn't want to tell him that he had forgotten to put the open sign on the door.

Only seconds after Daisy had left to go shopping, Dr Pearce appeared on the pavement outside and peered through the window. When she came inside, she was looking for a *High School Musical* book. Her youngest daughter has fallen under its malign spell. She told me that *High School Musical – The Show* was coming to the De Montfort Hall in Leicester and that she had obtained four tickets for the matinée next Saturday. She said that Robin had been meant to go but had decided to stay another week in Norway, and given that the tickets were so expensive . . .

She said, 'I'm sure your little daughter – Gracie, isn't it? – would love to go.'

Thinking on my feet, I said, 'Next Saturday, I'm afraid I'm working in the shop.'

Mr Carlton-Hayes, who was hovering near by, said, 'No, you must go, my dear. I'll cover for you.'

Dr Pearce rummaged in her copious handbag and a single disposable nappy fell out and on to the floor. She picked it up and rammed it into her bag before handing me two tickets.

Diary, like an idiot I took them.

Wednesday 10th October

Pandora rang when I was in the shower. Daisy answered and apparently told Pandora that we expected the results of the MRI examination at the end of the week. Pandora said that her constituents had demanded to see her in her surgery next Saturday afternoon and asked if we would 'give her supper' on Saturday night.

As I was getting dressed, Daisy said, 'What can I possibly cook for somebody who is godmother to Gordon Ramsey's youngest child?'

I told her that her shepherd's pie always went down well.

To be honest, Diary, I shared her apprehension. She is perfectly capable of starting a meal off, but she falls apart when it comes to serving it up and bringing it to the table. I have seen her in tears over a simple mushroom omelette.

I intended to ring Dr Pearce and cancel *High School Musical* but events overtook me. My mother came round and said that she had been surfing the internet and found somebody in America who claims that they can cure prostate cancer. All I have to do is send five hundred dollars to an address in Waco, Texas and I will receive my own personal crystal to wear in a bag around my groin. According to my mother, the crystal will neutralise the antibodies that are attacking my 'prostrate'.

I told her that I did not have five hundred dollars to

spare and that I was putting my faith in medical science and the National Health Service.

My mother said, 'We must explore every avenue, Aidy. Don't close your mind to alternative health. I've got your father on seaweed extracts and it's perked him up no end.' As I was seeing her out, she whispered, 'A producer from *The Jeremy Kyle Show* rang me this morning. They want me, Rosie and Lucas on the show in a couple of weeks.'

I begged her to reconsider and said that if she was so desperate to be on television, why didn't she apply for *The Weakest Link*? She told me that Rosie and her horrible boyfriend, Trevor 'Mad Dog' Jackson, were coming to stay for the weekend. I warned my mother that she should lock up any valuables and make sure that her purse and credit cards were hidden away. I reminded her that the last time Mad Dog came to stay he stole her gold locket, which contained a curl of my baby hair, and exchanged it for a wrap of cocaine.

She said, 'Poor Mad Dog, he was so distraught that he'd stolen from me. Put yourself in his place, Aidy. Imagine that you're an addict and have no money, what would you do?'

I said, 'It might surprise you, Mother, but I am unable to imagine myself in the hideous shoes of Mad Dog. The man is a total waste of space.'

My mother said, 'Perhaps we ought to tell Jeremy Kyle about Mad Dog ... he might be able to get him into rehab, find him work, put him on an anger management course, sort out his alcohol problems, do something about his kleptomania.'

I said, witheringly, 'And why not ask Jeremy to end world poverty and stop global warming while he's about it?'

Thursday 11th October

No word about my MRI results. I woke in the night and couldn't get my breath. This time next year, will I be lying six feet under in Mangold Parva graveyard? Which is, unfortunately, sited opposite Gracie's Nursery School classroom.

Friday 12th October

Mrs Leech rang from the surgery earlier this morning to say that my MRI results were in and that Dr Wolfowicz wanted to see me. I could not tell from her voice whether the news was good or bad.

I walked Gracie to school. She took great delight in kicking her way through the dead leaves at the side of the lane. I threw a branch at the horse chestnut tree at the boundary of the village and brought down half a dozen conkers. When I opened the outside prickly skin of one and showed Gracie the shining brown conker inside, she clapped her hands together in pleasure and said, 'Is it magic, Dad?'

I told her that the chestnut trees of England were dying of a tree disease and that when she grew up it was possible there would be no horse chestnuts left to throw a stick at.

She said, 'There'll be other kinds of trees left, Dad.'

After taking her into school, I tried not to look at the graveyard opposite but could not help noticing a fresh mound of earth covered in rotting flowers.

Dr Wolfowicz's waiting room was full. I was on nodding terms with most of the people in there but I did not feel like talking. When it was my turn to go into the surgery, I was reluctant to get to my feet. Was my tumour confined to my prostate, or had it spread to other more vital parts of my body?

Dr Wolfowicz said, 'Please sit down, Mr Mole. I have your MRI results.' He smoothed the creases of a letter with his massive hand. 'And I am going to say to you that the news is not good. I'm afraid that your tumour is more advanced than we had hoped. We need to start treating your tumour immediately, my friend. Is there anything you'd like to ask?'

I brought out the list I had scribbled down at breakfast.

1. How long have I got to live?
2. Will I have to declare my tumour when I renew my personal insurance on 1st November?
3. If I lose my hair due to chemotherapy will the National Health Service supply a wig?
4. Did Dr Wolfowicz know any patients who had totally recovered from prostate cancer?
5. Was it a painful death?

6. Would I continue to lose sexual function?
7. Would I be able to work whilst I was undergoing treatment?
8. If not, could I claim sickness benefit?
9. If the pain got too bad towards the end would he advise me to go to Switzerland and end my life in a clinic whilst listening to Mahler?

Dr Wolfowicz gave a deep sigh and said, 'I have a leaflet somewhere that should answer all of your questions, apart from number nine, that is. I'm afraid I cannot condone euthanasia. And yes, I know many young and youngish men who have been in remission from prostate cancer for many years. As for question number one, none of us know when we're going to die. We live with death from the moment we are born.'

I asked him if his Roman Catholicism gave him comfort.

He said, 'No, but my faith in human courage certainly does.'

When I left Dr Wolfowicz's surgery, I was pleased to see that Daisy was outside waiting for me but I did not know how to arrange my face. As we walked through the village, it started to rain and the leaves in the lane were soggy and gave off the smell of decay. I held her hand and told her exactly what Dr Wolfowicz had told me. We were passing the graveyard at the time. She threw her arms around me and big fat tears rolled down her face and on to mine.

When she could speak, she said, 'I can't bear it, Aidy.

It's my fault. I've been so vile to you. But I can't imagine a world without you in it.'

From the school we could hear the ragged sound of small children singing, *We plough the fields and scatter the good seed on the land.*

My parents were waiting at their living-room window and watched as Daisy and I walked up the drive. As we approached the Piggeries, they opened their front door and my mother pushed my father down the ramp towards us. My mother has never been able to wait for anything, even bad news, so we stood in a light drizzle around my father's wheelchair while I told my parents that I had an advanced tumour of the prostate and would be needing immediate treatment.

My mother went into a long emotional monologue about the day I was born and how happy she had been. My father reached up and took my hand and shook it, which, from him, was a gesture of paternal love.

When the drizzle turned into a downpour, we went inside and my mother searched for the cafetière and the Fair Trade ground coffee she had bought after seeing a programme about poverty in Kenya. We talked about how my bad news would affect all our lives. Daisy offered to get a job, my mother offered to take Gracie after school and my father offered to cash in his insurance policy to help us out with money.

I tried to cycle into work at lunchtime but the rain and weakness in my legs made me turn around before I reached the dual carriageway.

Dougie Horsefield took me to work in his Ford Mondeo taxi. During the journey he told me that there had been a lot of talk about my community play, *Plague!*. He said, 'Nobody wants to wear filthy rags and have boils all over them. Can't you write summat where all the women look sexy and all the men look handsome and we can have a laugh?'

I said, from the back seat, 'Dougie, life in the Middle Ages was grim. There were no antibiotics, soft toilet paper or Nurofen. Most people were dead before they were thirty-five. They didn't do much frolicking on the Village Green.'

He said, 'Well, all I'm saying is there's a gang of us who would rather do *Joseph and the Amazing Technicolor Dreamcoat.*'

I pointed out that in that case they would have to pay a performance fee to Andrew Lloyd Webber and Tim Rice, whereas I was providing my services as writer, producer and director for free.

He charged me £12.50 for the fare and didn't seem grateful when I gave him £13.

2 a.m.

Just realised I have not rung Dr Pearce to cancel *High School Musical*. What is wrong with me? I don't find the woman remotely attractive.

Saturday 13th October

Mr Carlton-Hayes has taken the news about my illness very badly. He held both my hands and struggled to find the appropriate words. Later that morning he gave me a copy of P. G. Wodehouse's *Blandings Castle* from the cabinet and told me that I must take as much time off work as I need. He said that he would ask Leslie to help out if necessary.

As arranged, Daisy brought Gracie to the shop at noon. Gracie was dressed in her *High School Musical* cheerleader costume and she enthralled Mr Carlton-Hayes by singing 'Breaking Free' and doing one of her cheerleading routines on the floor of the bookshop. It was truly a clash of two cultures.

After instructing me not to buy any more *High School Musical* tat, Daisy went to register with Executive Careers in Horsefair Street.

As Gracie and I trudged up the London Road, a sense of fatalism propelled me towards De Montfort Hall. Diary, why do I have no strong will of my own? I am easily bent, like a twig in a gale. I felt sure that my wife would not understand me in regard to Dr Pearce's kind gesture with the tickets.

Dr Pearce was waiting outside the hall with her daughter. She was wearing denim jeans, trainers and an orange cagoule with matching lipstick. Her little girl, who was costumed as Sharpay, held out her hand and said, 'Hello,

I am Ophelia. Who is your favourite character in *High School Musical*?' She sighed impatiently as she waited for my answer.

I found her quite intimidating. She wears heavy black-framed spectacles and has short black hair, which gives her an uncanny resemblance to Louis Theroux.

Entering the auditorium was painful on the ears. The audience was mostly female, the majority of them were under eleven years old and all of them were on the verge of hysteria. Men and boys were thin on the ground. Dr Pearce and I sat together and halfway through the energetic but baffling performance she leaned in close to me and surreptitiously took my hand. I wanted to remove it but couldn't work out how to do so without causing offence, so we sat holding hands until the lights came up and it was time to leave.

Once we had filed out of the theatre and bought a *High School Musical* mug and a Sharpay pencil case, I was ready to say goodbye to Dr Pearce and Ophelia. I had arranged for Dougie Horsefield to pick us up outside the venue because the last bus to Mangold Parva leaves Leicester at 5.15 p.m. on Saturday afternoons. To my horror I saw that he had Daisy in the back of the cab. Had she seen me saying goodbye to Dr Pearce and Ophelia?

As soon as we were in the taxi, Gracie said, 'Daddy was holding a lady's hand.'

Dougie Horsefield tried to conceal a snort of laughter.

Daisy asked, 'Who was she?'

I replied, 'A complete stranger, she was overcome with the heat and the noise and I simply felt her pulse.'

Daisy said, 'Why? You're not in the bloody St John Ambulance brigade.'

She was unnaturally quiet for the rest of the way home. Thankfully Gracie hardly drew breath as she told Dougie and her mother the convoluted plot of *High School Musical – The Show.*

As we prepared the shepherd's pie for Pandora, Daisy said very little apart from 'pass the mince', 'don't chop the carrots too thickly', etc. All I could think about was my narrow escape. I have to make it clear to Dr Pearce that I wish to return to our former relationship, i.e. bookseller and customer.

Sunday 14th October

Pandora was what she called 'fashionably late'. Eventually I put the shepherd's pie in the bottom oven to keep warm but it was certainly past its best by 9.07 p.m. when she finally arrived.

Earlier in the evening we'd had the usual clothing crisis. I told Daisy that she looked wonderful in the purple kaftan and she put it on, albeit reluctantly. But I must admit, Diary, that when Pandora strolled in, swathed in pale grey cashmere, Daisy looked a tiny bit vulgar in comparison. The atmosphere was as cool as the bottle of the 2005 Cuvée des Vignerons Beaujolais I had inadvertently put in the fridge.

Pandora wanted me to tell her the 'story' of my prostate. Halfway through she said, 'I need a fucking fag for this, I've left them in the bloody car.' Daisy pushed a packet of Silk Cut towards Pandora. It was the first companionable gesture the two women had shared all evening.

When I had finished, ending up with Dr Wolfowicz's philosophy that we are all dying from the moment we are born, Pandora started to sob, laying her head on the table and almost knocking over her wine. I waited for Daisy to comfort her but when she made no move to do this I got up, went to Pandora and stood by her side. She wrapped her arms around my waist and soaked my shirt with her tears. I must admit, Diary, I was close to tears myself but when I looked at Daisy I saw, with a chill in my heart, that she was dry-eyed and wore what a neutral observer would have called an expression of icy indifference.

Pandora stayed until two o'clock in the morning, long after Daisy had gone to bed. She talked about the old days, when we were both 13¾ and fell in love.

She said, 'I was totally obsessed with you. I could not think of anything else at all. I only lived for the next moment when I would glimpse your nerdy face. You were the first person to see my nipples.'

'No,' I corrected her, 'you only showed me your left nipple.'

I tried to get her to share some Westminster gossip. I particularly wanted to hear about Gordon Brown's state of mind. Did she think he was dangerously unstable, as some of the newspapers were saying?

She said, 'You have to be a bit mad, it's a bloody awful job. Do you think it's insane of me to want to be the first Labour woman prime minister one day?'

I said, 'I thought you must be sick of politics – you're hardly ever in your constituency.'

Pandora's eyes glittered and she said, 'But Westminster is intoxicating. One is loath to leave it for the dreary provinces.'

I bridled at this and said, 'It's the dreary provinces that made this country rich. Dr Johnson came from Lichfield, Shakespeare from Stratford-on-Avon. And the scientist who discovered DNA fingerprinting, Dr Alec Jeffreys, is a Leicester man!'

Diary, I was glad when she left. The day's events had exhausted me and the cheese from the shepherd's pie kept me awake for quite some time.

Went to The Bear for Sunday lunch. I am sick of their Sunday roasts so opted for the Thai Special. It tasted like the black soap my mother used to wash my hair with on Sunday evenings in a vain attempt to stop me from catching nits. Still, what can you expect from a chef called Lee who has only got a diploma in Cooking With A Microwave, from an FE college.

Somehow the news of my illness has spread around the village. I doubt Dr Wolfowicz is in the habit of talking about his patients and their afflictions so I suspect that the culprit is Mrs Leech. It can only be her. I have a good mind to complain to the British Medical Association. Several villagers came up to me and engaged me in conversation, all the while looking at me as if to measure me for my coffin. A small part of me enjoyed the attention.

Bumped into the Timbuktu woman when I was pushing my father and Gracie back from the pub. She

asked me if Gracie was an adopted child. I joked that, as
far as I knew, Gracie was carrying my DNA.

My father said, in a feeble attempt at being humorous,
'Though you never know in our family.'

The Timbuktu woman, whose name I have forgotten,
said, 'She looks nothing like you, she looks dark, very
dark, like a gypsy girl.'

My father took offence and said, 'Are we going home,
or what?'

Gypsies once tarmacked his drive in their old house in
Wisteria Walk while he was out and tried to charge him
£1,000. He was about to write a cheque when my mother
came home and reminded him he had no money in the
bank. The gypsies took their revenge by dumping a pile
of tarmac at the end of the drive so he couldn't get his
car out.

Monday 15th October

It was an effort to cycle to the bookshop today. In
between customers I tried to write a few scenes of *Plague!*.
However, my muse has deserted me and I realized that
I could not stage the play single-handedly. I wrote to
the vicar in his role as chairman of the Mangold Parva
players.

Dear Simon
    It is with great regret that I have to inform you that, due to
ill health, I am no longer able to write, direct and produce our

community play, *Plague!* I realise that this must come as a blow to you, but I have been told that there is a movement afoot to stage *Joseph and the Amazing Technicolor Dreamcoat*, which is perhaps more suitable to a church-based group.

I remain, sir, your most humble and obedient servant,

A. A. Mole

PS: Are there any vacant family plots available in your grave-yard, in an area not overlooked by the school?

Tuesday 16th October

Received an appointment in the post today. I am seeing the oncologist tomorrow at ten fifteen at the Royal Hospital.

Wednesday 17th October

My oncologist is Dr Sophia Rubik.

I said, 'Rubik? As in the cube?'

'Yes,' she sighed, 'as in the dammed cube.' She invited me to sit down and asked me how I wanted to be addressed.

There was initial confusion – I thought she said 'get undressed' so I stood up and started to unbuckle my belt – but once we'd sorted it out, I said, 'Call me Adrian.'

*

To be honest, Diary, I could not fully concentrate while she talked about suitable treatments. I was thinking about the day my father threw my Rubik's cube into the canal when I went fishing with him once. He said the constant clicking was scaring the fish away. But I must have heard a few options: watch and wait, radiotherapy, radioactive pellets, surgery, radioactive ultrasound and photodynamic therapy.

I got into a mild panic, just as I used to at the pick 'n' mix counter in Woolworths. I asked her which treatment she recommended.

She said, in her pleasant North Country accent, 'We decide together, Adrian.'

I said, 'But I'm not qualified. I only got a C grade in GCSE Biology.'

She said, 'But it's far better if our patients engage with us, Adrian. We find that patients who own their disease have a more satisfactory prognosis.'

I said, 'Well, which is the least painful treatment option?'

She said, 'None of them are painful, Adrian, though I suppose it depends on your tolerance, but some are uncomfortable and have unpleasant side effects.'

I said, 'Which treatment has the least uncomfortable side effects?'

She said, 'Watchful waiting, I suppose, but in your case we cannot watch and wait. You need treatment, starting in the next few weeks. Your PSA levels are higher than I would like.'

'What exactly is PSA?'

She rattled off, 'Prostate Specific Antigen. It's the liquid that carries and nurtures your sperm and it's essential for healthy sexual function.'

She gave me a booklet and said, 'Read this and discuss it with your family, and then we'll carry on from there.'

I sat down in the waiting room to sort myself out and heard an elderly man say to his wife, 'I wouldn't have a prostrate operation again for all the tea in China.'

As I walked to the hospital car park, I mentally crossed 'surgery' off my list of options.

I wish now that I had not discussed my treatment options with my family when I got home. Everyone had a different opinion on what was best for me.

Daisy said, leafing through *Prostate Treatment Explained*, 'Isn't it the bloody doctor's job to decide on a treatment? I mean, we're talking bloody *cancer* here.'

My mother said, 'I wish you wouldn't use that word, Daisy.'

Daisy asked which word.

'You know,' said my mother, 'the "C" word.'

'Cancer?' said Daisy.

'*Please*,' said my mother, 'don't say it.'

'But that's what it is,' said Daisy. 'There's no point in pussyfooting around, is there?'

'We used to call it "canker", when I was a kid,' said my father, smiling at the memory.

Thursday 18th October

Daisy offered to come to the hospital with me today. I told her I'd rather face it on my own. I had expected her to insist and was hurt when she did not.

I do not approve of tattoos so I was annoyed when Dr Rubik told me that, as I had opted to have external-beam radiotherapy, I would have to have permanent tattoos over the site of my tumour. Who will do the tattooing? Will I have to go to a parlour?

Dr Rubik said, 'A radiotherapist will collate your data and calculate where to direct the beam. Before you are tattooed you might like to tidy yourself up down there.'

When I got home, I asked Daisy what she thought Dr Rubik had meant when she said 'tidy yourself up down there'.

Daisy shuddered and said, 'My guess is it's something to do with pubic hair – as in, get rid of it.' I started to ask her for advice but she said, 'I'm sorry, I can't take part in this conversation. I don't do pubic hair.'

This is true, Diary. She once finished a three-year relationship because she found a single pubic hair of his embedded in a bar of her Chanel soap.

I did the best I could with a razor and a hand-held magnifying mirror. I must say, I quite like the look. Daisy said it's called 'a Brazilian'.

Friday 19th October

Mr Carlton-Hayes has kindly ordered *The Complete Guide to Overcoming Prostate Cancer, Prostatitis and BPH* by Dr Peter Scardino. He said, 'I believe this is highly regarded,' when he handed it to me, 'as is Professor Jane Plant's *Prostate Cancer*, which is considerably easier to carry.'

Saturday 20th October

My mother has fixed a date to go on *The Jeremy Kyle Show*! As if I don't have enough on my plate already. Also, Glenn is home on leave next month. I read on his Facebook page that he was in a patrol vehicle yesterday that narrowly missed being blown up by a roadside bomb. However, he saw a kid who was standing near by lose all the fingers on one hand. Glenn's patrol took the kid to a medical centre.

Glenn wrote: 'It ain't no joke having no fingers on your hand in Afghanistan. There ain't no National Health Service, and you need two hands to harvest the poppies what they make their heroin from.'

Sunday 21st October

Rosie and Mad Dog Jackson arrived at my parents' house today having hitched a ride from their squat in east Leeds. A lorry delivering chickens from Scotland to Plymouth (why?) dropped them off at junction 22, at Leicester Forest East services. They then persuaded an old lady in a red Corsa to bring them to Mangold Parva. The poor woman actually drove up our potholed drive and deposited them outside my parents' pigsty. My mother ran out and welcomed them all and felt obliged to ask the old lady in for a cup of tea. She soon regretted her invitation when Mrs Pearl took off her hat and bored everybody rigid by talking about the son and daughter-in-law she had been visiting in Derby.

Eventually my father cracked and said, 'You'd best be off now, Mrs Pearl. They close all the exit roads from the village at dusk. Mrs Pearl arranged her hat on her head, took up her car keys and left in a hurry.

Rosie burst out laughing and said, 'Dad, you're such a banger!'

Rosie and Mad Dog Jackson have switched their allegiance from hippy to goth. My mother said Rosie looked well, which Rosie did not take as a compliment as she was attempting to resemble somebody recently risen from the grave.

My father was wearing the idiotic smile he always has when Rosie is around. He said, 'You're like your dad, Rosie, we neither of us like to stick to the rules.'

Mad Dog sprawled himself on the sofa and rolled a cigarette, taking tobacco from a tin decorated with skulls. When my mother addressed him as Mad Dog he corrected her, saying, 'That was in a past life, Pauline. I'm called Banshee now.'

*

I Googled the name when I got home, and was disconcerted to find that a banshee is an unworldly being who screams when somebody is about to die.

Monday 22nd October

Rosie – who is still called Rosie, thank God – came round late last night to borrow some cigarettes from Daisy. In the warmth of the kitchen she gave off a pungent odour and constantly scratched her head.

I said, 'I hope you haven't got nits, Rosie. We've only just got rid of Gracie's.'

She said, 'No, my scalp's itching. I haven't washed my hair for over a year.' As she was leaving, she stopped in the doorway and said, 'I have prayed to our goth God to make you well again, Aidy.'

I asked her if her God was a compassionate sort.

She said, 'Not always. When a goth dies, God laughs. But you're a human, Aidy, he'll look after *you*.'

I said, 'We need to talk about *The Jeremy Kyle Show*.'

She said, 'I've got to sort it out, Bro. I've never felt as if I belonged in this family.'

I said, 'Neither have I. I've always felt as if my true family were aristocrats of some kind.'

She said, 'But you've got Mum's feet and George's nose.'

How sad, that she is now calling our dad George.

Tuesday 23rd October

Sometimes I forget I've got prostate cancer for minutes at a time. So, progress of a kind. It seems that every time my mother looks at me she has tears in her eyes. She should either toughen up a bit or stop wearing mascara, one of the two.

Wednesday 24th October

Mr Carlton-Hayes has started using a walking stick. I am suddenly aware that everybody I come into contact with has some form of physical or mental disability. Where are all the able-bodied people? It's a wonder the country is not bankrupt.

Thursday 25th October

Started my treatment today. Before I went into the X-ray department Dr Rubik said, 'Perhaps I should remind you about the possible side effects of radiotherapy.'

I said, 'There's no need. I've read the booklet twice, thoroughly, and there are very few side effects.'

Dr Rubik said, 'I have been a practising oncologist for seventeen years. I have been responsible for treating thousands of patients. I have done more than read a booklet, twice, so perhaps you'll allow me to inform you about the side effects of your chosen treatment. First, you must be very careful in the shower and do not use soap or gels. Your treatment area will be fragile and you must not expose yourself to strong sunlight.'

I gave a hollow laugh at this and said, 'If only.'

'Second, urinary incontinence. You could find yourself dribbling during or after the completion of the treatment. Thirdly, you could suffer from diarrhoea and rectal discomfort.'

'So I could find myself doubly incontinent?' I checked.

'Possibly,' she said, 'but no two patients are alike, and the size and the siting of a tumour vary incredibly. I have known patients have no side effects whatsoever, but I have also known a few unfortunate folk who are confined to the house with double incontinence.'

As she spoke, I had a vision of myself trapped in the pigsty, wandering from room to room wearing huge incontinence pants underneath voluminous tracksuit trousers. My wife and child had fled. My only visitor was the incontinence nurse bringing me fresh supplies.

A nurse took me to the radiotherapy department to familiarise me with the equipment, and then handed me over to the radiotherapist, a nice girl who looked more like a farmer's wife than a hospital technician. She held her hand out and said her name was Sally. She looked remarkably cheerful for someone who works with half-dead people all day. She told me that I would have to have a permanent tattoo in order to determine the position of the radiotherapy delivery.

I asked her if I could have something discreet – a small

bird perhaps or a flower, or even 'Daisy', my wife's name.

Sally said, 'This is not a tattoo parlour, Mr Mole. Your tattoos will be a series of tiny dots, barely discernable to the human eye. She asked me in the nicest possible way to remove my trousers and pants and put on a hospital gown. She then asked me to climb on to a high hard bed and to lie on my back.

I had dreaded the moment that my gown would be lifted to reveal my nakedness, but as she positioned the machine over my genitalia she chatted brightly about her weekend. She had spent it sailing in a dinghy on Rutland Water with her boyfriend, Anthony. She asked me if I was interested in water sports. I told her that I was morbidly afraid of water and that for me it took a large amount of courage even to swim in the shallow end of a swimming pool. I hardly felt the prick of the tattooing needle. Then Sally left the room and spoke to me through a loud speaker, urging me to 'keep absolutely still, Adrian'.

I did as I was told, terrified that the beam would miss my prostate and hit my penis. After a few minutes, Sally told me to relax and came back into the treatment room.

As she helped me down from the bed, she said, 'So, I'll see you at the same time tomorrow.'

While I was dressing I was relieved to think that Sally and I would get along, as I would be forced to see her nearly every day for the next eight weeks.

Friday 26th October

Treatment.

Saturday 27th October

Treatment.

Sunday 28th October

Treatment.

Monday 29th October

Treatment.

Tuesday 30th October

Treatment.

Wednesday 31st October
Halloween

Mr Carlton-Hayes in hospital with severe back pain. Hitesh is running the shop.

After treatment, and before I went to work, I reluctantly called in at Woolworths to pick up a witch's costume for Gracie to wear tonight when she is out trick or treating. The weather is so cold it will be completely hidden by her big Puffa.

I do not approve of this American practice. It is wholly un-English. However, given the state of my health, I need a quiet life. I filled a large bag with £5 of sweets from the pick 'n' mix, for the trick or treaters who call on us, though in the past two years few have dared to walk down our dark and inhospitable drive.

For some reason I always feel comforted when I am in Woolworths. When I was a child, I spent my first pocket money there. I was five years old and forked out twenty pence on flying saucers. It is good to know that whatever travails we may suffer in life, Woolworths will always be there.

Thursday 1st November

Hitesh rang me last night to say that he can't cope alone. He doesn't understand how Mr Carlton-Hayes's system works. Also, he is not qualified to give valuations on the second-hand and antiquarian books.

I went to see Mr Carlton-Hayes after my treatment, in Ward Seventeen. Leslie had just left. I did not want to worry Mr C-H but I suggested that I get in touch with Bernard Hopkins, who occasionally helps us out in emergencies, and ask if he can run the bookshop until Mr C-H and I are able to go back to work full time. It was strange seeing him in his nightwear. I didn't realize that they still manufactured blue and white striped pyjamas with a draw cord. He is in a lot of pain. A television hanging from the ceiling was showing *The Jeremy Kyle Show*.

Mr Carlton-Hayes said, sotto voce, 'I now understand your distress at the thought of your mother going on Mr Kyle's show. The poor guests are frightfully indiscreet about their troubled lives and relationships. I find it quite distressing, I cannot concentrate on my Socrates, though I admit that there are certain parallels with ancient Greece.'

I asked him if he wanted me to turn the television off.

'No, no,' he said, 'I'm mildly addicted to it now, I think.'

Friday 2nd November

Bernard Hopkins is currently living in a boarding house in Northampton. I rang him at ten o'clock in the morning but to my dismay his speech was slurred and at first he couldn't remember who I was. I should have put the phone down there and then but instead I went ahead and asked if he could help us out at the bookshop for a couple of weeks.

He said, 'I'd be delighted to leave this accursed place. I came here to top myself. I parked up on a farm track, connected a hose to the exhaust pipe, downed a bottle of Stolly, smoked a few fags, thought I'd die listening to the afternoon play on Radio Four, did the sudoku in the *Independent*, then the soddin' car ran out of petrol so I was fucked. Couldn't drive back to the boarding house, too pissed. Bloody cold it was. Had a row with a yokel who couldn't get his tractor by me. Shunted my motor into a ditch. It was dark by the time the AA pulled me out. Complete bollocks of a day.'

I asked him if he was up to running the shop on his own with part-time help from Hitesh.

He said, 'Piece of cake. Are you providing accommodation, young sir?'

I said that he could sleep in the back room.

He said, 'Ah, to sleep in the arms of Morpheus surrounded by books, what man could wish for more? I'll drive over as soon as the jalopy is back from the garage.'

I warned him that there were absolutely no free parking spaces in the whole of Leicester.

He said, 'In that case I'll jump on an omnibus and toddle over to you.'

As soon as I had put the phone down, I regretted my impetuous nature. Bernard Hopkins is the bookseller from hell. If he applies for a job at Waterstones his name triggers an alarm on their computer network. At one time Borders had his photograph up in their staff rooms with a notice saying: 'Do not employ this man'. But there is nobody to touch him when it comes to antiquarian books. He handles them with reverence and will not sell them to a careless owner – a bit like those women at Cats Protection who require you to have a degree in cat care before they will allow you to take one home.

Saturday 3rd November

Woke at 3 a.m. in a sweat. Lay awake, semi-paralysed by fear, thinking about death. What happens? Do we *know* we're dead? Do I want to be buried or cremated? Will anybody remember me after a few years of grieving? Should I make a will? How will Daisy and Gracie manage without me? Will any of my novels be published posthumously?

By 9 a.m. I was in the post office. Tony and Wendy Wellbeck were behind the counter drinking tea and eating toast, which I thought was most unprofessional.

When I asked for a do-it-yourself will form, Wendy Wellbeck said, 'Yes, I heard about your trouble down below.'

Tony Wellbeck said, 'Your mother came in yesterday. She was very upset. Wendy had to go round the counter and give her a cuddle.'

I said, 'I was not aware that my medical condition was the subject of village gossip.'

Wendy Wellbeck said, 'Don't be too hard on her. We mothers suffer when our children are poorly, Mr Mole.'

Tony Wellbeck asked, 'Does this mean the community play is cancelled?'

'It might be postponed,' I said.

'Only the Young Farmers are keen to do a traditional *Cinderella*.'

Wendy Wellbeck said, proudly, 'They've asked if they can varnish one of Tony's giant pumpkins.'

After I had paid for my do-it-yourself will form, Tony Wellbeck said, 'We've known half a dozen people suffering from your kind of trouble, haven't we, Wendy?'

Wendy Wellbeck smiled and said, 'Yes, and two of them are alive and well today, aren't they, Tony?'

When I reached work, Bernard Hopkins was sitting on the doorstep of the shop. He was wearing a navy overcoat on top of a green sports jacket, shirt and tie. His corduroy trousers were splotched with what looked like blackcurrant jam. His shoes looked like a cartoon tramp's. His shirt collar was frayed and filthy.

When he saw me, he threw his cigarette into the gutter and staggered to his feet, saying, 'Good morn, young sire. Fare thee well?'

I didn't want to tell him about my prostate trouble whilst we stood on the doorstep so I said, 'I've been better, thank you.'

Once inside the shop he started to prowl along the shelves, grunting and purring as he caught sight of familiar books. He pulled out a copy of Boswell's *Life of Johnson* and opened it at random. He handled it as other people might handle an exquisite treasure. He snorted with laughter at something he read, then replaced the book on the shelf and said, 'Your telephone call was very timely. Another couple of hours and I might have popped my own clogs.'

I said, 'Please don't talk about killing yourself. Your life is very precious.'

To my alarm his eyes welled with tears and he said, choking, 'Nobody has ever said that to me before. I've always felt that I was a bit of a nuisance. My mother and father gave the impression that I was a drain on their finances, and my wives seemed to turn on me as soon as they had the bloody ring on their fingers. It doesn't do much for a fellow's self-confidence.'

I went through the practical details with him of running the shop. I showed him the cash box, reminded him that the electric kettle sometimes boils over if the 'on' switch is not pressed down far enough, told him that our insurance company will not allow alcohol on the premises (a lie, but he will never know), warned him not to call Hitesh Gunga Din, reminded him that it is against the law to smoke in a public building and asked him to do a hard sell on Antony Worrall Thompson's new book (I had ordered a cartonful by mistake).

At 1 p.m. I suddenly felt ravenously hungry and went out in search of a plain cheese sandwich. After trawling round several sandwich shops in a fruitless search – all the sandwiches in Leicester seem to have been polluted by filthy mayonnaise – I went to Marks & Spencer and bought a crusty loaf, a pack of butter and a block of red Leicester, then returned to the bookshop to make my own.

When I arrived, Bernard was asleep on the sofa in full view of the window, Antony Worrall Thompson's book open on his lap. Hitesh told me that he had been asleep for over half an hour. Once again I regretted my mad impulse to ask Bernard to help out.

Hitesh said, 'Only two customers have been in. One

was asking for a book suitable for a person who loves cats, and a crazy guy came in and bought a copy of Philip Larkin's *High Windows*.'

Bernard woke up at 2 p.m. and asked for a sub of £10 from the till, then went out to look for a café that served 'proper English grub'. I went online and found a prostate survivors website where, to my alarm, I read that 'Karl in Dumfries' had suffered a loss of libido after he had finished his course of radiotherapy and 'Arthur in High Wycombe' had been unable to resume marital relations since his treatment. I posted an anonymous blog, calling myself Steve Hardwick, asking if impotence was inevitable after treatment with external-beam radio-therapy, adding, 'I am a young man, not yet forty.'

I busied myself in the shop for half an hour and then went back to the computer. A bloke called Clive had written:

Welcome to our blog, Steve. No, impotence is not inevitable. With the help and encouragement of my wife, Cath, we have devised ways to have a satisfactory sex life. So don't despair, keep your pecker up!

I replied:

Many thanks, Clive. You are certainly lucky in having such an understanding and loving wife. My own is impatient and has a quick temper (she is half Mexican).

Clive replied almost straight away:

Steve, she sounds fabulous. Perhaps Cath and myself can join you for a foursome. What do you think? Obviously we would wait until your treatment was complete. Have you got any pics of your lovely señora? It won't bother me if she is half or even fully naked. Me and Cath are open-minded OAPs. Hope to hear from you soon. We live in Frisby-on-the-Wreak, Leicester-shire, but with our free bus passes distance is no problem. Yours, Clive.

I heard Bernard's voice in the shop and shut down the computer. I could smell the beer on him from three yards away. I took a tube of Polos out of my pocket and gave him one, saying, 'Freshen your breath, Ber-nard.'

He shuddered at the sight of it and said, 'No fear, young sire. Got my tongue trapped in the bloody hole once. Never again.'

There was hardly any trade in the afternoon. Bernard fell asleep again and Hitesh gave himself what looked like a professional manicure with an emery board, an orange stick and a bottle of cuticle remover that he took out of what he calls his 'manbag'. He offered to sort my nails out but I demurred.

At four thirty I left the shop to visit Mr Carlton-Hayes. He told me excitedly that there was a programme on the television called *Loose Women*. He said, 'There are five ladies who have strong opinions on a variety of topics.

They are daringly frank and delightfully uninhibited.'

I told him that I had made a great mistake in inviting Bernard to help us out in the shop.

Mr Carlton-Hayes said, 'You mustn't blame yourself, my dear. We must look on the bright side – think how happy Bernard will feel knowing that he is needed somewhere.'

Mr Carlton-Hayes is having an operation on his discs on Monday. They are either taking two out or putting two in. I forget which.

I told him that I was having external-beam radiotherapy.

He said, 'My dear, if I could have the wretched treatment for you, I would. I think it is terribly unfair that the gods have given you what should be an old man's complaint.'

We watched *Sally Jessy Raphael* on his suspended television. A gigantic fat black man was boasting that he had fathered seventeen children with seventeen different mothers.

Sally Jessy, an elderly red-haired woman in Eric Morecambe glasses, was chiding the man and telling him that he should be using a condom.

The man said, 'Ain't no point in sucking on candy with the wrapper on!'

Mr Carlton-Hayes said, 'I do so like this programme. It's deliciously awful.'

I reminded him that BBC Four had a fine reputation for broadcasting respected cultural programmes, starting at 7 p.m.

He said, 'You are quite right to admonish me, Adrian.

I am in thrall to reality TV. I must wean myself off it before I leave hospital.'

I told him that my mother was also a captive of such shows.

As I rode home, I decided that I would use my illness to manipulate my mother into not appearing on *The Jeremy Kyle Show*. At the traffic lights on the Narborough Road a car papped its hooter behind me. I turned round but couldn't see who it was in the dark, then Dr Pearce wound down the window and motioned for me to turn left and pull in. As she overtook me, I saw that the whole of her back seat was covered in Sainsbury's bags full of groceries. She shifted, with some difficulty, to the passenger seat and opened the door. Then, as I leaned in, she pulled my head down and kissed me on the lips. After I had broken away, she said, '*Please* put your bike in the boot. I have to talk to you.'

It took for ever to take my bike apart. It was an unpleasant and difficult job, made worse by the commotion of the heavy goods vehicles as they roared through the rain towards the motorway. However, it went in the boot eventually. I reluctantly got into the car and Dr Pearce drove us to The Boat House in Barrow-upon-Soar.

We sat in the car park facing the dark river for a while and she told me that when her husband had arrived back from Norway last week, he had been very cold towards her. After a few days of near silence he had confessed that he had shared his hotel room in Trondheim with a geographer called Celia. She said, 'I was very surprised because he hasn't shown much

176

interest in sex since Imogen was born. I feel such a fool.'

I told her about the treatment I had embarked on. I was very conscious of the fact that I was thirty miles away from home and an hour late, but in the face of her obvious distress I switched my phone off and we went into the pub and ordered beef burgers, salad and fat chips.

Dr Pearce chose a bottle of Rioja and said, 'This place is lovely in the summer. We must come here, sit by the river and have a picnic, Adrian.'

I was very alarmed by this. Was she under the impression that our relationship would continue into 2008?

She dropped me off at the end of our drive and sped away to feed her children. To my dismay Daisy and Gracie were walking up the lane from the village and caught me putting my bike back together.

Gracie said, 'Why is your bike broken, Dad?'

I said, 'It suddenly fell apart.'

Even to my ears this sounded like a feeble excuse, and when Daisy said, 'You've been drinking,' I lied yet again and said that I'd called in for a glass of wine at a pub in town.

She said, 'Nobody calls in for a glass of wine, Adrian, they call in for a swift half.'

I found it impossible to reassemble my bike in the pitch black of the Mangold Parva night, so I took the frame and one wheel, Daisy took the other wheel and Gracie carried the pedals back to the pigsty. I didn't know who I felt more angry with – Dr Pearce, for manipulating me into a secret tryst, or myself, for my cowardice in going along with it.

177

Sunday 4th November

Spent a depressing morning making my will at the kitchen table. It was disheartening to realize that in thirty-nine years I had accumulated nothing of any value. Apart from my books and manuscripts, a few clothes and pairs of shoes and my Sabatier knives I have little of any worth. My bank account is overdrawn and even my bicycle is in pieces. And according to an estate agent my mother recently inveigled into giving her a valuation, both pigsties are already in negative equity. I did have an insurance policy but Brett persuaded me to cash it in and put £23,000 into a high-interest Icelandic bank account that I will not be able to touch for at least seven years.

Brett said, 'It's as safe as houses, Adrian. Local authorities and councils have been taking advantage of the ridiculously high interest rates.' It is great to have a half-brother who is also a financial expert.

I remembered that the funeral plan that my parents had paid into since I was born was kept in my Important Documents box, which is hidden behind the suitcases on the top of the wardrobe in my bedroom. I went out to the shed and had to move months of accumulated rubbish before I could reach the stepladder. I then had to knock a large spider from its web – no doubt it was looking forward to spending the rest of the winter there. After dragging the stepladder through the garden, it had picked up mud and leaves so I then had to unroll the hose. However, no water came out.

I asked Daisy where the stopcock was.

She said, 'Are you trying to be funny?'

I went next door to ask my mother.

She, loving a drama, however small, got herself involved and infuriated me by jiggling the hose about and saying, 'It was working last time I used it.'

In the end, Daisy fetched a damp cloth and simply wiped the mud and leaves away.

After carefully scrutinizing the funeral plan, I discovered that it was worth the risible sum of approximately £160.37. I lifted a bundle of marriage, birth and decree nisi certificates out and saw in the corner of the box a rusty key. I was immediately transported back to the day when Bert Baxter, the pensioner I used to visit when I was 13¾, pressed it into my hand. Where was Bert's trunk now? Did Pandora still have it? I put the key back into the box and put the box back on top of the wardrobe. I sat on the chair in front of the dressing table and tried to envisage the young Adrian. Some of the happiest moments of my life happened when Pandora, Bert and I were together. She was the only person, apart from me, who Bert trusted to cut his toenails.

When I joined Daisy and Gracie in the kitchen, Daisy said, 'I've been reading your will. Why have you left your Sabatier chef's knives to your father? You know I love those knives.'

She had the ingredients for lasagne on the table, perilously near to my will form. I was about to move it out of danger when Gracie reached across for her jar of felt tips and knocked a full bottle of passata over.

We all screamed when the tomato goo splashed over my morning's work.

I shouted, 'Why does this *always* happen? You can't be trusted near any form of liquid whatsoever!'

Gracie burst into tears. This made Daisy shout at me. I shouted back at her and made *her* cry. I then stormed out of the kitchen and sat on the side of the bed and made myself cry. I am dreading the days ahead.

Monday 5th November
Guy Fawkes Night

All the financial experts, including Robert Peston of the BBC, are predicting that we are in for a recession. Mortgage interest rates are due to rise.

Daisy said, 'I told your mother that we should have taken out a fixed-rate mortgage, but she wouldn't listen. She believed everything that smarmy mortgage broker told her. They're snake-oil salesmen, Adrian.'

I said, 'You were happy enough to move in here at the time.'

She said, 'I was pregnant with Gracie. It was move into a pigsty with a cesspit in the garden and your parents sharing a party wall, or be rehoused by the Council on a sink estate where even the babies have tattoos.'

I said sarcastically, 'I'm sorry that you are so unhappy with your lot.'

She replied, 'So am I.'

*

We did not speak to each other as we walked into the village. It was bitterly cold. Gracie complained that she couldn't move because of the layers of clothes we had insisted she wear, so we took it in turns to carry her to the roped-off bonfire on the little green opposite The Bear, where my parents and Rosie were shivering and waiting for the bonfire to be lit. Hugo Fairfax-Lycett and his oafish cricket team were in charge. While Fairfax-Lycett dispensed sparklers to the children, one member of the cricket club barked orders through a megaphone, warning us of the dangers of falling into the bonfire or being hit by a rocket, while another was attending to a whole pig on a spit.

I said to Daisy, 'They could at least have removed its head. Keep Gracie away from it or we'll be up all night.'

Daisy gave me that 'I'm not speaking to you' look and turned to talk to my mother, asking her where Banshee was.

My mother's face lit up in the way it does before she is about to pass on a piece of gossip. 'Well,' she said, 'all I said to him was, I don't see why you can't be a follower of your goth God *and* wash your hair. He gave me a funny look. And when he found out I'd put his black jeans on an extra heavy soil wash he went berserk — which doesn't look good when a man's in his Y-fronts — and called me a petty bourgeois housewife with an anal fixation. Your father shouted, "If only she *was* a house-wife!" and Rosie said, "Don't call my mum an arse!" Well, they went into the spare bedroom and had a row and the next thing I knew he'd stormed into the kitchen, dragged his jeans out of the washer, put them on – sopping wet – said, "I can't live in this suburban hell," and left.'

I glanced over at Rosie. She didn't look too bothered.

Out of the darkness Fairfax-Lycett appeared, holding aloft a burning taper. He had removed his Barbour and the fool was wearing a white shirt, open at the neck. I noted that he had also fallen prey to the ridiculous fashion of not fastening his cuffs à la Laurence Llewelyn-Bowen. A member of the cricket club hurled a Guy Fawkes on to the top of the bonfire and Fairfax-Lycett plunged the taper into the kindling at the bottom. A ragged cheer went up from the small crowd. I looked across at my father, who was sitting in his wheelchair waving a sparkler with Gracie, and I could have wept. Little did he know that his world was about to be shattered as a result of my mother's wish to validate her life by appearing on television.

As soon as Fairfax-Lycett starting carving the hog, I saw Daisy go over and join the small queue. When it was her turn to be served, he took for ever and I could tell that Tony and Wendy Wellbeck, who were behind her, were getting impatient. At one point, Daisy laughed out loud at something he said. When he passed her the pork-filled rolls, she offered him a £10 note but he waved it away. I watched carefully to see what would happen when he served the Wellbecks. He took their money.

The next time I saw Fairfax-Lycett, he had taken charge of the fireworks and was letting them off in a most irresponsible manner. There was little coordination. Expensive and cheap fireworks were intermingled during the display. Consequently there was no proper climax. When we were leaving, my father's wheelchair got stuck in the mud. In my weakened state I could not free it. To my chagrin, Fairfax-Lycett took over and with one huge shove propelled my father and the wheelchair across the grass, while my mother and Daisy simpered their thanks.

My father muttered, 'That toff in the shirt could have had me in the bonfire.'

We congregated in my mother's kitchen and she put some potatoes in the oven. While my father was in the toilet I urged the women not to mention *The Jeremy Kyle Show* or anything pertaining to it.

I said, 'Don't spoil Dad's Bonfire Night.'

They settled down around the kitchen table drinking a bottle of Asda's Chardonnay and eating curry-flavoured Twiglets. Because my mother wanted to listen to 'Whispering' Bob Harris's country and western show on Radio Two, it was some time before we heard my father shouting from the toilet that he was finished. After I had put him back in his wheelchair, I went home and climbed into bed without washing or cleaning my teeth, exhausted.

Tuesday 6th November

When I got to the shop, Hitesh told me that Bernard had been gone for two hours on a 'book-buying expedition'. I was alarmed at this, the shop is not short of second-hand books. The shelves are groaning with their weight and the back room is full of them. There is barely room for Bernard's blow-up single mattress. What we desperately need is somebody to *buy* our books, otherwise the shop will be certain to go out of business.

I dreaded going home and hung around the shop, tidying the books and even dismantling and cleaning the coffee machine.

When Bernard came back, I asked him what he had bought.

He said, 'Nothing, cocker. They were disgusting.'

'Pornography?' I asked.

'No,' he said, 'worse. Danielle Steel.'

I told him that I was delaying going home because my mother intended to tell my father that she was going on *The Jeremy Kyle Show* for a DNA test because she was not sure that Rosie was his.

Bernard said admiringly, 'Your mother would put Madame Bovary to shame.'

Wednesday 7th November
7.30 a.m.

Emotionally drained.

At 8 p.m. last night I went next door, to find my mother and Rosie sitting on kitchen chairs facing my father in his wheelchair.

My father was wittering, 'Why is the telly turned off? What's up?' He looked like a trapped animal and kept glancing from his wife, to his daughter, to me and back again. 'What have I done?' he pleaded. He lit a cigarette and dropped the spent match in the integral ashtray on the arm of his wheelchair.

There was a long silence.

I was furious with my mother and sister. They should have planned what they were going to say, and how to say it, but in the end it was left to me to remind him that Rosie's paternity had never been definitely proved and that there was a strong possibility that Mr Lucas, our ex-next-door neighbour, might be Rosie's biological father. And that he had recently been in touch with Rosie.

Since he had his last stroke, my father's mental acuity has lost its edge. I had to repeat my disturbing news several times before he fully understood the importance of what I was saying.

It's true that he looked unhappy – although I have seen him look unhappier when Leicester City lose at home.

My mother sobbed that she was sorry for hurting him, but went on to say, 'You're partly to blame, George. I was a red-blooded woman with sexual needs and you preferred to read your stupid cowboy books in bed. In fact, I remember one time when we were making love and I caught you reading *Bill the Bronco Buster* behind my head.'

I waited for my mother or sister to mention *The Jeremy Kyle Show*, but neither of them did. Once again, Diary, it was left to me to broach the subject. To my surprise my father looked quite pleased at the prospect of appearing on television. When I protested, saying, 'Aren't you worried about the invasion of your privacy?' he said, 'Adrian, nothing's private now. Everybody knows everything about us. You're living in the dark ages, son.'

My mother looked at me triumphantly and said, 'I knew your dad would cooperate.'

Rosie said, 'Nobody's mentioned me, yet. Don't you care if you're not my real dad?'

I felt sorry for her, and I said to my father, 'Haven't you got something to say to Rosie, Dad?'

My father looked baffled, stroked his ragged moustache and said, 'She knows I'm fond of her.'

'*Fond!*' shouted Rosie. '*Fond!* I hope Mr Lucas is my dad! He's dead handsome and he's got lovely handwriting.'

My father shouted back, 'I should have beaten him to a pulp while I had still had my strength. I should never have trusted that Taff bastard! And your mother wasn't the only woman he was knocking off!'

My mother said indignantly, 'Yes, I was!'

Rosie slammed into the spare bedroom. My mother went into the kitchen and we heard the sound of ice tinkling in three glasses, then the glug of the vodka bottle and the slight hiss as the tonic was poured. She came back in carrying a tray. For once I didn't refuse a drink. By the time my parents had refilled their glasses several times they were chatting quite amicably about what to wear on *The Jeremy Kyle Show.*

When I got home, Daisy asked me how my father had taken the news.

I said, 'Quite well,' and went to bed.

186

As I cleaned my teeth, I was alarmed to see there was a bit of blood in the washbasin.

7.30 p.m.

Sally said that my bleeding gums are probably a symptom of gum disease and not necessarily connected to my illness or treatment.

Went to see Mr Carlton-Hayes but he was asleep and I didn't want to wake him. The nurse said that Leslie had gone to the canteen for a cup of coffee.

I asked her if the operation had gone well.

She said, 'I'm not allowed to say due to patient confidentiality.'

I should have lied and said that I was his son.

Thursday 8th November

As if I hadn't got enough on my plate, Dr Pearce phoned and said plaintively, 'You haven't rung.'

I agreed that I hadn't.

She said, 'Why?'

I said that I had been busy.

She asked if we could meet up somewhere.

In the silence that followed I mouthed, 'No, no, no,' to myself. However, I said, 'Where?'

She replied, 'Anywhere. At any time.'

I told her that I would be at the hospital in the morning and in the bookshop all afternoon, hoping that she would take the hint, but she continued to try and pin me down. She said that she was lecturing until two thirty and then she had to take the children to a dental appointment but would be free by six.

I said that I had to get home to my wife and child.

She said, 'Why, are they ill?'

I lied and said, 'Yes, they are both very ill with . . .' The name of every illness fled from my brain.

Eventually Dr Pearce said, 'You don't want to see me again, do you?'

I blurted out that, should she come into the bookshop, I would be pleased to engage her in conversation.

She said, 'But nothing more?'

'No,' I replied, 'nothing more.'

I switched my phone off. I hope she is not going to become a nuisance.

Friday 9th November

This morning had treatment as usual. Sally very subdued, I asked what was wrong. She said that Anthony had taken another girl to Lake Windermere.

Sally said, 'It's a horrible betrayal.'

I couldn't work out whether Sally was upset because of the other girl, or jealous because he had taken her to a superior lake to the ones where he had taken her.

Robert Peston was on the *Today* programme reporting that some of the high street banks were in trouble. He took great pains to explain the complexities of the banking crisis in layman's language, but I was still baffled. I started to panic, then remembered I had no money in any of the high street banks. I thanked God that I had put my insurance money into that fail-safe Icelandic account.

Received a text message from Pandora tonight. It said:

I am thinking of you, my dear brave boy. I am gld u r benefitin 4rm the targets set by the Government 4 the NHS Cancer Care initiative. Will u do sum media wid me nxt tym I am in lester? Luv as ever, pan xxx

Saturday 10th November

Treatment.

Sally has got hold of Anthony's sailing logbook. Apparently, he has philandered his way across lakes, lochs, estuaries and coastal waters with a succession of female shipmates. She has put her wet weather gear and waterproof boots on eBay.

Called in to see Mr Carlton-Hayes. He looked about 110. He reacted badly to the anaesthetic and is being given frequent doses of oxygen. He is still wearing a hospital gown and is hooked up to tubes and drains, but he managed to convey through the transparent mask that the pain in his back was better. He asked me about the shop, and I lied and told him that business was brisk.

When I returned to the shop, I noticed with a sinking heart that Dr Pearce was loitering on the opposite pavement, ostensibly looking in Rackham's Christmas window. Before I could take my coat off she had crossed the road and entered the shop. She has had her hair cut and highlighted and now looks a bit like Ann Widde-combe, which is an improvement.

I asked her what the special occasion was.

She said, 'You.'

She claimed to be shopping for Christmas presents for her children so I tried to palm her off on Bernard, but he said, 'No can do, lad. Kiddiewinkies and me don't get along.'

Hitesh was on his break so I showed her some of the more expensive pop-up books. She eventually chose four, totalling £62.42.

After I had handed her card back to her, she said, 'I apologise if I've made a fool of myself.'

I felt so sorry for her that I almost cracked, but instead I summoned my resolve and said, 'Not at all. Have a good Christmas.'

I went home early and fell asleep on the bus.

Sunday 11th November

My mother has rung *The Jeremy Kyle Show* to say that she, her husband, her daughter and her ex-lover have agreed to appear on the show, which will be recorded on Tuesday 20th of this month. Rosie is spending her birthday with her possible new father, Lucas.

My mother has made her plans. She has booked a manicure at Top Tips, a hair appointment in the village and a stylist at Debenhams to help her choose a suitable outfit for the show. I pointed out to her that she was going to an unnecessary expense as the dress code for women over sixty on *The Jeremy Kyle Show* was a skimpy vest, sagging cleavage, pale pedal pushers and trainers with no socks. Hair is either lank or parted in the middle, or a tight pulled-back ponytail (otherwise known as a Croydon facelift). She said that she didn't want the audience at home (about three and a half million people) to think that she was any old slapper.

Once again I begged her to change her mind and cancel her appearance.

She said, 'It's all right for you, you've *been* on telly. I might never get the chance again.'

Nobody wanted to cook so we went to The Bear for Sunday lunch. I protested that in my fragile state of health I need good nutritious food, not the muck they serve at The Bear. Diary, incredible as it may sound, nobody offered to stay at home and prepare me something delicate and light to tempt my fragile appetite.

Gracie begged me to come so, reluctantly, I put on my Next overcoat, scarf and the fur-lined aviator hat with the flaps that Nigel bought me last Christmas.

Daisy said that she didn't want to be seen in public with me wearing the hat, but my mother said, 'He has to keep his ears warm. When he was a kid, I used to sit up night after night pouring warm olive oil into his earholes. He used to scream the place down.'

Diary, this is news to me – my memory is quite different. I remember the torment of earache but I do not remember my mother ever being in the same room as me. All I can remember is my father banging on my bedroom wall and shouting, 'Can't you suffer in silence? Me and your mother need our sleep.'

When we walked into The Bear, the room went quiet. I was conscious of people looking at me quickly and then looking away. How much worse will it be after my family have appeared on *The Jeremy Kyle Show*? Once again we were too late for the beef and the lamb so had to settle for pork. However, I have to admit that my Sunday lunch was quite good. Lee, the chef, has been sacked for sexually harassing Mrs Urquhart (i.e. her husband found out about their affair). Mrs Urquhart has taken over in the kitchen. Whenever the kitchen door swung open I could see her savagely dishing the food on to the plates, her face beetroot and her hair in damp tendrils sticking to her neck. She looked quite attractive. Her gravy was superb.

While we ate I listened to Tom Urquhart complaining to Terry Pratt, ex-landlord of The Feathers in Little

Snittingham, that The Bear was losing £500 a week. He said, 'It's bleddy Gordon Brown's fault, he's hand in hand with the supermarkets. You can buy a crate of Carlsberg for tuppence ha'penny in Tesco. Nobody's going to trek to a pub and pay two pound twenty a pint and then be told they can't have a fag, are they?'

When I went to the bar to order more drinks, Tom Urquhart said enigmatically, 'Sorry to 'ear about your trouble, Mr Mole. My father-in-law had a prostrate. He heard about it on the Tuesday and he was dead by Friday night.'

'I'd better book a trip away soon, then. I've always wanted to see the sun break over the Valley of the Kings before I die,' I said sarcastically.

Urquhart said, 'Me and Mrs Urquhart had a trip down the Nile a few year ago. I got the shits and 'ad to stay on the boat but Mrs Urquhart said she'd never seen anything like them pyramids, though she 'ad to physically attack some of the beggars who wouldn't get off her back.'

When I got back to our table with the drinks, I asked my mother if she had put a notice about my illness on the village notice board. When she denied it, I said, 'Perhaps you hired a small aeroplane to fly a banner over Leicestershire saying "Adrian Mole has got prostate trouble".'

My father, ever the pedant said, 'You wouldn't get a small aeroplane to fly a banner that long. There's far too many words.'

As we were finishing our drinks, I saw Hugo Fairfax-Lycett gesticulating to my mother through the window.

He was miming smoking a cigarette. My mother took her drink outside, saying, 'Won't be long.'

After two minutes Daisy went to join her.

When I paid the bill, I saw that Urquhart had added extras such as light, heat, staffing costs, use of cruet, milk, sugar, apple sauce. When I protested, he said, 'Those are my hidden costs. I'm not running a charity.'

I paid up reluctantly and manoeuvred my father's wheelchair outside. Daisy, my mother and Fairfax-Lycett were sitting under the patio heater laughing like maniacs.

When they saw us, they stopped laughing and Daisy said, 'Adrian, good news. Hugo has offered me a job as his PA.'

Fairfax-Lycett rose to his feet, pushed his floppy hair back, held out a large brown hand and said, 'Terribly sorry to hear about your prostate, Mole. Er, hope you don't mind me stealing your wife three times a week?'

I said coldly, 'What will my wife be doing for you three times a week?'

'This, that and the other,' he laughed.

My mother gushed, 'She'll be helping him to run the hall.'

'We're opening it to hoi polloi,' said Fairfax-Lycett.

I said, 'But, Daisy, you hate housework.'

Daisy snapped, 'I'll be Hugo's personal assistant, marketing person and special events organiser.'

I had a sudden vision of Daisy and Fairfax-Lycett standing on the steps leading to the ornate front door of his palatial country house. A pony trotted by with Gracie on its back.

*

As we walked up the muddy lane on the way home, Daisy talked to my mother about the clothes she would need for her new job. She said, 'Ideally, it will be a Vivienne Westwood suit with a cinched waist and a pencil skirt.'

My mother said breathlessly, 'But you're talking five hundred quid, aren't you, Daisy?'

Daisy said, 'Oh, that's all right. I'm getting a clothing allowance. Hugo said if I'm representing Fairfax Hall I ought to maximise my assets.'

Why does every event necessitate new clothes? Have none of them heard the Chinese proverb 'Beware of any occasion that demands new clothes'?

She starts on Tuesday.

Monday 12th November

Daisy dropped me at the hospital this morning. She is taking the train to London and then a cab to Selfridges, shopping for clothes.

Sally was back. She said she had taken a day off sick to try and get over Anthony.

I said, trying to be cheerful, 'Did you X-ray your broken heart?'

To my surprise she seemed to take offence and gave her instructions very brusquely. When she came back into the room, I apologised for appearing to make fun of her failed romance. She accepted my apology. I will be

195

more careful with her in future. I didn't think she looked like the sensitive type. She is small but sturdy.

Bernard Hopkins has hired a box van and driver to help him clear a house in Clarendon Park of its books. He assured me that 'amongst the dross are shafts of pure gold'.

Tuesday 13th November

Diary, how *could* I have forgotten that Glenn was back from Afghanistan yesterday! After radiotherapy I went to see him at his mother Sharon's house. I expected him to look tanned and fit but he was pale and haggard and said that he'd been sitting in a plane on a runway in Helmand Province for twelve hours due to 'an army cock-up'. He hadn't been able to sleep on the plane because of turbulence and the cramped seating.

When Sharon went into the kitchen to prepare his favourite meal, a full English breakfast, I asked him, 'What's it like out there, Glenn?'

His eyes shifted and he said, 'I don't want to talk about it, Dad.' Then he asked me, 'Why do *you* think we're fighting the Taliban, Dad?' It seemed as if he genuinely wanted to know.

I told him that the Taliban were religious fanatics who wanted to rule the country according to strict Islamic laws, which meant not allowing girls to be educated, forbidding music, haircuts and shaving.

He said, 'Trouble is, Dad, the Taliban and the ordinary

Afghans look exactly the same and none of 'em like us soldiers. It ain't surprisin' really, not when the Yanks are dropping bombs on their weddings and stuff.'

Sharon came out and said that she had burned the sausages, so Glenn's breakfast would be delayed.

How could she have burned the sausages when she was hovering over the stove for a quarter of an hour holding the handle of the frying pan? I know this was the case because I could see her through the open kitchen door. Sharon has always been fat but now she is on the way to being super morbidly obese. In another two years she will require a team of firemen to get her out of the house. Looking at her I could not believe that I had engaged in sexual intercourse with the woman and that, at one time, my heart had quickened when I saw her approaching. I even composed poems for her and left them on her pillow. She is currently in the throes of yet another disastrous relationship, with a younger man, namely, Grant McNally who is on probation for stealing a leg of lamb from Aldi.

Sharon defended Grant by saying, with a sob in her voice, 'He was only trying to feed his family. Nobody will give him a job.'

Glenn said, 'I wun't give him a job neither. He's a tosser who can't get his arse out of bed before three in the afternoon.'

As if on cue, sounds were heard overhead (Sharon has had laminate floors laid in every room) and Glenn's latest 'step-father' came into the room scratching himself and blinking in the daylight. He was wearing a wrinkled vest and boxer shorts. I noticed he had four names tattooed on his upper biceps – Britney, Whitney, Calvin and Cain – the names of his estranged children, apparently.

Sharon said placatingly, 'You're up early, Grant. Was we making too much noise?'

McNally whined, 'Yeah, I 'eard voices an' I cudn't get back to sleep. Is the kettle on?'

Sharon dashed into the kitchen (well, as much as a super morbidly obese woman can dash) and McNally sat down on the sofa, lit a cigarette and flourished the remote in front of the vast flat-screen television. He had still not addressed a single word to me or to Glenn.

I got up and, with exaggerated politeness, said, 'How do you do? I'm Adrian Mole, Glenn's father.'

McNally did not tear his eyes away from *The Trisha Goddard Show* where a thin man with a straggly grey ponytail was being berated by Trisha about his skunk dependency.

Glenn rose to his feet, went over to McNally and stood between him and the television screen. He hissed, 'Are you dissing my dad?'

McNally whimpered, 'I ain't dissin' nobody.'

'Well, say 'ello, then. And when you've done that, get your arse upstairs and get some clothes on.'

Sharon came in with a mug of tea which said on the side 'man of the house'. Her eyes darted from McNally to Glenn and back again. The tension was palpable.

McNally slurped on the tea and complained, 'It's too 'ot, you fat cow.'

Sharon said, 'Sorry,' and went back into the kitchen.

Glenn prised the mug from McNally's fingers and said, 'I'm the man of the house now, and I'll 'ave that, thank you very much. You shun't have called my mam a fat cow. Say you're sorry!'

What followed was most unpleasant. In the ensuing scuffle the tea was spilt and McNally was forcibly removed from the room. Sharon tried to intervene between her son and her lover, but a few blows were exchanged.

Personally, I loathe violence and confrontation but I could not help but be pleased that my son had stuck up for his mother. McNally ran upstairs and barricaded himself in the bathroom.

Sharon started to cry and said, 'You shouldn't have done that, Glenn. I'll pay for it later.'

Glenn said, 'Does he knock you about, Mam?' Sharon looked down at the floor and Glenn continued, 'Mam, he don't work, he lives off you, you're scared of him and he's an ugly bugger to boot. Why are you with him?'

Sharon sobbed, 'I love him.'

In the taxi, on the way back to Mangold Parva, Glenn said, 'I never thought my mam would choose a loser like 'im over me, her own son.'

I patted his shoulder and said, 'Love turns us all into imbeciles, Glenn.'

If Daisy was annoyed that Glenn was spending his leave sleeping in Gracie's room, she had the grace not to show it. When I went into our bedroom, I saw the suit of Daisy's dreams hanging on a pink satin hanger. Underneath it was a pair of plain black court shoes with the highest heels I have ever seen. She will never be able to walk in them.

Wednesday 14th November
7.30 a.m.

Daisy back at just after 7 p.m, yesterday, very excited about her first day at Fairfax Hall. I was listening to *The Archers* but she turned it off and made me hear all about her working day, which seemed to consist of being driven around the estate with Fairfax-Lycett introducing her to the staff and tenants. Apparently, they had a pub lunch in a nearby village and then returned to the hall for a brainstorming session on how to make money out of the general public.

She strode around the kitchen in her high heels, black suit and white shirt ensemble, flicking ash into the sink each time she passed it. I thought she looked like she used to look, when we first fell in love over five years ago. I couldn't believe my luck then – that such a beautiful woman had returned my love.

She said, 'I feel like myself again, Aidy!'

I said, 'Have you been struggling to walk in those court shoes?' and she said, 'No, Hugo bought me a pair of wellingtons.'

When I went into the hall, I saw the wellingtons standing by the front door. They were pink, with a floral pattern. My heart froze.

9.00 p.m.

Treatment as usual this morning. Sally distracted. She treated me as though I was just another patient. Perhaps it's her time of the month.

Went to the shop. Bernard has bought an old bloke's entire library of books about polar exploration. I asked him to catalogue the collection and type it into the shop's computer.

He said, 'No can do, duckie. I'm a pen and paper chap.'

I asked Hitesh if he could computerise the polar books and he jumped at the chance, he will do anything to avoid serving customers. I can't say I blame him. A large percentage of them seem to be suffering from a nervous disorder. It comes with the territory.

Thursday 15th November

Treatment.

Sally still quite distant. Does she regret telling me about her doomed relationship? Perhaps I shouldn't have said that I had always thought that Anthony was obviously a complete bastard and that she was well rid of him.

Pandora rang and said, 'It's a real drag, but I promised to take Mummy to Hambledon Hall for her birthday dinner on Sunday, so can we meet up on Saturday to talk about my cancer initiative? We can do some blue-sky thinking. It would be good to hear from you about what it's like to be at the cancer coalface.' I suggested Wayne Wong's and she said, 'Yes, book our usual table next to the fish tank.'

Went to bed at eight thirty. Fell asleep after rereading a page of *Rabbit, Run* by John Updike. By nine o'clock at night I am good for nothing.

Friday 16th November

Cycled to treatment in the dark. It was heavy going against an icy wind. Sally is back with Anthony. I only know because one of her colleagues congratulated her on her engagement.

Went straight home after the hospital. Daisy was out shopping with Glenn, Gracie at school, so I had the house to myself for a change. Read a chapter of *Rabbit, Run* then went next door to tell my mother about Sally's engagement, but she had taken my father to his Wheelchair Mobility class. I looked through a stack of letters on the kitchen table. I noticed that they had received a final demand from the TV Licensing Authority – my father begrudges paying it, because he mostly watches ITV – and there was a postcard from Rosie telling my parents that she was having a great time with her 'dad' in Burton-on-Trent. Underneath the letters was *A Girl Called 'Shit'*. I flipped through it and read a bit of chapter five.

By the age of fourteen I was living a double life. In the week I was a normal-looking schoolgirl in my uniform, although my home-made shoes (made out of old lorry tyres and baling twine) set me apart from my peers. When I returned from school, and at weekends, I was forced to change out of my uniform and made to wear dresses fashioned from old potato sacks. My mother did her best with the sacks. She sometimes added a gingham collar or a piece of lace from one of her old blouses, but nobody was ever fooled. My dresses were stamped with the words 'Maris Piper – Norfolk'. In the winter I had to wear a poncho-type garment made from an old horse blanket.

There were no books or magazines in the house but occasionally the seed potatoes would be wrapped in pages from the *News of the World* and I would read about the sex lives of the rich, the famous and the ordinary and dream that one day I would be written about in a similar fashion.

Me and my mother lived almost entirely on a diet of potatoes and mashed mangel-wurzels. My father would eat a twelve-ounce fillet steak every night, washed down with a home-made beer he forced my mother to brew for him. The smell of steak maddened me and was the cause of my eventual downfall. A lad called Eric Lummox lured me into a Wimpy Bar in Norwich. He knew I was destitute and said that if I had sex with him he would buy me a Wimpy Max.

The whole thing is a farrago of lies! Her mother and father are called Sugden and I know for a fact that they only ever grew King Edward potatoes!

When my parents came round this evening, I was

tempted to challenge my mother about her false memoir but I did not want a family row in front of Finley-Rose, so kept quiet. She is a lovely girl, beautiful, articulate and with eight GCSEs. I ascertained that her mother and father were still together, went to the Algarve for their holidays and owned their own house on a Barratt estate in Enderby. She has read *The Catcher in the Rye* and *Jane Eyre*! Glenn looked a bit baffled by our literary discussion, but Finley-Rose was very gracious to him when he told her that he had read *Tornado Down* in his compound in Afghanistan. As he talked, her eyes never left his face. He is less like Wayne Rooney now, and is almost handsome. His body is tanned and well muscled. I felt quite puny sitting next to him.

As Finley-Rose daintily ate her Morrisons lemon meringue pie, she told Glenn that she had decided to leave her hair and beauty course at Leicester College to take her A-levels, because she wanted to go to university and study to be a forensic pathologist. Her favourite TV programme is *Silent Witness*. Glenn obviously did not know what a forensic pathologist did, but he nodded in approval anyway.

My mother said, 'That's a drastic change, isn't it?'

Finley-Rose licked a crumb from her lower lip and said, 'They're both messing about with bodies. The only difference is that I won't have to ask a corpse where it's going for its holidays.'

Glenn said, 'We brung a corpse back on the plane.'

Finley-Rose said, 'You *brought* a corpse back, Glenn.'

She is certainly straight talking. I don't know if Glenn will be able to keep up with her.

Saturday 17th November

Had treatment. Went to see Mr Carlton-Hayes. He was sitting in a wheelchair and told me that, although he was out of pain, the operation had not been a total success in that he now has difficulty walking.

I said that we would have to build some ramps so that he could access the bookshop.

He put his hand on mine and said, very gently, 'My dear, I'm terribly sorry, but I fear the bookshop will have to close. We are not making any money from it. Leslie and I are struggling to make ends meet. We have used up all our savings and the bank has declined to make us a loan.'

I could not speak. Daisy and I have to find at least £600 a month to cover the mortgage, council tax, water, gas and electricity. But most shocking of all was the thought that I would not see Mr Carlton-Hayes on a daily basis.

Sunday 18th November

I haven't told Daisy that the bookshop is to close as I can't cope with another row about money.

I was reluctant to go home after treatment. Waited ten minutes for a bus, before deciding to walk into the almost deserted city centre. Many shops are boarded up and there is an air of melancholy about the place. On the way I went into the Newark Museum and had a look at Daniel Lambert's clothes and chair. I remembered my father encouraging me to break the rules and sit on the chair, and the argument that ensued between him and an officious attendant. My father said, 'He's only six years old, he's hardly going to break the bleedin' chair, is he? Daniel Lambert was fifty-eight stone, eleven pound.' On my way out I picked up a leaflet advertising the fact that Richard Attenborough, Leicester born and bred, had donated his collection of Picasso ceramics to the New Walk museum. Having time to kill before I met Pandora, I walked in the watery sunlight up New Walk to inspect the exhibits. Diary, I would love to have taken one of the bowls home. It would look magnificent on our sideboard with a bunch of bananas in it. As I was leaving, I spotted Dr Pearce trying to control three unruly children and shepherd them into the dinosaur room. Thankfully, she didn't see me.

I had told Daisy that I was going to see Wayne, who is one of my oldest friends, this afternoon. However, I omitted to say that Pandora would be there. I couldn't face the walk to Wayne's restaurant, and as my bus came and parked at the curb with its engine throbbing, Pandora rang and said, 'Shall I order your favourite – chicken in black bean sauce with crispy noodles?'

I informed her, over the noise of the engine, that since watching an horrific documentary about intensive chicken rearing I had given up eating the stuff.

She said, 'For God's sake, hurry up. I'm starving.'

*

When I got to Wayne's, there was a buzz of excitement at the far end of the room next to the large fish tank. I practically had to beat my way through the crowd of admirers and well-wishers. Pandora was having her photograph taken with a young man. He had spiky gelled hair, a ring in his nose and was wearing a Leicester City football shirt. His partner, a woman with multiple piercings, Leicester City football club tattoos on her arms and an unnatural tan, asked for Pan's autograph on the back of what looked like a social security envelope. As she was doing so, I had the chance to take a proper look at my childhood sweetheart.

Although she is in the Foreign Office, she has resisted the temptation to cut her beautiful treacle-coloured hair. It fell on to the shoulders of her fitted light grey suit. She is the only woman I know who can get away with wearing dark red lipstick. Her eyelids were smudged with black stuff and she has had something expensive done to her teeth. The little frown mark that used to be in between her eyebrows has gone.

I love her.

Wayne Wong said that Pandora had already ordered for the two of us so I could relax. He handed me a glass of Chinese beer and I sat down and listened to Pandora telling the pierced couple that she would talk to Gordon Brown himself about their damp problem. Eventually, after having her photograph taken several more times with customers and signing her name on a napkin for one of the waiters, people drifted away and we were alone.

She pressed my hand and said, 'Aidy, darling, you look incredible. One would never know that you had such a dreadful illness.'

The tiny mobile that was lying next to her chopsticks buzzed discreetly.

She picked it up and said, abruptly, 'I said no calls, I'm working!'

I was hurt by this. I said, 'So, this is *work* for you, is it?'

She looked away and studied one of Wayne's koi carp. It came up to the glass and seemed as much in awe of her as the humans had been previously.

Wayne was hovering near by, fiddling with a table setting. She asked him how the fish tank was cleaned. Wayne told her that he paid a pensioner in thigh-high waders to actually climb into the tank and scrape the sides. Pandora asked how much the pensioner was paid.

Wayne said, 'He don't get paid in money. He takes it in a week's worth of chicken chow mein and a big carrier bag of prawn crackers. He's happy, I'm happy, the fish are happy and the tax man don't have to be bothered.'

I was anxious to draw her attention back to me so said, 'How often do you think about death, Pandora?'

'Death?' she laughed. 'How did we get from cleaning fish tanks to death?'

'I think about it all the time now,' I said.

'Well, you would, wouldn't you? You've got a potentially fatal disease.' She looked at me and said, 'Did you know that certain men get better looking as they get older?'

I said, 'No, all the men I know have aged very badly. My father's face looks like a fossilised scrotum.'

She said, 'You've grown to be an incredibly attractive man. You've kept your figure and, thank God and hallelujah, you've finally had a haircut that suits you. I'm so glad to see the back of that dreadful side parting, and you've finally taken my advice and stuck to dark clothes. Any man in pastel clothing looks like he's on holiday in Majorca.'

I said, 'You're such a snob.'

She said, 'I *love* Majorca. I've been there several times, as a house guest of Prince Felipe and his wife Letizia.'

A waiter came up with a bowl of prawn crackers. Pandora spoke to him in Mandarin and they had a long conversation. When he'd gone, I asked Pandora what they had been talking about.

'He asked me if I could speak to Gordon Brown about his visa,' she said.

I said, 'Hasn't Mr Brown got better things to do than to be bothered with damp and visa problems?'

Wayne brought us two bowls of liquid in which floated something from the poultry genus. I asked him what it was.

He said, 'It's duck's foot soup. It's a delicacy.'

I said to Wayne, 'You're having a laugh, aren't you?'

He said, 'Are you mocking my cultural heritage, Moley?'

He and Pandora exchanged a few words in Mandarin, which made them both laugh. As a non-Mandarin speaker I was beginning to feel excluded.

I said, 'Am I actually supposed to eat these toenails?'

Pandora said, 'The toenails are meant to be an aphrodisiac.'

When Wayne had gone, I said, 'That was cruel, Pandora. You know my sexual function is not a hundred per cent at the moment.'

She took my hand and said, 'I'm sorry, Aidy. Is there anything I can do to help?'

I pushed my duck's foot soup away.

She did the same with her bowl and said, 'I'm quite prepared to help you in any way I can.'

I asked, 'Is that a proposition?'

She said, 'I was at dinner the other night with a sex therapist called Marsha Lunt, I could get her number.'

'No, thank you,' I said tersely.

There was an awkward silence. We both stared into the fish tank. Eventually she said, 'My mother had her loft insulated the other day and when she was clearing all the junk out she came across a box with Bert Baxter engraved on the lid.'

'What was inside?' I asked.

'I don't know,' she said. 'It was locked.'

I said, 'I think I may have found the key to that box.'

She looked me directly in the eye and said, 'Then we must get together soon and you can put your key into my box.'

Wayne brought several dishes and laid them on to the lazy Susan in the middle of the table. I did not recognise anything.

I said, 'It looks as though somebody has stir-fried the droppings from an abattoir floor.'

Pandora said, 'Try something different, broaden your horizons.' She took up her chopsticks and with great expertise dropped some pieces of unrecognisable food into my empty bowl. 'This is the food the Chinese eat,' she said. 'Go on, try it!'

I reluctantly picked up my own chopsticks and attempted several times to put a slimy morsel into my mouth but only succeeded in dropping the food on to my lap. Pandora reached across and fed me with her own chopsticks. Her nearness, the scent of her perfume and the unsettling cleavage she displayed made it hard for me to swallow.

The food wasn't too bad but not a patch on chicken in black bean sauce. I was glad when Wayne brought out a dish of recognisable noodles.

When we were drinking Wayne's terrible coffee and Pandora was talking about the prostate awareness campaign she is involved with and how I could be of help to her, I only half listened. I was studying her beautiful face and had an overwhelming need to stroke her hair and tell her that I loved her when she was thirteen, loved her now, and would always love her.

Later, over complimentary brandies, I told her about my various problems, Daisy's unhappiness, the closure of the bookshop and my mother's imminent appearance on *The Jeremy Kyle Show*.

Pandora said, 'Oh, I *adore* Jeremy Kyle's show. It keeps one in touch with the underclass without having to visit their dreadful council estates. I'll definitely watch it.'

I said, 'Apparently, it's pre-recorded but I'll ring you when it's due to be broadcast.'

'Yes,' she said, 'we must keep in touch, mustn't we?'

I agreed that we must.

*

She gave me a lift home, driving like a lunatic down the country lanes. Had we met a tractor coming in the opposite direction we would have faced certain death but, as she pointed out, nobody would be driving a tractor at one o'clock in the morning.

When we drew up outside the house, Pandora said, 'You'd better go in, Daisy's still up.' She sighed. 'I wish there was somebody waiting up for me.'

I said, 'But you're so clever and beautiful. Men must be throwing themselves at your feet.'

She replied, 'I terrify most men. And the rest are either married, gay or bipolar.'

Diary, she looked so desolate that I wanted to take her in my arms. Instead I said goodnight, and went into the house. Daisy was sitting in the kitchen. There was a full ashtray in front of her, an empty bottle of wine and a half-empty glass.

She said, 'That was her, wasn't it?'

I said, 'Yes, we bumped into each other at Wayne Wong's.'

She shouted, 'To think I had that woman in my house, eating my shepherd's pie.'

We slept in the same bed, but it was as if I was at the North Pole and she was at the South.

Monday 19th November

Woke with a heavy heart at 6 a.m. Worries crowded in on me. Got up to make coffee. Glenn was sitting at the kitchen table in his boxers and a camouflage T-shirt.

I said, 'You're up early.'

He said, 'I'm used to it, Dad. We 'ad to leave the compound before the sun came up.' While we waited for the kettle to boil he said, 'Dad, can I ask you something? Why don't you write to me every week like the other parents do?'

I said, 'To be honest, Glenn, there's not much to write about. Nothing interesting happens here.'

Glenn said angrily, 'I'm interested in everything, it don't matter how small. An' I want to know how you are, don't I? I'm worried about you. I don't want you to die, Dad.'

Gracie came in and climbed on to Glenn's knee. She stroked his unshaven chin and said, 'You know that dead hedgehog we saw, Dad. Is it in heaven?'

I was about to explain the points of difference be-tween the proponents of creationism and intelligent design when Glenn said, 'Yeah, course it is, Gracie. It's in 'eaven. And it's 'appy.'

While we were eating breakfast Daisy appeared wear-ing incredibly high-heeled boots. She was carrying a large black patent bag that was also new to me. I offered to make her a bacon sandwich.

She said, 'I've got a breakfast meeting with Hugo.' She kissed Gracie and Glenn and went out.

I went to the living-room window and watched her circumnavigating the potholes in the drive. She could have been walking down Oxford Street.

Gracie's school uniform was laid out on a chair next

to her bed, but she refused to wear it and was sitting unconcernedly in the living room watching a DVD of *High School Musical.*

I shouted, 'Gracie, we have ten minutes before we have to leave this house!'

I ordered Glenn to find the hairbrush, picked Gracie up and took her into the bathroom. Then, while I cleaned her teeth, Glenn brushed her hair and pulled it into an untidy ponytail. We wheedled, cajoled and bribed her to wear her school uniform, but eventually I gave in and let her wear her Little Mermaid outfit. She wouldn't wear her school cardigan with it until I pointed out that it was only the bottom half of a mermaid that was a fish. She conceded that this was true.

Because we were late I put the child seat on the front of my bike and cycled her to school, even though I was worried that the fishtail would get caught in the spokes. I then cycled to the hospital for my treatment, arriving drained of every last drop of energy.

Sally said that I looked exhausted and ought to give the bike up until my treatment was finished.

When I got back, after calling in at the bookshop, Glenn told me that a car had arrived to take my parents to Manchester, where *The Jeremy Kyle Show* is recorded. My heart sank. I had been hoping that fate would intervene to stop them from making the Mole family a laughing stock.

Tuesday 20th November

My mother rang early this morning from her hotel room in Manchester. She said that Lucas and Rosie were in the same hotel but they would be going to the studio in different cars. She told me that she and my father had hit the mini bar last night and, after getting drunk, they had talked at great length about their marriage, i.e. was it worth saving?

I asked her what conclusion they had come to.

She said, 'Neither of us can remember. I told you, we were drunk.'

I pointed out to her that the reason she was going on *The Jeremy Kyle Show* was to ascertain Rosie's paternity.

She said that, after talking to a researcher on the show, they had decided to 'widen the brief' and had agreed to take lie detector tests about their respective marital affairs.

As the years go by I grow more and more suspicious about my *own* paternity. I have absolutely nothing in common with my parents.

Glenn has taken Finley-Rose to a hotel in Birmingham for a few days. He wants to buy her a present from Harvey Nichols.

Wednesday 21st November

Treatment.

Went home, and at twelve thirty had a phone call from the school. Headmistress wanted to see me urgently. Cycled to school. Went to headmistress's office.

Mrs Bull is ridiculously young to be a headmistress. She said, 'Thank you for coming in, Mr Mole. I'll cut to the chase, shall I? We have had some concerns about Gracie for some time now. We've tolerated her quixotic apparel. We've bent over backwards to humour what we thought was a phase, but I can no longer allow my teaching staff to give so much attention to one child.'

I said, 'Has it crossed your mind, Mrs Bull, that Gracie might be a gifted child?'

Mrs Bull replied, 'No, it has not crossed my mind for a moment. This morning, when the other children were in the classroom waiting for registration, Gracie was sitting on the shoe rack in the cloakroom wearing that mermaid costume. When I asked her to walk with me into the classroom, she said, in a very patronizing tone, "Fish can't walk." When I insisted that she walk, she again refused. She said that the shoe rack was a large rock and that the floor of the cloakroom was the "specific ocean". I managed to get her into the classroom by allowing her to "swim" on her belly, but she was infuriatingly slow. I quite lost my patience with her, I'm afraid, and handed her over to Miss Nutt. However, at morning break I glanced out of my window to the playground and saw Miss Nutt carrying Gracie in her arms. Your daughter was shouting, "Fish can't walk," and it wasn't long before most of the other girls in the playground were shouting the same and begging Miss Nutt and the other teachers on playground duty to pick them up. This can't be allowed to go on, Mr Mole. This is not an aquarium. This is a school.'

Inside my head I said, 'Oh, I do beg your pardon, I thought it *was* an aquarium, which is why I sent my daughter to school wearing appropriate dress.' What I actually said was, 'I'm sorry, Mrs Bull. I will make sure that Gracie wears her school uniform tomorrow.'

Went to post office to pay my parents' newspaper bill. Knocked Christmas tree over on my way out. Several baubles smashed. Why can't they use plastic baubles like everyone else?

This *is* 2007.

When I got back, the lights were on in my parents' house. After taking several deep breaths, I called in to question them about *The Jeremy Kyle Show*. My mother was working on her misery memoir and my father was still in bed.

'I don't know why your father's sulking,' said my mother. 'It was him who got the audience's sympathy.'

I asked why.

'A sobbing man in a wheelchair who finds out that his precious daughter was fathered by another man? You'd need a heart of stone not to feel sorry for him.'

'So Lucas *is* Rosie's father?' I said.

'Yes,' said my mother. 'When Jeremy Kyle read out the DNA result, Lucas leapt to his feet, punched the air, ran around the stage, embraced Rosie, took the card from Jeremy Kyle, kissed it and then sat down and burst into tears. Your father tried to wheel himself over to Lucas to punch him in the face but couldn't get near enough. Then Jeremy Kyle turned on me and said that I was a "disgrace". Then Rosie had a go at me, saying that her whole life had been a lie. Lucas said he wanted to make up for lost time and asked Rosie if she would go and live with him. He bragged to the studio audience and the watching millions that he lived in a mansion in Burton-on-Trent and had an indoor swimming pool and that he had already prepared an en-suite bedroom for Rosie. Rosie fell into his arms and sobbed, "I *will* come and live with you, Dad."'

My mother's eyes filled with tears. She choked, 'I was booed off the stage, but your father was cheered and got a standing ovation. I wish now that I'd never agreed to go on the bloody show.'

I patted her shoulder, it was the least I could do. I then went to the bedroom to see my father. The lights were off and the curtains were drawn. My father was in bed. I knew he was awake. I could hear his wheezy breathing.

I said, 'I'm really sorry, Dad. It must be terrible to find out that you are not related to Rosie.'

He said, 'She'll soon get tired of swimming in that pool. She's allergic to chlorine.'

Before I left I asked my mother when the show was going to be broadcast.

She said, 'The producer said she would ring and let

us know.' She then started to cry and held her arms out to me and said, 'I'll be the bloody laughing stock of England.'

'Great Britain,' I corrected her. 'In fact, the world. You can get *The Jeremy Kyle Show* on the internet, and once it's on the World Wide Web it will be there for ever, until the end of time.'

She thrust me away from her, saying sarcastically, 'You're such a comfort, Adrian.'

When I got home, I rang Rosie on her mobile.

A stranger answered and said, 'She's in the pool.'

I am very hurt that she hasn't returned my call. I was there at her birth.

I wanted to talk to Daisy, but she has told me that Hugo has asked her to keep her mobile switched off because he doesn't want her distracted when they are working.

Thursday 22nd November

Treatment.

Got home in time to see Daisy leaving for work. She was showing far too much cleavage. I asked her to fasten a couple of buttons on her shirt. She did so, but when she got to the lane I saw her undo them again and adjust her bra straps. I dressed Gracie in her school uniform and sent her to clean her teeth. When she came back, she was wearing her Spanish flamenco dress and shoes and was carrying a Spanish fan. In the struggle to remove the red and black spotted dress the zip broke and Gracie screamed so loudly that my mother came round to find out what was going on. She ordered me out of the kitchen and after ten minutes appeared with Gracie, who was fully dressed in her school uniform and was wearing her hair in two plaits with ribbons at the end. My mother said that she would be taking Gracie to school in future.

I don't know what she said to Gracie but it certainly worked.

Spent the day sorting out my old manuscripts. Perhaps now is the time to resubmit my serial killer comedy *The White Van* to the BBC. Wrote a covering letter to the head of series and serials suggesting Russell Brand for the serial killer and Amy Winehouse for his wife. His victims could be: Kate Winslet, Barbara Windsor, Billie Piper, Jodie Marsh, Carol Vorderman, Colleen Rooney, Kym Marsh, Charlotte Church, Lily Allen, Cheryl Cole and Dot Cotton.

I parcelled up the manuscript and took it to the post office. Wendy Wellbeck handed me an invoice for the three baubles I had smashed.

She said, 'I know you've got a very serious illness, Mr Mole, but Tony and me are facing an uncertain future and we can't afford to have our possessions smashed up.'

She was proposing to charge me £2.50 per bauble! I asked her when she had purchased the glass baubles.

She said, 'Christmas, 1979.'

I said, 'Please write out another invoice quoting 1979

prices, then take off the years of use you have had from the baubles. Then, and only then, will I consider re-imbursing you.'

I pushed my manuscript under the glass.

She weighed it in silence then read the address, gave a scornful laugh and said, 'The BBC!'

On my way out I was careful to avoid the Christmas tree.

Friday 23rd November

Somebody has hung a piece of tinsel over the radio-therapy machine. I feel sure that this must infringe NHS guidelines in some way.

Sally told me that Anthony is going to buy her a dog for Christmas.

I asked Sally if she liked dogs.

She said, 'No, but Anthony does.'

I asked her what kind of dog Anthony liked.

She said, 'Big ones. He'd really like a wolf.'

I said, 'From what you've told me about Anthony, he's hardly leader of the pack material.'

Sally said, 'Anthony can be very forceful. He made his parents vote Conservative at the last election.'

I begged her to put her foot down and tell Anthony the truth, that she would prefer a 'nice watch'.

Went upstairs to see Mr Carlton-Hayes on the ward. A nurse was packing his little suitcase. He is going home today. He told me that Leslie has organised ramps at home and widened the doors downstairs in order to accommodate his wheelchair.

I asked him when the shop would be closing.

He said, very quietly, 'In a matter of weeks, my dear.'

I went to the shop. Bernard was there telling a tall stooped man that all of the Booker Prize winners had won because they had slept with the judges.

The tall man said, 'Surely not Anita Brookner?'

'How else to explain it,' said Bernard. He steered the man over to the prize-winning books section and said, 'Have a shufti through this little lot. Then tell me they won their prizes on merit, because I don't think so.'

I went into the back and started to look through the books that Bernard had bought in a house sale, but after only ten minutes I had to sit down. I couldn't face hanging around for the bus so I called a taxi. When I got home, I went straight to bed. I phoned my mother and asked her to pick Gracie up from school.

At 3.10 p.m. I had to leap from my bed and run to the toilet. Urination painful, stinging. I rang the radiotherapy department and spoke to Sally.

She said, 'These are almost certainly side effects of your treatment. You've been lucky so far.'

Saturday 24th November

Daisy went out early this morning with Fairfax-Lycett. They are on a reconnaissance visit to a rival establishment, Belvoir Castle, where they hope to pick up ideas on how to attract the public. When I said goodbye to Daisy, adding, 'Have fun,' she said defensively, 'I won't be having *fun*, Adrian, I'm working.'

I didn't have the energy to argue with her.

I took Gracie round to my parents, then tried to cycle to my treatment. Halfway down the lane I had to return and ring for a taxi. Can't afford taxis twice a day. How will I get to the hospital in future?

The taxi back from treatment cost me £14.50. When I protested that I had paid £10.80 for exactly the same journey this morning, the taxi driver said, 'My cab uses more fuel in the afternoon.'

I let it go but ever since have been wondering if this is a scientific fact. I went round to collect Gracie and then changed into my pyjamas and dressing gown, although it was still daylight. I feel like an invalid today – even ate a tin of rice pudding.

When Gracie took all the cushions off the sofa and built a playhouse with the clean sheets from the airing cupboard, I was too weak to protest.

I was still in my dressing gown and pyjamas when Daisy returned. She went crazy when she saw the state of the living room and even crazier when she found Gracie inside the playhouse wearing her vintage Vivienne West-wood cocktail frock. I wanted to help her tidy up, Diary, but I did not have the energy. Is this the start of my decline?

Gracie was sent to her room, but this is hardly a pun-ishment. She has got more toys in there than Hamleys.

Sunday 25th November

Taxi to treatment. Taxi back. Changed into pyjamas. Went to bed. Only got up for painful urination.

Gracie came into the bedroom and told me that she had just watched *Titanic* with Mummy. She said, 'Mummy cried at the end.'

I said, 'Well, it's a very sad film, Gracie. I'm surprised that Mummy let you watch it.'

Gracie said, 'She's still crying.'

I got up reluctantly and went to find Daisy. She was in the bathroom sobbing into a bath towel. I said, 'Don't cry, Daisy, it's only a film.'

Daisy threw the towel into the bath and shouted, 'Do you think I'm crying over a stupid film? I've been crying on and off for three weeks!'

I said, 'If it's me you're worried about . . .'

She said, 'Not everything's about you, Adrian. I do have a life, you know!'

I noticed that she wasn't wearing her wedding ring.

When I asked about it, she said, 'You may not have noticed, but I've lost a lot of weight. It keeps falling off.'

Monday 26th November

After treatment I was met by my mother. She was parked illegally outside the oncology unit in a Mazda that had been sprayed a shade of green that was new to nature's pallet. As she was negotiating the speed bumps on the roads within the hospital grounds, she told me that she had decided to empty the old-fashioned sweet jar of the mixed coins she has been collecting for the last three years and take them to the bank.

She said, 'As long as I've got enough to bury him, I don't care.' She went on, 'I can't bear to see you struggling to get to your treatment. So from now on I will take you there and pick you up.'

I – genuinely – protested, saying, 'No, Mum, I can't possibly impose on you.'

She said, 'I'm your mother, Adrian, and you are a very sick boy. I'd walk over hot coals for you, I'd swim across a shark infested sea, I'd wrestle with a polar bear . . .'

The thought of being trapped inside a car with my mother twice a day fills me with dread. After a few minutes she switched on Radio Two and James Blunt's 'You're Beautiful' blasted out from the four stereo speakers inside the car.

While I was in the car Pandora rang me on my mobile to tell me that I must sell any stocks and shares I have.

She said, 'The whole financial market is going to crash.'

I told her that my mother had predicted the very same thing months ago.

Pandora said admiringly, 'How prescient! I always said that your mother was a witch.'

My mother took my mobile from me and said, steering with one hand, 'Pan! How *are* you? Are you seeing anybody?'

Whatever Pandora replied made her laugh.

She said into the mobile, 'There are worse things than a man having a little willy. You shouldn't let that put you off, especially if he's loaded.'

We stopped at a red light and a policeman knocked on the driver's side window. Due to my mother's unfamiliarity with the car it took her for ever to wind it down. The policeman was mouthing something, James Blunt was wailing that his lover was beautiful and Pandora was now on speakerphone telling my mother something salacious about Peter Mandelson.

The policeman said, 'Are you the owner of this car, madam?'

'I am,' said my mother. 'I picked it up this morning.'

'Can I see your driver's licence?'

My mum dragged her handbag on to her lap and handed my phone back. It slipped from my grasp and fell between the gear column and my seat. I scrabbled to find it but only succeeded in knocking it further underneath. Pandora's voice, louder than ever, could be heard complaining about the head of the Metropolitan Police. It took my mother a horribly long time to find her driver's licence. The policeman stared at her photograph, then stared at my mother.

Meanwhile Pandora was shouting, 'We're almost living in a police state, Pauline.'

Eventually the policeman said, 'Do you know why I've stopped you, madam?'

My mother said that she didn't.

The policeman said, 'You were driving erratically and speaking into a mobile phone.'

My mother said, 'My son here is suffering from cancer,

Constable. I was trying to get an urgent appointment . . .'

The policeman said, 'An urgent appointment with the female person who is slagging off a fine public servant!'

From her position below the passenger seat Pandora was telling the three of us that Harriet Harman was a sanctimonious ball breaker who had had a humour bypass.

By now I was crouched upside down in the foot well and trying to get a grip of my phone.

My mother said to the policeman, 'I'd completely forgotten about the mobile phone law. I'm in the final stages of the menopause. My hormones are all over the place.'

I shouted under the seat, 'Pandora! Get off the phone! My mother is being interviewed by a policeman.'

Pandora shouted back, 'Good luck with the filth, Pauline!' Then, mercifully, she disconnected the call.

My mother was given a fixed penalty notice. She had to pay a fine of £80 on the spot. This is literally highway robbery. The modern policeman is as much a highwayman as Dick Turpin.

Tuesday 27th November

Had to drag myself out of bed this morning. My mother drove me to treatment. She insisted on coming into the radiotherapy room. Said she wanted to meet Sally.

I don't know why people like my mother so much. Sally ended up giving my mother her telephone number and email address. During their short conversation my mother advised Sally to leave Anthony, told her where to go for a great haircut and that she was B6 deficient.

She also informed Sally that the hospital tunic she wore did nothing for her. 'Wear it with a belt,' she said. 'Cinch that waist in!'

When my mother had gone to sit in the waiting room, Sally said, 'Your mother is fantastic. I'd give anything to have a mother like her. My own mother hardly speaks to me and she has nearly bankrupted my father. She's spent a fortune on Cliff Richard memorabilia. She squandered a month's salary last week on an early 45 rpm copy of "Living Doll".'

After the hospital we went to the bookshop. My mother parked illegally on double yellow lines. To deter traffic wardens she put a scribbled note behind a windscreen wiper.

Dear Traffic Warden

I have parked on double yellow lines because my son is currently having treatment for prostate cancer and he is too frail to walk even a short distance. Should you need me to move the car in an emergency you will find me in the bookshop.

Yours sincerely,
Pauline Mole

Bernard Hopkins took my mother into his arms, shouting, 'Pauline, you're a proper bobby-dazzler.'

She said, 'Bernard! Adrian told me that you'd tried to top yourself.'

Bernard laughed and said, 'I was down in the dumps because I'd run out of fags. Let's find a pub with tables outside so that we can smoke and I'll tell you all about it.'

So off they went, arm in arm, leaving me to look after the shop. An hour later a traffic warden came into the shop and asked me if I knew a Pauline Mole. When I replied that my mother had been called away on an urgent errand, the traffic warden said, 'Would you be the son who can't walk a few yards?'

I admitted I was. Unfortunately I was at the top of a ladder at the time sorting through the highest shelf of the poetry section. He gave me ten minutes to move the car. When he'd gone, I immediately phoned my mother. She said that she and Bernard were sitting outside the Rose and Crown and had just ordered their second round of drinks. When, after ten minutes, she still hadn't returned, I phoned her again.

She said, 'We're halfway through our ploughman's lunch,' and told me to move the car myself. When I pointed out that I was not insured to drive her car, she said, 'You're such a *pedant*!'

There was a strange crunching sound on the line.

I said, 'What's that noise?'

She said, 'I'm eating a pickled onion.'

A few minutes later I saw the traffic warden taping a fixed penalty notice to the Mazda's windscreen. This will cost her £60 she can ill afford.

She can't carry on at this rate.

Wednesday 28th November

To hospital in the Mazda. My mother suggested that we visit Melton Mowbray after my treatment. She wants to buy some chickens from the cattle market. She says she has got a feeling in her gut that civilization, as we know it, is due to collapse. I have just realised that my mother's offer to drive me to and from the hospital was not entirely selfless. I am an excuse for her to get out of the house and escape from the tedium of looking after my father. When she saw the parking ticket, she threw it into the gutter, saying, 'I shall go to court and fight them every inch of the way.' She didn't buy any chickens – she said they weren't attractive enough. Instead she spent £7.50 on a giant pork pie.

Daisy didn't get back from work until eight thirty. When she was in the bath I looked through her handbag. Something made me check her phone texts. There were over thirty messages from Hugo Fairfax-Lycett. How dare he badger my wife when she is at home with her family!

I went to bed and reread *Just William*. At 3 a.m. I woke and crept out of the bedroom, leaving Daisy asleep. I went through her bag more thoroughly this time and found a receipt for a bottle of champagne, a book of matches from Bon Ami (a restaurant in Loughborough I have never heard of), a taxi receipt for £19.50 and a new bottle of mouth spray. Now I know how Othello felt.

I went back to bed and watched my Desdemona while she slept. She looked beautiful with the moonlight on her face.

Thursday 29th November

Pandora rang at 7.30 a.m. to ask me if I would agree to be filmed with her on Saturday as part of the government's new Cancer Reform Strategy.

I asked her where she was.

She said, 'In London, in my office. The early worm catches the promotion.'

After we had disconnected the call, Daisy said, 'What did that bitch want – apart from my husband?'

I was quite pleased at this sign of jealousy.

Another tantrum from Gracie regarding her school uniform. Thankfully my mother papped the hooter of the Mazda outside so I grabbed my coat and left Daisy to deal with our daughter.

On the journey to the hospital I asked my mother if she thought Gracie needed to see a child psychologist.

My mother said, 'No, all she wants is her arse smacking.'

I said that I didn't agree with hitting small children.

She said, 'It didn't do you any harm.'

I said, 'On the contrary, I am a mass of neuroses.'

My mother now strolls in and out of the radiotherapy department as if she owns the place. When I told her

231

this, she said, 'I *do* own the place, the government keeps telling me that I'm a stakeholder.'

Phoned Mr Carlton-Hayes this afternoon and asked him about the closure of the bookshop. Did he have a particular date in mind?

There was a very long silence, then he said, 'I think perhaps it ought to be a Saturday.'

I asked which Saturday.

There was another very long silence. 'The first Saturday after Christmas would be sensible,' he said.

There were many questions that I wanted to ask him, such as how would we dispose of the books? Did we need to notify the Council? Should we arrange for electricity, gas and water to be turned off? I also wanted to know if I would qualify for redundancy pay. Should I give notice to Bernard and Hitesh? And what should I do for the rest of my life?

However, I asked none of these questions.

Gracie brought a letter home from school.

Dear Principal Carer

As you are probably aware, Britain is under threat from terrorism. As part of the government's war on terror Mangold Parva Infant School proposes to construct several concrete bollards in the playground to stop a possible suicide bomber driving a vehicle into school premises.

Construction is due to begin next week. I ask for your cooperation. However, should you have any concerns about the measures we are taking to protect your child/children please do not hesitate to contact me at the above address.

Please note any parent or child walking within one metre of the building work must wear a hard hat and a fluorescent vest.

Yours sincerely,

Mrs Bull (Head of School)

Friday 30th November

In the bath this morning I noticed a sore patch on the site of my radiotherapy tattoo.

On the way to the hospital my mother kept stopping the car to forage for holly and ivy. She could not reach the mistletoe growing on the very top branches of the large poplar tree, but tomorrow she is proposing to bring some tent poles, which she will screw together until she achieves enough length to reach the white berries. According to her they are selling for a ridiculous price this year. I pointed out to her that the mistletoe trees are on the Fairfax Hall estate, but she said that she didn't 'believe in the private ownership of trees'. I reminded her that she had sung to a different hymn sheet when Mangold Parva Parish Council asked her to cut down the leylandii she had planted on the border of our land. Then she had threatened to chain herself to those thirty-foot monsters if the council workmen came anywhere near them with their chainsaws. She said leylandii don't count as trees.

*

When we were queuing to get into the hospital car park, Pandora rang and told me to meet her on Saturday afternoon in Town Hall Square at 2 p.m. for a photo opportunity with the Leicester Prostate Awareness Group. It was not a request. It was an order. She knows I cannot say no to her.

Daisy came home at 10 p.m. claiming she had 'forgotten the time'. One of the buttons of her shirt was missing.

Saturday 1st December

Worked on the first draft of my Christmas round robin.

Dear Family and Friends

What a start to 2007! The pipes at the Piggeries froze! The call-out charge that most plumbers asked for was prohibitive so it was three days before we had running water and flushing toilets. Eventually my mother rang a friend of a friend, Noah Clapham. He wasn't a plumber but he had once worked at Homebase and had an impressive tool box. He charged £25 an hour and was with us for five days. My father claimed he caught Clapham asleep on the bathroom floor but Clapham denied it, saying he was 'visualizing the problem'.

In February I surprised Daisy on Valentine's Day by presenting her with tickets for a coach tour of Wales – stopping overnight at bed and breakfast establishments. Unfortunately, it rained every day and it was impossible to see outside the coach windows. Daisy had a panic attack when she had to crawl along a tunnel to the coalface during a Mining Experience day at the Coal Board Heritage Centre. However, she managed to climb to the top of Snowdon – the first woman to do it in high heels, apparently!

Due to a venue mix-up my parents attended the Society of Electric Storage Heater Salesmen's Christmas Dinner in March. My mother won a Christmas pudding in the raffle! We took Gracie to A&E after she swallowed what turned out to be a briefcase belonging to Business Barbie.

Health
Gracie has had a few colds and sniffles throughout the year and her temper tantrums continue to give us cause for concern. There was a particularly unpleasant episode in Pizza Hut earlier this year caused by Gracie making three unauthorised visits to the salad bar and monopolizing the pineapple chunks. However, Pizza Hut has agreed to lift their ban, providing Gracie is 'kept under control'.

Poor Daisy had menstrual trouble this year and her PMT has worsened to such an extent that she stays in our bedroom alternately weeping and raging for at least three days a month, bless her! The good news is that she is working again. Hugo Fairfax-Lycett, whose family home is Fairfax Hall, has appointed her as his PA and events organiser. She is currently trying to source two giraffes for the proposed safari park. Yes, giraffes!

It is a relief for all of us that my mother is, at last, through the menopause. It's three months since she had her last hot flush. She is worried by her increasing hairiness and has started on a course of laser exfoliation, so fingers crossed! The bunion on her left foot is playing her up but she is afraid of an operation.

A life of inaction and self-indulgence has caught up with my father. He is confined to a wheelchair and is dependent on medical equipment hired from the Red Cross. His bowels are still a bit sluggish – he only manages to pass a motion approximately every three days. No homespun remedies, please! We have tried everything legal and nothing works.

Daisy came in and read the letter over my shoulder. She said, 'Have you gone completely mad? I absolutely forbid you to send it. Nobody wants to know about our gruesome ailments. And the safari park is top secret.'

I wore my best suit, shirt and tie for my treatment. Sally was not there. I showed my sore patch to Claire, who only works weekends when her husband is at home to look after their two-year-old triplets. She said I mustn't worry about the sore patch on the site of my radio-therapy and told me that it was normal at this stage. She reminded me that I must not rub it or use soap in the bath, and told me to eat seaweed, an organic egg a day and lots of garlic.

She said, 'Wash the infected area with water only, using a very low power shower. Use olive oil or the leaves of aloe vera on the skin but no creams – even herbal ones – as they could contain irritating preservatives.' She added, 'I'm surprised Sally didn't tell you all this.'

I asked her if she was a believer in alternative medicine and mentioned that my father-in-law is Michael Flowers, who owns the health food shop in the market. She said, 'Yes, I know him all right. I bought a flagon of his

Orgobeet. It was me who alerted the Environmental Health Inspectorate.'

I went to the bookshop and me, Bernard and Hitesh decorated the shop window with Christmas books and some of the holly, ivy and mistletoe my mother had plundered on the journey in.

Bernard asked me what I was doing for Christmas. I told him that I would be spending it at home with the family.

He sighed and said, 'Ah, the family! What a cracking institution that is. Bloody useful for high days and holidays.'

When I asked Bernard where he would spend Christmas, he said, 'Drawn a blank there, lad. Inside a bottle, I suppose. I shall lie doggo until the festivities are over and normal life resumes.'

I couldn't bring myself to tell Bernard and Hitesh that we will cease trading after Christmas.

I walked to the town hall and arrived as the town hall clock struck two. There was a display of large wooden stands concerning cancer, stalls with literature and a poster showing a diagram of the prostate. Pandora was already there, surrounded by middle-aged men. The Lady Mayor was very colourful in her sari, ceremonial robes and mayoral chain. She made a speech about how good Leicester hospitals were. The small crowd applauded politely.

Pandora took the microphone and gave a rabble-rousing speech about the NHS. She implied that the

Conservatives would have us all dependent on BUPA and that they would, if elected, charge for admission to doctors' surgeries. She then called on cancer sufferers to make themselves known and to join her at the microphone. A surprising number of quite healthy-looking people left the crowd and joined her, including myself. She asked for volunteers to talk about their experiences of the NHS. When nobody came forward, she asked me by name and pulled me in front of the microphone. I said a few halting words about my treatment at the Royal Hospital. At the end I was clapped disproportionately and some people in the crowd whooped like Americans. I commented on this later to Pandora when we were having a cup of tepid coffee in the mayor's parlour.

Pandora said, 'Your speech was crap, yes, but people were applauding your courage.'

I said, 'But I'm not at all courageous, I often cry under the duvet and feel sorry for myself.'

She said, 'Every cancer sufferer is courageous, every cancer sufferer is fighting the disease, every cancer sufferer has dignity. People don't want to hear you're snivelling under your duvet, Aidy.'

I would have liked to have spent more time with her, but she had an appointment with Keith Vaz MP to tour the new theatre, The Curve. I might send the theatre *Plague!*. I'm sure the management would welcome a new play from a local playwright.

Sunday 2nd December

Woke at 5.30 a.m. and made a mental list of my worries. Felt quite miserable until I thought that at least I don't have to look after two-year-old triplets today.

At 7.30 a.m. I walked into the village with Gracie to buy the *Sunday Times* and *Observer*. As we were passing St Botolph's, Gracie asked me what all those 'grey things' were. I told her that they were called headstones. She wanted to see one up close so we went through the lych-gate and walked up the path. She asked me what was written on 'this stone'.

I read, 'Here lies Arthur Goodchild, diligent servant of the Lord, died aged sixteen, 23rd December 1908.' I said, 'Sixteen, that's so sad.'

She said, 'Where is Arthur Goodchild?'

I said, albeit a little reluctantly, 'He's under the ground.' She said, 'Does his mummy miss him?'

I said, 'Oh yes, a lot.'

Gracie said, 'Well, she should have dug him up, then.'

Booked a telephone conversation with Dr Wolfowicz. I asked him if he could prescribe a stimulant to keep me awake so that I can finish *Plague!*.

He said, 'I am not going to give you amphetamines, Mr Mole. Isn't it traditional for English writers to use vodka, cigarettes and black coffee?'

Monday 3rd December

Treatment.

Sally was wearing reindeer horns on her head. It is the radiotherapy department's Christmas party today. None of the patients are invited. I was quite hurt by this.

Later, in the bookshop, a man wearing a woman's fur coat came in and asked if we sold electronic books.

I said, 'No, and we don't provide electronic coffee either.'

He said, 'Why are booksellers so bloody rude?' and went out, slamming the door.

Hitesh said, 'Electronic books are the future. They're selling them on Amazon.'

Bernard said, 'Fuck that for a game of soldiers. You can't *smell* an electronic book or *read* it when the soddin' batteries have gone!'

A woman with a thousand carrier bags came in asking if we had a decent copy of *Ulysses*. She said, 'Have you got a first edition signed by James Joyce?'

Bernard shouted, 'The ignorance of the public never fails to amaze me. You're talking seventy thousand quid, woman. However, I do have a signed Penguin edition.'

The woman sat on the sofa and arranged the carrier bags around her. Bernard went into the back for a few minutes and came out with the Penguin *Ulysses*. He opened it at the title page and showed the woman the author's signature, which, to my eyes, looked remarkably like Bernard's distinctive handwriting.

He said, 'Abso bloody marvellous, isn't it? To think that the master himself has touched this page with his pen.'

The woman said, 'I don't read books myself. It's for my son. He's a bit of a bookworm. His room is so full of musty old books that I can hardly get in to clean. I offered to buy him a cashmere jumper for Christmas but, oh no, he had to have *Ulysses*. According to him, it's a masterpiece.' She laughed indulgently.

I should have intervened, but instead I watched Bernard take £30 from the woman. As he was at the till, she said, 'Does James Joyce ever do a reading at Waterstones?'

Bernard said, 'He'd have a job, madam, as he's been dead since 1941.' Bernard sighed, 'The thirteenth of January, a dark day indeed.'

When she had bustled out with her bags, Bernard watched her through the window and shook his head. He asked me if I had read *Ulysses*.

I said I hadn't.

He said, 'Nor me, couldn't get past the third page.'

Hitesh said, 'You should try again, Bernard. It's a bit like assembling an IKEA wardrobe. At first it looks like a lot of bits of wood and screws and bolts and stuff, but if you persevere and study the diagram and you've got the right screwdriver . . .'

Bernard snarled, 'For Christ's sake! What's bloody IKEA?'

He is the most unworldly man I have ever known.

Tuesday 4th December

My mother came round with a copy of the *Leicester Mercury* open at page three. There was a photograph of me standing between Pandora and the Lady Mayor and flanked by cancer sufferers. The headline said: 'Brave Victims Tell Of Cancer Fight.'

I had my eyes shut, my mouth open and a limp left wrist. When Daisy saw it she laughed and said, 'You look like Graham Norton halfway through a sneeze.'

Diary, I have never seen a single decent photograph of myself. The camera does not love my features. My mother looks like Scarlett Johansson in photographs, in real life she looks ninety-three.

Wednesday 5th December

To treatment in the Mazda.

Sally told me that Anthony has taken leave from his job and flown to Canada, where he plans to do voluntary work with a man who is petitioning the Canadian government to finance a wolf breeding programme in the hope that tens of thousands of wolves will be born and allowed to roam freely throughout the tundra.

I asked if their engagement was off.

She said, 'I can't trample on his dream, can I, Adrian?'

Personally I hope Anthony gets torn to pieces by a pack of resentful wolves. Harsh, I know, but everybody has to die and I'm sure Anthony would die happy amidst the slathering beasts.

Got a Christmas card from my mother and father in the post. Why waste a stamp? They only live next door.

Slept all afternoon, then had to run to school to pick Gracie up. She was in Mrs Bull's office crying. Apparently, she had told Mrs Bull that she had not eaten for a week and that there was no food in our house. I denied it, of course, and invited Mrs Bull to come home with us and inspect our pantry and refrigerator. She declined, but I could tell she thought that we neglected Gracie in some way. On the way home I interrogated Gracie and asked her why she had told Mrs Bull such a black lie.

All she would say was, 'I was hungry.'

I am dreading parents' evening at the school tomorrow.

Thursday 6th December

Treatment.

Sally was very quiet. She asked me not to talk about Anthony or Canada.

*

Went to the bookshop. When I asked Bernard to move a carton of Nigella Lawson's cookery books, which were blocking the entrance to the door, he said, 'No can do, old cock. I've done my back in. You'll have to wait for the whipper-snapper Hitesh to come in.'

At two thirty Hitesh texted to say that he had broken his ankle falling out of bed.

When I told Bernard, he said, 'Where's the lad been sleeping – on the top of a bleedin' crane?'

So, due to my debilitating weakness and Bernard's back, Ms Lawson's books remained inside their carton. Unfortunately, whilst Bernard and I were in the back room sorting through the new stock, Nigel and Lance Lovett came in and fell over the box. I don't know why Nigel went so mad. It wasn't as though he physically hurt himself, and I thought it was an hysterical overreaction when he threatened his oldest and best friend with civil action for damages.

However, Lance was very gracious and accepted my apologies, saying, 'I'm always falling on my arse. We blinkies are clumsy buggers.'

Under my instructions and guidance Lance picked the carton up and dropped it in the back room.

When Nigel kept going on about his tripping over the box, I told him that it was his own fault and in future he should not go out without his dog, his white stick or a sighted person to show him the way.

Nigel said, 'We came here to buy our Christmas presents, but I'm now thinking I may give my money to Marks & Spencer instead.'

After he had sat down on the sofa and had a cup of

coffee, he relented and, ironically, bought six copies of *Nigella Express*.

Daisy was not home in time for parents' evening so I went on my own.

Miss Nutt said, 'In many ways Gracie is a delightful little girl. Despite her ... well, eccentricities, she makes friends easily and seems to enjoy her work.' Then her brow furrowed and she said, 'However, last week I asked each child to talk about their family and dictate a few sentences to go with the picture they had painted.' She pointed to a large painting on the back wall, where a stick figure in spectacles was lying horizontal on what looked like grass next to another stick figure with a red mouth and high heels, holding a bottle. Miss Nutt had written (to Gracie's dictation): 'My mummy and daddy do drink a lot of vodka and they do lie down and shout at me.'

I glanced at the next picture, drawn by Abigail Stone. The caption said: 'My family went to Alton Towers and we had a picnic. We did sing in the car.'

I said, 'I can assure you, Miss Nutt, that neither my wife nor I drink vodka. I'm surprised that Gracie even knows the word.'

Miss Nutt said, 'Well, she's heard it from somewhere and she obviously knows the effect of drinking too much. She is the only child in the class who has painted her parents in a state of collapse.' She went on, 'Yesterday Gracie came to school in rags.'

There was an accusatory tone to her voice that I did not care for. I said, 'That was her Cinderella dress, Miss

Nutt. If you had turned it inside out you would have seen it transformed into a ball gown.'

Miss Nutt said, 'In future, unless Gracie is wearing her uniform she will be suspended from school. We have been ridiculously indulgent with her so far, but it has to stop.'

I left with a heavy heart and battled through the wind to The Bear. I had intended to have a quick drink and then go, but Tony and Wendy Wellbeck called me over to their table and insisted I join them.

I said, 'About the baubles . . .'

Tony said, 'Never mind about the baubles. Let bygones be bygones. It's Wendy's birthday – what will you have?'

For some reason I blurted out, 'Vodka.'

When he had gone to the bar, Wendy said, 'I'm glad we ran into you. I wonder if you would mind reading something I've written. You're almost a professional writer, aren't you?'

To my dismay she pulled out a typewritten folder from her commodious bag and pushed it in front of me. It was titled *Primroses and Puppies*. I read the first few sentences.

I had a happy childhood. Laughter ran around the cottage where I was born. Father was gruff and tough but he had a heart of pure gold. Mother had a twinkly smile and soft hands that were always busy.

I closed the folder with an inward sigh. I knew that when I got to the bit about the primroses and the puppies, I would want to vomit.

Wendy said, 'I've so enjoyed writing it. Would you read it for me and tell me what you think of it?'

I mumbled that I would.

'But you must swear to tell me the truth,' she said, wagging a finger in my face. 'You must be brutally frank.'

Tony came back with what looked like a triple vodka in a Smirnoff glass. I was taking my first sip when Miss Nutt entered the pub with her fellow teachers. She walked past our table and gave me and the glass a piercing look.

When I got home, I found Daisy sitting in the dark listening to Leonard Cohen. I went into the kitchen and found a note on the table.

Dear Adrian

The Jeremy Kyle Show is on tomorrow so I have asked Dougie Horsefield to pick you up in the morning.

Love,

Mum

Friday 7th December

Dougie was annoyingly early. He sat outside with the engine running while I was showering, dressing and fighting with Gracie and her uniform.

*

On the way to the hospital Dougie said, 'I'm going to drop you off then get home fast for the Kyle show. My missis has invited some of the neighbours round.'

Sally noticed my agitation and I told her that my parents, sister and my mother's ex-lover were on *The Jeremy Kyle Show* this morning.

I had expected her to be shocked, but she said, 'I do so admire your mother.'

Is there such a thing as privacy now? At one time people kept their problems to themselves.

When I lay on the high bed, having my nether regions zapped, I thought that I would like to stay there for ever. All my energy seemed to have seeped away. Sally had to help me down. She took me into the waiting room and made me sit on a chair. For once I was sorry that my mother was not there to take me home. After half an hour I felt slightly better and made my own way to the bookshop. As I walked past the Sony shop on the High Street, I saw my parents on a huge television screen. My mother looked extremely glamorous and my father looked utterly pathetic in his wheelchair. Lucas and Rosie were sitting next to each other holding hands. There was a close-up of my father's face as a single tear rolled down from his left eye. Eventually the tear trickled into his moustache and disappeared.

My legs propelled me into the shop and over to the television section. I was surrounded by hundreds of screens, each one showing *The Jeremy Kyle Show*. An assistant sidled up to me. His name badge said that he was Mohammed Anwar. He murmured, 'Are you all right there, sir?'

I lied that I was interested in purchasing a 50-inch plasma television.

He led me over to a gigantic screen and said, 'You pay nothing for the first year –'

I interrupted him, saying, 'I would like to hear the sound quality.'

He produced a remote control and turned the sound up.

On the screen Rosie was shouting, 'You've lied to me all these years, Mum.'

My father shouted, 'Yes, Pauline, and how do I know that Adrian is mine?'

Jeremy Kyle said, 'Adrian is your son, is he, Pauline?'

My mother nodded.

My father shouted, 'I want a DNA test. I need to know if Adrian's mine!'

Jeremy said, 'Pauline, are you sure that Adrian is George's?'

My mother sniffed and said, 'I'm seventy per cent sure.'

'Seventy per cent!' I said. 'Is that all?'

The assistant next to me laughed. 'Where do they get these people from?' he said.

'God knows,' I said.

He tried to talk me into buying the 50-inch plasma screen. I told another lie and said that I would think about it.

He sighed and said, 'Nobody's buying nothink any more. Everybody's already got everythink.' For a moment he looked stricken, saying, 'What will happen if people stop buying? I'll be out of a job.'

*

As I walked to the bookshop, I tried to remember a conversation I had once had with my mother. It concerned a maggot farmer called Ernie who she had been very fond of. She reminisced about the love poetry he had written for her. She had been going out with Ernie when she first met my father. Was I the son of a maggot farmer? Was it from him that I inherited my literary talent? It is true that I have absolutely nothing in common with my father. He thinks that only poofs and nancy boys write poetry. However, I am quite fond of him. It would be a bit of a blow to find out that I do not share his blood.

Midnight

Can't write much. I am distraught. My mother could give me no guarantees that the man I have been calling Dad for the last thirty-eight years might be only a person my mother had married. She has asked me to contact Ernie the maggot farmer and ask him to provide a sample for DNA testing.

Saturday 8th December

Treatment.

Bernard took an order from a prematurely bald young man for a book published in America called *The Audacity of Hope* by somebody called Barack Obama. When the customer said his name was 'Roger Mee', Bernard laughed and said, 'Bit of a bum moniker to drag through life, isn't it?'

Roger Mee looked puzzled. 'I beg your pardon?' he said.

'Your parents obviously had it in for you,' said Bernard. 'Did your mother have a hard labour?'

Mr Mee's mouth slackened. He glanced at me, silently asking for help.

I said, 'Bernard is referring to an archaic term for sexual intercourse: "to roger", as in, "Will you *roger me*?"'

Mee – who was, I'd guess, in his early twenties – said, 'I've never heard the term before.'

'I used to use it all the time,' said Bernard unhelpfully. 'I'd ring up one of my lady friends and say, "Hello there, Gladys (or Marcia or whatever her bloody name was), will you come round and roger me?"'

Roger Mee's face had drained of colour. I could tell that he was reassessing his previous social interactions. He said, 'I had to give my name at the library yesterday. I now know why the elderly librarian sniggered. And my wedding ... the vicar ... when he asked, "Do you, Roger Mee ..." the congregation laughed out loud.'

After Mee had left, I reproached Bernard, saying, 'In future, Bernard, please don't make personal remarks about our customers. They are few and far between as it is.'

Bernard said, 'You're telling me. I've seen more customers in an hour in an Eskimo's brothel than we get through here in a day.'

When I queried Bernard's knowledge of an Eskimo's

brothel, he said, quite huffily, 'I'll bring in documentary evidence.'

Sunday 9th December

Bowing to pressure from Gracie, I agreed to go out and buy a Christmas tree (I think it is wrong to put up a tree and decorations until the last week before Christmas). I borrowed the Mazda and Daisy drove us to the first of three garden centres. My mother still refuses to put us on her insurance. I was a nervous wreck throughout, expecting at any minute to be flagged down by a police car. Most of the Christmas trees were trussed up like turkeys in bags of green netting so that it was impossible to tell whether their branches were even and symmetrical.

At the third garden centre Daisy put her foot down and said, 'If we don't choose one from here, Adrian, I swear I will go out tomorrow and buy a plastic one from Woolworths.'

We were sitting in the café surrounded by middle-aged people in sensible car coats and shoes. I was so tired I could easily have slept with my head on the table. I told Daisy to choose a tree, any tree, and that I would wait with Gracie in the car. Daisy stalked through the automatic doors into the outside area and was soon lost amongst the conifers. It was dark by the time she emerged. The Christmas tree was too large for the car, we had to tie it to the luggage rack with some rope we found in the boot.

Query: Why does my mother keep bits of old rope in the boot of her car? Isn't that what serial killers do?

The tree is ridiculously tall. The top branch brushes the ceiling. The fairy is stooped like Quasimodo. The tree lights worked brilliantly until all the baubles and decorations had been meticulously placed on the tree. When we were sitting back and admiring our work, the tree lights failed.

Can nothing go right for us?

Monday 10th December

Treatment.

Sally is trying to book a seat on a plane to Canada. She wants to sit by Anthony's bedside in hospital. I told her that doctors can perform wonderful reconstructive surgery these days. All the same, I hope she cannot get a ticket. I need her here in Leicester.

Mr Carlton-Hayes rang today and asked how Bernard and Hitesh had taken the news that we were going to close. I admitted that I had not yet told them anything about the closure.

He said, 'Oh dear. Then I must do it myself.' I apologized and he said, 'I shouldn't have asked you, my dear, you have a kind heart and I should have known that such a distressing duty would have caused you pain.'

I told Mr Carlton-Hayes that, by the end of business,

Bernard and Hitesh would be told that they will not be employed in the New Year.

Midnight

I couldn't do it. I'll tell them tomorrow, first thing.

Tuesday 11th December

After treatment my mother drove me to the bookshop and dropped me off. Hitesh was clumping about in his plaster cast while Bernard was sitting on the sofa reading *Vanity Fair* (the book not the magazine). I called them together and broke the news to them that the shop was closing.

Bernard's face collapsed. He said, 'Well, that's it, then. I'll go ahead and do the deadly deed. England doesn't want old farts like me hanging around with our haemorrhoids and halitosis. The blue birds over the cliffs of Dover are –'

Hitesh interrupted, 'Am I entitled to any redundancy money?'

I said, 'I'll look it up for you.'

Bernard said, 'It will be Christmas in the workhouse for me, then.'

I told him that he was welcome to spend Christmas with me and my family.

Why? Why? Why did I open my mouth and let that invitation escape my lips?

Bernard said, 'I'm much obliged to you, young sir. I shall bring a bottle.'

Later on I Googled 'redundancy pay UK Law' and told Hitesh that he would not be entitled to anything because he had not been working for Mr Carlton-Hayes for two years.

Hitesh said, 'My cousin owns a franchise for KFC. I'll ask him for a job.'

Bernard said, 'What's KFC? Kettering Football Club?'

Hitesh and I laughed longer than Bernard's display of ignorance warranted. I suppose it was a release of tension.

My mother came into the shop and asked if she could leave her Christmas shopping in the back room. I helped her carry the bags through. She gave me strict instructions not to look inside a Marks & Spencer's bag. On her way to the front door she said, 'There's a terrible atmosphere in here. Have you girls been quarrelling?'

I told her that the shop was closing.

She said, 'I'm not surprised. Where's your chick lit and your celebrity biographies? Your front window looks like Miss Haversham's bloody library. The berries have fallen off the mistletoe and your holly and ivy are as dry as a nun's crotch.'

Later I looked inside the Marks & Spencer's bag. She had bought me a pale lemon 100 per cent acrylic V-necked sweater in a large size.

I hope she has kept the receipt.

Wednesday 12th December

Had a conversation with Daisy about Gracie's Christmas presents. I suggest that we buy her something modest – felt-tip pens perhaps – and we donate a sum of money to Save the Children or a similar worthy charity. I also suggested buying my parents an Oxfam goat between them.

Daisy said, 'Don't even think about buying *me* livestock.'

I haven't told her yet that I have invited Bernard for Christmas.

I went to bed at 7.15 p.m., weary and downcast, leaving Daisy in the kitchen bad-temperedly making a North Star costume out of aluminium foil and wire coat hangers for the nativity concert next week.

When Daisy came to bed, just after midnight, she stroked my back and whispered, 'Are you OK?'

I pretended to be asleep and eventually she turned over and tuned in to the World Service on the radio. There was a documentary about child mortality in Africa.

I resolved to buy everybody farmyard animal tokens.

Thursday 13th December

Treatment.

Anthony's insurance company have agreed to fly him back to England. I told Sally that I was surprised that

Anthony hadn't invalidated his insurance. Surely there was a clause somewhere in the policy advising against befriending wolves?

Rang Parvez for advice on unemployment pay and sickness benefit, but he was away at a Building Societies Association conference. He is giving a talk on 'Sharia law and the Muslim housing market'.

I can remember the time when Parvez was too shy to blow the candles out on his twelfth birthday cake. He ran out of the house, leaving me and my fellow party guests to comfort his mother (who had been up half the night decorating the cake with a Porsche racing car on the track at Silverstone, complete with pit and mechanics – not an easy thing to do with marzipan and an icing bag). Now he's doing public speaking and is a prominent member of the Rotary Club (Leicester Branch). *Plus ça change!*

Friday 14th December

The dirty washing has piled up and I had to search for a pair of clean underpants this morning. In my search I opened Daisy's underwear drawer and found three new pairs of matching bras and knickers in black, red and white lace. They were a class above her old off-white knickers and her turned-grey-in-the-wash bras.

Eventually found a pair of boxers in the ironing pile.

When is Daisy going to see to the laundry? It's easy enough – all she has to do is throw it into the washing machine, put a tablet of detergent inside the little mesh bag and press a knob. What's so difficult about that? And as for the ironing, any fool can run an iron over pieces of cloth, can't they?

On the way to treatment I asked my mother what I should buy Daisy for Christmas.

My mother said, without hesitation, 'A Marc Jacobs bag – a Bruna quilted tote that combines classic cool with its metallic hue and gold hardware.'

I said, 'It sounds expensive.'

My mother said evasively, 'It does, doesn't it? But it's what she wants.'

I was grateful to her. She has saved me hours of trailing around the shops. I asked her if she would order the bag for me on the internet and gave her my Visa card.

Anthony is in the BUPA hospital in Leicester having skin grafts. His parents have sold one of their greengrocer's shops to pay for it.

I said to Sally, 'That's very kind of his parents.'

She said, 'Not really. They're frightened of him.'

Saturday 15th December

On the way to treatment my mother said, 'When are you going to give me some petrol money?'

I was flabbergasted. How mercenary can you get?

I pointed out to her that I will be unemployed soon and needed every penny of my wages at the moment.

She said, quite nastily, 'You can afford to splash out on a Marc Jacobs bag for your working wife.' She handed me back my Visa card and said, 'Securicor are delivering the bag this morning. Your father will sign for it and make sure it is hidden somewhere so that Daisy doesn't see it.'

Securicor! Why are they delivering a *handbag*? Surely they only deliver really expensive items.

Glenn and Finley-Rose are engaged. He rang me while I was on my way to treatment.

He said, 'If I cop it in Afghanistan, Finley will get a widow's pension.'

I think this is taking pragmatism too far.

Sunday 16th December

As I was spooning hot goose fat over the roast potatoes, I asked Daisy what I should buy my mother for Christmas.

She paused from chopping carrots and said, 'She'd like a silver necklace with a rose quartz pendant.'

I said, 'Where would I get one of those?'

'From the Tiffany's website,' she said.

I said, 'Tiffany's, as in "breakfast at"?'

'Yes,' she said. 'Your mother has been waiting for your dad to buy her something from Tiffany's since they went to see the film in 1961. Apparently, as they were leaving the cinema, he made a promise to her that, if she married him, he would buy her a piece of Tiffany's jewellery for every birthday.'

259

I shoved the potatoes back in the oven and said, 'One more broken promise to go with the others.'

I asked Daisy in passing if she would mind chopping the carrots more evenly. I pointed out to her that some of the slices were almost wafer thin whereas others were on the chunky side. My wife cannot take any criticism whatsoever. To my absolute amazement she went berserk and started stamping round the kitchen, gesticulating wildly with our sharpest paring knife. She went from 'carrots' to my 'self-absorption' to 'Dr Pearce', then to 'Pandora'. She paused a while on my obsession with 'stinking old books' and then galloped forward again with 'you've lost interest in me, emotionally, sexually and romantically'. She stopped and burst into wracking sobs.

Gracie came in and gave me a reproachful look and said, 'If you make Mummy cry, you'll go to prison.'

I told the child that she was being ridiculous, that nobody went to prison for shouting.

She said, 'Yes they do. I saw it on *The Bill*. It's called a Section Five.'

Daisy shouted, 'We can't even have a row in peace! Either Gracie interrupts us or your parents listen through the party wall!'

I shouted back, 'Why have you suddenly taken to buying matching lace underwear?'

This allowed her to go on another protracted rant about my 'meanness', my 'antisocial and suspicious behaviour' and then, unforgivably, she shouted, 'And your writing is a joke. You make Barbara Taylor Bradford look like a Nobel laureate. You couldn't write

your way out of a plastic bag. Think about it, Adrian —
why has nobody wanted to publish or broadcast anything you have written for over twenty-five years?'

I did not deign to answer her. I took my warmest coat,
my gloves, my scarf and balaclava and left the house,
saying, before I slammed the door, 'I may be some time.'

Unfortunately, it was 3.30 p.m. and almost dark so I
walked up and down the lane a few times and went back
into the house, where I was surprised to see that it was
only 4.05 p.m.

I did not speak to Daisy that night apart from giving her
my Visa card and saying, 'For the necklace.'

Monday 17th December

At treatment I told Sally that I am experiencing severe
discomfort when passing water.

She said, 'How severe is severe out of ten?'

I said, 'I am a writer, Sally. I choose my words very
carefully.'

She said, 'You are also prone to exaggeration, Adrian.'

Why are all the women in my life so difficult? Men
do not correct your speech or criticise your character or
accuse you of sexual indifference.

After treatment I went to the bookshop and was
surprised to find quite a crowd in there. They turned out
to be Bernard's drinking mates. He promised to give

them a discount of 50 per cent on all Christmas books. I noticed that many of the selected titles were alcohol related. One of Bernard's mates, a man with a seasonally suitable red nose, bought the screenplay of *The Days of Wine and Roses* for his mother.

Tuesday 18th December

I am feeling the strain of not talking to Daisy. We are like two deaf mutes. We communicate in signs and little grunts. I shall have to break my silence soon because I need to talk to her about the Christmas arrangements.

On the way to treatment I asked my mother if she thought I was a good writer. She didn't answer for a long time, then a fox ran across the road in front of us and she slammed on the brakes. When we were driving again, I repeated my question, saying, 'Am I a good writer, Mum?'

She said, 'I like some of your stuff.'

I challenged her to name one piece.

She said, '"The Tap". I liked that.' And she quoted, 'The tap drips and keeps me awake in the morning, there will be a lake.'

I said, 'You like a banal poem I wrote when I was thirteen and three-quarters! What about my later canon?'

Diary, I was very tempted to confess that I had read *A Girl Called 'Shit'* and advise her to discontinue the inevitably doomed project, but I kept shtum.

*

Later that morning I went to Mangold Parva Infants for the nativity play. Daisy was already there on the front row sitting next to my father in his wheelchair. He was holding his camcorder. I sat in between them. To my annoyance Daisy's father, Michael Flowers, was also there with his horrible beard and hand-knitted sweater with the reindeer design. My mother sat down clutching a disposable camera. Mrs Bull stepped on to the raised platform and quietened the audience. She was wearing her usual ill-fitting green suit and had applied a dab of orange lipstick for the occasion. When her order was not instantly obeyed, she raised her voice and shouted, 'Can I have your attention, *please!*'

The audience, a cross section of the village, i.e. chavs and Barbour-wearing parents, fell silent.

Mrs Bull said, 'I have a few announcements to make before our festive play begins. I would have liked to call it a nativity play but, unfortunately, due to the sensitivities of the Muslim community I am not allowed to do so.'

My father muttered, 'It's political correctness gone bleedin' mad.'

Michael Flowers said loudly, 'It's a bloody disgrace.'

Everybody in the audience looked around the hall trying to spot a Muslim.

Mrs Ludlow, who runs the pensioners' group on Wednesday afternoons, was wearing a headscarf but she is a fervent member of the Church of England.

Mrs Bull continued, 'I'm afraid that those of you who have brought cameras and video machines with you will not be allowed to use them. This is to prevent our children from being exploited and posted on the internet for the purposes of adult titillation.'

My mother said, 'Nobody is going to be titillated by a load of kids wearing bed sheets and tea towels on their heads.'

Mrs Bull glared at my mother and said, 'And finally, toddlers and babies who shout or cry out will be asked to leave. Our children have been rehearsing this performance for many weeks and I am determined that they will be heard in silence.'

A small boy walked on wearing a striped brushed-cotton sheet and a white and blue tea towel with 'GLASSES' written on it. What followed was a travesty. The children were obviously under-rehearsed and had no stagecraft. When Joseph fidgeted with his headdress, causing it to slip from his head and fall on to the floor, and then started to cry, from somewhere in the audience a woman shouted, in a cut-glass accent, 'Don't worry, Benedict darling, carry on without it.'

It went downhill from there on. When the thirty snowflakes made their entrance, the cows, sheep, wise men and shepherds were pushed to the very brink of the platform, causing Mrs Bull and various teachers to link arms to prevent the children from falling into the audience. The recorded music was not coordinated with the action on stage.

I whispered to my mother, 'God save us from amateur productions.'

After twenty tedious minutes, Gracie (the North Star) had still not made her entrance.

I forgot that we were not speaking and whispered to Daisy, 'Surely the North Star should have been there from the beginning, else it makes a nonsense of the wise men scenario. I mean, what are they supposed to follow?'

Daisy whispered back, 'It's a bloody fiasco.'

Eventually, towards the end, the North Star made her entrance to loud applause from the Mole family and from her Granddad Flowers. She announced to the audience that she had been on the toilet for a long, long time. This was met with laughter and applause, though I noticed Mrs Bull did not join in.

My parents disobeyed instructions and videoed and photographed my little girl, who should have announced, 'Morning came and the North Star faded in the sky,' but instead waved to her family on the front row. By now Mary was absent-mindedly swinging Jesus (a Baby Annabelle doll) by one leg. One of the three wise men fell off the platform and lay at my father's feet still clutching his box of frankincense.

Michael Flowers got up and helped the boy back on to the platform, whereupon Mrs Bull shouted, 'Please don't manhandle the child!'

My father-in-law said, 'Madam, I do not follow Strasbourg's dictates on how to pick up a child!'

After a ragged rendition of 'Jingle Bells' the audience filed out. I tried to apologise to Mrs Bull on behalf of the Mole family. I told her that my father-in-law was a man of extreme political views.

Mrs Bull said, 'I happen to share his views, Mr Mole, but this was not the occasion on which to express them.'

*

After waiting for the North Star to change into her normal clothes, we walked home. Michael Flowers insisted on pushing my father's wheelchair. Was it my imagination or did he deliberately push my father through the deepest puddles? We were forced to invite him to share our evening meal. Flowers drank a bottle and a half of red wine and went into a long lament about his first wife, Daisy's Mexican mother Conchita. He moaned that he had never stopped loving her and still hoped to win her back. He then proceeded to tell me that I was a damn fool to have been bullied by the doctors into having radiotherapy for my prostate cancer.

He said, 'Adrian, let's face it, your poor diet and unhealthy lifestyle are to blame for your cancer. If you are serious about regaining your health you should revolutionise your diet. Daisy, tomorrow morning you must go out and stock up on blueberries and raw vegetable juices. He needs green tea and antioxidants. And it's *essential* that you make up a poultice from a mash of passion fruit, lentils and papaya and apply this to Adrian's genitals.'

I said, 'How am I supposed to keep a poultice on my genitals?'

He said, 'Use cling film but make sure you apply it to your testicular sack.' He added, 'I have noticed that you do not have a window open.'

Daisy said, 'Dad, it is December.'

Flowers said, 'We were not meant to live in overheated dwelling places. It's not long since we came out of the caves.'

After advising me to hang upside down for at least an

hour and a half every day, he took his leave. We stood at the door to wave him off.

When the lights of his Volkswagen camper van had disappeared down the lane, Daisy said, 'Remind me to put cling film on the shopping list.'

We laughed and went to bed and slept in the spoon position until I had to get up to go to the toilet.

Wednesday 19th December

Daisy was getting ready for work – she is arranging a New Year's Eve party at Fairfax Hall. Tickets are £75 a head! She asked me if I wanted to go. I said I would.

At treatment I asked Sally if there were any medical benefits from the poultice/cling film method. She said one of her patients fell under the influence of a person they found on the internet who advised them to stop chemotherapy and instead live entirely on a diet of seaweed and mackerel. She knew of another who spent their life savings on crystals, which were placed in every room.

'And how are these patients?' I asked.

'Dead,' she said.

Thursday 20th December

Four days to Christmas! I have done no Christmas shopping and I have not told Daisy that Bernard Hopkins is to be our house guest.

My mother came round to use our phone. She threw her own against the wall and smashed it because BT sent her a bill for £2,376,215.18. When she rang to query this extraordinary amount, a person at the BT call centre told her to hold. After my mother had listened to the whole of Vivaldi's *Four Seasons*, the phone was cut off. My mother redialled and spoke to another call centre operative 'in India'. According to her, 'I could hear an elephant trumpeting and a Bollywood soundtrack playing.' However, my mother is prone to exaggeration so I'm not sure I can trust this part of her narrative.

Friday 21st December

Treatment.

Sally is very sad. Anthony has postponed the wedding indefinitely, saying the wolves must come first. Apparently, as soon as his skin grafts have taken he's returning to Canada.

Had an appointment with Dr Rubik this morning. She said that my latest blood tests showed that I am slowly responding to treatment. She said that my prognosis is 'quite good'.

Only *quite* good?

Pandora rang while I was still talking to Dr Rubik. She said, 'I would like to talk to her myself. Put her on, will you?'

Dr Rubik took my phone and was soon deep in conversation with Pandora about me and my treatment.

I felt like an interloper. At one point Dr Rubik turned her back on me.

When she handed the phone back to me, Pandora said, 'I might be in Leicester for Christmas. If I am, I'll drop in and see you.'

My heart soared.

My mother picked me up from the hospital. The back seat of the Mazda was piled high with multipacks of Heinz baked beans, corned beef, dried milk and a jumbo bag of long-grain rice.

I said, 'That's peculiar food to buy at Christmas.'

My mother said, 'That's my hoarding food. The Christmas stuff is in the boot.'

When I asked her why she was hoarding food, she said, 'I don't like the signs, Adrian. Houses are not selling and Gordon Brown is denying that there is a credit crunch.'

Credit crunch! Where does she get these terms?

I asked her what my father would like for Christmas.

She said, 'Six white handkerchiefs or six pairs of black socks or a Dolly Parton CD.'

I know for a fact that my father has got two drawers entirely devoted to white handkerchiefs and black socks and he prides himself on having every song that Dolly Parton has recorded including those when she was a bare-footed hillbilly.

Saturday 22nd December

Woke in the night sweating. Had a dream that I was dead and lying in a coffin. Friends and relations were filing past me.

My mother passed the coffin and said, 'He was a terrible writer.'

Pandora laid her head on my cold chest and wept, saying, 'He was my only true love.'

Nigel barged into the coffin and I fell out.

Then I woke up. I told Daisy about my dream (I missed out the Pandora part).

She said, 'When we were first married, we made a promise that we would never talk about our dreams. I expect you to honour that agreement.'

Three days to go. I must tell Daisy about Bernard Hopkins. Mr Carlton-Hayes rang this morning and invited me, Bernard and Hitesh round on Monday evening for Christmas drinks and a mince pie.

At last! I have never been to Mr Carlton-Hayes's house before or met Leslie. I hope he/she will be pouring the drinks.

Gracie dictated a note to Santa Claus.

A real dog
A real cat
A real fish

A real bird
A real pig
A real cow
A real horse
A real baby

We waited for Daisy to come before we burned Santa's letter in the fireplace. Gracie fell asleep at 8.30 p.m. but Daisy didn't arrive home until 11.05 p.m. She said there was some paperwork she had to finish. She brought a bag full of pine cones from Hugo Fairfax-Lycett's estate.

Sunday 23rd December

Daisy's mood is increasingly erratic. This morning, as I was enjoying a bowl of cornflakes, she said, 'Do you *have* to open your mouth when you eat?'

I replied, 'Actually, I do. It's the only way I know to get the food inside.'

Five minutes later she hurled herself into my arms and said, 'Do you think it's possible for us to *be* happy?'

An interesting choice of tense.

Monday 24th December
Christmas Eve

Treatment.

I gave Sally a festive box of After Eights. She gave them back to me, saying that in the code of practice hospital staff are not allowed to receive presents from patients.

I tried to hand them back to her and said, 'Put them in your bag, nobody will know.'

She said, '*I* will know, Adrian.'

Sometimes I can see why Anthony prefers the wolves to her.

There was the usual Christmas Eve rush in the book-shop. At 5 p.m. people started running in and panic-buying. We sold out of Jamie Oliver and Nigella and one distraught woman hammered on the door at five thirty, after we had closed, and begged to be let in.

When I took pity on her, she blurted out, 'My sister's coming down from Scotland, she rang me this morning. She's leaving her bloody awful husband – again. She's got five children ages one to seven. Why me? We don't get on and she knows I can't stand kids. Derek and I were going to have a quiet Christmas – a little smoked salmon, a couple of glasses of champagne and the *EastEnders* special.'

I invited her to sit on the sofa and compose herself. I then chose five suitable books and had Hitesh gift-wrap them.

The woman said, 'This is very kind of you. I will give you my custom in the New Year.'

Bernard said, 'You'll have a job, madam, this venerable old shop is closing. It's the end of an era. Will Waterstones and Borders open their doors to you, madam, and gift-wrap your books? Will you receive such service from the pimply youths they employ?'

When she'd gone, I rang for a taxi and was told by a surly man on the end of the line that the fare would be double because it was Christmas Eve.

The taxi driver was wearing a Father Christmas hat.

Bernard said, 'Excuse me, chap, but aren't you a follower of Islam?'

The driver turned to Bernard, who was in the back seat, and said, 'Yeah, but Christmas is for the kids, innit?'

Hitesh said, 'Christmas ain't like what it used to be.'

Bernard patted his arm and said, 'Hitesh, old flower, Christmas is exactly the same, it's you who have changed.'

Mr Carlton-Hayes lives in a huge Edwardian house in Stoneygate. Many of the houses in the street have been turned into residential homes for the elderly or into probation hostels. A sprightly elderly man with an abundance of grey hair and wearing a white polo-neck jumper opened the door to us. He was wearing yellow washing-up gloves. He pulled one off and shook our hands, saying, 'I'm Leslie, Mr Carlton-Hayes's friend.'

We stepped into the large hall. Books lined the walls.

Mr Carlton-Hayes shouted, 'Show them into the drawing room, my dear.'

Leslie ushered us into a room which was hung with gaudy Christmas decorations. Mr Carlton-Hayes cut an incongruous figure sitting in his wheelchair wearing a quilted dressing gown and cravat. He was illuminated by an artificial silver Christmas tree behind him with flashing primary-coloured bulbs.

He said, 'Hello, my dears. Do please sit down.' After we were seated, he said to Leslie, 'Champagne, I think, my dear.'

Bernard said, looking around at the paper chains, garlanded mantelpiece and bunches of balloons hanging from the ceiling, 'It's very cheerful in here, Mr C.'

Mr Carlton-Hayes said cautiously, 'Yes, it is rather jolly.'

Bernard said, 'I like a bit of vulgarity myself. I despise that minimalistic, arty-farty, tight-arsed, bare-floorboard, Habitat foolery.'

Hitesh said, 'My mum has a string of coloured lights nailed to the picture rail all year round.'

'Quite right too!' said Bernard.

As a fan of Habitat and bare boards, I kept quiet. We made small talk between us. Leslie came back with a bottle of Marks & Spencer's champagne and four glasses. Thereafter the conversation grew more and more stilted until it eventually dried up and there was an uncomfortable silence.

Nobody had mentioned the elephant in the room — the fact that Carlton-Hayes's new, second-hand and antiquarian bookshop had gone out of business. Bernard saved us by recounting the anecdote about his most recent failed suicide attempt. He tried to make it sound amusing. Nobody laughed but at least it passed a few minutes. Leslie went out and came back with a tray of what he called 'bonnes bouches' which were tiny beef burgers and minuscule mince pies.

There was so much I wanted to say to Mr Carlton-Hayes: how much I loved him, how I would miss him, how much I respected his knowledge of books, how much I admired his unfailing good manners. For something to do I gathered up the plates and glasses and took them into the kitchen, where I found Leslie slumped over the sink with his head in his hands.

I asked him if he was all right and he turned a tear-stained face to me and choked, 'This could be his last Christmas with me and yet he still will not properly introduce me to his friends. Why? Is he ashamed of me? I've always kept the house nice for him. He's always had a good meal waiting for him when he comes home. I don't know what will happen to me when he dies. I can't start all over again, not at my age.'

To my horror he removed his hair and wiped his bald head with a handkerchief. I stared down at the grey curly wig. It had certainly fooled me. He put it back on his head and checked his reflection in the shiny microwave door. He said to himself, 'Right, shoulders back, Leslie,' and returned to the drawing room.

To give myself time I rinsed the glasses and plates and looked around the kitchen. There were more books on the shelves than kitchen equipment. Reluctantly I went back into the drawing room, where I found Hitesh —

who was unused to champagne – telling a story about one of his college lecturers whose wig had been blown off in a high wind on the campus. I saw Leslie touch his hair and exchange a look with Mr Carlton-Hayes.

Bernard said, 'I don't know why the silly fuckers wear a wig. You can always tell.'

I rose to my feet and said, 'I'd better get home. Can I call a cab?'

Leslie said, 'I'll give you a lift. I've got to buy a packet of Paxo for tomorrow.'

I wished Mr Carlton-Hayes a very merry Christmas.

He said, 'We'll talk after the festivities, my dear.'

I meant to shake his hand but instead I bent down and kissed him.

Leslie's car stank of the pine tree he had hanging from his rear-view mirror. We dropped Hitesh off at his parents' semi-detached house in Evington and watched him walk unsteadily to the front door. As we drove out towards the countryside, I remembered that I had not yet rung Daisy about Bernard. I could hardly ring her in Bernard's presence so it was not until Bernard walked into our kitchen that Daisy knew we had a Christmas house guest.

Midnight

It is officially Christmas Day. Daisy greeted Bernard very frostily, but when my parents came round and a few bottles had been opened Daisy relaxed and, after ordering him to wash his hands, allowed Bernard to stuff the turkey. After we had laid out a saucer of milk and a half-eaten carrot for the reindeers and a nibbled mince pie and a glass of whisky for Santa in the fireplace, my parents went home and I made up a sleeping-bag bed on the sofa for our guest. Bernard had not brought pyjamas, a toothbrush or a change of clothes or underwear with him, so I went next door to borrow a few items from my father who is the same size as Bernard. My mother was still up. Her hair was in giant rollers and she was wearing a green face mask, made of seaweed and cucumber, she said. She told me that she thought Bernard was a 'riot' and that he would liven up Christmas. She tiptoed into my father's room and gathered together some toiletries and pyjamas.

When I got home, Bernard was asleep on the sofa with Wilde's *The Happy Prince* on his chest.

Gracie's main present was a mini trampoline. When we opened the box from Toys 'R' Us we discovered that it contained eighty separate components and that it lacked the special tool with which to build the soddin' thing and which was vital to the trampoline's successful self-assembly. So the boast on the outside of the box that 'Within minutes your child will be having healthy, happy, bouncy fun!' was a lie. At one thirty in the morning, when we were practically weeping with tiredness and realized that we had connected the springs upside down, Daisy gave me a look of pure hatred and said, 'A proper man would have *realized* that the springs were on upside down,' and stomped off to bed. It was 3 a.m. by the time

I had successfully assembled the bloody bastard soddin' thing.

Tuesday 25th December
Christmas Day

Daisy and I leapt out of bed at 6.05 a.m., woken by a loud crash and a shout of pain from Bernard Hopkins. As we struggled into our dressing gowns, Daisy said, 'Six bloody o'clock! I can't face Christmas at this god-forsaken hour!'

When we went into the living room, we found Bernard trying to fit together the pendant light which had fallen from the ceiling. The light bulb had shattered and tiny shards of glass were scattered over the dark blue canvas of the trampoline (reminding me, Diary, of Van Gogh's *Starry Night*). Bernard's left leg had slipped between the canvas and the springs. He was holding a red velvet cushion in front of his genitals – otherwise, he was naked.

'Sorry, old cock,' he said. 'I got up for a jimmy riddle and couldn't resist a jump on the bouncy contraption. Must have misjudged the hellish ceiling height, hit my bonce on that craperoony Habitat light fitting.'

Daisy went to fetch the vacuum cleaner while I extricated Bernard from the springs. Once he was free he threw the cushion away and I was forced to glimpse his private parts. God, will mine look like that when I am an old man?

After I had checked his feet for broken glass, he climbed back inside his sleeping bag and was instantly asleep. Not long after all the glass had been scrupulously sucked up Gracie came bursting in and Christmas Day had officially begun.

Daisy loved her handbag and immediately transferred all the junk she carries around with her from her old bag to the new.

Disappointingly she had bought me a boxed set of *The Office* DVDs. Apparently, I had once mentioned that I sympathised with the anti-hero, David Brent. On this flimsy evidence Daisy assumed that I would be delighted to be given hours' worth of the stuff. She was wrong.

My mother bought me a CD, *The Best of Katherine Jenkins*. She had written on the gift tag: 'I know you like opera.' Diary, this is true. I do like operatic arias. But I like my opera sung by neurotic tortured women, who sound as though they are about to throw themselves off the leaning Tower of Pisa (perhaps). Ms Jenkins is pink and pretty and has a bosom like two marshmallows. I prefer my singers to be swarthy and have rather more aggressive breasts.

The turkey was too big to fit into the oven. I went out to the shed and searched for the lump hammer. When I found it, I used it to batter the turkey and break its breastbone. Then I went for treatment. My mother was wearing the gift I had bought her and said, 'I have never had such an expensive piece of jewellery. Your father always went to Ratners.'

Sally was down in the mouth. Anthony has not given her a Christmas present. Instead he has donated £100 in her name to the WPSOC (Wolves Preservation Society Of Canada). She is spending Boxing Day with her parents in Wolverhampton.

When we returned home, Daisy told me that I was banned from the kitchen. She said, 'The dinner is under control and I don't want anybody in here until it is time to serve up.'

When I went out to the wheelie bin to dump the Christmas wrapping paper and packaging, I glimpsed a corner of a box that said 'Aunt Bessie's roast potatoes'. On delving in further I found the following:

Aunt Bessie's stuffing balls
Aunt Bessie's mashed potatoes
Aunt Bessie's chipolatas and bacon wraps
Aunt Bessie's bread sauce
Aunt Bessie's buttered parsnips
Aunt Bessie's Brussels sprouts
Aunt Bessie's julienne carrots
Aunt Bessie's Christmas pudding
Aunt Bessie's custard.

Such deception! What else is she hiding from me?

I will not give her away but I am deeply disappointed in her. Christmas dinner is not the same unless the cook has sweated and panicked and slaved over a hot stove. My mother's only contribution to the meal was to provide the Mole Christmas gravy, which she concocts using a secret recipe passed down through the generations by senior Mole women.

When our guests gushed that the dinner was delicious, and my mother hugged Daisy and said it was the best Christmas dinner she had ever tasted, I looked Daisy in the eye – expecting to see her glance away – but she brazenly stared back at me and accepted the compliments. I wonder how she disguised the ping of the microwave? Was that why she had the radio on at full volume?

When the dinner had been cleared away, the Mole men washed up, as is the custom. Later, we played Leicester Monopoly. My father made a serious misjudgement regarding his property on the Clock Tower and lost all his money buying the Grand Hotel in Granby Street. Bernard kept getting the 'go to Leicester jail' card and my mother hogged all the free parking. Daisy won, but she almost certainly cheated. I did not play. I do not believe in competitive games. I was quite glad when my mother and father went home. There was not enough room in our living room to accommodate a wheelchair and a trampoline. Fell into bed at 9.30 p.m., exhausted. Lay awake wondering how to get rid of Bernard. He's homeless, jobless and penniless.

Wednesday 26th December
Boxing Day

Treatment.

Had an Estonian radiotherapist called Stefan. He told me, in perfect English, that he sends home half of his wages to his mother and his large extended family.

I said, 'Families are a nightmare, aren't they?'

Stefan said, 'I would die for my family. I have not seen my mother's face for two years.'

Ate cold turkey and baked potatoes. My father went a bit mad when he realized that Bernard was wearing his clothes. He whined, 'I've lost my independence, I'm not long for this world and now my wife is giving my bleedin' clothes away. Can't you wait until I'm dead, Pauline?'

Bernard patted my father on his back and said, 'I'd take them off, George old chap, but my own clothes are in the wash.'

My mother said, 'You're a selfish sod, George. You've got a wardrobe full of stuff you never wear. Surely you don't begrudge Bernard a change of clothes?'

My father shouted, 'I do begrudge him. He had the biggest baked potato and he got to sit next to Gracie! *I* sit next to Gracie.'

My mother shouted back, 'You're showing yourself up, George. Bernard's potato was not bigger than yours.'

Daisy jumped to her feet and shrilled, 'For Christ's

sake! Do I have to take a bloody tape measure to the potatoes now?'

But my father could not stop himself. He yelled, 'And where was the red cabbage? You know I love the stuff. It's a Boxing Day staple.'

Diary, I could not believe that my father was ruining Boxing Day with quibbling complaints about red cabbage and the size of baked potatoes. A horrible silence fell and all that could be heard was the scraping of cutlery on plates and the sound of mastication. Then there was a banging on our door. I got up with a sigh to see who it was.

It was Brett.

I looked behind him for his car but it wasn't there. I asked him how he had journeyed to the Piggeries.

He said, 'My car ran out of petrol at Leicester Forest East Services and I couldn't afford to fill it up. I've lost everything, Adrian.'

In his haste to get to his second son my father jammed his wheelchair in the kitchen doorway. Brett dropped the plastic Harrods bag that he was holding and rushed to my father. He knelt down at the side of the wheelchair and threw his arms around my father's neck.

After a while my father said, 'You'll have to let me go, son. You're choking me.'

Brett sobbed, 'I'll never let you go again, Dad. I'm going to stay by your side and devote the rest of my life to looking after you.'

My mother looked alarmed at this proclamation and said to Daisy, '*I* look after George.'

I managed to free the wheelchair and push my father

back into the kitchen. Brett was wearing one of his expensive pinstriped suits but his white shirt had a dirty collar and he was unshaven. He sat down at the kitchen table, burrowed his face in his hands and sobbed.

Bernard went behind him and said, 'Pull yourself together, lad. I'm also on *my* uppers but I'm managing to keep myself together.'

Brett lifted his head and said, 'You stupid old fart. You've obviously had nothing to lose in the first place. I've lost three prime apartments, a Lamborghini and a fucking hedge fund!'

Bernard poured himself a neat vodka and sat down.

I said, 'Bernard is a guest in my house, Brett. Apologise.'

Gracie broke the brief silence by saying, 'I had to apologise for saying Mummy was fat.'

My father said, 'You've got a bed in our house for as long as you need it, son.'

I was extremely annoyed. I had intended to ask my parents if Bernard could lodge in their spare room. Now it was to be occupied by my bankrupt half-brother.

Daisy said, 'You can't have lost everything, Brett. Not in such a short time.'

Brett (who still hadn't apologised, I noticed) said, 'The properties were mortgaged, the car was leased, and the hedge fund collapsed. The fucking banks turned me away. I lived on my credit cards for a while but the bastards closed me down.'

Gracie said, 'You mustn't swear. If you do, your tongue will fall out.'

All the smokers lit cigarettes. Only Gracie and I did

not. I was, of course, a little sorry for Brett but a tiny seed inside me was delighted at his downfall.

Daisy said, 'Brett, you've got a first from Oxford. You'll soon find another job.'

Brett said, 'The attendant in the petrol station at Leicester Forest East had a degree in astrophysics so save your platitudes, Mrs Mole.'

Rage swept over me. I said, 'How dare you call my wife platitudinous!'

Brett said, 'Do you know what the worst thing is about my crash?'

None of us knew.

He said, 'It's having to live in the fucking East Midlands amongst provincial doltheads with tight-arsed sensibilities who teach their children that swearing will cause their tongues to fall out.'

My mother shouted, 'I'm not provincial! I went to London three times last year!'

Brett said wearily, 'Any chance of some food?'

It was a stupid question. Every surface was crammed with food.

Since nobody else made an effort to assemble a plate of food for him, I got to my feet and carved some slices of turkey and then added to the plate a shrivelled baked potato and pickles. I was about to add salad when Brett said, 'No salad, I never eat salad!'

Gracie said, 'You have to eat salad. It's the law.'

Thank God, it wasn't long before my parents took Brett next door. When they'd gone, Bernard said, 'What a tosser!'

We spent the evening watching Gracie's DVD of *The Sound of Music*. Unfortunately, she insisted on singing and dancing during the musical numbers. Bernard was enchanted but Daisy and I have seen her performance many hundreds of times. By the time we went to bed we had half-eaten a family-sized tin of Roses chocolates.

Daisy has started undressing and putting on her pyjamas in the bathroom. I used to love to watch my wife undress and at least twice a week it was a prelude to our marital relations.

Had to get up many times in the night to go to the loo. By the time morning came I was exhausted and had to drag myself out of bed to go for my treatment.

Thursday 27th December

As if things weren't bad enough! Michael Flowers invited himself to lunch today. It was me who took the phone call.

Daisy said, 'You're so slow witted lately, Adrian. Why didn't you tell him a lie and put him off? Or you could have given the phone to me. I'm a brilliant liar, almost a professional.'

I was scandalised. I said, 'That's nothing to brag about, Daisy, truth is the greatest virtue. Without truth we are nothing but farmyard animals.'

Daisy turned on me and said, with a smile, 'So what's the truth about you and Pandora fucking Braithwaite, eh, truth boy?'

This was so unexpected that I was flummoxed for a while. Eventually I stammered, 'We are just good friends.'

Daisy said, 'That's not what you wrote in your Boxing Day text to her.'

She went to her green bag on the table and took out her notebook. She rifled through the pages and then pointed to:

Very disappointed not 2cU at Xmas.

I said, 'She was my first love, Daisy. One never properly gets over one's first.'

Daisy said, 'Oh, one can. My first love was a dodgem car attendant at the fair. He had lank black hair and spider tattoos across both sets of knuckles. I got over him the day the fair left our village.'

Friday 28th December

Nine of us sat down to lunch yesterday, plus one child. God knows how – there are only four chairs at the kitchen table. We had to use two garden chairs, the plastic stool from the bathroom, a milk crate from the shed and bring Gracie's old highchair down from the attic. We were all at different heights. A couple of us could barely see over the table. We ate Daisy's traditional curried turkey, basmati rice and the delicious chapattis that Parvez's wife has taught Daisy how to cook. To cater for her father, Daisy made a vegetarian curry using all the squashy vegetables at the bottom of the fridge.

NOTE TO SELF. Why does our fridge do the opposite to every other fridge I have known? I.e. it does not keep the food fresh.

Flowers turned up with Daisy's sister Marigold and Brain-box Henderson, her husband, who presented everybody but Brett and Bernard with a Star Trek mug. Marigold said to Brett, 'We didn't know you'd be here. We thought you'd be in the Sandy Lane Hotel in Barbados like you are every Christmas.'

I said, 'Brett has had a change of fortune.'

Bernard said, 'I don't mind not having a mug. I have boycotted American goods since the McCarthy trials.'

Brett, sitting on the milk crate, looked up at us all and said, 'Isn't anybody going to open the wine?'

Michael Flowers had brought four bottles of his quince and plum wine. I did not drink the filthy stuff but everybody else seemed to enjoy it, or at least endure it. Before the food was served, Flowers handed out Christmas crackers he had made himself. To my eye they were pathetic, made of handmade paper with bits of bark in it, and none of them had a satisfactory snap. The small presents inside were tiny biscuits covered in unrecognisable seeds. There were no corny jokes either. Instead there were strips of paper with quotations from Nelson Mandela, Kant and Nigel Farage of UKIP. It was thoughtful of Flowers to have made the party hats. But there was something dispiriting about hats made out of the financial pages of the *Independent*. My mother's hat read: 'NORTHERN ROCK: BROWN STEPS IN.'

My father's newsprint was upside down but I managed to make out what it said: 'AVERAGE BRITON IN DEBT FOR £12,700 PLUS MORTGAGE.'

I took my own hat off and read: 'UNEMPLOYMENT TWO AND A HALF MILLION.'

My mother said, looking at Daisy's paper hat, 'What is a sub-prime mortgage?'

Brett looked up at my mother and said, 'It's a mortgage given to morons who can't afford to pay it.'

'We can't afford to pay ours,' said my mother.

Michael Flowers said, 'Personally, I'm glad that capitalism is on the slide. It means we can withdraw from Europe and live a much simpler life. I saw this coming and turned my investments into cash,' he dropped his voice, 'which I don't mind telling you I keep under my mattress. Anybody with money in a British bank is a fool and deserves to lose it.'

Brett wriggled on his milk crate and said, 'You're talking out of your arse, you stupid bearded tosspot.'

My father, who hates Michael Flowers almost as much as I do, said, 'Now then, Brett, "tosspot" is going a bit too far.'

Daisy had overdone the chillis in the curry and before long our eyes and noses were streaming, but at least it shut everybody up – apart from Gracie, who had declined the curry and opted for spaghetti hoops and a mince pie. She took advantage of our silence to sing some of the more monotonous songs she had learnt at school. Each time one of us stopped smiling and looking at her she banged on the table with her fork and spoon and shouted, 'Pay attention!' – an expression she must have picked up from her teacher.

Diary, I am glad that Christmas is now officially over.

Saturday 29th December

The bookshop closes today.

Didn't have radiotherapy. Sally sent me for an ultrasound and blood tests. When I returned to the radiotherapy department, I asked Sally if she had enjoyed her Christmas in Wolverhampton.

She said that she had left her parents' house on Christmas Day night because she could not bear the way her father said 'lovely jubbly' after every mouthful of food. I asked her when my radiotherapy would continue. She said, 'It depends what your scan and PSA results are.'

Went to the shop. Mr Carlton-Hayes and Leslie were already there. They were both wearing white gloves. Leslie was taking out the antiquarian books from the glass-fronted cabinet and handing them to Mr Carlton-Hayes in his wheelchair. Mr C-H was dusting them with a dry shaving brush and wrapping them in tissue before placing them inside a fireproofed cardboard box. I went into the back room and made some coffee. I could not bear to see the bookshop being dismantled of its stock.

Daisy had urged me to talk to Mr Carlton-Hayes about my redundancy pay but I could not bring myself to do so.

Bernard turned up at 10 a.m. and soon got stuck into sorting the wheat from the chaff. I admired his single-mindedness. I would have dithered over which books to keep and which books to give away. Bernard said, 'It's a doddle, old cock. Anything with a gun, a cat or a swastika on the front is chaff, as is a large-breasted girl with a castle in the background.'

My work rate was very slow. I kept finding books that I had been meaning to read, as did Mr Carlton-Hayes. Leslie had to speak sharply to him several times when he noticed that he had become engrossed in a book. At four o'clock a market trader came to collect the chaff. Mr Carlton-Hayes let the lot go for £275. By five o'clock I was exhausted and had to lie down on the sofa. At five thirty Leslie shook me awake and said that he was taking Mr Carlton-Hayes home. It was too late to mention my redundancy pay. When they had gone, I rang my mother and asked her for a lift. As I was speaking, I noticed that my voice had a slight echo from the empty shelves.

My mother parked illegally outside the shop. When she came in, she said, 'It looks bigger with most of the books gone.' She put her arm around my shoulders and said, 'You don't look well.'

I admitted that I was feeling quite poorly. She took the keys from me, locked up and turned the lights off.

We looked back through the shop window at the almost-empty shelves. I said, 'They're turning it into a Tesco's.'

She said encouragingly, 'If you play your cards right you could get a managerial job. You'd make a good Tesco's manager.'

I did not have the strength or inclination to argue with her. The stress of meeting Tesco's daily targets would surely kill me. Why didn't she understand that?

My own mother does not know me at all.

Visits to loo: thirteen.

Sunday 30th December

I normally feel guilty if I'm in bed past eight thirty in the morning but today I didn't care. At 2 p.m. I had a lightly boiled egg and some bread and butter soldiers, then I got up and watched *Antiques Roadshow* in my pyjamas.

My mother came round to complain that Brett has been harassing them for money. He says that all he needs is 'a few K' so that he can trade. He has already blackmailed them into installing a Sky dish so that he can follow the money markets.

My mother said, 'He keeps whining that your father wasn't "there for him" when he was growing up. He says that you were always his favourite.'

'Me?' I said.

'Yes,' my mother sighed, 'he said that George was always boasting about your achievements. Your father said, "You're wrong there, Brett, you could fit Adrian's achievements on the back of a small matchbox." I defended you. I informed him that you'd achieved a lot in your life – you've been married twice and fathered three children, and have had countless letters from the BBC.'

I said, 'Rejection letters.'

My mother said, 'It's still a letter.'

Monday 31st December

I lost count of how many times I had to get up in the night to urinate. Each time I dragged myself out of bed and stood in front of the lavatory I prayed that it wouldn't hurt, but each time it seemed to get more painful, a horrible niggling stinging pain. What a way to start the New Year – and we are meant to go to Fairfax Hall to see it in. It is almost a certainty that when Big Ben strikes twelve I will be in one of Fairfax-Lycett's many lavatories.

I wore my best navy suit, white shirt and the tie with the elephant design. Daisy was wearing a black dress with a plunging neckline that I had not seen before. It looked expensive but Daisy said, 'This old thing? I got it on eBay. It's vintage Versace. I got it for virtually nothing.'

Diary, can this be true?

I rang Dougie Horsefield and booked him for eight o'clock. He said, 'I'll have to charge you triple the fare. It's New Year's Eve, you know.'

Diary, I am sick of people telling me things that I already know.

I said, 'Dougie, do you honestly believe that I don't know that it is New Year's Eve? Do you sincerely think that this significant date has passed me by?'

When he found out that we were going to Fairfax Hall, he moaned, 'It's only a bleedin' mile. Can't you walk it? It's hardly worth me turning my engine on.'

When I put the phone down, I said to Daisy, 'I've a good mind to cancel him and ask my mother for a lift.'

She said, 'Your mother's been drinking all day, and you're not insured to drive her car – and nor am I, she made sure of that.'

Dougie turned up at 8.35 and he had Tony and Wendy Wellbeck sitting in the back. I was annoyed that we had to share the car and make conversation. I like to have a period of silence before I enter a social situation. The Wellbecks looked as though they had dressed themselves from the 'occasion wear' section of TK Maxx. She was in an orange sequined top, he in an acrylic white dinner jacket and bow tie. Daisy had failed to tell me that the dress code was 'black tie' so I started the evening at a considerable disadvantage. Horsefield charged us £6 a head!

When I remonstrated with him, Tony Wellbeck said, 'It *is* New Year's Eve, Mr Mole.'

I paid up and we got out of the car.

Horsefield said, 'Enjoy your party. Think about me driving through the night with a load of drunks spewing up in the back.'

The exterior of the hall was lit with flaming sconces. They cast dancing light on the ivy-clad walls.

As we climbed the steps towards the imposing front entrance, I said to Daisy, 'I hope they're insured, if they're not careful that ivy will catch fire and they'll have a serious conflagration on their hands.'

Hugo Fairfax-Lycett was waiting in the cavernous entrance hall to greet his guests. A huge log was burning in the black marble fireplace.

He kissed Daisy on both cheeks and said, 'Mrs Mole, you look absolutely stunning.'

I didn't like the way he said 'Mrs Mole'. It was as if he and Daisy were sharing a private joke. A waitress in a black and white uniform offered us glasses of pink champagne from a silver tray. A glance around the hall confirmed that I *was* the only male present not wearing a dinner jacket.

Fairfax-Lycett said, looking at my suit, 'Daisy mentioned you were a bit of a non-conformist. I must say I admire a chap who is not afraid to show that he is anti-establishment. I'm afraid I am an entirely establishment figure.'

Daisy laughed and said, 'Hugo, you have been known to cut loose.'

Daisy was attracting many admiring glances. I have to admit, Diary, that my wife looked magnificent. I knew she felt triumphant that, by wearing Spanx magic knickers, she had been able to squeeze into her size 14 eBay dress. After a few more minutes of banter with Fairfax-Lycett, Daisy took me on a tour of the house, throwing doors open and switching on lights as though she was the chatelaine. She showed me the office she shares on the first floor with Fairfax-Lycett. Their desks were very close together. She sat in her black office chair and swung round. She had a photograph on her desk of my parents, me, Gracie and herself. It had been taken in the garden of The Bear the summer before last. I was wearing baggy shorts and the brown sandals that Daisy has since thrown away in the rubbish. The others were laughing but I had my face in a grimace and my eyes were closed against the sun.

I said, 'So what is it you do in here all day?'

She said, 'I project manage the renovation and restoration of the hall. I plan events, I act as Hugo's PA, I pay the staff, and at the moment I am trying to source secure fencing for the safari park and buy a pair of giraffes.'

I asked her how much giraffes cost.

She said, 'In the States a young giraffe can be had for twenty-five thousand dollars, but keep it to yourself. Hugo doesn't want the villagers to know his plans yet. He doesn't want them getting up a petition – not until we've been granted planning permission.'

I said, 'He'll never get planning permission for a safari park. They forced the church to stop ringing the bells because of the noise. They won't stand for the row of lions roaring, elephants trumpeting and giraffes ... making whatever noise giraffes make. And there was Pamper Yourself, they had to pull down the shed at the back where they had the tanning machine.'

When we got downstairs, Daisy took on the role of hostess, ushering people into the dining room for the buffet. I got stuck with the Wellbecks, who told me in minuscule detail about their last holiday in Wales. Eventually I managed to extricate myself and went next door to the drawing room to listen to the music of the string quartet and watch the dancers as they tried to dance to Handel's *Where'er You Walk*.

At ten o'clock carloads of Fairfax-Lycett's friends arrived from London. I was surprised to see that Daisy knew some of them. She was soon in the middle of a group and they appeared to be hanging on her every word. Having nothing to contribute to the conversation I sidled out and went into the library, where I spent a pleasant hour looking through the books.

Then the disco started with the opening chords of 'Brown Sugar'. This was followed by a loud cheer, and on opening the library door I saw people coming from all parts of the house to cram into the large drawing room to dance to the Rolling Stones.

A memory of my father dancing at my first wedding came to mind and brought a tear to my eye. He danced so violently to 'Brown Sugar' that he dislocated his back and had to be taken home strapped to a door. When I next saw Daisy, she was in the middle of the dance floor with Fairfax-Lycett dancing to 'I Will Survive'. However, such was the collective vocal force of the women singing along with Gloria Gaynor that the males soon left the dance floor – apart from a few obviously gay men – and stood around drinking and watching. The DJ (Craig Puddleton from the garage) shouted into the microphone, 'C'mon, girls! Let the bastards have it!'

Then – to my astonishment, because I knew there had been no rehearsal – the women made eye contact with the men and shouted, 'I DON'T WANT YOU ANY MORE!'

After the song ended, there was a lot of female solidarity going on, hugging and kissing each other. Even Wendy Wellbeck raised a fist to her husband. A few minutes later, when I was coming out of the downstairs cloakroom, I heard a car screeching to a halt on the gravel. I went to the entrance and saw Pandora throwing her keys to a waiter and heard her say, 'Park it for me somewhere, would you, darling?' She walked in wearing a tight red dress with diamanté straps. Her hair was at least three times its usual size. She looked very beautiful indeed.

I said, 'What have you done to your hair?'

She said, 'It's called *hairdressing*, Adrian. What are you doing here? Hobnobbing with the gentry?'

I said, 'Daisy is Fairfax-Lycett's personal assistant.'

Pandora looked around at the other guests and drawled, 'Are you wearing that suit as a sort of protest?'

We went and stood in the doorway of the drawing room.

She looked across at Daisy and said, 'Are her breasts *meant* to be on the outside of her dress?' Then she turned her attention back to me and asked, 'So how goes the big C?'

Before I could answer, a small fat man with an

aggrieved face came up to Pandora and said, 'They've still not mended that pothole in Cossington Lane. You said you would write to the Council.'

Pandora purred, 'Those dreadful council people. I will bring it to the attention of the Minister for Roadworks and Potholes as soon as parliament reconvenes.'

A woman in a green sequined top gushed, 'I saw you on *Question Time*, Miss Braithwaite. You gave that Norman Tebbit a run for his money.'

Pandora gushed back, 'Oh, Norman is a big pussycat.'

When the woman had gone, Pandora said, 'I haven't been on *Question Time* for over a year. She's confusing me with somebody else.'

I said, 'How could anybody confuse you? There is nobody else remotely like you in the whole world.'

Craig Puddleton bellowed, 'Make sure you've got a drink. It's nearly midnight.'

I looked at my watch. It was 11.55 p.m. I excused myself to Pandora and hurried to the downstairs lavatory. Finding a queue I then ran upstairs to the lavatory next to Daisy's office. However, the door was locked and so I ran down endless corridors until I could hardly hear the disco music from downstairs. By now my need was urgent and I grew increasingly desperate to find a lavatory. I began opening doors and switching lights on, but none of the bedrooms were en suite. I ran up a further flight of stairs and eventually came to a series of smaller rooms, obviously servants' quarters. In one of these I found a washbasin and, Diary, though I am loath to confess it, I relieved myself in the said receptacle. I had almost finished when I heard the first strike of the church bell. It took another three strikes before I *was* finished. I ran out of the room and down the stairs, tugging my zip up as I went. I had reached the top of the last flight of stairs when I heard the twelfth bong and the cheers that followed. As I was crossing the hall to go into the drawing room to find Daisy, one of the waiters said, 'Excuse me, sir, but your shirt is poking out of your flies.'

By the time I had jiggled my zip and released my shirt and tucked myself in, I was too late to join the circle for 'Auld Lang Syne'.

Later, when I began to tell Daisy what had happened, she said, 'Don't tell me any more. I hate lavatorial jokes.'

At 12.30 my father rang me on my mobile and asked me to return home. He said, 'Your mother is out cold, Brett is wandering about outside in his shirtsleeves, pissed as a newt, the bloody church bells woke Gracie up, and she is asking me for cheese on toast.' He whined, 'She knows I can't reach the grill, you'll have to come home.'

I explained that Dougie Horsefield was not due to pick us up until 2.30 a.m, and told him to order Gracie back to bed.

He said, 'You know I'm scared of Gracie.'

I said, 'Gracie is a little girl. Pull yourself together.'

He said, 'That vein in my neck is throbbing. I think I'm about to have another stroke.'

I disconnected the call and immediately rang Dougie Horsefield.

He said, 'Hello,' and then I heard him yell to one of his passengers, 'Puke on my upholstery and you'll pay a twenty-quid penalty.' When he said, 'Ugh! You dirty bastard!' I switched my phone off, told Daisy I was leaving and left.

As I was crunching down the gravel drive, shivering in a bitter wind, Pandora ran after me, shouting, 'Where are you going?'

I explained my domestic problem. She said, to my amazement, that she would walk home with me because she couldn't stand being harangued by her constituents.

She said, 'They're bad enough when I see them in my constituency office, but when they're half pissed they're impossible.'

I said, 'You'll freeze to death in that dress.'

She said, 'Then we'll have to run to keep warm, won't we?'

She took my hand and what with the exhilaration of her company and the way she urged me on, we started to run. How she did it in high heels and how I did it in my state of health, I don't know.

It didn't take long. As we turned from the lane and jogged up the drive to the Piggeries, it started to rain and we came across Brett. He was trying to find the front door of his 'office', and seemed to be under the impression that he was in Canary Wharf. We dragged him through the house and put him to bed. Thank God, Gracie had gone back to sleep. I placed her in her princess bed, then came back and helped my father retire for the night. He took his teeth out and asked me to clean them, but I refused.

*

When we went next door, Pandora ordered me to put some dry clothes on. While I was changing into my pyjamas and dressing gown she cooked bacon and eggs and made a pot of coffee.

When we were eating, she said, 'You've got to take better care of yourself, Aidy. You have to learn how to be selfish, like me.'

We sat in the kitchen talking and waiting for Daisy to come home, until a lone bird started to sing. Eventually I made a bed up for Pandora in Gracie's room. I looked in on Bernard. He was sleeping soundly on the sofa with a copy of Anthony Powell's *Casanova's Chinese Restaurant* over his face. Before I went to bed I stood over the lavatory and tried to pee. After two long minutes I had only succeeded in voiding an acorn cup's worth, but within only a short time I was back. I don't know at what time I finally fell asleep but quite a lot of birds were singing and Daisy was still not home.

2008

Tuesday 1st January 2008

Woke up to find a text on my mobile.

**Taxi did not come. Forced to stay here.
Back soon Daisy X.**

I had just digested this news when Pandora came in wearing Daisy's dressing gown. She had brought me a cup of tea.

I showed her Daisy's text.

Pandora said, 'It's a plausible excuse, I suppose.' She went to fetch her own tea and then sat down on my side of the bed and said, 'Is your marriage in trouble, Aidy?'

I told her that Daisy seemed a lot happier recently, since she'd gone back to work.

Pandora raised an eyebrow and said, 'She certainly looks quite beautiful lately. She's lost weight and she has a new wardrobe. Does she work odd hours?'

I said, 'They work late a few times a week.'

Pandora sighed and said, 'You can't see the rhinoceros in the room, can you?'

I corrected her, saying, 'You mean *elephant* in the room.'

She said, 'I cannot bloody bear misquotations. The quote was taken from Ionesco's play *Rhinoceros*, which is an absurdist allegory of the rise of Nazism in Germany!'

What a woman she is, Diary!

She said, 'One last question. Is she buying matching bras and knickers?'

I said, 'Yes. Why?'

Pandora said, 'Ha! Thought so!' She got up and went out of the room.

The next time I saw Pandora she was wearing her clothes of the previous night and she was allowing Gracie to brush her long heavy hair.

Gracie said, 'You've got hair like a princess.'

Pandora said, 'Not Princess Anne, I hope.'

Bernard Hopkins laughed and said, 'I met Her Royal Highness at a book do in 2002. She has a remarkably equine face. I was tempted to give her a lump of sugar.'

When I started to prepare breakfast, Pandora ordered me to sit down and said, 'You look like shit, Aidy. Why don't you go back to bed?'

I sat down but didn't go to bed. I wanted to look at her loveliness and be in her company.

Wednesday 2nd January

Daisy came back at lunchtime yesterday. Hugo Fairfax-Lycett gave her a lift. He didn't come in and Daisy said that he had to supervise the clean-up of the hall. She said, 'You wouldn't believe how some of the partygoers behaved. Some dirty bastard, it could only have been a man, peed into a blocked-up sink in one of the bedrooms!'

I changed the subject and discussed with Daisy what we were going to do with the carcass of the turkey. 'Shouldn't it be thrown away?'

Daisy said, 'Take it into the spinney and leave it for the foxes.'

I said, 'Isn't Fairfax-Lycett a fox-hunter? Aren't you showing divided loyalties?'

She said, 'It's the one thing I don't like about him.'

Diary, *one thing*.

Brett came round this morning with my father.

I said, 'Are you growing a beard?'

He said, 'No, I can't be bothered to shave. There is a difference.'

He sat at the kitchen table next to Bernard, who had just informed us from the pages of the *Independent* that we were heading for a depression to rival that of the thirties.

Brett said, 'And oil's risen to a hundred dollars a barrel, which is unprecedented.'

I said, 'Why should you care? You haven't got a car any more.'

He said, 'Yes, but I will make another fortune. That's the difference between us, Adrian. You've never made any money and you never will – you're a provincial loser!'

My father said, 'Come on now, lads, shake hands and make up.'

I would have shaken Brett's hand for my father's sake, but Brett slammed out of the front door and ran down the drive.

My father watched him through the window. 'Look at him run!' he said admiringly. 'He's like a young gazelle.'

Bernard said, 'My father walked from Jarrow to London to bring the government's attention to the fact that we were starving up north. I can remember my mother boiling a marrowbone with a few carrots and a leek for Sunday dinner.'

I said, 'Bernard, I thought you came from a middle-class family. Didn't you go to Cambridge?'

He said, 'I was a scholarship boy. It broke my father's heart. He wanted me to go down the mines.'

Thursday 3rd January

Daisy has gone back to work. Before she left, I asked her when she would be paid, whether she was on an hourly rate, what her hours were and was she paid overtime? I advised her to insist on a contract of employment.

She said, 'Why do you have to drain the fun out of *everything*, Adrian?'

I said, 'I don't want that Hugo Fairfax-Lycett exploiting you, Daisy.'

She said bafflingly, 'If anybody exploits anybody, it will be me exploiting him.'

I have got nothing to do until my next hospital

appointment. At some time I will have to go to the storage place where the contents of the bookshop are kept in a container, but I am not up to it and I don't want Bernard to go without me.

In the afternoon Glenn and Finley-Rose came round to show us Finley's engagement ring – a surprisingly chunky white gold band with a large white stone that flashed under the kitchen light. They had spent Christmas and New Year in Scotland with Finley's grandparents.

Glenn said, 'I din't like to tell you before, Dad, but I've gotta go back to Afghanistan at the end of the week. I know you worry, I din't want to spoil your Christmas.'

I took Glenn into the living room under the pretext of showing him Gracie's trampoline. After closing the door, I said, 'A few words of advice from a twice-married man. Women don't actually say what they want you to do. For example, if they want you to empty the dish-washer, they might say, "I think the dishwasher has finished its programme." Do not say, "Really?" Or they might say, "My back hurts every time I bend over to empty the dishwasher." Do not say, "Poor you." And when a woman sighs and you ask her what is wrong and she says, "Nothing," do not believe her – there is always something wrong and you must stick at it until you find out what it is.'

Glenn nodded and said, 'Now we're talkin' man to man, Dad . . . this prostrate. 'Ave I got one?'

I said, 'Of course, all men have one.'

Glenn asked 'What's it there for, Dad?'

I took a deep breath, my knowledge about the form

and function of the prostate is on the sketchy side. I said, 'It's a gland situated near to the bladder and its job is to alkalinise semen and let some semen out now and again.'

Glenn said, 'You've lost me already, Dad.'

I said, 'The *prostate* is like the Bank of England, but instead of it having money in it, it has sperm, OK?'

Glenn blushed. 'OK.'

For a soldier, he is incredibly prudish. Then he said, 'So *that's* why they call it a sperm bank. I always wondered.'

I went next door to ask my parents to join us for a celebration of Glenn's engagement. I found them both asleep, my father in his wheelchair and my mother in the armchair next to the fire. They both looked old and frail, and I wondered what it will be like to be without them when they are gone. Brett was in the spare room, lying in his bed smoking a cigarette, in his vest and boxer shorts.

I said, 'Isn't it time you got dressed?'

He said, 'I've got nothing to wear. All my shirts are in the bin.'

The wastebasket next to his bedside table was over-flowing with pure white cotton shirts. I pulled them out and counted them. There were ten. I said, 'You can't throw these away, all they need is a hot wash.'

He said, 'Nobody washes shirts on the trading floor. We buy them in packs of ten and chuck them at the end of the day.'

I took the shirts and put them in my mother's washing machine, turned the dial to sixty, placed a tablet of Ariel in the soap dispenser and turned the machine on. When

I went back to Brett's bedroom, I asked him if he had any plans.

'I can't stay here for long,' he said, 'they haven't even got Bloomberg.'

Monday 7th January

Appointment with Dr Rubik.

She was wearing a bright red cardigan. When I complimented her on it, she told me her husband had bought it for her for Christmas, although, she said, 'I don't know why – he knows I only ever wear black, grey or white.' She told me that she had received my latest blood results from the lab, and that my PSA was over ten, 'Which is a little worrying,' she added.

I felt the blood from the rest of my body collect in my feet. 'So I'm back where I started,' I said.

'It's certainly a setback,' she replied, 'but remember, we have a little while to wait yet for the optimum results. And it's not uncommon – quite a high percentage of men with prostate cancer need several treatments before we can give the all-clear.'

I told her about my latest symptoms, and she nodded and said, 'Yes, that's quite normal,' and began to go through the various 'roads we can go down'.

I thought, 'No, it's not a road *we* can go down, Dr Rubik, it's a lonely road that I will be going down alone. You are merely waving to me from the safety of the pavement.'

When I left, I realised that I had not taken in what she

had said about treatment options. I went down the corridor to see Sally in Radiotherapy, but the light was on outside her door, signifying that she was delivering deadly rays to another poor sod. Eventually I went into the waiting room to meet up with my mother. She asked me how I'd got on. I made a non-committal noise in my throat and forced a smile. I didn't want to tell her my bad news, not until she'd driven us safely home.

When she pulled up outside the Piggeries, I broke the news to her that the radiotherapy had not cured my cancer. She headbutted the steering wheel, sounding the horn. My father opened their front door and wheeled himself down the ramp. I got out of the car and he said, 'What's up with your mother?'

I told him about my appointment with Dr Rubik.

He said, 'Your poor mother. Help her out of the car, Aidy.' Then he started to beat his thighs with his fists and shouted, 'You should sue the bloody National Health Service. They've obviously done a crap job.'

To prevent further self-flagellation from my parents I went into my house and hoped that they would not follow me. I had wanted to have a few quiet moments to think and to ring Daisy, but my parents insisted on staying to keep me company.

My father asked, 'Do they do prostrate transplants? Cos if they do, you can have mine, kid.'

My mother sniffed, 'You should have tried that crystal next to your groin. It wouldn't have done any harm, and it might have helped.'

Eventually I persuaded them to go home and I rang Daisy.

She answered immediately and said, 'Adrian! What did she say?'

I told her that my cancer 'was not quite cured'.

She said, 'What do you mean "not quite cured"? That's like saying I'm not quite pregnant. You're either cured or you're not.'

I said, 'Not.'

I heard her say to Fairfax-Lycett, 'Hugo, I have to go home.'

I heard him say, 'Can't we just finish . . .'

She shouted, 'No, I have to go home.'

He gave her a lift in his Land Rover. I noticed him crawling up the drive, avoiding the potholes with exaggerated care. I thought, perhaps unreasonably, that he was comparing our drive to his, which has its gravel raked every morning. When he had stopped his four-by-four, he got out and opened Daisy's door. They exchanged a few words and he put his hand on her shoulder before Daisy ran in and threw herself into my arms.

I have spent happier afternoons. We tried to cheer ourselves up by lighting a fire in the living room using Zip firelighters and kindling. Daisy went outside and brought in some logs, but they were damp and the fire soon went out. We walked together to pick Gracie up from school. I noticed that we both averted our eyes from the graveyard opposite.

*

Gracie talked non-stop on the way home about snow-flakes. She told us there are millions and millions and millions of flakes and not one of them is exactly the same. Watched television after dinner but didn't see or hear anything. Went to bed early. Daisy joined me and we lay in each other's arms until we went to sleep.

Thursday 14th February
Valentine's Day

I should have made more of an effort with Daisy's Valentine's Day present. I am unable to get to the shops independently lately, so asked my mother to choose something for me from the city centre. She came back with a bag of toiletries that she had bought from a stall in the covered market. When she handed it to me, she said, 'It's Chanel, but I got it for seven pounds ninety-nine.' There was a block of pink soap so pungent that it made your eyes water before the cellophane wrapping was taken off. There was a nailbrush for a dwarf, a moisturising cream that wouldn't rub into the skin, and an exfoliating pad so harsh it could have scrubbed down an industrial turbine. My mother had obviously been duped by a crooked market trader – on closer examination I saw that 'Chanell' was spelt with two thin 'l's.

When I handed Daisy the Chanell gift set, she was polite and said thank you. But later, when she was in the bedroom on the phone to Nigel, I overheard her say, 'It's as fake as our marriage at the moment.' She gave me an earthenware mug with a heart on it and a card featuring a black Labrador sitting by the side of an armchair at his master's feet. Inside she had written 'Love as Ever, Daisy'. My card to her had been made by Gracie. It showed me and Daisy at our wedding. I only came up to knee height on my bride – is that how Gracie sees our relationship?

Friday 15th February

Went out to the bin after lunch to dispose of non-recyclable food packaging and found a family of foxes gorging on yesterday's chicken bones. How did they drag the carcass out of the bin?

The largest fox, the father presumably, gave me a contemptuous look and then carried on eating. How dare he? Are these wild creatures no longer afraid of us humans? I shouted, 'Boo!' and clapped my hands together, but the ginger beast smiled and carried on eating. The mother and two cubs strolled a few yards away, then sat down and proceeded to groom each other.

I shouted, 'Clear off!' and clattered the lid of the wheelie bin down, hoping to startle them into flight, but all four remained where they were. Eventually I got cold and went inside.

Brett had been watching me through our front-room window and said as I went into the living room, 'You should have taken a spade to their filthy verminous heads.'

Bernard looked up from his book and said, 'You're a complete bastard, aren't you, Brett? Why don't you toddle off next door?'

Brett said, 'This is my brother's house, you stupid old fart. I have more of a right to be here than you, you ligging old bastard.'

I should have said something to Brett but, quite frankly, Diary, I do not have the energy for any more confrontations. I went into the bedroom and lay down on the unmade bed.

Saturday 16th February

My mother and father came round to ask if they could do any shopping for us. While I compiled a list my mother carried on with the argument she'd been having with my father earlier.

She said, 'George, promise me you won't give in and lend Brett that money.'

My father said, 'It's hard to deny the boy a chance and it's not doing anything, is it? You have to speculate to accumulate, Pauline. Who dares wins, remember.'

I said, 'Dad, if you've got some money in the house, Brett will sniff it out.'

My mother looked worried and said, 'Adrian's right, George. It's not safe where it is.'

Later that night she came round carrying a giant tin of Heinz beans. She gave me the tin and tapped the side of her nose, saying, 'This is a very, very *valuable* tin of beans. Do you get what I'm saying? These beans are in a very *rich* juice. They will be a great *asset* on your pantry shelf.'

Before she could make any more clumsy financial analogies, I took the tin from her and put it on the tinned food shelf.

Wednesday 27th February

Diary, you have been a cruel mistress. I am enslaved by you. But it is increasingly difficult to find sufficient energy to report to you on a daily basis since I started chemotherapy. I have been subsumed by my illness and its treatment.

Wednesday 5th March

Went to see the NHS wig supplier today at the hospital. Daisy drove us there in the Mazda. (My mother still refuses to put us on her insurance, so we have been forced to buy our own extortionate policy.) She said, 'You can't be trusted to buy underwear for yourself, let alone a wig.'

The wig bloke was called Malcolm Daltrey. I asked him if he was related to Roger Daltrey, the singer in The Who. He looked at me in a puzzled way and said, 'No.'

Diary, why do I feel the need to make conversation with health professionals? Is it because I hate being a patient and need to reassert my status?

He examined my scalp and said disapprovingly, 'You should have come to see me weeks ago *before* your hair started to fall out.'

Daltrey's hair looked suspiciously like a wig to me. It resembled a piece of roadkill – a stoat, perhaps.

I asked, 'Did you make the wig you are wearing yourself?'

He said huffily, 'I'm not wearing a wig. This is my own hair.' He measured my head and asked, 'Do you have any preferences? Colour? Shape? Style? Length? Curly? Straight?'

I said, 'Since I started chemotherapy, I've been unable to make a decision about anything.'

Daisy said, trying to be helpful no doubt, 'Now is your chance to have the hair you've always wanted, Aidy.'

Daltrey said, 'Do you want to try a few on?'

The first wig I tried on was black and parted to one side and made me look like Gok Wan. The second was blond and curly.

Daisy said, 'Take it off, you look like Harpo Marx.'

The third was a mousy short-back-and-sides apology for a wig.

Daltrey said, 'Well, that's your basic Anglo-Saxons. Do you want to look at the wigs for "persons of colour"?'

I said, 'I might as well, while I'm here.'

After inspecting a black wig with tight curls and something he called an 'oriental standard', Daltrey said, 'We can mix and match colour and length but we are restricted by NHS guidelines.'

I said, 'Do you do a Boris Johnson? I think I might suit that.'

Malcolm Daltrey said, 'You're asking the impossible, Mr Mole. If it's a celebrity intellectual style you're after, you may have to go private.'

I resented him suggesting that Daisy and I were so impoverished that we could not afford a private wig so we left without choosing one.

When we got outside, Daisy said, 'Aidy, why don't we go and see Lawrence at Pamper Yourself? He'll know where we can go for advice.'

We drove back to Mangold Parva and parked outside the salon. Lawrence was lounging in a chair in front of a mirror reading *Vogue*. Mrs Lewis-Masters was underneath a drying hood, her head was covered in huge rollers the size of sewage pipes. She was reading *Country Life*. She raised an eyebrow in greeting.

Daisy and Lawrence fell on to each other's necks and Lawrence said, 'Where have you *been*, Daisy?'

Daisy said, 'I've been washing and trimming it myself, at home.'

Lawrence threw his sinewy arms back in exaggerated alarm. 'You're a *bad* girl! I know you're a bit short of the spondulicks at the moment but hair always, *always* comes first!'

Daisy explained why we were there.

Lawrence said, 'I'd heard that you were doing chemo.' He sat me in the chair he'd just vacated, stood behind me and looked at my reflection in the mirror. He picked up odd clumps of my remaining hair and said, 'You could go the whole hog and let me shave these bits off. They're not doing much, are they? They're just hanging around on your head.'

319

Daisy said, 'I like a shaved head.'

I was reluctant to lose the little hair I had left but Daisy said, 'You're losing handfuls of it every day in the shower, Aidy. If the pipes clog up, we'll be having to pay a plumber to unblock them.'

While I equivocated Lawrence brought Mrs Lewis-Masters to the next chair and began to take out her rollers.

She said, 'The men of the desert regarded baldness as being a sign of wisdom and sexual potency.'

I said, 'All right, Lawrence, shave it off.'

While Lawrence blow-dried Mrs Lewis-Masters' hair, I glanced through her discarded *Country Life* and was startled to see Daisy's happy smiling face staring out at me on a half-page devoted to a photographic account of the Belvoir Hunt Ball. She was arm in arm with 'The Honourable Hugo Fairfax-Lycett'. Other large-toothed members of the hunt were holding champagne glasses aloft. One would have thought that they were congratulating Daisy and Hugo on their engagement. I showed the page to Daisy. She blurted out, 'I did tell you about that, Aidy – remember?'

I said, 'I remember it well. I was in hospital overnight after having a very unpleasant, painful biopsy.'

She lowered her voice and said, 'Hugo had nobody to go with. He'd been let down at the last minute.'

I said, 'I didn't mind you *going*, Daisy. But did you have to look quite so *happy*? You told me that you had a miserable time having to listen to a "load of tossers" bragging about how they had tortured several helpless foxes.'

When Mrs Lewis-Masters' hair had been teased into

her usual helmet style, Lawrence left her with his junior (who I remember Daisy told me had to be taught how to use a sweeping brush) and turned to me. 'So,' he said, 'I'll shave your head and I've got some fabuloso Andre Agassi products that will keep that scalp gleaming.'

It took only a few minutes to shave and moisturise my head. I stared at my reflection. My skull shone under the spotlights and my glasses looked very prominent.

Daisy said, 'It'll look better when it's had a bit of sun.'

Lawrence only charged me £5 for the head shave, but by the time I'd bought Agassi moisturizer, toner and serum it cost me the best part of £40. I didn't give him a tip.

When we got home, my mother said that she had always liked bald men ever since she had seen Yul Brynner dancing around a ballroom with Deborah Kerr in *The King and I.*

My father laughed and said, 'By Christ! You look like a billiard ball on legs. If I were you, I'd keep clear of The Crucible in Sheffield. If Ronnie O'Sullivan claps eyes on you he'll take your head off your shoulders before you can say "pot black".' He laughed himself stupid and had to be given a drink of water in order to calm him down. Did my father's over-elaborate analogy hide his true feelings? Was his first instinct to weep? If so, he hid it very well.

When Gracie came home from school, she said, 'I like your new hairstyle, Dad.'

I was very tired and my mouth was sore. I said irritably, 'How can it be a hairstyle, Gracie? I haven't got any hair.'

Her lip trembled but I managed to divert her by telling her that she could polish my head with a duster if she wanted.

She said, 'Can I use Mr Sheen?'

When I said no, she carefully laid herself down on the rug in front of the fireplace and had a tantrum. I didn't have the energy to do anything so I watched her thrash about until, after five minutes, she calmly got up and walked away.

Sunday 9th March

My mother gave me a lift to the hospital this afternoon. On the way she drove down the High Street and parked outside the bookshop. We got out and looked through the window. The builders were in and had already knocked down the walls between the shop area, the back room and the store rooms beyond, making one large space.

My mother said, 'It's going to be a Tesco Metro. I thought about applying for a job. I've got a few hours spare while you have your chemo.'

Diary, how insensitive can you get?

When I was hooked up to the machine, I called Daisy at work. Hugo Fairfax-Lycett answered the phone and told me that she was on the other line to the States. He said,

'Sorry, Adrian, but I don't want to interrupt her, she's closing a deal with a Yank travel agent.'

I said, 'Yes, she told me that you're going all out to get American coach parties in.'

He said, 'The Yanks are very nervous travellers lately. We have to convince them that Al Qaeda are not likely to bomb them while they're taking tea in the orangery.' He went on, 'I'm sorry if I've taken up a lot of your wife's time lately, but we're trying to prepare the hall for our opening in April. We're spring-cleaning thirty-four rooms, mowing eight hundred and forty acres of deer park and dredging a moat. I'm sure you know what it's like.'

I was longing to discontinue the call but didn't know how to.

He said, 'I hear you've been under the weather lately.'

I agreed that I had.

He said, 'Daisy must be a great comfort to you. She's a marvellous girl.'

I said that I had not seen a lot of Daisy recently, but that my mother was being extremely helpful.

'Good, good,' he said. 'One's family is terribly important.'

There was a very awkward silence. I expect he was waiting for me to say something, but I could not find anything *to* say apart from, 'Would you ask her to ring me when she's free? Thank you.'

Tried to eat the orange segments my mother had prepared for me but couldn't, my mouth was too painful. I'd been warned that this would happen.

Sally came in to see me and thought that my bald

head looked 'edgy'. I am an ardent follower of the ongoing saga of her relationship with Anthony. It is obvious to me that Anthony is fooling around with other women but Sally seems to be oblivious to his licentious behaviour.

Today she said, 'We were meant to go away for the weekend to Wolf Edge in the Peak District, but by the time he'd stashed all the camping gear in his car there wasn't room for me in the passenger seat.'

I said, 'So he's gone alone?'

'Yes,' she said, 'he sounded so disappointed on the phone.'

I said sceptically, 'Just how big *is* his tent, or are we talking marquee here?'

She said, 'It's a four-man tent but the sleeping bags take up a lot of room.'

I said, 'What is he driving – a bubble car?'

'No,' she said, 'it's a four-by-four, but he's taking a lot of food.'

I said, 'Sally, you're only five foot three. You take up hardly any room.'

She said, 'Yes, but there's his camping stove and wet weather gear, his wellingtons, the water containers, the ice boxes, the groundsheet, the inflatable raft, the paddles ...'

Diary, I gave up, she obviously does not want to see what is under her nose.

On the way home my mother said, looking intently into my face, 'Daisy's putting in a lot of hours at the hall. I hope she's getting overtime.'

Daisy was home at 10.30 p.m. She has had trouble with the workers who are digging out the moat.

I said, 'Well, it must be difficult for them, working in the *dark*.'

Monday 10th March

A Mexican email from Daisy's mother.

Hello to you, my daughter. Daddy tells me that you have a job in an English country house. This is good news. When will you bring your husband and little Gracie to see us? Arthur is working in Mexico City. He has two shops now, both of them selling pig meat. We have many high-up customers: the chief of police, two cardinals and the nuns who care for the orphans who work on the rubbish tip. I hope that you are still not angry with me, Daisy. I had to run away from your father. He would talk to me for three hours every night without stopping. Every day he bought me presents. When he was at work, always he ring me on the telephone and tell me that he love me and that I am beautiful. That is why I left. What woman could stand it? I am happy with Arthur, he does not treat me good, I must serve him dinner every night at the dining table and I must eat alone in the kitchen but I am happy.

Love from your mother,
Conchita

When Daisy showed it to me, I said, 'I will never understand women.'

Daisy said, 'My father suffocated her.'

I asked Daisy if she would like to visit Conchita and Arthur, her stepfather, in Mexico City when I am better.

She said, 'No, Hugo needs me, and anyway, we couldn't possibly afford it.'

I was relieved, the murder rate in Mexico City is amongst the highest in the world.

Tuesday 11th March

Had a visit from the Environmental Crime Unit. The 'unit' consisted of two people – a young woman with a sulky mouth and an older man in wet weather gear. The woman showed me her ID and asked if they could come inside 'for a chat'.

'Chat' is a word I detest so I said, 'You may come inside and talk to me, but I don't have time for a "chat".' I made them stand in the hallway because Bernard was in the kitchen wearing a too-small rummage-sale dressing gown that kept falling open, and my father was in the living room having his toenails cut by my mother, using my special cutters.

It transpired that the Environmental Crime Unit is employed by our District Council. They had been 'out on patrol' and had noted that our two bins had been in the lane at 10.17 a.m. – 'a full two hours after they had been emptied at 8.16 a.m.' – and the unit reminded me that this was an infringement subject to a penalty of £100.

'And what's more,' said sulky lips, 'the lid of one of the bins was open by six inches.'

When I protested that I was too weak to bring the bins back to the house and that I had instructed my wife not to overfill said bin, the duo exchanged what I took to be a professional glance.

The woman said, 'We've heard every excuse going, Mr Mole. This is an official warning. Remember, no bins are to be put out before seven thirty in the morning, and bins are to be brought back to the house by eight thirty. Understood?'

They left shortly after Bernard came out to see what was causing voices to be raised. He said, when they'd gone, 'Reminds me of living in East Berlin after the war, the neighbours reported you to the Stasi for coughing in the night.'

Wednesday 12th March

Couldn't get out of bed this morning. Daisy took Gracie to school. They were late leaving the house because Gracie behaved disgracefully. She was perfectly pleasant until she saw the contents of her lunch box.

She whined, 'Yuck! Horrible brown bread with bits in and horrible grapes with pips and horrible water with bubbles. Why can't I have a Curly Wurly and crisps and a bottle of Coke?'

I fear that our daughter has inherited my father's bad food genes. He almost starved to death once when he mistakenly booked into an all-inclusive macrobiotic hotel on an otherwise deserted Greek island.

*

At 9.35 a.m. the house phone rang. I staggered out of bed to answer it.

A robotic voice said, 'If you are the parent or guardian or principal carer of Gracie Mole press one.'

I pressed one.

'This is Alerter Truant acting for Mangold Parva Infants and Junior School. Your child, Gracie Mole, is not at school. If your child is ill, press two. If your child has an authorised absence note, press three. If your child left for school and has not arrived, press four. If none of the above apply, press five. If you wish to speak to a member of staff, do not ring between the hours of . . .'

Here, Diary, the robot gabbled, 'Eight thirty and nine ten. Eleven ten and eleven thirty-five. Twelve fifteen and one thirty. Three fifteen and three thirty-five. Please note that school closes at four p.m. Enquiries about lost property must be made in between the times stated above.'

I pressed six to see what would happen.

The robot barked, 'Mangold Parva Infants and Junior School cannot be held responsible for any accident or mishap that may befall a child outside the boundary of the school.'

I disconnected the call and tried to ring Daisy but only got the robot back. I tried ringing her on my mobile but she was engaged. There was nothing for it but to go to the school and find out what had happened to my daughter. Had Daisy abandoned her in the lane, having been pushed to breaking point by Gracie's awful behaviour?

Bernard offered to go in my place but a person of Bernard's dishevelled appearance turning up in the playground and asking about Gracie would have sent every police car in the county screaming to the school – especially since he bought an old mackintosh from the village hall rummage sale.

Daisy and I met outside the locked school gate. Neither of us could speak due to shortness of breath. It's some time since I attempted to run anywhere. As soon as I stopped, my knees buckled and Daisy had to help me to the wooden bench covered in carved initials near the bus stop. After she had buzzed and panted her name into the intercom and she had been let into the playground, I tried to recover myself.

I was sitting with my head in my hands when Simon, the vicar, put his Spar bag down next to me and said, 'Adrian, don't give way to despair.' He sat down and put his arm around me. To my horror his eyes were full of hideous compassion. 'Wherever there is life, there is hope,' he murmured, 'and if you share your burden with God he will listen.'

It sounded as though he was recommending I contact BT Customer Services.

I took the opportunity and asked him if there were any family plots left in the graveyard. 'I'd prefer a side view,' I said, 'out of sight of the school. And if possible I'd like the plot to catch the evening sun.'

Simon said he admired my pragmatism but that, sadly, there was a long waiting list for interment. However, in the event of my death, should I decide to be cremated, my family members would be allowed to scatter me on to the rose bed by the church porch.

When Daisy came out, angrily denouncing the school's faulty Alerter Truant system, the vicar stood up and said, 'Mrs Mole, these must be difficult times for you.'

She said, 'Too right! You try finding a giraffe-keeper who'll work for the minimum wage.'

I stared down in embarrassment at the contents of the vicar's Spar bag: a jar of Vaseline, a tin of apricot halves, a head of garlic and a packet of cotton buds.

When he'd gone, Daisy said, 'You look awful, Aidy. I'm going to ring your mum to come and pick you up.'

I'm not ashamed, Diary, to inform you that I allowed my mother to take me home and put me to bed with a cup of tea and two marshmallow tea cakes.

Bernard offered to open a tin of soup after he returned from The Bear. When they'd both gone, I gave way to tears and cried for two minutes and thirty-one seconds.

Friday 14th March

Chemo.

I have decided to make full use of my six hours in hospital. Went to the shed and dug out my old Linguaphone Russian course. I hope to be fluent enough by the end of my treatment to say, 'Could you please direct me to Dostoevsky's grave?'

Sunday 16th March

Found a discarded receipt in the kitchen bin today. On the back (in Daisy's distinctive hand) she had written:

Mrs Daisy Fairfax-Lycett
D. Fairfax-Lycett
Daisy Fairfax-Lycett
Mrs Hugo Fairfax-Lycett
DFL

Diary, this can only mean one thing.

I searched for her diary but couldn't find it. Sat on the edge of the bed and stared at the wall. Phoned Pandora but only got her answerphone.

Hello, you have reached the Right Honourable Pandora Braithwaite BA, MA, DPhil, MP. If you consider your call to be of sufficient importance, please leave a brief concise message, no longer than thirty seconds. If I concur that your call is worthy of a reply, I will ring you back.

I left a message saying that I had lost my hair, was confined to bed, had a painfully sore mouth and that I thought my wife was in love, possibly having an affair and was fantasizing about marriage to Hugo Fairfax-Lycett.

*

331

Pandora rang back half an hour later and said, 'Aidy, you sound as though you're wallowing in self-pity. Force yourself out of bed, have a shower and pull yourself together. Ask Daisy outright if she's in love with that pea-brained wanker, Fairfax-Lycett.'

I did everything she said, until Daisy came home. Diary, perhaps if I had Latin or Mediterranean blood I might have found it easier to confront my wife and accuse her of adultery, but my pure English blood was of no help to me. I didn't quite know how to tackle the subject. She was very kind to me during the evening and brought me some ice cubes for the ulcers in my mouth.

Monday 17th March

Chemo.

Woke with a feeling of dread, knowing that I would have to speak to Daisy about Hugo Fairfax-Lycett today. However, when Daisy brought me a cup of tea in bed she was dressed in her business suit and high heels and said that she would have to go into work 'to finish the brochure', which had to be at the printer's in the morning. She said she was taking Gracie with her because Hugo's girls from his first marriage were visiting and they had offered to take Gracie on a pony ride.

I said, 'So you'll be playing happy families, will you?'

Daisy said, 'Certainly not, you know I hate card games.'

I said, 'You know what I mean, Daisy.' She looked as

though she was about to say something, then appeared to change her mind and left without speaking.

When they had gone, my mother came round to 'look after me'. I protested that I was perfectly able to look after myself but she stripped the bed and remade it with clean linen and helped me change my pyjamas. She washed my face and hands with a soapy flannel and was about to clean my teeth when I wrestled the toothbrush from her and did it myself. While she was tidying the bedroom, tut-tutting over Daisy's discarded clothes, she kept shooting nervous glances at me.

I asked her what was wrong.

She said, in that unconvincing way that women have, 'Nothing, nothing.'

After she had given several deep sighs, I tried again, saying, 'Something *is* wrong, Mum. What is it?'

She said, 'No, Aidy, don't make me tell you.'

I tried yet again. I said, 'I can see that you're bursting to tell me whatever it is.'

She threw a pile of Daisy's dirty underwear into the linen basket and said emotionally, 'Don't think it gives me any pleasure, Adrian. This is breaking my heart.'

'This what?' I asked.

'This Daisy situation,' she said. 'The whole village is disgusted. Does Daisy think we're all blind and deaf?'

I said, 'I presume you're talking about Daisy and Fairfax-Lycett?'

It was like a dam breaking. She told me that everybody had their own Daisy and Fairfax-Lycett story to tell. Wendy Wellbeck had seen them holding hands in his car outside the post office, Lawrence the hairdresser had witnessed a close embrace in a lay-by on the A6, a woman who cleans at Fairfax Hall had found Daisy's NatWest debit card in his bed, and Tom Urquhart had heard him boasting in the lounge of The Bear about his 'adorable half-Mexican firecracker'.

Bernard came to the bedroom door and said, 'You're not the first man to be cuckolded, my old flower. If you marry a bobby-dazzler like Daisy, it's always a risk that some bounder will want to take her away from you.'

My mother defended me, saying, 'Aidy was a good-looker, until he lost his hair.'

Bernard said, 'The man is a complete bastard. He wants horsewhipping. He told me that he's got a magnificent library. When I asked him about the collection, he said, "Oh, I know nothing about the books. I never read, but I do love my library."'

When they'd gone, I lay back on my pillows. Any normal man would have been angry but all I felt was sadness and a dreadful apprehension. I got up in the afternoon and peeled some potatoes and carrots for dinner. I found a minced steak and shortcrust pastry pie in the freezer. I made some Oxo gravy. It was only when I poured the gravy into Daisy's favourite little blue and white jug that I started to cry.

When my wife and daughter returned home, they were both flushed and happy. I sat on the lid of the lavatory and watched as Daisy bathed Gracie.

Gracie said that 'Hugo' had given her a pony 'that is my very own'.

I said, 'What? Fairfax-Lycett has given Gracie a pony? Isn't that ridiculously generous?'

Daisy splodged L'Oréal No Tears on to Gracie's wet hair and said, 'Hugo has got half a dozen ponies hanging around doing nothing. He can easily afford to give one away.'

As part of the bathtime ritual Gracie threw herself backwards into the clear blue water so that her hair streamed out and the soapy bubbles floated away. When she was upright again, I asked her what the pony's name was.

She said, 'I've called him Daffodil.'

Daisy said, 'You should *see* the daffodils at Fairfax Hall, Aidy. Talk about "beside the lake, beneath the trees, fluttering and dancing in the breeze".'

I continued, '"Continuous as the stars that shine, and twinkle on the Milky Way, they stretched in never-ending line, along the margin of a bay."'

We exchanged a quick smile.

I left them and went to put the dinner on.

Gracie fell asleep before it was ready and was put to bed, and Daisy said that she couldn't eat a thing. Hugo had provided lunch and afternoon tea. At 9 p.m. my mother rang and asked if I had confronted Daisy yet. I said no, put the phone down and went to bed.

Tuesday 18th March

My mother drove me to hospital this morning. After treatment I sought Sally out and told her that my wife was having an affair with the local landowner.

She said, 'It sounds a bit like *Emmerdale*.'

I said, 'No, it's more Mills & Boon. Intellectual cancer-stricken husband betrayed by half-Mexican wife with fox-hunting floppy-haired lord of the manor.'

We both laughed, although I'm sure neither of us thought it was the slightest bit funny.

After dinner Glenn rang from Afghanistan to say that 'it wasn't him who was dead'. When I asked him what he was talking about, he said that he was the third in a convoy of vehicles and that the second vehicle had been blown up by a roadside bomb. One of his mates had been killed and another had had a leg amputated.

He said, 'It'll be on the news tonight, Dad. I didn't want you to see it and think it was me what was dead.'

I said, 'But, Glenn, you know the army always tells the next of kin before they announce it to the media.'

There was a long silence, then he said, 'I just wanted to tell you, Dad.'

I said, 'It must have been a horrible experience.'

He said, 'It was, Dad. I get on with everybody at home, Dad. It ain't nice being in a country where people hate you and want to kill you.'

We said our goodbyes and I was just about to discontinue the call when he said, 'Quick, Dad, before you go, remind me, why *are* we fightin' in Afghanistan? I keep forgettin'.'

I babbled something about democracy, freedom, women's rights, defeating the Taliban and that, according to Gordon Brown, 'Alky Aida' were training their followers to attack us here in England.

Glenn said, 'But ain't they got training camps in other countries in the world, Dad?'

I had to agree with the boy that this was probably the case.

He said, 'Thanks for that, Dad. Cheers.'

When Daisy returned home from work, she was very subdued. Her eyes were puffy and her mascara had smudged. She looked as though she'd been crying for hours. I asked her what was wrong.

She said, 'Nothing.'

She took a bottle of wine out of the fridge and fetched two glasses from the shelf. After she had poured the wine and lit a cigarette, she sat down and traced a pattern on the tablecloth with a fingernail.

My heart went out to her and I said, 'It's Hugo, isn't it?'

She laid her head on the tablecloth and started to sob.

I said, 'Are you in love with him, Daisy?'

She nodded her head, then she lifted her face and said, 'It's horrible being in love with him. I can't enjoy it and neither can Hugo. We're both so worried about *you*.'

I said sarcastically, 'I'm sorry I'm spoiling your fun.'

She said, 'Don't be horrible, Aidy. We are genuinely worried about you. Hugo thinks the shock of finding out could *kill* you.'

I said, 'Hugo probably *hopes* it could kill me.'

She said, 'You've got him wrong, Aidy. He's a very sensitive and caring person. We didn't *ask* to fall in love.'

I said, 'Are you sure he loves *you?*'

'Oh yes!' she said. 'He's never felt like this before. He loved me from the moment he saw me lighting a cigarette outside The Bear. He says that I'm the most beautiful woman he's ever seen. He adores me. And we can *talk* to each other, Aidy. He admires my intellect.'

'Well, he has very little of his own,' I said.

'Hugo is extremely clever in his own way.' She said, 'Can you skin a rabbit? Do you know how to drive a quad bike? Could you manage a staff of twenty-five? Just because he's not got his head stuck in a book all day . . .'

I said, 'I could tell you'd been crying when you got home.'

'Yes,' she said, 'I've been crying in his arms. He's asked me to live with him. I told him that I couldn't possibly leave you. Not while you're so ill.'

I said, quite calmly, Diary, 'I don't want you checking my pulse as soon as you wake up in the morning. You'd better go to him, Daisy. Why should my cancer keep you here against your will?'

I pleaded with her but she refused to leave. When she'd gone into the bathroom to repair her make-up, I took her mobile out of her bag and speed-dialled Fairfax-Lycett.

He answered immediately, 'Darling.'

I said, 'It's not your darling, it's your darling's husband.'

He said, 'Ah! Splendid! How *are* you, old chap?'

I said, 'I know everything. I'm sending my wife over. You can keep her.'

He said, 'Look, this is terribly decent of you, Mole. When my first wife left me for a National Hunt jockey, I went after the leprechaun with a riding whip. The bastard couldn't sit on a horse for the rest of the season.'

I said, 'We Moles bide our time, but when our wrath is directed at you its force is devastating. The woman in the Spar shop who short-changed my mother had to move to the next village.'

He wheedled, 'Look, I think we should meet and talk about this man to man. May I come over?'

Diary, this was the last thing I wanted, a night of dramatic confrontations and hysterical declarations of love and tear-soaked protestations of guilt. But that's what I got. When Fairfax-Lycett arrived, we greeted each other with icy politeness but the meeting soon deteriorated into a dissection of mine and Daisy's marriage.

At one point Daisy accused me of causing her 'mental anguish' by 'telling her things about politics'. She ranted, 'I'm really not interested who said what on some parliamentary select committee. You must be the only person in the whole of Britain who watches BBC Parliament. You only watch it because you want to letch over that hard-faced slapper, Pandora soddin' Braithwaite.'

Diary, this was only partly true. I actually *enjoy* being informed of the finer details of the Finance Bill.

She said, 'When I first fell in love with you, I thought you were fashionably geeky, but I've since found out that you're not fashionably *anything*, you're just a geek!'

It was here I lost control and picked up her Tate Modern mug and threw it at the party wall. It shattered very satisfactorily.

Daisy screamed, 'That mug was a precious link to my old life, you cruel bastard!'

Fairfax-Lycett mostly kept his mouth shut, but when my mother came round to find out what was going on and called him 'an inbred twat-face with a chin like an illegal banana', he roared, 'I'm taking Daisy away from this low-life hellhole.'

Daisy turned to my mother and said, 'Will you look after Adrian, Pauline?'

My mother said, 'I've looked after him for almost forty years. I was thirty-six agonizing hours in labour for him because of his unusually big head. I'm hardly going to give up on him now, am I?'

Daisy went into our bedroom and I heard the suitcases being pulled down from the top of the wardrobe.

Bernard came in from 'visiting a friend' and found the kitchen table occupied by me, my mother and Fairfax-Lycett, none of us speaking to the others. He proceeded to cook himself eggs, bacon and toast and eventually ate his meal reading *Anglo-Saxon Attitudes* by Angus Wilson, which he propped up against the fruit bowl. Bernard seemed to have a calming effect on us, and when Daisy came out of the bedroom carrying two obviously heavy suitcases, we all said our goodbyes courteously enough, though Bernard did say to Fairfax-Lycett, 'I can remember a time when a man who stole another man's wife would have to take her to one of our colonies. You are a *disgrace*, sir.'

After Daisy and Fairfax-Lycett had gone, my mother cried a little, saying, 'I loved Daisy. She was the daughter I *should* have had.'

Bernard said, 'I used to be in love with Princess Margaret. I wrote to her every day, had a standing order at Interflora to send her a dozen dark red roses every Thursday. I couldn't bear it when she married that little fellow with the gammy leg, Antony Armstrong-Jones. I went to Beachy Head, wrote a last letter to Margaret and was about to chuck myself over the edge when it started to rain. So I walked back to the car and drove home.' He turned to me and said, 'Don't worry, kiddo. You've still got me and your mother.'

So, Diary, the nightmare begins. My health and happiness are now in the hands of my mother, Bernard Hopkins and the National Health Service.

Wednesday 19th March

When I went into the kitchen early this morning, I found Daisy sitting at the table. She had made a large pot of coffee.

I said, 'You've come back. I knew you would.'

She said, 'We didn't talk about Gracie. I want to take her with me. *You* can't look after her, can you?'

I had a vision of Gracie riding Daffodil and shouting, 'Daddy, look at me!' to Fairfax-Lycett.

'No,' I said, 'Gracie stays here, with me.'

Daisy poured me a cup of coffee and said, 'Gracie won't be happy without me. And quite honestly, Adrian, I don't think you, your mother or Bernard Hopkins are fit for purpose. I'm going to wake her up in a few minutes, get her dressed and take her to school and it will be me who picks her up this afternoon.'

Thursday 20th March

I should have fought harder for her but I could hardly have *dragged* the kid out of Daisy's arms, could I? I had to pretend to Gracie that she was going on a holiday to Fairfax Hall and was forced to smile as I waved her goodbye.

So it's just me and Bernard Hopkins who inhabit this house now. How did it come to this?

Brett came round at lunchtime and offered to 'take Fairfax-Lycett out'.

I said, 'I take it that you don't mean "out" for a meal or "out" to the theatre?'

Bernard said, 'It's criminal parlance for murder, Adrian.'

I said, 'I know what it means, I have read about the Kray brothers in some depth.'

Brett said, 'I'm only trying to help, Bro.'

Bernard said, 'As a matter of interest, how much would it cost to take somebody out?'

Brett said, 'In the provinces? Frighteningly little.'

*

Later, as we were driving to the hospital, my mother said, 'Daisy'll soon get tired of living at Fairfax Hall with all those servants.'

After overtaking a tractor on a blind corner, she said, 'And who wants to trek over to Paris to buy clothes, when you can buy stuff in Leicester that's more or less the same?'

'Paris?' I queried.

'Yes, he's taking her for the weekend. He "wants her in Dior".'

I said, 'I liked her in Monsoon.'

My mother patted my hand and said, 'I'd like to see his face when he walks into his bedroom and sees her haute couture thrown all over the floor.'

When I got home, I found a letter on the mat. It was an invitation to Nigel and Lance's wedding. It was addressed to Mr Adrian and Mrs Daisy Mole. There was an RSVP so I wrote back:

Dear Nigel and Lance

Thank you for inviting myself and my wife to your wedding on 19th April. I will be delighted to attend. However, I cannot speak for my wife as she is now living with her lover, Hugo Fairfax-Lycett. Her new address is: Fairfax Hall, Mangold Parva, Leicestershire.

Yours sincerely,

Adrian

Daisy

It's not your eyes I miss,
It's not your hair.
Your lips I'd like to kiss,
But you're not there.
It's not your skin I need,
It's not your face.
With every book I read,
I feel your grace.
I scan a newspaper,
I watch TV.
But I see nothing there,
Return to me.

I'll burn my cardigans,
Update my glasses.
Eat crisps another way,
I'll join the masses.
Learn to rock 'n' roll,
Watch *EastEnders*.
Like R & B and soul,
And gender benders.
I'll watch *Big Brother* live,
And the repeat.
I'll educate myself
By reading *Heat*.
I will embrace *The Wire*
And ditch my *Newsnight*.
Oh, Daisy, light my fire,
And soothe my Dark Knight.
                    A. A. Mole
            (husband of Daisy Mole)

Friday 21st March
Good Friday

What is so good about it?

Since Daisy left, the house is dead. It was she who turned the lamps on at night and put flowers in the vase, she who straightened the rugs and plumped up the cushions. I miss her clutter of lotions in the bathroom and the glossy magazines she kept next to the lavatory. Does she have them delivered to Fairfax Hall now?

And I didn't think I would miss Gracie as much as I do. I miss the physical presence of that indomitable little girl, trying to make her mark on the world. The feeling of those small strong arms around my neck. I miss the made-up songs she used to sing in the bath, I miss the certainty of her world. She knows nothing of nuclear proliferation or the misery that comes from loving somebody too much.

I cannot imagine my wife with another man. What do they talk about? Does Fairfax-Lycett know that she likes Pulp but can't stand Coldplay? That her favourite number is six? That her porn name is Cindy Arnez? That her first memory was being stung by a wasp at a picnic? Does he know that she rates Tracey Emin but thinks Damien Hirst is a wanker? Does he know she hates milky tea? Has she told him that she is allergic to hyacinth bulbs, biological soap powder and prawns? How will he cope with her premenstrual tension or her fear of ants?

Does he know how lucky he is?

Saturday 22nd March

Nigel rang and said, 'Sorry about Daisy, Moley, but do you reckon we can get mate's rates if we have our wedding at Fairfax Hall?'

I said, 'Quite frankly, Nigel, I'm disgusted at you. I can't hear Daisy's name without a small piece of my heart breaking off, and all you can think of is saving a few pennies on your not-quite-a-wedding wedding reception.'

Nigel said, 'C'mon, Moley. I love you to bits but she was bound to leave you some time. You can't pluck a hot-house plant like Daisy Flowers out of tropical London and transplant her in the cold soil of Mangold Parva. She's gonna wither and die, man.'

Before he could carry on with his horticultural analogy, I said, 'Phone Daisy on her mobile,' and hung up.

Who can I talk to who will sympathise with *me*?

Sunday 23rd March
Easter Sunday

No Easter egg from Daisy this year. I felt the loss keenly.

Gracie is staying with my parents while her mother is in Paris. A letter arrived yesterday.

To the parent/guardian/principal carer of
GRACIE PAULINE MOLE

An appointment has been made for the aforementioned child to attend **Dr Martin Hazlewood's Educational Psychology Clinic** at 2.30 p.m. on **Friday 27th June**.

At Sigmund House
113 Cockfoster Lane
Leicester
LE2 1SZ

When I showed my parents the letter, my father said, 'There's nothing wrong with our Gracie that a bloody good thrashing wouldn't cure. You're too soft with her, Adrian. She walks all over you. You've got her footprints on your face.'

My mother said, 'She doesn't need an educational psychologist. All under-fives are mad. When you were Gracie's age you used to talk to the moon. You invited it to your birthday party and cried when it didn't come. Remember, George?'

My father doubled up with laughter. When he could speak, he said, 'As it got dark and the moon came up, he went in the garden and threw a sausage roll at it.'

It was quite nice to see them laughing together again, even if it was at my expense.

Monday 24th March

My mother brought Gracie round this morning. Apparently, she had behaved impeccably. There had been no tantrums, no answering back and no delusional behaviour, i.e. talking to the moon.

My mother looked years younger. I asked her if she had been using Boots No. 7 Protect & Perfect Beauty Serum (I had heard that women were going wild for it).

She said, 'No, but I've got my name on the list. I look better because I slept for eight hours last night. Since Gordon has nationalised Northern Rock me and your dad can rest easy.'

I said, 'You talk about our prime minister as though he is an intimate friend of yours.'

She said, 'I know that Gordon is secretly on the side of the working class and that when he's settled in a bit he'll show his true colours.'

This made me laugh quite a lot. I said, 'A few years ago you were bragging that you were middle class.'

She said angrily, 'I've never called myself middle class. That was your father. He thought that selling electric storage heaters gave him a key to the executive toilet.'

When my mother had gone, I interrogated Gracie about life at Fairfax Hall. She told me that, 'Hugo and Mummy sleep in a big bed with a curtain hanging round it,' and that, 'Hugo has bought me a puppy which is called Snowball cos it is white all over,' and that, 'Hugo teached me to canter on Daffodil and I sleep in a princess bed from IKEA.'

I asked her if she missed me and Grandma and Granddad Mole when she was at Fairfax Hall.

She said, 'No,' and turned her attention to Bernard, who was dealing the Happy Family cards in preparation for a game.

At a crucial point (I was only waiting for Mr Bun the Baker to win the game) Brett burst into the kitchen shouting that Bear Stearns had crashed. Bernard, Gracie and I looked at each other with mutual incomprehension.

Brett said contemptuously, 'You don't know what it is, do you?'

I said, 'No, but you're going to tell us, aren't you?'

He said sarcastically, 'It's one of America's largest investment banks, one of Wall Street's most prestigious names.'

Bernard said, 'Oh dear.'

Brett said, 'You won't be saying, "Oh dear," when the world's financial institutions have collapsed and you are rioting in the street and looting Sainsbury's in order to survive.'

Bernard said mildly, 'Look, cocker, I've reached my three score years. I'm not really up to rioting. I'd just quietly drink myself to death and leave the looting to the young folk.'

Bernard took and rejected a card. It was Mr Bun. I fell on it like a slathering dog and shouted triumphantly, 'I've won!'

As Brett sorted through the Sunday papers and extracted the business sections, he said, 'Illiquidity in global capital is as bad as when the markets froze in August last year. How much further do central banks have to go to support a system that is so obviously broken?'

None of us could answer his question. He left after saying that he had a fail-safe system, if only he could raise the capital. Was it my imagination or did his glance fall on the tinned goods shelf?

As I microwaved three Morrisons cottage pies and opened a packet of petits pois, I wondered if Daisy was sitting at a table on the Champs Elysées watching Parisian life go by whilst eating escargots and sipping her vin rosé.

In the afternoon Bernard took Gracie for a walk to see the bluebells in the wood. I lay down on my bed and slept with my arms around Daisy's pillow. When I woke up, there was a jar of wilting bluebells on the kitchen table and Bernard told me that the world's finances had fallen a further 3 per cent and that financial experts were predicting mass unemployment and homelessness due to mortgage foreclosures. He spoke these words as though they were foreign to him.

Tuesday 25th March

My mother took Gracie to school this morning, then came back and took me to the hospital for my treatment. As I was being hooked up to the infusion, she said, 'I'm starving, I'm going to the canteen to buy a cheese cob.'

She came back minus her two front teeth, having bitten into the bread with what she admitted was 'unusual force'. She rang her NHS dentist, Mr Little, from the hospital and was told by a receptionist that he had died four years ago.

My mother said, with her hand over her mouth, 'I need an urgent appointment.'

'I could get you in to see Mr Sturgeon at three,' said the receptionist.

As we were walking to the car park, my mother said, 'I can't show my face to the world until I've got my replacement teeth.'

I said, 'Mum, you're being ridiculously oversensitive.'

However, when she uncovered her mouth to put the car into gear and turned to me and smiled, it gave me quite a shock. With the green light from the sun visor on her face, her untidy hair, wrinkled smoker's lips and missing teeth she looked like the Wicked Witch of the West.

Mr Carlton-Hayes rang this afternoon and asked if Bernard and I could help him catalogue the remaining books that were still in storage. I told him that tomorrow morning would be a good time.

On hearing this, Bernard rubbed his hands together and said, 'Christ, kiddo, I'm looking forward to getting my hands on those beauties,' rather as other men might react on being invited to a topless bar.

I often think that Bernard's relationship with books is

not entirely healthy. Perhaps he has substituted books for sex and sometimes confuses the two.

Wednesday 26th March

I had never been to a storage depot before. It was a series of huge containers. Some of the doors were open as we passed by. Some seemed to hold the contents of a house. One was full of life-sized mannequins who were striking various attitudes, while another was stacked to the container ceiling with old newspapers.

Mr Carlton-Hayes and Leslie were already working methodically, placing books with the value of over £25 in a tea chest and those over £50 in a small cardboard box. After Bernard and I arrived, the work slowed down.

Leslie said, 'Bernard, we do not have time to discuss the merits or otherwise of the books. We are here this morning to sort them according to their price.'

Bernard said, 'I can't just handle them without giving them their due, can I, cocker? I mean they're not inanimate objects, are they?'

Leslie said, 'But they *are* inanimate objects, Bernard. They can't see or think or feel, can they?'

Mr Carlton-Hayes, who seemed to be shrinking by the day, said, 'I know how Bernard feels. Every book seems to be a living breathing thing, I've always hated to see books kept in a dark cupboard.'

At lunchtime we broke off and went to The Clarendon Hotel for a drink. Naturally the talk was of books and booksellers, and we did actually talk about cabbages and kings. When I pointed this out, we all laughed. It was the happiest I had been for a long while.

On the way back to the storage depot, I pushed Mr Carlton-Hayes in his wheelchair and told him about Daisy and Hugo Fairfax-Lycett.

Mr Carlton-Hayes turned round in his wheelchair and said, 'My dear boy, how absolutely dreadful. You must win her back. There is a volume of John Donne's poetry in the over-fifty-pounds box.'

Poor Mr Carlton-Hayes. Does he honestly think that a metaphysical seventeenth-century poet can compete with a manor house, a canopied bed and sexual fulfilment with a handsome aristocrat?

When we got back to the container, he rummaged inside the box and brought out John Donne's *The Love Poems*.

He said, 'These poems are wonderfully sensual. When I was a young man, they were never far from my bed.' He quoted, from memory:

> License my roving hands, and let them go
> Before, behind, between, above, below.
> O my America! My new-found-land,
> My kingdom, safeliest when with one man manned . . .

He handed the book to me and said, 'I'm distantly related to the Fairfax-Lycetts. They're a bad lot. They made their money transporting African slaves.'

It took the four of us until about 7.30 p.m. to finish sorting the books. Just before we were about to leave, Mr Carlton-Hayes pointed to the 'valuable' boxes and said, 'Adrian, these are yours. You must regard them as your redundancy payment.'

I was overcome and could hardly stammer my thanks.

Bernard slapped me on the back and said, 'You deserve it, kiddo.'

Mr Carlton-Hayes said, 'I haven't forgotten you, Bernard. You will find some of your favourites among them. They are marked with your name.'

When my mother came to pick us up, she had a scarf wrapped around the lower part of her face. She had been to see Mr Sturgeon and he had told her that he only saw private patients. To have two new front teeth would cost her at least £2,000.

She said, 'I had no choice but to tell him to go ahead. The only National Health Service dentist I could find was on the Isle of Wight.'

When we got home and she removed her scarf, I examined the new teeth. To my mind they did not look right. They towered over the rest of her mouth, a bit like Canary Wharf and the Lloyd's building tower over the City of London. Whenever she enunciates sibilants, she whistles like the sheep farmers on *One Man and His Dog*.

Thursday 27th March

No energy today, feel ill, mouth sore, am nauseous. Bernard panicked and sent for Dr Wolfowicz. When he came in, I was taken aback by his height and girth. I had forgotten that he was so huge. He seemed to completely fill the doorway of the small bedroom.

After taking my blood pressure, temperature and shining a little torch into my eyes, he said, 'You are in no immediate danger. Your vital signs are, I think, good.'

Bernard, who was hovering near by, said, 'He's not himself, doctor, he can't even pick a book up.'

Dr Wolfowicz sat down on the side of the bed, almost crushing my legs under the now tightened bed clothes. He asked me if there was anything else I wanted to tell him. Did I have any worries?

I told him that my wife had left me and that I was worried about the world's financial situation.

He said, 'There is nothing modern medicine can do for these unfortunate occurrences, Mr Mole.'

I asked him if I was depressed.

He said, 'I don't know, are you?'

I said, '*Clinically* depressed?'

He said, 'You are sad, I think, but that is fine. I am sad when I think of my homeland.'

He stared at a reproduction of Van Gogh's *The Potato Eaters*, which hangs on the wall above the bed. I wondered if he was thinking about Warsaw and rye bread. Eventually he said, 'If your sadness continues, I will refer you to our practice counsellor.'

I said that I had seen therapists in the past and had either fallen in love with them or bored them with my problems. I told him about my last therapist, who had yawned throughout the fifty-minute session.

He said, 'Martha Richards is a different pan of fish. She is a good woman. Now, tell me about this prostate? How is it doing?'

He made it sound as though my prostate had a life of its own, went shopping, had a relationship.

I said, 'I hope it's shrinking.'

He said, 'Let us wish so. You must grow your hair back for the winter.'

As he was leaving, he said conspiratorially, 'Mr Mole, next time marry an ugly woman. Nobody will take her from you then, I promise.'

Friday 28th March

Had to leave my bed and go for chemo. Bernard came with me because my mother is having her hair cut at Toni&Guy. She has not used the salon in the village since Lawrence said she should have a 'feather cut' because it was 'kinder to the ageing face'.

Bernard had brought *The Human Factor* by Graham Greene to read in the waiting area. He offered to come into the treatment room and read aloud to me. I thanked him but said I would listen to a recording of Melvyn Bragg's *In Our Time* on my little Sony tape recorder.

He said, 'You're a bugger for self-improvement, aren't you, lad?'

I said, 'Due to parental neglect I missed out on a good education and was forced to become an autodidact.'

The bloke who hooked me up to the chemo drip was from the Philippines.

I asked him if he had lived in Leicester for long.

He said, 'Unfortunately, I have lived here for fourteen years.'

I asked him why he didn't go home.

He said, 'I was chosen by my father to be educated. Now I must send my wages home. They feed seventeen members of my family.'

Later, when I was listening to Melvyn quizzing a panel of academics about the dissolution of the monasteries, I reflected that to be alive in England in the twenty-first century was comparable to winning the lottery of life.

When I went to the waiting room to meet up with Bernard, I found him wiping his eyes with a filthy white handkerchief.

He said, holding up his book, 'You must read it, lad. Mr Greene's hero is so noble, so decent, so fucking *English*.'

I was struck by the reciprocity of our thoughts.

I rang my mother on her mobile and she said that there had been a problem with her highlights but that the salon was trying to rectify the mistake.

I heard an altercation, then a man with an Australian accent said into the phone, 'Just to put you in the picture, sir, it was not the salon's mistake. Your mother lied about having a skin test, and she has since admitted that she bleached her hair at home seven days ago, therefore this salon cannot be responsible for the mess that your mother's scalp is now in.'

I asked to be reconnected with my mother and said, 'Mum, why can't you follow the rules?'

She said, 'They're getting their knickers in a twist over nothing. My scalp always reacts to bleach. I have an agonizing twenty-four hours, then it settles down and starts to heal. What's the problem?'

I asked where she had parked the car.

'In the disabled space outside the shop,' she said.

When I protested that the space should be kept free for invalids, she said, 'I *felt* like an invalid this morning. Me and your father downed a couple of bottles of White Lightning each last night.'

Later, as Dougie Horsefield was driving us home in his taxi, I said, 'Bernard, what is White Lightning?'

Bernard said, 'If you should see a homeless gentleman who stinks of urine and has an open wound above the bridge of his nose you can be sure that White Lightning is his park bench drink of choice.'

Dougie laughed and said, 'Your mum and dad are on a slippery slope, Adrian.'

I went straight to bed as soon as I got home. Bernard brought me some ice for my mouth and offered to heat up a can of chicken noodle soup.

Got up at ten to watch the BBC news with Bernard. The new Terminal Five at Heathrow opened yesterday. The TV showed chaos, traffic gridlocked around the perimeter, planes cancelled, computerized baggage handling not handling any baggage, passengers near to rioting, staff hiding in offices.

Bernard sighed, 'Nothing's been the same since our chaps stopped using Brylcreem.'

Saturday 29th March

Glenn rang me early this morning in great distress. He had heard from my mother that Daisy and I had separated and she was now living with Hugo Fairfax-Lycett.

He said, 'I tell you what, Dad, this world what we live in is a horrible place. When I get home, I'm going to give that Fairfax-Lycett bloke some big beats.'

I said, 'Violence never solved anything.'

He said, 'Tell me about it. I'm in fucking Afghanistan.'

I asked him exactly where he was.

He said, 'I'm shelterin' behind the wall of a compound.'

'From the sun?' I asked.

'No, Dad,' he said with a flat voice, 'not from the sun.'

Michael Flowers came to visit me this afternoon.

He said, 'I'm on my way to Fairfax Hall for tea but I thought I'd drop in and see you first.' He talked for a full hour about UKIP and its leader, Nigel Farage, saying, 'I am hoping to stand as a candidate at the next election.'

He blames the European Union for the failure of his

Orgobeet business. He said, 'It was European red tape that did for me. A man should be able to sell his produce without being stifled by ludicrous health and safety legislation.'

I said, 'But are you quite sure, Michael, that Orgobeet is safe to drink after being stored for months in your garage without refrigeration?'

He shouted, 'Beetroot is a natural food and the juice contains organic chemicals that keep it fresh for ever!' He said that he was hoping to persuade Fairfax-Lycett to allow him to have a stand at the medieval jousting tournament that Fairfax Hall was hosting in August. He added, 'I've commissioned a crafts person to manufacture some rough-hewn goblets.'

Just before he went, he said, 'Awkward business this Daisy and Hugo thing.'

Bernard said, 'It's bloody heartbreaking.'

Michael said irritably, 'She must have left for a reason,' and then glared at me as though I was a wife beater.

I said, in a pleasant tone, 'By the way, Conchita wrote and invited Daisy to visit. Apparently, Arthur, her second husband, is supplying the chief of police in Mexico City with his pork.'

I later watched five minutes of *Sexcetera* but its content left me cold. Will I ever have a sex life again?

To My Organ

Oh staunchèd rod of old,
Why art thou now so limp and cold?
Has desire fled from thee?
Or art thou anxious to be free
Of love's quick flame so
Quickly quenched?
Will you lift your head again?
And if 'yes' please, rod, tell me when.

A. A. Mole

Tuesday 1st April

Woken at 7 a.m. by a foreigner on the line telling me
that he had met me in Moscow many years ago. He said,
'You invite me to stay with you in England, yes? So I am
bringing my wife and children to live in your house.
Please collect me from Heathrow Airport.'

I said, 'Nigel, you have deprived me of sleep for a
not-at-all-funny April Fool's joke.'

Nigel said, 'Keep your hair on, Moley. You're such
a party-pooper.'

Bernard and I were at breakfast this morning when
my mother came in, laughed and said to us, 'How's the
odd couple?'

I looked down at the table. Bernard's half was littered
with toast crumbs and blobs of marmalade, he had

361

slopped his coffee on to the tablecloth, and his boiled egg was a mess of yolk and egg shell. My half of the table was pristine. There was nothing spilt on the cloth and the top of my boiled egg had been surgically removed. It was not me who had dunked a knife into the marmalade jar, removed it and returned it to the butter dish.

When Bernard had gone to perform what he calls 'his ablutions', my mother said, 'How long is Bernard staying with you? He only came for Christmas.'

I said, 'He won't leave until I'm well again.'

She said, 'Christ! He could be here for ever.'

Wednesday 2nd April

I am FORTY TODAY.

What have I done with my life? I have lost two wives, one house and one canal-side apartment, a head of hair and my health.

The gains have been few: two sons, one daughter, some first editions and a body of literary works that nobody will publish or produce.

My presents were the usual rubbish, apart from a Smythson A4 moleskin notebook, which came in the post from Pandora. Nigel and Lance thought it amusing to have a blow-up rubber doll wearing a French maid's uniform delivered by Parcelforce, together with a card saying: 'Rubber up the right way and she'll blow your mind!'

I had told my mother that, due to my depression, I did not want any kind of celebration or party. She agreed, although she looked disappointed. I spent the day quietly with Bernard, both of us reading and occasionally putting down our books to make a cup of tea.

At about six o'clock my mother came in. She had a febrile edgy look about her. She said, 'Your dad wants to take you to The Bear for a birthday drink.'

I told her that, although I appreciated my father's offer, I would prefer to stay at home.

She said, 'No, you can't stay at home on your fortieth. It's not natural, is it, Bernard?'

Bernard said, 'I spent my fortieth in a brothel in Marseille, caught the clap from a comely wench called Lulu.'

'See,' said my mother approvingly, 'Bernard knows how to enjoy himself!'

After half an hour of badgering I reluctantly agreed to be driven to The Bear and to change into 'that lovely Next suit you never wear'.

The Bear was in darkness when I walked in ahead of my parents, my brother and Bernard. Then the lights were turned on and there was a roar of 'Happy Birthday!' and I realized that I was the unlucky recipient of a surprise party.

My mother screamed above the din, 'I've been planning this for weeks.'

I slapped a fixed grin on my face and looked around at a room full of familiar faces. Nigel and Lance were sitting at the bar. Wayne Wong came out of the kitchen with a platter of Chinese titbits. Marigold and Brain-box

Henderson were talking to Michael Flowers. Gracie ran up and hugged my legs. Mr Carlton-Hayes and Leslie were at a table together, with three old men who I knew by sight. (Tom Urquhart told me later that they were regulars who had refused to budge 'just because it's a private party'.) The Wellbecks were standing under a plastic banner which said 'Happy Fortieth'.

I looked around for Daisy but she wasn't there. However, at about half past eight Pandora swept in wearing a long buttery cream sheepskin coat and dark brown suede knee-high boots. It was the first time she'd seen my bald head but she didn't flinch.

She said, 'The motorway was horrendous. Full of idiots in their little family runabouts. There should be a lane for *serious* people like me.'

I said, 'Isn't that the fast lane?'

'No,' she said, 'it's not fast enough.'

A fawning Tom Urquhart brought her a glass of champagne. She swigged it back as though it was lemonade. Urquhart attempted to talk to her about the brewery, which was threatening to close The Bear.

He said, 'There's twenty pubs a day going under,' but she cut him off, saying, 'I'm here in a private capacity, Tom. Would you be a darling and fetch me another glass of fizz?' As he scuttled back to the bar, she fixed me with a glittering eye and said, 'I want a progress report on this bloody prostate of yours.'

I told her that the tumour appeared to be shrinking and that the oncologist had said there were 'grounds for optimism'.

She didn't look impressed. 'Alistair Darling said much

the same thing about the economy before the pound took a dive.' Tom Urquhart handed her another glass of champagne and she said, 'And bring me up to date on this ridiculous Daisy/Hugo thing.'

I told her that they were still together and the last time I'd seen Daisy she was in the post office in the village wearing Dior.

'Dior!' she laughed. 'Not in the *country*. How vulgar is *that*?'

All through our conversation people had been circling, hoping for a chance to talk to Pandora. I was under no illusion that it was me they wanted to spend time with. At about nine the lights went out and my mother appeared from the far end of the bar carrying a large cake in the shape of an open book and decorated with icing and forty candles. After I had made a silent wish (for Daisy to come back), I blew the candles out. There were a few ragged attempts to sing 'for he's a jolly good fellow', then my mother clapped her hands together and shouted for quiet. My heart sank. She was going to make a speech. She started by bursting into tears and fanning her hands in front of her eyes – something she has learnt from *The X Factor*. I have never seen anybody do this in real life. Several women rushed to her side and offered tissues and comforting pats, etc.

My father shouted, 'Buck up, Pauline!' and eventually she managed to compose herself.

She started off conventionally enough. 'Thank you all for coming and for keeping it a secret from Adrian.' But then it went downhill. 'I can hardly believe it was forty years ago when I gave birth to him. My God! I've never had pain like it! It was thirty-six hours of excruciating agony, and I had nobody to hold my hand or rub my back. To this day I don't know where George was.'

Disapproving female eyes were turned on my father.

He protested, 'I was on a fishing trip. It was well before mobile phones.'

'You could have kept in touch,' said my mother. 'Your mam had a phone.'

No doubt to stop this exchange from deteriorating further, Mr Carlton-Hayes said, 'May I say a few words?'

My mother nodded, clearly reluctant to give him the floor.

Mr C-H wheeled himself until he was facing the small crowd. He said, smiling, 'I'll try not to be a bore. I'd just like to say that Adrian is possibly the kindest person it has been my privilege to meet. You know, work in a bookshop can be very taxing – we seem to attract a somewhat unusual clientele. Adrian was always patient with our customers. He has suffered many blows recently and has coped quite magnificently, with hardly an ounce of self-pity. Happy birthday, Adrian!'

After the applause had died down, my mother took centre stage again. 'So after thirty-six hours struggling – the size of his head amazed the midwives – he was born. After a few months of him screaming day and night we realized we'd got the wrong size of teat on his bottle,' she laughed. 'It was no wonder he couldn't get anything out and was losing weight!' She chuckled again at the memory. 'Well, then we started to enjoy him. At six months he was sitting up on his own.'

Pandora muttered, 'Christ! Is she going to take us through your forty years month by fucking month?'

My mother broke down several times throughout her speech, but still she went on and on and on. People looked at their watches. Some of the lucky ones standing near the door slipped out unobtrusively. Eventually, urged on by Pandora, I interrupted my mother while she was mid-anecdote about the time I was fourteen and she took me to A&E with a model plane stuck to my nose.

I got up and made a short speech thanking my mother, Wayne Wong and the woman who had made the cake. Later, because she was tired, Gracie knocked a can of Vimto all over Pandora's creamy sheepskin. Pandora was unperturbed and laughed it off, saying, 'It doesn't matter in the least, I can claim it back on expenses.'

'Parliamentary expenses?' I asked. 'Isn't that illegal?'

'Not at all,' she said. 'It's within the rules, we're paid like fucking paupers. The expenses supplement our measly salaries.'

I asked her if the Smythson notebook she'd bought me would be claimed on expenses.

She said, 'Of course, it'll go down as office stationery. But if your scruples won't allow you to accept it I'll gladly take it back.'

I thought about the luxurious moleskin cover and the heavy satin-like pages. I visualised myself writing something extraordinary in it: a groundbreaking book. Could the Smythson notebook and I together revive the English novel?

'I'll keep it,' I said.

My mother persuaded Tom Urquhart to play some music through the pub's loudspeakers. He chose Frank Sinatra's *Songs for Swingin' Lovers!*

Bernard Hopkins and Mrs Lewis-Masters were the first to take to the floor. I was astounded at the nimbleness of their footwork. Nigel and Lance were up next, which baffled a few of the unsophisticated Mangold Parvians.

When Pandora asked me to dance, I said, 'You know I can't dance, Pandora.'

She pulled me to my feet and said, 'Nonsense! One just takes to the floor and simulates sexual intercourse, but one holds back from actual penetration.'

I allowed her to take me in her arms and we shuffled around the small area in front of the bar. My mother danced by with Brett, who laughed and said to Pandora, 'This is what passes for a big night out in the provinces.'

Thursday 3rd April

SOMETHING AMAZING!

At ten thirty last night I told Pandora that I was exhausted and would have to go home.

She said, 'I can't face the drive back, can I stay with you?'

I told her that Bernard was in the spare room, but that she was welcome to sleep on the sofa.

She stroked my bald head and said, 'I don't do sofas, I'll share your lonely marital bed, shall I?'

I nodded, unable to speak, because I had forgotten to breathe.

When we got home, there was a birthday card on the mat. It was from Daisy. A man was leaning over a stone bridge smoking a pipe and staring down at a river. I recognised the card – it had been on a shelf at the post office for at least four years. Why did Daisy choose that card? She knows I hate smoking, am nervous of bridges and afraid of deep water.

Before we got into bed, Pandora said, 'By the way, Aidy, I'm trying sexual abstinence for a year.' She went on to tell me that the last time she'd had sex had been behind the Speaker's chair with a Tory frontbencher.

'Not while the Commons was sitting?' I gasped.

'No,' she said, 'but I was so disgusted with myself – I mean, a *Tory*!'

I put my pyjamas on and we climbed into bed. I was relieved that there was to be no sex. My spirit was willing, but for my reproductive organs it would have been a bridge too far.

Bernard brought me a cup of tea in bed this morning. He did not seem surprised to see Pandora there.

He said, 'Best thing to do, cocker. If you fall off a horse, you get right back on and ride it hard until its bloody hooves fall off.'

Pandora said, 'Are you calling me an old nag, Mr Hopkins?'

Bernard tugged on his moustache and said, 'Madam, you are a thoroughbred, a filly sired from the crème de la crème of bloodstock merchants.'

Before she left, Pandora kissed my head and said, 'I had a great night's sleep, Aidy. Perhaps I'll come again.'

Bernard and I watched from the front window as she swayed down the drive in her boots and the stained sheepskin, on her way to retrieve her car from outside The Bear.

Bernard sighed. 'Beauty and brains, and thighs you could crack a nut with,' he said.

Overheard at the party:

Bernard to Nigel: *'I had a brief spell as a homosexual, but I had to give it up.'*

'George Mole is not deaf, Wendy. He's choosing not to hear you.'

Friday 4th April

Treatment.

Sick many times.

Saturday 5th April

Slept until noon. Gracie gone to Longleat Safari Park with Daisy and HFL.

Sunday 6th April

Got up, had shower, shaved, ate one Weetabix – or should that be Weetab*i*?

Watched the Olympic torch being relayed around London flanked by ten Chinese security guards and two Metropolitan policemen. It was carried by celebrities that Bernard and I had never heard of.

In Downing Street Mr Brown came out to look at the flame. However, he did not touch it.

Bernard said, 'By touching it, cocker, he would have condoned the occupation of Tibet and given his blessing to the slaughter in Tiananmen Square.'

I am very worried about the Olympics. I cite Wembley Stadium and Terminal Five, which is still not working. Will the world be laughing at us in 2012?

In the afternoon I felt well enough to walk to the wood nearest our house. Bernard came with me. The ground was dotted with bright yellow flowers showing through the dead leaves.

Bernard said, 'Celandines! They make you feel that all is not lost, don't they, kiddo?'

Monday 7th April

Princess Diana – the latest.

The inquest jury returned with a majority verdict of nine to two. They found the Duke of Edinburgh not guilty of murdering Princess Diana. I was slightly disappointed, he looks fully capable of murder. Is it beyond the realms of imagination that the duke smuggled himself into France and, in disguise, hired a car – a Fiat Uno, perhaps – and forced Diana's car off the road and into the wall of the tunnel, then made his escape back to England? Can he account for all his movements that night?

Tuesday 8th April

Treatment.

Blood results back. Dr Rubik said my PSA levels had dropped, which indicates the chemo is working. She is worried about my weight, though.

I told her that my appetite is poor.

She said, 'Get your wife to tempt you with small amounts of your favourite foods.'

I told her that I was not living with my wife and that my principal carer was Bernard Hopkins.

She raised her eyebrows but did not comment.

I said, 'Bernard and I are just good friends.'

She said, 'It's nothing to do with me. You don't have to explain your living arrangements, Adrian.'

I said, 'But I think you've misunderstood –'

She interrupted, 'I'm really not concerned. He's obviously doing you good, and that's all I care about.'

The next time I see Doctor Rubik I'm taking Bernard with me. Perhaps then she will realise – the idea that he and I could be anything more than friends is laughable.

Wednesday 9th April

Bernard has been missing since breakfast. My mother came round with some chicken soup she had made herself. As I was eating, she told me there was a rumour in the village that he was 'knocking off' Mrs Lewis-Masters.

I was outraged. I said, 'Can't the small minded busybodies accept that there is such a thing as friendship between a man and a woman?'

My mother looked doubtful and said, 'I've never managed it myself, I've always had a problem with boundaries.'

I said, 'But Bernard is ancient and so is she.'

My mother said, 'Des O'Connor fathered a child and *he's* ancient.'

I said, 'But Mrs Lewis-Masters is a refined woman.'

'She's not that refined,' said my mother. She picked up my empty soup bowl and washed it under the hot tap. There was something about the set of her shoulders that signalled she had more to tell. It was not long in coming. As she dried the bowl, she turned and said, 'The refined Mrs Lewis-Masters has got an illegitimate son in Timbuktu. His father is a rich African – rich in camels, that is.'

'And who told you?' I asked.

'Wendy Wellbeck,' she mouthed, though there was nobody in earshot. 'The son keeps writing to her saying he wants to join her in England; apparently, he's got lovely handwriting.'

I said, 'Wendy Wellbeck could end up in prison for intercepting the Royal Mail.'

I waited up for Bernard. When he came in, at 11.35 p.m., I asked him if he'd been with Mrs Lewis-Masters.

He said, 'Cocker, you're looking at the happiest man in the world! I asked Dorothea to marry me tonight and she said yes!' He smiled, showing his tobacco-stained teeth. 'Of course, there are conditions. I've got to shave my moustache off. Shame, but there it is. I'm not allowed an alcoholic drink until lunchtime, and I mustn't bother her for sex more than twice a week. Oh, and I've got to smarten myself up generally.'

I said, 'So when are you and Dorothea getting married?'

Bernard said, 'Oh, not for years. I'll be moving in with the old girl, though. It should be a comfortable billet.'

Diary, I should have been happy for him but I only felt jealousy. However, I said, 'Congratulations, Bernard.' He wanted me to stay up and drink to his happiness but I played the cancer card and went to bed. As I lay awake in the dark, I wondered if Bernard knew that he would be a step-father to a middle-aged man in Timbuktu.

I reflected that nobody truly knows anybody else and that everybody's life is mysterious.

Thursday 10th April

Therapy day.

My mother gave me a lift to the surgery this morning. As we passed the school, we saw a group of stout middle-aged women demonstrating outside the school gate. Some were waving placards. One said: 'GORDON BROWN HAS DONE US DOWN.' Another: 'TEN PENCE TAX SHOULD BE MAX.'

My mother waved and sounded the hooter in support. She said, 'Gordon must have gone mad. Why is he making the dinner ladies pay more tax?'

I said, 'I can't talk politics with you. The chemotherapy has neutralised my political opinions, I can no longer see a difference between the main parties.'

When we had parked outside the surgery, I asked her to pick me up in an hour.

Before she drove off, she said, 'When you talk to Martha about your depression, you won't blame me, will you? Only I know her a bit from Wheelchair Mobility – her mother's in the Latin American formation team.'

Martha laughed when I told her what my mother had said, and after a few minutes I was completely relaxed in her company. My IKEA chair and matching footstool were incredibly comfortable. I liked the room's seaside decorative theme. The scented candle on the little white mantelpiece burned in a lighthouse candlestick. Within my reach, on a distressed coffee table, was a jug of water, a glass and a box of pastel-coloured tissues. I recognised some of the framed photographs on the walls.

'Martin Parr,' I said. 'We used to sell his books.'

We stared at a photograph of an old couple sitting opposite each other in a seaside café. They were ill at ease and not speaking. It captured the desolation of growing old and of having nothing left to say. I felt my throat constrict and, to my horror, tears started to gather.

At the end of the session the tissue box was almost empty and the waste bin was half full of damp tissues.

Martha said, as we stood at the door, 'You are depressed for very good reasons, Adrian. Perhaps next week we can actually talk.'

I assured her that I would not be sobbing for the full fifty minutes next week and went out, closing the door quietly behind me.

I like women like her. She hasn't got the thin wrists and ankles I require but she has curly brown hair and an old-fashioned face. She was draped in different shades of grey layers so it was impossible to make a judgement on her figure.

When I got into the car, I asked my mother what she knew about Martha.

'She's got grown-up children,' she said, 'and her husband was killed in an avalanche.'

'Unfortunate,' I said.

'Yes, but it's a classy way to die, isn't it?'

I said, 'It depends which ski resort he was killed in. Some of them are simply a sub-zero Blackpool.'

'You're such a bloody snob,' she muttered.

'You're the one who calls herbs "*'erbs*". It's not as if you're French, is it?'

We drove the rest of the way home in silence.

Before I got out of the car, she said, 'Aren't you going to tell me what went on in your therapy session?'

I said, 'No.'

She yelled, 'Well, I hope you're not blaming *me*. I might have rejected you for your first year, but I've tried to make up for it, haven't I?'

I got back in the car, 'What do you mean "rejected me"?' I asked.

She said bleakly, 'When the midwife gave you to me, I handed you back. I couldn't look at you; I didn't know what to do with you. I'd never held a newborn baby before. I had big plans for myself.'

I said, 'So who *did* look after me?'

'Your dad,' she said. 'He took a year off work. A lot of men would have buggered off — other men called him a big jessie. Men didn't have anything to do with babies in those days.'

As I let myself into the house, I reflected that there would be a lot to tell Martha at our next session.

Friday 11th April

The Bear has closed!

Yes, Diary, our ancient pub, whose name and situation commemorate the time when Mangold Parva was the very epicentre of bear-baiting, has been closed down by the property company who own it. The Urquharts have already left and gone to Kirkby New Town to be relief managers at a pub that was featured in the TV series *Britain's Toughest Pubs.*

This sad news was passed on to us by Justine from the Equine Therapy Centre. She put the brakes on her horse and stopped in the lane. Ironically we were on our way to The Bear to have a drink with Bernard and Mrs Lewis-Masters.

'Serves the Urquharts right,' said my father. 'The gradient of that ramp to the disabled toilet was so bleddy steep you needed oxygen to get to the bleddy summit.'

My mother said, 'It's a tragedy for the village. There's nowhere left now where you can get drunk in public and walk home.'

Justine said, 'I celebrated my engagement, marriage and divorce in there.' Her big black horse started to shake his head from side to side and shuffle his fetlocks – or whatever horse's feet are called. Justine shouted, 'Behave yourself, Satan!'

I asked, 'Is he one of your clients?'

Justine kicked the horse into submission and said, 'My

378

clients are stressed and unhappy *people*. The horses help them to recover their equilibrium.'

I said, 'I thought it was horses you nursed back to health.'

She laughed and said, 'We're full of sad cases from the financial services industry at the moment.'

I said, 'So the masters of the universe are mucking out your stables?'

'Yes!' she laughed, 'and they're paying through the nose for it!'

When she and Satan had trotted off, my father said bitterly, 'Talk about money for old rope! Introduce a rich nutter to an 'orse, give him a shovel and let him get on with it.'

When we got to The Bear, we found a small disconsolate group standing at the locked front door, Bernard and Mrs Lewis-Masters among them. I was quite touched to see that they were holding hands.

Bernard said, 'Poor old England is under attack again. The distinction being that this time the enemy is not the Luftwaffe, it's our own government!'

There was a rumble of agreement from the crowd. One of the ancient ex-regulars piped, 'We should do summat about it!' The crowd agreed loudly. However, after a few moments of unfocused grumbling we drifted away from each other and went our separate ways.

When we got home, I told my mother I wanted some time alone with my father. She brought him round after his tea. She had already changed him into his pyjamas, cleaned his teeth and brushed what is left of his hair. He looked like a crumpled boy.

He said. 'What's up? I'm missing my programmes.'

I said, 'I wanted to thank you for what you did when I was a baby. Mum told me that she couldn't cope.'

My father fumbled in his pyjama jacket for his cigarettes. He said, exhaling smoke, 'Your mother was very highly strung, son.' He frowned. 'You've been to Norfolk, seen those horrible big skies, that land that goes on and on – imagine living there, in the middle of a potato field, without a telly.' He shuddered, 'Is it any wonder that your mother's nerves were bad?'

'Well, thank you, Dad,' I said and patted his shoulder.

'It's all right,' he said. 'I took to you straight away, and I knew your mother would come round in the end.'

Monday 14th April

Had Gracie after school. Cooked her current favourite food – grilled sweetcorn, cubes of Red Leicester cheese and sweet pickled onions. I don't mind indulging her now that she is no longer my full-time responsibility. I will let Daisy struggle to get vitamins and minerals into the kid.

Fairfax-Lycett came to pick her up. Diary, did Gracie have to be quite so pleased to see him?

Tuesday 15th April

Worried about money. Sickness benefit does not cover my half of the mortgage, and Bernard will be gone soon, together with his pension.

I was sitting writing at the living-room window when I saw Simon, the vicar, turn into our drive. It was raining and he was sheltering under a huge black umbrella. My heart sank. Simon is one of those people who make you yawn before he has opened his mouth.

He made an annoying fuss about where he could put his dripping umbrella and wet overcoat. When all that was sorted, he said, 'I've been wanting to talk to you for a while.'

I invited him into the kitchen and put the kettle on the stove.

He said, 'You know the church roof is in a dangerous condition and needs completely replacing?'

I said, 'Before you go on, Simon, I'm a penniless atheist.'

He said, 'No, no, it isn't money I want from you. It's too late for that. The bishop has had three estimates and they are all exorbitant. So I'm afraid St Botolph's is to be deconsecrated and put on to the open market.'

'No!' I said. 'It can't be a *Grand Designs* project! It's so absolutely beautiful – the stained glass, the worn-down flagstones, the ancient smell!'

Simon said sadly, 'The tiny congregation, the frozen

pipes in winter, the Harvest Festival produce consisting of old tins from the back of the pantry.'

I blushed a bit at this, remembering that we had sent Gracie to the last Harvest Festival with a tin of stuffed vine leaves we'd bought at Athens Airport before she was born.

He said, 'I wanted to warn you because I know you've set your heart on being laid to rest at St Botolph's ...'

I assured him that I would sort out another resting place when the time came and thanked him for his thoughtfulness in letting me know.

When I told Bernard that St Botolph's was closing, he said, 'Shame. As you know, cocker, I'm a red-in-tooth-and-claw agnostic, but St Botolph's was a grand place for a sit down and a quiet think.' He lit a cigarette and said, 'I sometimes have a word with that poor sod, Jesus, hanging there on that God-awful cross.'

I asked, 'What do you say to him?'

Bernard said, 'I usually say, "Cheer up, cocker."'

Wednesday 16th April

Glorious sunshine and a baby-blue sky. I walked to the end of the drive and about twenty-five yards along Gibbet Lane. The hedgerows were heavy with the sight and scent of white and pink hawthorn. The birds were making a lot of noise and were busy doing something in the trees. Grasses by the verge were waving in the breeze together with unidentified wild flowers. I found a long stick, used it to help me walk back, then sat outside when I got home and really *looked* at the land surrounding the pigsties. There is a lot of it. Felt a primeval urge to cultivate the soil. This has never happened to me before. Some of my most angst-ridden teenage hours were spent in garden centres trudging behind my mother as she barged a clanking metal trolley into the innocent legs of passing customers.

Thursday 17th April

Walked around the perimeter of our land with Bernard. We sat by the little brook on the trunk of a fallen tree while Bernard smoked a cigarette. I have always regarded the brook as a nuisance before, something to cause flood anxiety, a hazard for Gracie and a burden on our house insurance. But as I watched the sparkling water rushing over the stony bed, I saw that it was the very opposite. My little waterway was a most delightful asset. I said as much to Bernard.

He bent down and scooped some water between his cupped hands. 'It's nectar, cocker,' he said, 'it puts that poncey designer stuff in the shade.' He scooped some up for me. It had a faint taste of nicotine.

Friday 18th April

Slept all night with my arms wrapped around Daisy's old Puffa jacket. It smells of her – a mixture of perfume and stale cigarette smoke. Woke this morning to find the coat on the floor, smelled bacon frying, so knew Bernard was up. Went to the bathroom and looked in the mirror above the sink. My ghostly twin looked back at me. He had a gaunt pale face and a bald head. His eyes were dark smudges. I said aloud, 'Daisy, Daisy, Daisy.'

When I went into the kitchen, Bernard was at the stove pushing bacon round the frying pan with a teaspoon. With the other hand he was reading a book, *Out of the Woods: The Armchair Guide to Trees.*

'After breakfast, cocker, we'll walk round the perimeter of the land and catalogue the trees,' he said.

Suddenly it became important that I knew how old Bernard was. I asked him.

'Born the second of the ninth, nineteen forty-six,' he said promptly. 'Why do you want to know, old son?'

I could hardly tell him the truth – that I was scared he would die soon – so I said, 'You're the same age as Joanna Lumley.'

He said, 'Champion.'

P.M.

Apart from the hideous leylandii, which I intend to cut down at some point in the future, we have thirty-nine mature deciduous trees.

'All English natives, cocker,' Bernard said proudly.

Saturday 19th April
Nigel and Lance's Wedding

Walked to Fairfax Hall with my mother, who was pushing my father in his wheelchair. He grumbled that if God had wanted two men to marry each other he would have married Jesus off to John the Baptist. My mother and I exchanged a worried glance. He is constantly making religious references lately. Is it a sign of senility? Will he soon be deluded into thinking it is 1953 and demand to have tea in his Coronation mug?

We had to stop several times to rest and were glad when Fairfax Hall was glimpsed through the trees. We were in time to see Nigel and Lance arrive in a chauffeur-driven limo. They looked quite good in their matching pale blue suits but I could tell that Nigel was in a bad mood. When I asked him why, he told me that at seven thirty this morning Lance had got cold feet and wanted to cancel the wedding.

Lance said, shrilly, 'Tell him *why*!'

Nigel yanked on his guide dog's harness and spat, 'All I said was, don't stand at the altar with your mouth gaping open. It makes you look as though you live in sheltered accommodation!'

'How do you know when he's got his mouth open?' I asked.

Nigel snapped, 'I can hear him breathing! I asked him to have his adenoids seen to before the wedding!'

It was an awkward moment but my mother took

charge and told them that she had lost her nerve on the morning of her wedding. She said, 'The night before, George told me that he didn't want to have children. He said children ruined your sex life and wrecked a woman's figure.'

My father said, 'And I was right, wasn't I, Pauline?'

My mother said quietly, 'What he didn't know was that I was already pregnant with Adrian.'

The ceremony was conducted by an avuncular registrar who told us that it was Fairfax Hall's first civil marriage. It was a bit too sentimental for my taste.

He gushed, 'Alone you each have a heart that beats like the wings of a tiny bird but when you agree to this union you will have one strong eagle's heart, and like that noble creature you will soar into the sky together!'

Personally I would not have left the dog in charge of the rings. I was the Best Man and that should have been my duty. It was not a pretty sight to see the dog snarling and baring its teeth when various people tried to take the rings from the gold pouch around its neck.

At one point in the ceremony I had to look away – Lance's laboured adenoidal breathing, together with the look of open-mouthed idiocy on his face, was too much to bear. I could see the vein in Nigel's temple throbbing like a convulsed worm.

When I turned, I saw Daisy in her black suit standing at the back holding a clipboard. She gave me a half smile and looked away. I was extremely proud of my wife. It was her first wedding at Fairfax Hall and she had arranged everything beautifully. Not easy when half of the guests were gay men with very exacting standards.

When I stood up in the reception to make my Best Man's speech, I got a standing ovation. It took me completely by surprise.

Nigel muttered at my side, 'They're applauding the cancer, Moley, and the fact that your wife's scarpered. It's got nothing to do with you.'

I kept the speech short but humorous, saying that Nigel was the only boy in the school to apply moisturiser before he went out on to the football field. I also read aloud a text from Pandora.

Sorry can't be there, am in the Forbidden City.
Masses of love to Mr and Mrs Nigel and Lance.
Pandora.

I quipped to the guests, 'By "Forbidden City" Pandora doesn't mean Liverpool. She is leading a trade delegation in China.'

My mother laughed but not many people joined in.

Sunday 20th April

Spent the morning with Gracie, colouring at the kitchen table. She was drawing a succession of princesses, I was drawing my ideal garden.

Bernard cooked us his all-day breakfast. Gracie asked

me for a napkin before she started to eat. When I handed her a piece of kitchen towel, she frowned and said, 'Don't you have proper linen?'

In the afternoon I took her to see the brook, and allowed her to take her socks and shoes off and paddle in the ankle-deep water. We made a dam with some of the smooth stones off the bottom.

When Daisy came to pick her up, I said, 'You look tired.'

She said, 'I'm working a fourteen-hour day.'

I said, 'I hope he's paying you well.'

She said, 'We don't take a wage, all the money we make goes back into the business.'

So he is employing my wife for nothing!

Monday 21st April

My mother has got a meeting in Leicester with a commissioning editor from Melancholy Books Ltd. To talk about *A Girl Called 'Shit'*!

She said, 'They want to change the title but I've told them, it's *A Girl Called "Shit"* or nothing!'

P.M.

My mother back from meeting. She is calling her book *The Potato Farmer's Daughter*.

I asked her if she would show some of my unpublished work to Melancholy Books. She agreed, but she could have been more enthusiastic.

Tuesday 22nd April

My father rang from next door and asked me to bring 'that tin of beans' round.

I said, 'What do you want it for?'

He said, 'What's this, an interrogation? Are you working for the bleedin' CIA now?'

A ludicrous overreaction to a simple question. I took the tin of beans round. My father was there with Brett. My mother wasn't, but she had attached a sheet of A4 paper to the door of their fridge and had written in huge black letters:

GEORGE! DO NOT MAKE ANY DECISIONS WITHOUT ME!

I brought his attention to the notice.

'I've decided to ignore it,' he said defiantly.

Brett said, 'I've been sickened by how Dad's so-called family have treated him. Try to see beyond the wheelchair, Adrian. Dad is fully capable of making decisions, he is an intelligent man.'

I said, 'Is that why he thinks the actors on *Coronation Street* make up their own dialogue?'

Thursday 24th April

Why is everyone using the word 'unacceptable' lately? An irate woman on Five Live phoned in this morning and said that it was 'completely unacceptable that the banks were gambling with our money'.

Tonight, on *East Midlands Today*, after a disturbing report about a sawn-up body found in a wheelie bin in a Nottingham suburb, a policeman said, 'This is a quiet residential area and, as such, this crime is totally unacceptable.'

A neighbour who was interviewed in the street said, 'I noticed the bin had been out on the pavement for three days, which is obviously unacceptable.'

Saturday 26th April

Watched Bernard running up our drive this afternoon. He saw me at the window and waved what turned out to be a Rupert Bear annual above his head. As soon as I saw the cover, I knew why Bernard had been running. Rupert was brown and it was the 1973 edition.

The publishers that year had changed Rupert's colour to white after only a few brown copies had been printed. Consequently those rare brown Rupert editions are a book dealer's Holy Grail.

Bernard said, 'I found it in the vicar's rummage sale. I was looking for a decent pair of trousers when I spotted it. It's in perfect nick, never been opened by the look of it.'

He handed it to me, it was in pristine condition.

'Whoever it was given to must have shared my opinion of young Master Bear,' said Bernard.

'Which is?' I asked.

'Well, he was a bit of a degenerate, wasn't he? That bear had a serious drug habit. I'd guess at hallucinogenics, wouldn't you?'

He leafed carefully through the pages. Rupert seemed to be undergoing increasingly bizarre adventures, in what could only be described as Dali-esque landscapes.

I logged on to the book dealers' website and started to put in the information. 'How much did you pay for it?' I asked while I typed.

'The crone behind the trestle table only asked ninety pence for the Rupert annual, a pair of cavalry twills and a regimental tie,' he said.

When I saw how much the last 1973 brown Rupert had sold for at auction, I said to Bernard, 'If you're on heart tablets take one now . . . sixteen thousand pounds!'

Bernard sat down and lit a cigarette. He said, 'It can't be true, I was always last in the queue when Lady Luck came to call.'

I offered him a celebratory drink but he said, 'Better not, I'm on the wagon.'

We clapped each other on the back in a manly way. I made him wrap the precious book in a kitchen towel and put it inside a carrier bag.

He said, 'I owe you board and lodging since Christ-mas.'

I protested that he had paid me something out of his pension every week.

'Then I should buy you something for your land,' he said, 'cocker.'

I rang Mr Carlton-Hayes and told him about the 1973 brown Rupert annual. He gasped, and said he knew of a collector in America who would 'dearly love to complete his collection'.

I asked him how Leslie was.

After a short pause he said, 'Leslie is extremely well, and how are you, my dear?'

I told him that I was feeling better and that I was spending a lot of time cultivating my land.

He said, 'You've read Thoreau's *Walden*, I expect?'

I said, 'It's on my bedside table.'

After I'd put the phone down, Bernard said, 'Are you up to sorting the books we were given by Mr C-H?'

I said I was.

So we spent the afternoon going through the boxes of semi-valuable books from the shop. After taking out the books we wanted to keep, we agreed to sell the remainder online.

'So, cocker, we can call ourselves booksellers again,' said Bernard.

Sunday 27th April

Brett has not been seen for two days! I fear that the baked bean tin and his absence are not unrelated.

My mother thinks that the tin of beans is still in my pantry. My father has begged me not to say anything to her.

I asked him how much was in the tin.

He said, 'Too much.'

Monday 28th April

I was in the post office with a parcel for Glenn in Afghanistan (a shoe box full of socks, toothpaste, Fruit Pastilles, Wotsits, a drawing from Gracie, a letter from my mother, shaving cream, Ritz biscuits and a Walker's pork pie) when Kathleen Boldry, one of the militant dinner ladies, came in with a petition condemning the Council's decision to grant planning permission in support of a safari park in the grounds of Fairfax Hall.

Wendy Wellbeck said, 'None of us will be safe in our beds, with lions and tigers roaming free.'

'And think of the traffic!' said a sour face in the queue.

'I've heard there are going to be giraffes,' I said.

'Giraffes!' said the queue as one.

Mrs Golightly said, 'We don't want giraffes in the village with their long necks looking over our hedges.'

'This is not Africa!' said an old bloke with a bent back.

Tony Wellbeck said, 'We should march to Fairfax Hall

and tell that Fairfax-Lycett that the village is against it.'

I said, 'It would be far more effective to march at night, with flaming torches.'

Much to my alarm there was whole-hearted support for my suggestion. The bloke with the bent back said that he'd been in charge of making flaming torches when he was props master for the Mangold Players' outdoor evening performance of *The Phantom of the Opera* held in and around the moat at Fairfax Hall.

I said, thinking of Gracie and Daisy, 'I suggest we don't actually burn the hall down.'

A few hotheads in the queue were keen on a scorched earth policy, but Tony Wellbeck talked them out of it. We agreed to rendezvous at 8 p.m. on the green in front of The Bear.

Tony Wellbeck said, 'That's twenty hundred hours, check your watches.'

When the queue had dispersed, I noticed that the shelves looked bare and the government leaflets advising us on every aspect of our lives had gone. When I remarked on this, Wendy Wellbeck said, 'We're on the list for closure, we've put an appeal in but we don't hold out much hope.'

I told them that I had a great deal of influence with Pandora Braithwaite, our Member of Parliament.

Wendy Wellbeck said, 'Yes, we'd heard that you were knocking her off.'

Tony said angrily, 'Wendy! I know you're worried but there is no need to let your standards slip and use such offensive language to a valued customer.'

Wendy said, 'I apologise, Mr Mole. We're not ourselves lately. This place is our livelihood *and* our home.'

What was meant to be a torch-lit delegation of Mangold Parvians grew via the internet to include groups from: The World Wildlife Fund, Child Poverty Action, The Badger Protection League, People Against Zoos (PAZ), The Socialist Workers Party, Friends of Giraffes (UK), Ratepayers Alliance (Leicester Branch), Wildlife Aid, The Leicester Bat Group, Greyhounds in Need, World Parrot Trust and Tiger Awareness.

Protestors started to arrive in the late afternoon. It wasn't long before cars were parked on both verges of Gibbet Lane and surrounding roads.

My parents went to the end of our drive to watch as the protestors went by on their way to the meeting place in Mangold Parva. My father was able to fully indulge his prejudices against 'alternatives' as every possible type of non-conformist passed him by.

My mother was the happiest I had seen her for years. She kept saying, 'At last, something is happening in Mangold Parva!'

A police car went by, then an ambulance with its siren screaming.

'Ay up!' said my father, his eyes shining. 'Trouble!'

My mother rang Wendy Wellbeck to find out what had happened. It seemed that somebody from The Badger Protection League had harangued an activist from Child Poverty Action saying that they had no legitimate right to be there. A Socialist Worker fanned the flames by stating that badgers were riddled with TB and didn't deserve their place in the countryside. A policeman intervened and charged them both with a Section Five. The ambulance was for a man from Tiger Awareness who had fallen into a ditch full of stinging nettles.

I was beginning to feel sorry that I had suggested a torch-lit procession. When I arrived at the green, I was amazed at the multitude of people waiting there. Bernard was holding two flaming torches. He handed one to me and we set off. The Socialist Workers were chanting, 'Capitalism! Out! Out! Out!' Other groups tried to find a rhyme with 'safari park' but failed. Many of the older marchers sang 'Born Free'. We picked up my mother and father as we passed the end of our drive. As we got nearer to Fairfax Hall, I started to regret the whole thing and I began to think that it could be quite nice to have a safari park near by. Bernard told me that the animals' dung would make an excellent fertiliser for the roses I intended to grow – and wouldn't the village benefit from the jobs that the safari park would provide? I was relieved to see a police car parked near the gates. A traffic policeman got out of the car and addressed the crowd.

'Ladies and gentlemen,' he shouted. 'As you know, this is still a free country and as citizens of this country you are allowed to make a peaceful protest providing you inform the police of your intentions. However, I have to tell you that no such notice was given, therefore I am instructing you to turn round and go back in a peaceful manner to your cars and leave the area.'

I was about to turn back when Tony Wellbeck pushed to the front and made an impassioned but illogical speech about how money could be found for safari parks yet his post office, which had served the area well for seventy years, was being forced to close.

I told Bernard that I wanted to go back.

He said, 'Don't spoil the fun, cocker, I'm looking forward to giving that wife-stealer Hugo Fairfax-Lycett the fright of his privileged life. His sort live in dread of the mob.' He went up to the policeman, saluted and said, 'Colonel Bernard Hopkins retired here, sir. You have my word as an officer and a gentleman that I will lead these people in a peaceful protest.'

The policeman said he was off duty in five minutes and got back inside his car. The mob passed through the gates and started to process down the drive to Fairfax Hall.

My phone rang and Daisy said, 'Adrian, I don't know what to do. There is a crowd of people walking down the drive. They've got flaming torches and they look angry.'

I said, 'Daisy, I'm here with them.'

She said, 'Well, tell them to go back. I'm here alone with Gracie. Hugo is out somewhere on his quad bike, in fact I'm worried about *him*. He's not answering his phone.'

Diary, it all ended in confusion, low farce and tragedy. After a few speeches by ardent animal activists, who railed against keeping wild animals in captivity, the crowd dispersed and most of them started to walk back into the village. At nine thirty, when Fairfax-Lycett had still not been contacted, Bernard, Tony Wellbeck and a few of the villagers set out to look for him in the grounds. Me, my mother, father and Wendy Wellbeck went into the hall and sat in the little room Daisy called 'the snug'. It was a comfortable room with a lot of old brown antiques and modern sofas.

Daisy said, 'I get agoraphobic in the rest of the house. I'm not used to such large spaces.'

My mother said, 'That's what living in a pigsty does to you.'

I can't get used to the new Daisy. It still seems wrong to me that a woman would wear a two-piece tweed suit indoors.

At ten thirty Tony Wellbeck phoned to say that they had found Fairfax-Lycett under his quad bike. He was alive but unconscious. It hurt me to see Daisy's obvious distress.

Before she got into the ambulance, she said, 'He could be brain damaged.'

I said, 'How could they possibly tell?'

Tuesday 29th April

The village is ankle deep in litter. Mrs Lewis-Masters has organised a litter pick. Fairfax-Lycett regained consciousness an hour after arriving at the hospital last night. When the doctors tested his cognitive skills by asking him the year, the name of the prime minister and his birth date, he answered 1972, Mrs Thatcher and 1066, so they are keeping him in for observation.

Daisy is not at all pleased with him. When she asked him how the accident happened, he said that he was fleeing from the mob. She came to the Piggeries to leave Gracie with me so that she could spend more time at the hospital.

I said to her, 'Daisy, if he has to answer a few general knowledge questions accurately he may never get out. He's so thick.'

She said, 'I don't mind that in a man. The thickos are easier to control.'

In the afternoon Gracie wanted to paddle in the brook again so we took a few sandwiches, a packet of Jaffa Cakes and a flask of tea and had a picnic. I pointed out to her that the tree swaying over the brook was called a weeping willow. She wanted to know the names of the other trees near by and I was so happy that I was able to tell her.

My mother came down to join us but left after a few minutes saying that she couldn't stand the midges. Within a quarter of an hour she was back. She sat on the tree trunk and lit a cigarette.

When I objected, she said, 'I'm smoking for *your* sake, Adrian. I don't want the midges biting your bald head.' She slid a postcard out of a pocket in her denim jacket and said, 'I'm glad I found this before your father saw it.'

There was a moody photograph of an old brewery in Burton-on-Trent on the front. On the back Rosie had written:

Dear Mum

Just to let you know that Dad and I are fine. We have got a lot in common, not just our looks! I send you my love and please give my regards to George and Adrian.

Love from,

Rosie (Lucas)

Gracie played happily with twigs and stones and bits of stuff she found at the side of the brook.

My mother said, 'You could make a nice water feature out of the brook if you tidied it up and planted some colourful shrubs along the banks.'

I said, 'It's staying exactly as it is.'

Wednesday 30th April

Mrs Lewis-Masters came for tea today. I followed Delia Smith's recipe and made both cheese and fruit scones.

She no longer uses a Zimmer frame. When I congratulated her on this, she said, 'I have Bernard's support.'

I said that I was also grateful for Bernard's support.

She snapped, 'I am not talking *generally*. Bernard literally supports me when I walk anywhere.'

I said I would be very sorry when Bernard left the pigsty.

Mrs Lewis-Masters said that she expected 'a difficult period of adjustment' when Bernard moved in with her.

Bernard said, 'I've got some filthy habits, cocker, like

turning my underpants inside out on alternate days.'

Mrs Lewis-Masters said, 'I don't give a fig about personal hygiene. I lived with the desert people, they only bathed twice a year, in sand.'

After tea we went for a walk so I could show her the land. When we stopped to rest at the brook, she said that she would lend me her gardener and her rotovator for a couple of days.

Before he left to take Mrs Lewis-Masters home, Bernard asked if I would be in tomorrow. I told him that apart from therapy, I was always in.

Pandora rang at 1 a.m. to wish me goodnight. I didn't tell her I'd been in bed since half past nine.

She said, 'I've been thinking about you a lot recently. Do you think about me?'

I told her that I had been thinking about her since I was 13¾. What I didn't tell her was that my recent thoughts had been almost exclusively about my land and how best to cultivate it.

Thursday 1st May

A GREAT DAY!

Cancelled therapy.

Bernard has given me a present of four chickens, a coop and a fox-safe compound! It all arrived this morning together with two men who put it all together. They finished at noon.

My father has been sitting in his wheelchair, staring through the wire mesh and watching the chickens' every move. According to him, the hens have distinct personalities. 'That one's shy, that's a cocky bastard and the one standing in the drinking bowl is a gormless sod.'

Friday 2nd May

Fairfax-Lycett is out of hospital and is recuperating at Fairfax Hall. When she dropped Gracie off, I asked Daisy if he had sustained any brain damage.

'How would I know?' she laughed. 'He was turned down by *The Weakest Link*.'

I said, 'I don't know how you can live with such a pea-brain.'

'He is a bit thick,' she said, 'but I don't mind that. You either had your head stuck in a book, or you were writing in that bloody diary. You weren't there, Adrian!'

Saturday 3rd May

Woke with a feeling of happy anticipation. Put dressing gown on and went outside, found Bernard and my father smoking, drinking tea and watching the chickens. I gave them some clean water and food – the chickens obviously, not the old men.

I asked my father if my mother was OK.

He said, 'She's all right. She's working on her shit book.'

I said, 'I expect you know her book is a tissue of lies, don't you, Dad?'

Bernard said, 'Talking of lies, kiddo, I've been telling a few porky pies myself lately.'

I said, 'Colonel Bernard Hopkins, retired?'

'No,' he said. 'That's true, but what isn't kosher is that I'm a single man. My wife is hale and hearty and living in Northamptonshire.'

I urged him to tell Mrs Lewis-Masters the truth, hoping that she would break off the engagement, thus causing Bernard to stay and help me with the land.

Sunday 4th May

Another present from Bernard! A pig and a sty! I saw the Land Rover and trailer arriving slowly up our drive and thought that perhaps it was the saplings I'd ordered on the internet.

When Bernard and I went outside, I heard a grunting from the trailer. When I looked inside, a small pig looked up at me. Diary, I am not a sentimentalist, and I have never particularly liked animals, but I am not ashamed to say that it was love at first sight. I loved everything about the pig: its cheerful expression, its piggy eyes, its pink skin, its corkscrew tail.

Bernard said, 'It's an inherently comical animal, old cock. I thought it would cheer you up.'

He was right, it has.

Monday 5th May
Bank Holiday

Woken by the rotovator. Looked out to see that quite a lot of earth had been turned over. The bloke pushing it was a giant with muscles like small Welsh hills. He calls himself 'Cash in Hand', or 'Cash' for short.

Later he helped me and Bernard construct a wheelchair-friendly path to the pigsty so that my father can feed the pig, who is called, after much deliberation – Rupert.

My mother is having a lot of trouble finishing her book. She said that Melancholy Books Ltd are disappointed that she didn't beg on the streets or have a heroin addiction.

She said, as we were watching Rupert roll in the mud, 'I got a bit dependent on Nurofen in the eighties, but I didn't go into The Priory.'

I said sarcastically, 'It's a shame Dad didn't knock you about and keep you chained to the kitchen sink.'

My mother sighed and said, 'Not even a few slaps, he's frightened of me.' Then she looked up at me and said, 'Aidy, your hair's growing back! I can see it in the sun!'

Bernard shouted to say that Glenn was on the phone from Afghanistan. I hurried up to the house.

Glenn said, 'Dad, something great 'as 'appened. Finley-Rose is 'aving a baby. You'll be a granddad.'

Diary, my first thought was that I couldn't possibly be a grandfather, I was only forty years old. My second thought was that I wanted to live long enough to see this child grow up. There was a lot I wanted to teach it.

I congratulated Glenn and handed the phone to my mother, who had been hovering near by. She was beside herself with joy at the prospect of being a great-grandmother. 'And I've still got my legs,' she said after putting the phone down.

I went to the brook and said a secular prayer for my son, asking whoever was in charge of the universe to keep Glenn safe from roadside bombs, snipers, missiles and friendly fire. I was still there, sitting under the swaying willow, when Pandora's Audi sped up the drive, bouncing over the potholes, and drew to a halt outside the house.

I got up and started to walk towards her.